AN·ECHO·OF·THE·ASHES

PREQUEL

KEEPER

✦ OF THE ✦

FLAME

Cover by Fay Lane

Maps created by Charles Thompson @whitehawkcreekforge

Internal design by Coven Press www.covenpress.com.au

Printed in Australia

First Printing: July 2025

Paperback ISBN 978-0-6451842-6-6

eBook ISBN 978-0-6451842-7-3

 A catalogue record for this work is available from the National Library of Australia

Distributed by Lightning Source Global

AN·ECHO·OF·THE·ASHES
PREQUEL

KEEPER
·OF THE·
FLAME

· ANTHONY KEARLE ·

An Echo of the Ashes

-

Keeper of the Flame
Blood of the Eagle
Shadow of the Nightingale
Song of the Raven

Dedications

-

For Georgie.

My light. My heart. Always.

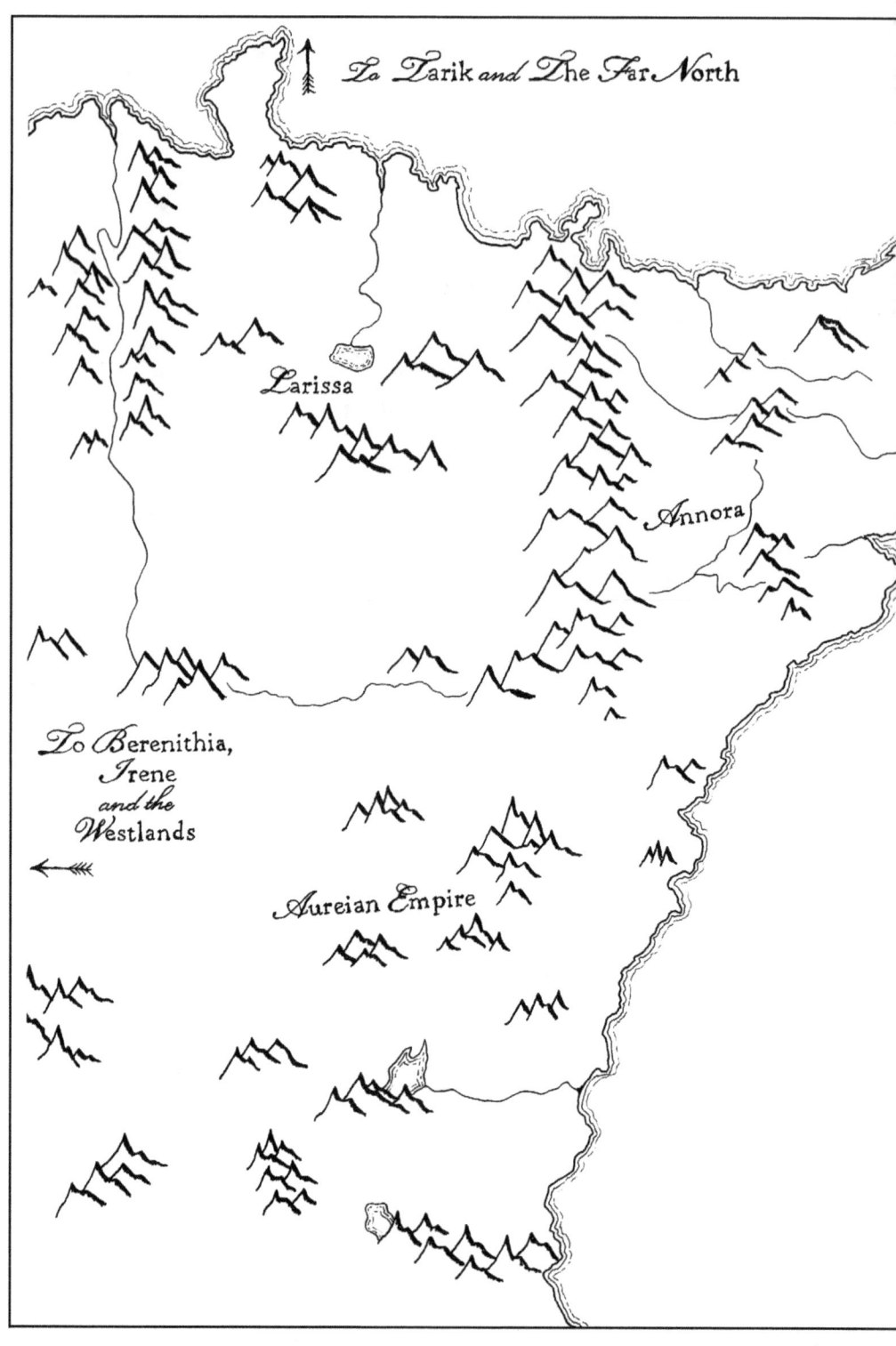

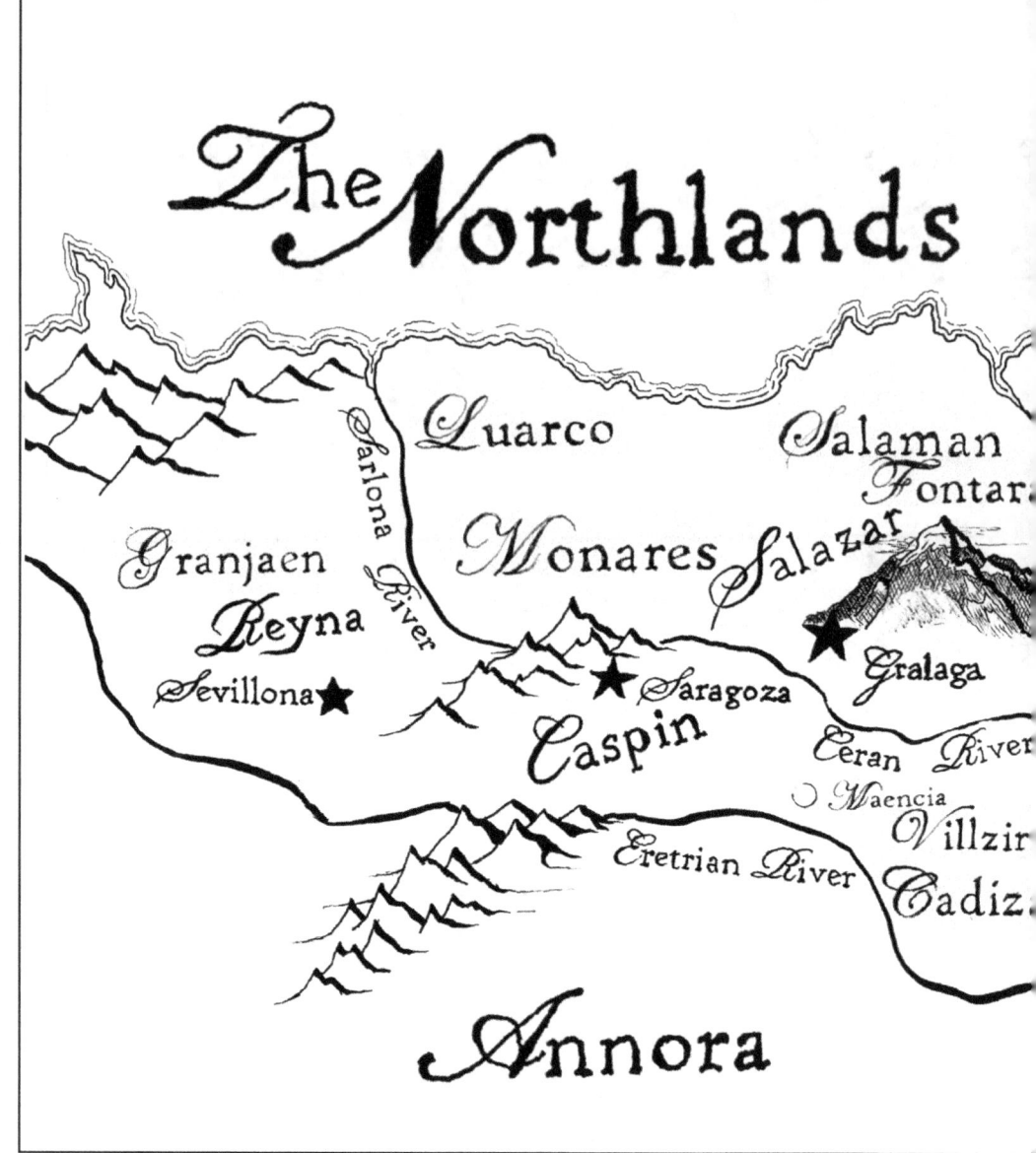

To Tarik and The Far North
Mithramir Sea
Jarez
Villaviedo
Granadix
Linair
Valengos
Karcera
Panala River
Patchi
Genilabra
Torovia
Palanza
Canaeric
Bailon
Gonaelric
Alvillia
Algelance
Cordojar
Marelva
Lintera
Bandujar
Arutilla
Cacera
Tolgoza
Vallgena
Aloys
Valcas
Lajera
Alusia
Yecala
Monocena
Sergova
Ciras
Malcia
Adrestia
Arzarlan

Salvaar
Noyon
Aldor
Faolan
Oryn
Caelis
Sacred Grove
Irwan River
Argon River
Blaithin
The Rift
Lake Thirlryda
Vadon
Roricsford
Barona
Moonwatch
Miera
Chausac
Rinar River
Imalric
Phoenix River
Ruins of Israfil
Idrisir
Carlian
Harren River
Cardna
Iribian Alps
Loxford
Vanhair

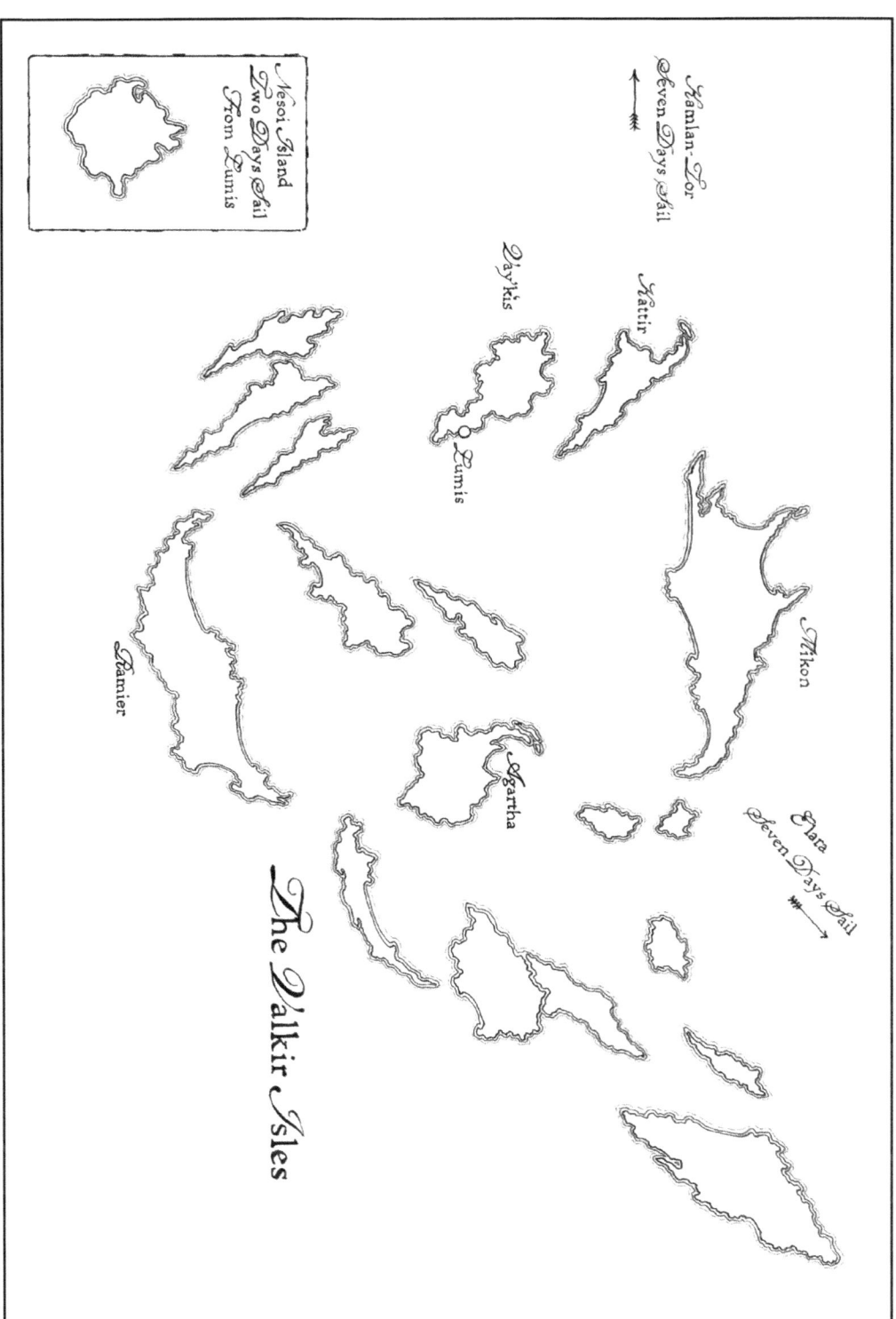

Nesoi Island
Two Days Sail
From Lumis

Tamlan-Tor
Seven Days Sail

Daykis

Lattir

Lumis

Nikon

Lamier

Agartha

Mara
Seven Days Sail

The Dalkir Isles

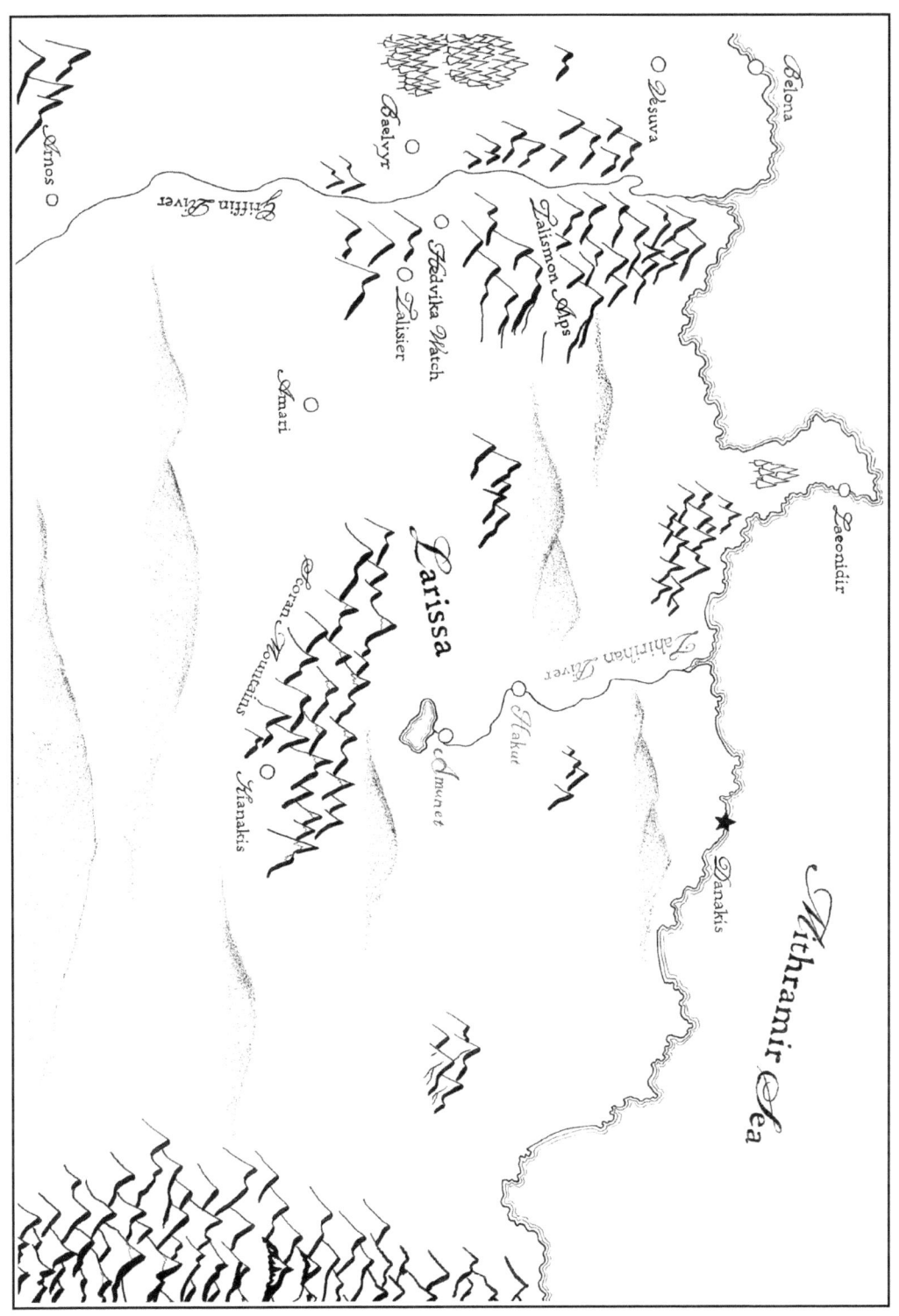

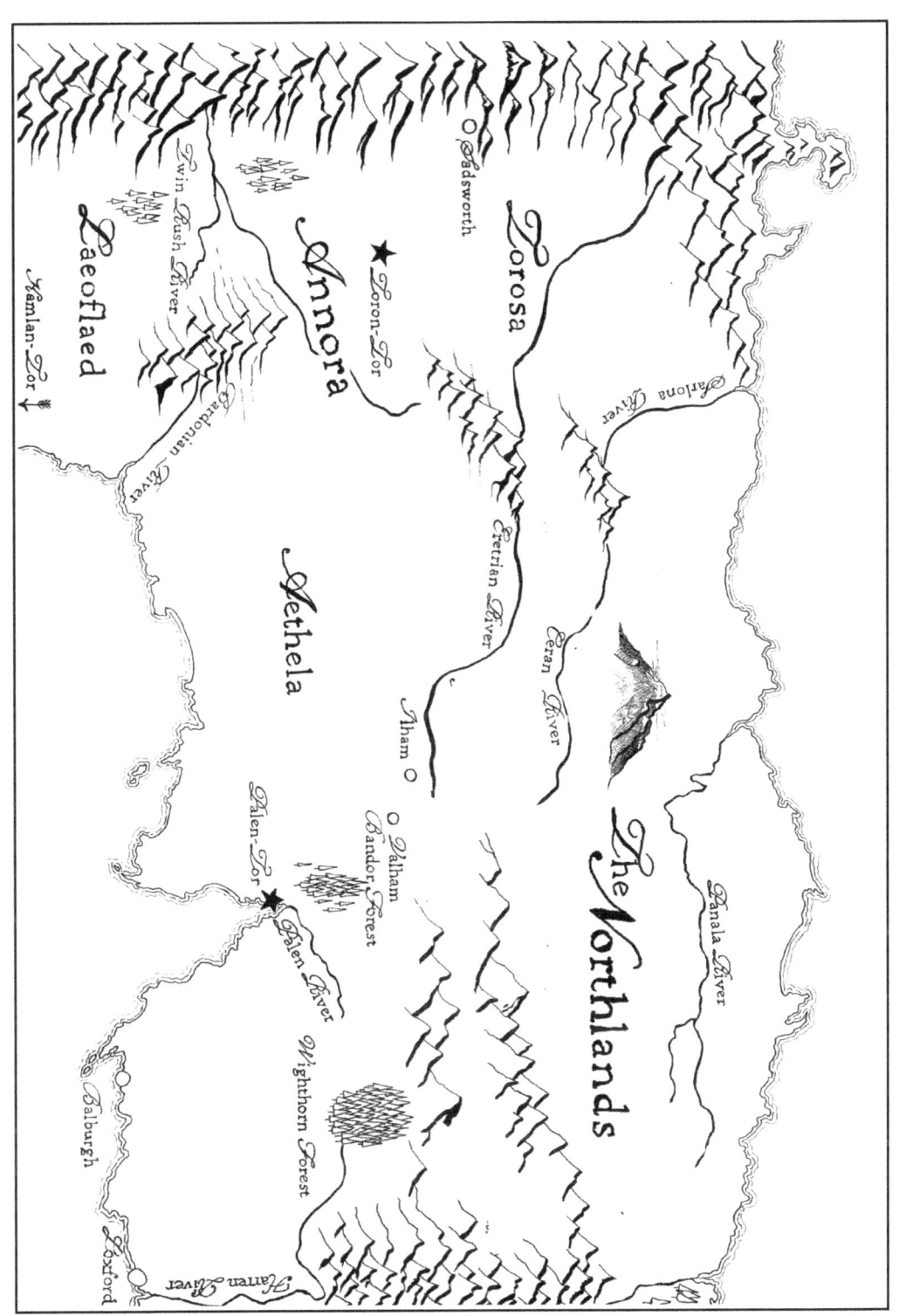

PART ONE

FALL

ONE

Forest of Salvaar

The cool north wind slipped through the trees. It caressed the wildflowers that grew along the banks of the great river. Songbirds filled the forest with their music. The sun kissed the earth with warmth. A young girl's laugh echoed through the woodland. Her skin was fair and her hair as white as winter snow. It hung over her shoulders like a waterfall of crystal, broken only by the braid that hung before her right ear. Ears that, in turn, tapered into points. She wore grey pelts and skins, and underneath her clothes were as fair as the girl herself. She was thirteen summers, young and strong like the rest of her elven kin. Her eyes, bluer than any ocean, shone with joy as she glanced at the woman beside her.

Nevra was seven years older. Like her sister, she was elven. Like her sister, her hair hung in a river of white. Her elven body was lean and strong. She held a fishing spear in one hand and her sister's in the other. Unlike her sister, a pair of thin braids hung down the left side of her face.

"Naidra." Nevra called her sister's name.

Naidra looked up expectantly.

"Here." The older sister held out the spear.

Naidra took it. It fit her hand as though it was forged for her. She was an elf, born of Sylvaine's tears. They were the Great Queen's warriors, trained in the ways of combat from the time they could walk.

"Close your eyes," Nevra said with a smile.

Naidra raised her eyebrows but did as she was bid. "Would you like me to dance?" she joked.

Naidra could hear her sister moving around. She could hear the hum coming from Nevra's lips. It was the melody of a song, a song that her sister had raised her on. A song of safety. A song of hope. A song of home. Naidra smiled as it echoed through the greenwood.

"Open your eyes," Nevra said, moving towards her sister.

Naidra's gaze flickered open. She glanced up at her sister and saw the crown of wildflowers in her hands. The green leaves and stems that held it together were broken only by the rainbow of petals that ringed the crown. Nevra placed it upon her sister's brow.

Together they continued through the forest. Together they hummed the song. When the sun reached its peak, they arrived at the Arwan River. It spanned from the Mithramir Sea in the north to southerly Miera. Crystal clear waters lapped at Naidra's legs as she stood in the gentle current. She used a net while Nevra used a spear. They spent hours fishing in those waters. A small pile of the fish grew on the bank. The elves would take enough for a few days, no more than that. There were only the two of them.

Fish swam by Naidra. Some found their way into her net, others continued down the stream without worry. They bumped into her ankles and legs. Naidra had grown used to the feeling many years ago. The net shook. She glanced down to see that a tear had ruined the rope.

"It's broken," she told her sister with a frown.

"That can't do," Nevra replied. "A fisherwoman without a net?"

"I'll fix it," Naidra stated, leaving the river.

Drops of water fell from her legs and soaked pants as she made her way up onto the bank. Her bare feet found purchase upon the warm earth. Naidra sat at the water's edge, fixing the net with hand and needle. She had made and fixed nets a thousand times before. Naidra was good with her hands, she always had been. She watched the birds flying overhead as she worked. She watched the sun and the clouds.

"Naidra!"

She glanced over at her sister. There was panic in her voice and worry painted upon her pale face. It was only then that Naidra realised why. She stared at the net with horror. She had been mending it ... but not with her hands.

She had been fixing the net with her mind.

It fell onto her lap as Nevra rushed towards her. A chill ran down Naidra's spine. She had seen the horror in her sister's eyes. Whatever it was, it was bad. She covered her eyes in shock. Nevra fell to her knees beside her sister. She held her tightly.

"What is happening to me?" Naidra murmured.

The birds stopped singing.

Sparks flew as Nevra brought a fire to life. The last of the sun's rays had slipped beyond the horizon and the moon shone high above. She looked to her younger sister. Naidra had not moved from the riverbank. She did not understand what had happened. She was too young to have been told. The shock that had overcome Nevra transformed into something new. Something darker. Fear. Not of her sister, but *for* her.

Elves were nomads that spent their lives traversing the trees of eastern Salvaar to the western lands ruled by the families. Dozens of families, dozens of barons. Humans. A race not so very different from the elves, yet one that watched them warily wherever they went. The further an elf travelled, the more this wariness grew. People feared what they didn't understand.

It was not the elves alone that they feared; it was the magic that they brought with them. A magic that so few of the elves could ever touch. A magic that even Sylvaine's kin had good reason to fear.

Nevra made her way to her sister. She sat beside her at the riverbank and gazed towards the horizon.

"You are autieyar." Nevra's voice was quiet but firm.

"I just wanted to help," Naidra replied.

The young girl looked to her sister. Nevra could see the fear in Naidra's eyes. She didn't understand. The older sister said nothing as she moved behind Naidra.

"Am I a monster?" Naidra murmured.

"No."

Nevra pulled her sister into her body and wrapped her arms around her. She placed her chin gently upon Naidra's shoulder and pressed her cheek into her sister's. She held Naidra as though she was scared that if she let go her sister would vanish. Slowly Naidra felt the fear seep away as her sister's warmth enveloped her. Slowly she started to feel whole again. She felt safe in her sister's arms. She felt at home. They were her home.

"Your name, what does it mean?" Nevra asked.

"It means Snowflame," Naidra replied.

"And mine?

"Flamekeeper."

"That means that I will always be there to watch over you," Nevra told her. "No monster is going to hurt you while I'm here. We will get through this. Together."

The next morning was sombre. Naidra felt numb. The power within – the *magic* within – terrified her. She had seen the pain in Nevra's face, heard it in her words. They packed their camp and stowed the fish in the net that had been transformed into a makeshift bag. Nevra slung the bag across her shoulder and gripped her spear tightly. She said nothing, but Naidra could see the tensing in her sister's jaw and the whiteness of her knuckles upon the shaft. She was scared too. Nevra's voice snapped the numbness away as fast as a man could snap his fingers as she began to sing:

"Tears of life and tears of snow,
gifts from the Mother for the Iceborn to grow.
Tears of life and tears of snow,
we will find home where the north wind will blow.

We will find home, we will find home,
we will find home where the north wind will blow.
We will find home, we will find home,
we will find home where the north wind will blow.

Tears of pearl and tears of sapphire,
hope is born at the Great Queen's desire.
Tears of pearl and tears of sapphire,
songs that echo across our new empire.

We will find home, we will find home,
we will find home where the north wind will blow.
We will find home, we will find home,
we will find home where the north wind will blow."

It was the song that she had hummed earlier, a song that every elf knew. When at last Nevra's voice trailed off, the world didn't seem too dark. The birds sang in the trees. Sunlight broke through the forest canopy. Each verse had awoken Naidra from her dark dream. She smiled as she ran her hand through the long grass. Naidra felt the strength of the forest flow through it, she felt it flow through her. Nevra wrapped an arm around her young sister's shoulders and gave her a squeeze. She said nothing, but in that moment it was enough.

The smell of campfires was the first sign that they were nearing home. It was not long before the cries of elven voices echoed all around. A village of white tents emerged beneath the trees. There was no clearing nor break in the woodland. The elves were nomads who preferred to live in the wild and their camp showed as much. Some lounged in the branches of the trees while others danced beneath them. Their horses ran free. A pair of warriors trained with wooden staffs. It was a simple life, but the elves did not value material possession, wealth or great houses. This was all they needed. This was all they wanted. They all had the same white hair and the same blue eyes. Some wore their locks in braids, others tied it back or let it hang free.

"Naidra," a boy's voice called.

She turned to see him gesture to her. Behind him there was a group of six elven children all around her age, standing beside a barrel. Upon it a bucket was perched. The children held coins in their eager hands. It was a game. Naidra grinned and glanced at her sister.

"Go on," Nevra said, nodding towards the children.

Naidra's smile widened. She raced off to join her friends. The boy, Riven, tossed her a single silver coin. She caught it with a laugh. A line was drawn in the earth with a stick, and then the children formed up around it. Riven was first. He stepped up to the line and flipped a coin towards the bucket. It spun end over end. Wood rang as the coin hit the side of the bucket and bounced towards the ground. The children laughed as Riven shook his head. One by one, they took turns flipping their coins towards the bucket. Their target was far, and not easily could a coin fall within, either bouncing off its lip or hitting the barrel. Some flew well beyond or far too short. The children shouted and cheered.

Naidra stepped up to the line, her blue eyes locked on the bucket. The sun warmed her cheek. Slowly she brought her arm around. It rose and she flipped the coin. The children watched it spin with bated breath. The coin glanced off the edge of the bucket, bouncing up onto its rim. The coin rolled like a wheel. Naidra's lips curled in anticipation. Then the coin fell. It had not stopped ringing upon the lid of the barrel when the children roared with amusement. Naidra clicked her fingers and stepped back with a chuckle.

Riven clapped her on the shoulder and moved forwards to have his second turn. A small crowd of elves, mostly adults, some hundreds of years old, had gathered. This time, Riven's coin found its mark. The crowd applauded and joined in with the cheers. Naidra watched as her companions took their turns. She saw her sister amongst those who looked on. All too soon it was Naidra's turn again. She raised her eyebrows at Nevra and took her position. She felt the wind caress her hair. She felt its breath upon her face. The coin danced through her fingers as she stepped up to the line. The jeers of her companions faded into nothing. The music of songbirds vanished. Her eyes were keen, dancing with blue flame. Naidra took a slow breath and sent her coin forth. It flipped end over end, carving its way through the air. Her gaze never left the silver as it dropped into the bucket.

"HA!" she cried, her hand balled into a triumphant fist.

It was only then did she realise that there were no cheers. It was only then did she see the horror on the faces of the adults and the fear in the eyes of the children. A shiver ran through her body. She couldn't just see their fear. She could *feel* their fear. She could see inside of their hearts, inside of their souls. She felt it all. They were all scared. They were all scared of *her*.

Naidra looked around, her limbs shaking. Silver shone near her face. The coins had left her friends' hands and they hovered in the air around her. A tremble ran through Naidra's body as the cold tendrils of panic descended. The coins crashed to the ground. Her breathing grew fast. Naidra saw her sister's face pale.

She ran.

The long grass tried to trip her and branches whipped at her cheeks, tore at her hair. Naidra did not care. She had never been so afraid.

She did not know how long she had been curled up at the foot of a willow tree when Nevra found her. Her tears had long since dried. All she felt now was cold.

"I'm scared," Naidra murmured.

Nevra sat beside her. Her sister had the right to know. She *needed* to know.

"I know," Nevra replied sadly. She nodded behind her shoulder. "When they find out what you can do, it is going to change everything. I have seen it before. The people out there, our people, they will be scared."

"But why?"

Nevra took her sister's hand.

"The autieyar were blessed by Sylvaine with magic," she said. "Their power can mend and heal, it can shield and protect, and can also be used as a weapon. They are revered by us, by the ruskalan, for their abilities. But they are also feared for them. Listen to me, Naidra, these abilities come with a cost, and it can be a great one. It has rules. It has limitations. Tap into this power and it can leave you weakened. Tap into this power for too long …"

She trailed off, unable to finish her words. Nevra had seen it before. Her heart had not yet healed from the experience. She set her jaw, determined to tell her sister the truth.

"When an autieyar taps into this power for too long, when an autieyar takes too much, the spirit world demands its price. It comes from here." Nevra tapped her brow.

"What are you saying?" Naidra breathed, an edge of panic clawing into her voice.

Nevra felt her sister's fingers tighten around her hand.

"If you use it too much … if you use it before you are ready, it will claim your mind," Nevra said quietly.

Tears rolled down Naidra's cheeks. Nevra could see the war

being fought in her sister's eyes. She had to tell her, she had no right not to. Not now.

"Our father was autieyar." Nevra's memories flooded back. "I saw what it did to him."

Naidra's jaw shook. Tears continued to flow freely.

"When we return home, they will come for you," Nevra said as she held back her own tears. "They will teach you to use it, teach you to control it. Its limits – your limits – you must learn for yourself. This power *must* be your last resort."

Their father had forgotten that. He had grown to love the feeling of the magic coursing through his veins. It had cost him. It had cost their family. Because of that, Naidra had never known her father. She had never known her mother. Her sister was all she had. In the space of a few moments, she had turned from a young girl into something that the whole world feared. The young girl's jaw trembled.

"Can't I just be your sister?" Naidra pleaded.

The sorrow in her voice broke Nevra's heart.

"You are my sister," Nevra told her fiercely as she pulled Naidra into her arms. "Nothing will ever change that."

That was the last day that the other children played games with Naidra.

The autieyar came for her within days.

The moon danced in the heavens. Silver light shone across the forest. The sisters watched and waited, for the call had been sent. Five walked towards the sisters' tent. They wore simple clothing that fit their lean forms. Sleeves and bracers covered their arms, and their robe-like dress split at the front to reveal their trousered legs. Wide sashes of blue adorned their waists, and fine swords hung from their hips.

Naidra clutched at her sister as they approached. The lead autieyar stepped forwards. He pushed back his hood. A waterfall of white fell down his shoulders as his face was revealed. It was akin to any other elf. He had no fangs nor eyes that held dark intent. The only thing that separated him and the other autieyar from the rest of their kin were their black tattoos. The swirling patterns ran down from their brows to their throats and then disappeared beneath their robes. The spiralling lines covered from the edge of their right eyes to their ear behind. They were not monsters. They were elves like any other.

The man held out a hand.

"You must come with me."

His voice was strong yet kind. Naidra could not tear her gaze from his eyes. She stepped forwards and the man placed an arm around her shoulders. Naidra glanced behind her as the autieyar lead her away. Only when she saw her sister did she realise what was about to happen. The autieyar were going to teach her their ways. They were going to guide her hands and help her to control the power within. They were going to separate the sisters. Naidra did not know for how long. She struggled against the autieyar's arm, but he held her tight. She could not escape. They would not let her go. Her terrified gaze locked with Nevra's. There was pain in her gaze. There was worse. They both knew that this was the only choice. Without training, Naidra could become the very thing her people feared. She could hurt her sister. Nevra did not look away until Naidra had vanished into the dark.

Naidra gasped as she tore free of her nightmare. She pushed herself up and fought to control her ragged breathing. Her mind swam with visions. She remembered her last days as a girl. Her childhood had ended the moment that she had fixed that net. Naidra held a hand to her throbbing temple as she composed herself. It had been seven years since the autieyar had come for her. Seven years of learning. Seven years of discipline and training. The black tattoos of the autieyar now covered the right side of her face. Now her hair was pulled back into a single thick braid.

"Naidra?" Nevra's voice broke the silence.

She had been back with her sister for years, but the nightmares still came and went like the tides. Naidra glanced at Nevra across the tent. Now it was just the two of them. Now there was no village. The others had left when she had returned as autieyar. Naidra glanced across the tent and met her sister's worried gaze.

"It's nothing," Naidra said. "Just a dream."

TWO

Holy City of Rovira, Aureian Empire

The dawn light of the Aureian sun cast its golden rays from horizon to horizon. From the grand temple to the cardinal's tower. From the great fortress of the Order of Kil'kara to the eastern river that led to the sea. Banners of the sun and moon flew in the breeze. Silver armour shone in the light. Midnight-blue surcoats emblazoned with the white sun of Durandail covered the chests of dozens of knights. The training yard at the fortress was filled with knights. They stood in a great circle, many rows deep. Their shields faced the open sands around which they formed a ring.

Grand Master Valdur Delrovira watched on. Kaladin Galad, the Sword of Kil'kara, stood at his side. Alseige, the battlemaster, and the warden, Sir Vortigern, were there. An eagle cried out overhead as two combatants entered the circle. One wore the armour of a knight. His armour and shield bore the emblem of his creed. The crest of his helmet was as blue as the sky. A younger man entered the sands opposite. His armour was without sigil or embellishment. A mail shirt sat atop a faded-blue gambeson. Pauldrons covered his shoulders and a gorget his neck. Bracers and greaves of steel armoured his forearms and shins. A shield was strapped to his left arm and he held his sheathed blade in the same hand. With his right he pressed his crestless helm onto his head. The wall of shields born by the knights of the Order closed at his back as he entered the circle. Like them he was strong.

Like them he was a warrior, a soldier of his faith. The amulet of the sun and moon hung at his throat. His eyes swept to the man opposite as he reached for his sword. Amber eyes. Eyes from the north. Eyes from Adrestia. He was thousands of miles from the village he had come from. Thousands of miles from the place that had long since ceased to be home. The Adrestian's hand tightened upon the hilt of his blade. Steel glistened in the sun as he pulled it forth. He tossed the sheath to the side; his eyes never left his opponent.

Armoured fists slammed upon shields.

The Adrestian remembered as his opponent marched towards him.

"FIRE!"

Screams filled the streets of Adrestia. Flames of the blazing fire clad the workshop in a ring of red. Timber charred and burned. Even the rain could do nothing against the fire's wrath. The smithy was all but gone, and the house beside it wreathed in flame. The blacksmith's apprentice sprinted through the growing crowds that descended upon the smithy with buckets of water. The rain soaked his clothes to the skin. His long hair was plastered across his face. Horror gripped the boy as he saw the destruction of his home.

"GRANDMOTHER!" he roared as the roof of the house began to collapse.

He turned his fear into a weapon as he surged towards the falling house. All he could think about was his family. Thunder crackled and lightning webbed across the dark skies. Mud splashed across his boots. An arm shot out of the blackness and wrapped around the apprentice's chest.

"She's gone," the man snarled, heaving the apprentice back.

"NO!" The boy shoved the man aside.

His family was trapped within the blaze. His parents had died long ago. His grandparents had taken him in, given him a home.

"If you walk through those doors, you die!" the man roared.

Hooves pounded upon the earth. Shouts and cries lit the air as a company of riders surged free of the stables beside the burning house. Flames had taken hold of the stable roof. It would be next. The horsemen did not stop. They charged out into the storm and barrelled away from the villagers. Away from the fire. The apprentice saw a wisp of white hair, and then the riders were gone. Flame danced upon the stables. A shadow darkened the doorway. A man stumbled out into the rain. A sword was held in his grip. His dark hair was greying.

"Grandfather," the boy called.

The sword slipped from the old man's grasp. He fell to his knees, crashing into the mud.

"GRANDFATHER!"

The boy raced towards his grandfather. The rain poured. The wind lashed his icy face. Fire burned. He could no longer see it. He could no longer feel it. The boy fell to his grandfather's side. No burns covered the old man's body as he struggled to breathe. His white shirt was stained red. A vicious wound had torn through him. It had been the riders. All of the Adrestians knew it long before the final words slipped from the dying man's lips.

"Elves ..." he murmured.

His eyes glazed over as life left his body.

The boy held his grandfather. Tears spilled from his eyes. Blood covered his hands. His family's blood. Twice an orphan. He bared his teeth as the fear set in, as the *rage* set in. His hate-filled gaze swept north in the wake of the riders.

He would see them to justice.

"GRANDFATHER!"

The word echoed through the Adrestian's mind ten years after it had left his lips. He had never forgotten. He could feel the heat of the fire on his face even now.

Knight circled Adrestian.

Boots crunched upon the sands. Light danced upon steel as the first blow came. The Adrestian saw the thrust driving towards his face. He deflected with his shield and countered with his longsword. The knight took it on his own shield. The Adrestian circled and feinted. He did not stop moving, and every move had purpose. The feints disguised his attacks. He came from different angles again and again. He *created* new angles. Steel kissed steel. He lunged left and then angled right, creating traps in his web of steel. The Adrestian drove forwards. Shield locked with shield. They fought for advantage. The Adrestian saw everything: he read his opponent's speed, measured his strength, anticipated. He punched his sword over the lip of his shield and thrust it into his opponent's helm. Steel slid across the armour, and then the crossguard cracked heavily into the knight's head. The knight staggered. The Adrestian followed through. He cut through the knight's defence in three blows. He ducked a hastily thrown thrust, stepped under, and then threw the knight to the ground. The dust had not yet settled when the Adrestian stepped back. His sword and shield came up. His eyes swept the circle. They never left the ring of shields that surrounded him. Sand crunched. The Adrestian spun, hearing the steel before he saw it. His sword came up and blocked the blow aimed at his head. Countering, he changed angles. He feinted high and then went low. His footwork changed; his stance changed. Steel met steel once, twice. The Adrestian shifted his feet. He thrust with sword. He thrust with shield.

Sword, shield.

Sword, shield.

Sword.

The knight slid back and made to counter the thrust he knew was coming from the Adrestian's shield. A trick.

Instead of pulling his sword back as he had three times before, he sent it to the right and into the side of the knight's helmet. It was a light blow, yet enough to take the knight's focus. The Adrestian's shield came up and around, followed the sword through. The knight had no chance to react as the rim of the shield crashed heavily into his cheek. He fell. The Adrestian spun as he heard sword slice through the air. His shield came around in time to stop steel from finding his back. The Adrestian continued his spin, his momentum taking him close to the knight. He deflected sword. One foot hooked behind his opponent's feet, and he threw a kick with the other. His leg flicked up and around. It cracked into the knight's chest. He had one way to go: backwards. The Adrestian drove his full weight into the kick. They both fell.

They landed side by side. The Adrestian was faster. He rolled on top of the knight and drove his shield hard into his opponent's chest. His foot stamped down on the knight's sword arm, while his own blade came to rest at the fallen man's neck.

It was over.

Thud.

Thud.

Thud.

Fists beat upon shield again and again and again. The knights ringing the circle created a wall of sound that echoed across the sands. It rang throughout the fortress, throughout Rovira. The Adrestian slowly rose to his feet. He beat his sword into his chest as the song of sound grew. For years he had searched for meaning. For years he had searched for purpose among the ranks of the Order of Kil'kara. He roared as he raised his sword high. He looked to the heavens, towards his gods.

Grand Master Valdur Delrovira stepped into the circle. The three defeated knights rejoined their brothers and beat their fists upon their shields. The grand master drew his sword and the thudding grew louder. It grew faster.

"Initiate, you have passed the final trial to gain entrance into the Order of Kil'kara. Kneel."

The Adrestian fell to his knees as the moment gripped him. Years of blood, sweat and tears had led him to this moment. From a blacksmith to an initiate. He had taken the hard road, and it had forged him into something better.

"Those who are soldiers of our creed are soldiers of the gods. Will you stand with us?"

"I will."

"We rise to the call of the gods. We are Durandail's steel. Without fear in the face of his enemies. We are Azaria's grace. A shield to protect the defenceless. We are guardians of the truth. Will you take up arms for your faith?"

"For the beaten and the broken. For the lost and the forsaken. I will bear my blade for this creed."

Valdur placed his sword upon the Adrestian's right shoulder.

"By the will of the Father of all Fathers."

The blade touched his left shoulder.

"And by that of the Silver Lady, I knight thee Sir Duran Cormac. Arise now as one of Durandail's chosen. Arise a Knight of Kil'kara."

"Knight of Kil'kara," the soldiers of the Order thundered.

Duran Cormac rose to his feet as cheers resounded around the training yard. He pulled the helmet of an initiate from his head for the final time. Elation gripped him as he pushed his coif back. He was barely sixteen when he had arrived at the steps of Rovira half dead from exhaustion. All of the training and all of the trials had led to this moment. All roads had led here. From a boy who had lost everything to a man with a new family. From a blacksmith to a knight.

Valdur extended an arm. Duran took it and gripped it tight.

"Welcome, brother," the grand master said.

One by one, the other knights clapped Duran on the back and congratulated him. Despite their ranks, they were all equal. They were all brothers.

The day was late when Duran Cormac at last found his way back to the halls and corridors of Rovira. The fortress city was the oldest in all of the empire. It had been born of stone centuries before the Delions had come, before Nykalous Gaedhela had claimed it barely sixty years before. Now Delios was gone. Now Rovira belonged to its people again. If one listened closely enough, they could almost hear the whispers of history that echoed through the walls of the city. Statues lined the corridors of the fortress citadel. Statues of great knights and statues of the gods. When Duran had first walked these stone corridors, he had been as scared as he had been excited. Now they were home. His rags had been replaced by the garb of an initiate, and now the armour of a knight. The white sun of Durandail burned upon his chest. The warrior god was his namesake, and that name had served him well. Duran walked the hallways until he reached a door that he had opened thousands of times before. He knocked and made his way inside.

Sir Kaladin Galad sat behind a simple wooden desk. The walls were lined with weapons and artefacts from across the entire world. From Tarik to Berenithia, Miera to Larissa. That was the only decoration. It was the only embellishment needed for the greatest swordsman in the world. Kaladin glanced up from the letter in his hand as Duran entered his office. He rose to his feet and clasped his hands.

"Do you know what it means to be Sword of Kil'kara?" Kaladin asked.

Duran frowned for a moment as he thought. He gripped his hands behind his back.

"It means that being ready is not near to enough," Kaladin continued. "It means that being prepared to fight is nothing. Every man within this Order is prepared to fight and die. No, to be the

Sword, you must know in your heart that you *will* win whatever fight comes to meet you. This fight is fast approaching, and it is a fight as close to you as any, my apprentice."

"The north?" Duran asked. In his heart he knew that it was the truth.

Kaladin nodded and held aloft his letter. "There was a rider today, a rider from Estevan Bailon," he told his apprentice. "The letter speaks of a war in the north that is almost inescapably coming. You know of what I speak."

A chill ran down Duran's spine. It was not the cold of winter nor the wind that caused it. It was something more, something darker.

"The houses have been tearing themselves apart for centuries," Duran replied. "Every year a new baron arrives. Every year there is a new fiefdom. Yet that is not what Bailon wrote about, is it? He speaks of the elves, of the ruskalan, of their ever-growing shadow."

Kaladin slowly nodded.

"You will have heard, no doubt, that tensions have been rising," the Sword said. "They say that the ruskalan have been turning the houses against one another. They say that the ruskalan and their magic has infiltrated the houses themselves – that the barons *willingly* align with them. There are those who trade with elf and ruskalan, those who fight beside them, those who wed them. There are also those who fear them. Tensions have been rising for some time. Messages arrive at the palace every day, and so far, the emperor and the courts have chosen peace. So far there have been no attacks, yet I believe that this time is coming to an end. You are from the north. What is your mind?"

Duran pursed his lips. He remembered the fire and the deaths of his grandparents.

"I have met elves," Duran told his mentor. "I have seen the ruskalan."

"Tell me about them." Kaladin gestured for him to continue.

Duran shrugged.

"In many ways they are just like us. There are good ones and bad ones," he said. "My grandparents were killed by elves ten years ago and I have not forgotten that. In the years and days before that moment, I drank with them and shared stories with them. They are led by their hearts, but I never had reason to fear them. I have seen the evils of men, and to suggest that the elves or ruskalan are any worse would be a lie."

"You speak true, even after what the elves did?"

"I can never forget what they did but blaming them all for the actions of a few is the mark of a coward."

"Then we are of like mind," Kaladin replied thoughtfully. "You fought well today, but where we now travel will require more than just your skill with a blade."

Duran watched his mentor curiously. He had been apprenticed to Kaladin for years and had grown to know him as well as he knew himself. There was an edge of wariness in the Sword's eyes.

"We are to leave Rovira?" Duran asked.

"We travel for Aureia," Kaladin explained with a nod. "Northerners have ridden for the Silver Court to petition the emperor on the behalf of their people."

"Who commands them?"

"No one," Kaladin replied. "They go at their own volition. The court will see them and hear their words. What those words will be, well, that remains to be seen. I believe they will speak of war. They will know that the dark forces of the world have struck at the throne before, and perhaps they will try to convince Emperor Janus to do something about it."

"Do you think he will choose to fight?"

"No, my brother knows war." Kaladin's tone was laced with memory. "He knows its cost. The elves, the ruskalan or whoever strikes at the throne from the shadows is not aligned with any race. The emperor will not risk the lives of his people in a foolish crusade against an enemy who may not be the enemy. No, Duran, my brother desires peace, not war. That is why we go to Aureia. The Order in days gone had a seat on that council. Until this dispute is settled, so it will again. The Circle has decided who better to advise the court than the emperor's own brother, and I will not be going alone. You passed your test with the sword, you have passed your tests of judgement and healing, yet this court is different. There those who oppose you don't look you in the eye or carry a blade. Their greatest weapons are their words. Lies, schemes, deception. That is the way of politics."

"Is that why you left?" Duran asked him with a grin.

Kaladin allowed a brief smile to grace his lips.

"In part," the Sword replied. His voice was grave as he continued, "Prepare to travel and do not pack light. We may be gone a long time."

THREE

The Northlands, Fiefdom of Cadiza

Even in winter the burning sun of the Northlands warmed the skin. Its people were hardy and weathered, made strong by the heat as much as they were by the ever-constant warring of the barons. Naidra had long since lost track of how many fiefdoms spread across the land. Some were no larger than the town within and its surrounding lands. Some covered dozens of miles, some hundreds.

The Northlands, an unnamed nation that the humans called home, was ringed by natural walls. The mountains of Larissa to the west, the Eretrian River to the south, Salvaar to the east and the Mithramir Sea to the north. Here in the north, war was a part of negotiation and blood was the common currency. Fiefdoms changed hands as quickly as coin. Few barons were ever able to hold onto their power, and fewer still passed it onto their descendants. Such was the way of the Northlands.

The elven sisters rode side by side as they made their way down the earthen road. Their horses were heavily laden with packs filled with tents, cooking pots, fishing equipment, bedrolls and food. Bows and their quivers hung from the saddlebags alongside waterskins. Despite the heat and the lack of clothing that the Northlanders favoured, the elves wore far different garments. They were nomads, but they were also warriors.

Naidra wore a short-sleeved tunic of grey, wraps covering her wrists and forearms. A short cloak of the same colour, with its hood pushed back, hung down her back and chest. It appeared no more than a small poncho that stayed clear of her arms. Darker boots and trousers covered her legs and feet. A glaive rested through the straps of her saddlebags. Half curved sword, half spear. A weapon that served her well. An autieyar weapon. Runes were etched upon the steel and wood. A knife was sheathed at her back.

Like her sister, Nevra wore grey-toned clothing. Unlike her, she wore a sword at her side.

Naidra closed her eyes and took a breath as the warmth of the sun caressed her face. In the years since she had returned to her sister, things had changed. They were still nomads; however, now it was just the two of them. Those they used to travel with hadn't forced them to leave, but Naidra understood their fear. To keep her people safe, to keep her sister safe, she had decided to leave. Nevra had joined her. Now they wandered beneath the trees of Salvaar and the great plains of the Northlands. Humans were scarcely found venturing beneath the woodlands of home, whereas out here both peoples lived in harmony. There were few elves, and fewer still ruskalan, yet they were still occasionally seen travelling and living with the humans. Despite the endless wars and fighting between the barons, out here they were all free. The sky was clear and the sun warm. It was all anyone could want. The rolling hills and meadows were broken only by rivers, lakes, the smoke of faraway towns and groves of trees. The road led them into a small forest.

A tingle rolled through Naidra's blood as they rode beneath the trees. She pulled her reins and brought her mount to a halt.

"Naidra?" Worry laced Nevra's voice.

The blue of Naidra's eyes danced as the magic that flowed through her veins spoke to her.

"There are people ahead," Naidra replied. "Humans. They are concerned. Scared. One is in pain. I can feel it."

Such was a gift of the autieyar. Nevra nodded as the sisters stared down the woodland road.

"They need help," Naidra said.

"Then we should help them," Nevra replied.

For the sisters it was the only option. The older sister clicked her tongue and urged her horse forwards. Naidra followed in her wake.

They smelt the smoke long before they found the people. Wagons had been pulled from the road to clear it. Small campfires had been freshly lit, while tents were still going up. Naidra swept her gaze around the camp. There were eight carriages that all bore the same bright colours. The strong draft horses that pulled them had been picketed far from their heavy loads. Word spread as the elves came into sight. Northlanders clad in vibrant colours emerged from the tents, wagons and trees. There were over twenty of them. The menfolk approached. Naidra could see few weapons, yet the humans' hands stayed near knife and spear. They all bore the same dark expression. A man paced back and forth at the end of one of the covered wagons. Whatever had stopped the company, it lay within.

"Good day," Nevra called with a smile.

Eyes went to the white hair, pointed ears and blue eyes. The humans knew who they were and to whom they held allegiance long before any of them spoke.

"What do you want?" one of the men called.

"We're heading north," Naidra replied. "To the market at Maencia."

"And you?" Nevra asked.

"West," came the curt reply. "You'd best be on your way if you wish to reach Maencia by nightfall." He was direct. He wanted them gone and gone quickly.

Nevra glanced at the man then looked past him to a break in the canopy towards the sun.

"What misfortune causes you to make camp at midday?" she asked as she looked back at the travellers.

"None that concerns you."

A scream came from the covered wagon. Naidra had heard those cries before. She knew what it meant – both the sisters did. Her eyes flicked to the carriage. Jaws tensed and fists curled as suspicious gazes lingered upon the elves.

"That sounds like something that might," Naidra told the man. "The woman is giving birth."

"You're a long way from a town," Nevra said, dismounting. "The baby is coming early, isn't it?"

The humans moved to block her as she started towards the wagon. Naidra read their emotions without needing to use her gifts. She could see it clear as glass in their faces.

"You have no physician, do you?" Naidra murmured.

More screams came from the wagon. It was bad and they all knew it.

"I am a healer," Nevra told them.

"You are well armed for a healer," came the suspicious reply.

"These are dangerous times." Naidra said. "We are nomads. Nothing more."

"Please, let me help you," Nevra continued.

"To what end?"

They distrusted the elves. They would have distrusted any travellers approaching and seeking to help. The man was right: Naidra and her sister were too well armed to be simple healers. There were many who would prey upon the weak; the humans were showing faces of strength.

"To save a life," Nevra told him.

"We have no coin nor great wealth in which to pay a healer," the man said.

The wall was beginning to come down. Naidra could feel his desperation.

"Good work is its own reward," Nevra said. "Please. I can help."

The humans could hear the sincerity in her voice. The elves cared and that was enough. At last, one of the men nodded. Nevra pulled a satchel from her saddlebags and slung it across her shoulder. Nevra glanced at her sister before following the man towards the wagon. Naidra dismounted and led their horses from the road. She had no cause to tie them off, for they would not run. Naidra made for the wagon in her sister's wake. The flap was pulled aside and then she clambered up. The stench of sweat hit her. Candles were lit to provide some light. Nevra knelt beside a woman prone atop damp and tattered bedding. Her belly was bare and bloated, her skin pale from exhaustion and her breathing was ragged between the screams. Nevra had a gentle hand upon the woman's belly.

"The baby has turned," Nevra said quietly.

The concern was in her voice as much as it was in her eyes.

"And if it cannot go back?" the man asked.

Nevra shot him a look. If the baby was not turned, then they could both die.

"You've done this before?" the man asked.

"Yes."

The man's hand did not stray from his amulet of the Twins.

"Her husband?" Naidra asked him.

He nodded. The autieyar gently touched his arm and then moved further into the wagon. She sat by the woman's side. Naidra reached out and stroked her cheek.

"What is your name?" she asked.

"Lana."

"Lana, I need you to do something for me," Naidra told her as she pulled a small strip of leather from Nevra's satchel. "Bite down on this. Can you do that?"

Lana dipped her head and bit down hard on the leather. Naidra took Lana's hand. She glanced at her sister, and then Nevra went to work.

The sun had begun to lower when Naidra dropped down from the wagon. The travellers sat around the grove quietly. They were nervous, and who could blame them? They had done nothing but listen to the screams of a dear friend for many hours while strangers tended to her. Nevra descended to her sister's side. All eyes went to the wagon as the flaps were flung wide and Lana's husband appeared. In his hands he held a baby wrapped snugly in blankets.

"MY SON!" he roared, holding the child aloft.

The humans leapt to their feet and cheered. Cries of joy and the sound of clapping filled the woodland.

"Tomorrow, we make for Saragoza," the man continued. "Tonight, we celebrate our new guests!"

The cheers grew louder. Cups were raised towards the elves. It was not long before the music of lutes, drums, flutes and pipes echoed through the forest. Then came the dancing. Drink flowed and the fires burned hot. The flamelight lit up the grove as the humans celebrated. Naidra found a seat upon the edge of a wagon as she watched the party unfold.

"We did a good thing today." Nevra approached with a pair of cups.

Naidra took the one offered. The sisters knocked them together and took long draughts. Naidra relaxed as the warmth of the ale hit her.

"These are good people," Naidra replied.

She couldn't help the grin that spread across her face as she watched the travellers dance beneath the trees. They spun and twirled, clapped their hands and stomped their feet. They laughed. The sound of their music would travel for miles, yet they didn't care. They were happy. One of the women gestured to the elves. Naidra raised her eyebrows and gave her sister a sidelong glance.

"Go on," she said.

Nevra's lips curled. She placed her cup on the edge of the wagon and, with a laugh, joined the throng of dancers. Naidra shook her head and raised her cup before she finished its contents with a single draught.

"Where are you from?" a young man called as he approached.

Naidra pursed her lips for a moment, thinking.

"I was born beneath the trees in Salvaar," she replied happily. "But as for home, I'm not so sure. I'm a traveller. I belong to the world, I would say." Naidra spread her arms wide.

"Indeed," the man replied, pulling himself up onto the wagon to take a seat beside her. He took a sip from his own drink and followed Naidra's gaze out across the dancers.

"And you?" Naidra asked as she looked at him.

He had dark hair like all the northerners. His accent was rich and his eyes richer still. They shone like amber in the firelight. Light stubble covered his sharp jaw.

"Oh, we're from all over," he said and gave her wink. "We're wanderers as well. Performers. Minstrels. Call us what you like."

"Really?" Naidra chuckled. "Tell me. What do *you* play?

"Many things. I play the lute, I sing."

"You sing?"

The man nodded. "You like music then?" he asked.

"I do."

"And do you sing?"

Naidra smiled. "On occasion."

"I'm not surprised," he said. "You have a beautiful voice."

"And you can tell that from one conversation?" Naidra sensed that he was flirting, and she couldn't help herself.

"Yes," he replied smoothly. "What do they call you?"

"My name is Naidra. And you?"

"Leonardo."

Naidra leaned closer to him. "And, Leonardo, what takes you to Saragoza? It is quite some way."

The northerner met her eyes and did not look away. "We are to perform at the Festival of Lineao for the Caspin family themselves," he told her proudly.

Naidra raised her eyebrows. Everyone knew that the House of Caspin was one of the greatest in the entire north.

"A great honour," she said.

"There are few things more so."

"These few things that you speak of," Naidra said mischievously. "What are they?"

Leonardo finished his drink with a grin and dropped from the wagon. He extended a hand towards her.

"Would you honour me with this dance?"

Naidra beamed, took his hand and dropped down beside him. She could feel the happiness that spread around the grove as Leonardo led her into the ring of dancers. They were joyous, impassioned and wild. They were *free*. She could not tear her gaze away from them as their joy became her own. The music whispered in her ears and called her name. It spoke to her as much as it did to the performers. Through it they created bonds stronger than any stone. Naidra's skin glistened as the warmth of the fires washed across it. Leonardo laughed, pulling her faster and then turning back to face her. She took his other hand, and they began to move. Naidra flowed into the dance, the music taking control. Her braid streamed through the air like white fire as she spun and twirled, her feet moving, fast and graceful, across the earth. The wind kissed her cheeks. It pulled at her clothes and hair. With every step the movement grew faster. With every step it called her soul. A laugh left Naidra's lips as she looked to the heavens and spread her arms, twirling. Partners changed with every heartbeat. She danced with the humans, she danced with her sister. Naidra's eyes found Leonardo through the crowd. They lingered for but a moment, long enough to catch his gaze, before she flitted away. Strands of wild hair pulled free of her braid. A hand found her own. The strong but gentle grasp pulled her from the centre of the party.

Leonardo. The light of the fires danced across his face, casting it half in orange and half in shadow. He handed her a flower, as white and pale as her hair.

"I don't believe that this is part of the dance," Naidra remarked as he led her away from the party.

She raised the flower to her nose and smelt its sweet scent.

"It is not," he replied.

His dark eyes sparkled. Naidra gave him a knowing look.

"Unless you would like to remain?" Leonardo continued playfully.

"My sister can have the attention."

Naidra observed him from behind half-closed lashes. She could see the look in his gaze and the curl of his lips. Step by step she allowed herself to be led further from the light, further from the music. Naidra stopped in her tracks and pulled him closer.

"I think she will probably be alright," she murmured as she at last looked into his eyes.

His breath kissed her cheek and Naidra drew him closer. The strands of his hair tickled her skin. She let the flower fall, forgotten, as she slowly pushed him back into the tree. She tasted his lips. The kiss was slow for but a moment before she melted into him hungrily.

FOUR

The Silver River ran fast and strong from Rovira to the empire's great capital and the Lupentine Sea beyond. Aside from a few small villages, little lay between the holy city and Aureia save for the endless green plains and rolling hills that sprawled through the heart of the great empire. With the river on their right and the fields on their left, Duran and his long-time mentor rode east. It was not long before Rovira was nothing but a speck on the horizon, and then the holy city faded into nothing. They did not stop until nightfall. Bedrolls were unfurled beneath trees under the watchful gaze of the stars. A fire was brought to life.

Duran leaned back against the trunk of a thick yew. His eyes slowly scanned the pages of the book in his hands.

"Little over seven day's ride and we will reach Aureia," Kaladin said as he pushed a log into the flames.

"This is the furthest I have travelled since I left Adrestia," Duran murmured, closing his book.

He remembered the grief that had driven him south. The deaths of his last family. Hope was the only thing that had kept him going. That hope had sent him to the gates of Rovira. After months in the saddle alone, he had fallen from his horse before the gates, exhausted and half-starved. Duran remembered it as if it was a fever dream. He had finally reached his destination and his mind and body sung that he could finally sleep. His clothes were travel-stained with dirt long before he crashed to the earthen ground. His eyes lingered above the gates and could not be drawn away from the banner of the sun and moon. It was the last thing he had seen as the hands of knights pulled him from the road.

"A long time ago," Kaladin replied, taking a seat by the fire.

"Ten years," Duran said. "Ten long years, yet they have passed in the blinking of an eye."

"Do you remember much of your home?" Kaladin asked curiously.

"Home?" Duran questioned. "So much for home. It is not so clear in my eyes. I have been in this life nearly as long as the other. Adrestia … I remember, but Rovira is my home now."

"You're not a boy anymore," Kaladin said. "You're a man. A knight of the Order of Kil'kara."

Duran slowly nodded. For ten years all he had done was study the sword and the ways of combat.

"Tell me about Aureia." Duran looked to his mentor.

Kaladin shrugged. "It is a glorious place, Aureia," he replied. "Civilised, a union of every culture. Travellers from Berenithia and even faraway Tarik frequent the streets. The bazaar is always open for trade and filled with finery from every corner of this world. The Festival of Lineao is soon upon us. You have seen it on Rovira, but in Aureia it is far more grand. Have you heard of fireworks?"

"No." Duran frowned and shook his head.

"Ah!" Kaladin clapped the younger man on the shoulder. "A great roar and the sky lit up in a great explosion of colour!"

"Is that so?"

"You will see."

"How long have you been gone?" Duran asked.

"It has been nearly eight years to the day since I last saw the Silver Palace," Kaladin told him seriously. "Thirty since I gave up my crown."

"Do you regret it?"

"Regret it? No. I hardly even remember making the choice," Kaladin said. "I have given my soul to the sword. This life … it chose me."

They rose before the sun. The light of the fire danced across the swords of master and apprentice as they moved through the motions of the sword dance of tarkaras. Every move Duran made was to perfection. Every stance and every form was as beautiful as it was deadly. He had been trained in the Tariki way of duelling since the day Kaladin had chosen him as an apprentice. That had been six years ago. When first he had moved through the dance of the far north, he had been sloppy and brutish, despite his skill with the blade. Now everything was precise. The two men danced side by side in perfect harmony. It was not long before the faint glow of the dawn sun crept across the horizon. It was not long before Duran and Kaladin were once again in their saddles.

The days came and went as they rode east along the river. The closer they got to Aureia, the more travellers they met upon the roads. Traders and pilgrims alike. Many were making their way to the great empire's capital for the Festival of Lineao. On the seventh day, a city emerged before the riders. A city so large that it dwarfed even Rovira. Fertile farmland ran for miles in the surrounding fields. Massive walls spread out from both sides of the mighty Silver River. Duran brought his mount to a halt as his eyes landed on the city. The rooftops of huge houses emerged from behind the walls. Towers ran through their midst, yet the city continued to grow larger towards the centre. A second wall, higher than the first, surrounded the imperial palace. The court of Emperor Janus sat on a massive island that grew within the heart of the river. Huge bridges of stone joined the palace to the northern and southern townships, while the castle itself soared into the heavens. The palace, like its walls and bridges, was as white as ivory. Its rooftops were so grey that they appeared blue.

"Welcome to Aureia," Sir Kaladin remarked.

The Sword of Kil'kara kicked his heels in, and the knights thundered towards the capital of the empire.

Purple banners emblazoned with the silver griffin flew atop the gatehouse. Guards in their steel armour with crests and cloaks of violet stood sentinel. Stares were directed towards Duran and his mentor as the people saw their garb and the sun insignia. The Order's reputation was well known; it had been forged by the founding knights well before the Delions had come. Their zeal and skill in battle had helped to turn the tide against the sons of Nykalous. Even now, sixty years since the Delions had been cast aside, the Order commanded huge respect among all who called Aureia home.

Duran fought against the instinct to show his awe at the sights that surrounded them. White houses that stretched as far as the eye could see. The great bazaar, a gigantic market that spread for near a mile. People of a thousand nations lined the city streets. They laughed and talked, traded and worked their crafts. Flags hung from rope above the paved roads. Performers showed their skill at every corner. Musicians, acrobats, jugglers, singers and more. They were all preparing for the great celebration to come. The city was filled with life.

The entrance to the bridge that led to the palace island was protected by two manned guard towers. These soldiers were different. They wore cuirasses that shone in the sun and were embossed with the symbol of the griffin. Their gambesons beneath were as violet as their capes. Their shields were round. Swords and axes hung at their belts. Their crests were purple, and the metalwork that held them was carved into the shape of a griffin. Long beards spilled from their chins. The Arkin Garter – the emperor's private guard.

"Light of the gods be with you, brothers," Kaladin called as warriors of the Garter approached.

"And with you, sir knight," the captain replied. "What brings you to Aureia?"

"An audience with Emperor Janus. We are expected."

The captain of the Garter frowned beneath his helmet.

"What names do you carry?" he asked.

"This my companion, Sir Duran Cormac." Kaladin gestured to the northerner. "And I am Sir Kaladin Galad."

The men of the Garter froze. They all would have known that the emperor's blood served with the Order, yet none could have expected that Janus' own brother rode before them. The captain bowed his head in deference and extended an arm down the bridge.

"Welcome home, my lord."

Stone echoed beneath hoof as the knights made their way across the vast bridge. The carved pillars that supported the bridge were topped by stone griffins that sat proudly on their hind legs. The deep waters of the river flowed beneath and around the castle. White stone walls towered into the sky and thick dark gates were wide open. Soldiers and warriors of the Garter patrolled the walls and gatehouse while more stood sentry in the courtyard below. A pigeon soared overheard from whence they had come. The soldiers who greeted them had sent word to those within the palace that the former prince had returned.

Duran and his mentor passed beneath the dark gates and crossed into the courtyard. The perfectly laid cobblestone was broken by one thing: the statue that rose in its heart, carved so beautifully that it could not possibly be anything but flesh turned stone. Atop the white stand was a griffin rearing. Its beak was opened to scream a wicked roar. Its great wings were spread, and its talons outstretched. Upon its back was an armoured rider. A long spear was clasped in his right hand and a crown was laid upon his brow. Duran knew the rider's name.

Auris, the *first* king of Aureia.

The man who had founded this city and forged the nation that would one day become an empire.

A man clad in the fine robes of the nobility emerged from the palace doors and strode down the steps towards them. His hair was neatly cropped and his jaw clean-shaven, and a purple half-cloak trimmed in silver hung over his left arm. Duran and his mentor dismounted at the base of the steps.

"Greetings, noble knights," the man called.

"My lord," Kaladin replied, dipping his head.

"My lord," Duran echoed.

"I am Dresige Vesper," the Aureian said as he bowed in return. "Steward of this great city. The emperor has been informed of your arrival and will see you in his court."

Dresige gestured to a stablehand who watched from the corner of the courtyard. Without a word, the man approached. Duran and Kaladin removed their helmets and stowed them in their saddlebags.

"Adrastos here will take your horses and see that your belongings are taken to your quarters," Dresige continued. "Now, please, this way."

Up the stairs and into the imperial palace they went, through the maze of white stone hallways and corridors. Servants, Aureian knights, members of the aristocracy and the Arkin Garter flitted about the halls as if they had been born within them. Perhaps some had. Two soldiers of the Garter stood before huge wooden doors. They saw the steward approaching with the knights and silently opened the doors.

The floor was polished and smooth. The tiles were of varying colours and arranged to form beautiful spiralling patterns. Huge pillars formed two rows through the throne room. They were topped with arches that reached to the vast ceiling. Chandeliers covered in candles hung high above, while a long violet carpet stretched from the doors to the dais. Three steps led to the raised stone platform, while two more led to the throne. Stained glass windows on either side of the room filtered in rainbow light, and a banner of the empire hung behind the throne. The throne itself was beautifully carved silver wood with armrests shaped into griffins. The tall back rose well above the one who would sit upon it, stretching out to either side like a pair of wings. Duran's gaze flicked to the people within the grandiose room.

Dozens of nobles lined the hall. Most were Aureian, yet there were those from Berenithia and Larissa.

Strong men of the Garter stood at the foot of the dais. One, with armour far grander than his brothers', stood at the right hand of the throne. The commander of the emperor's private guard. To the left stood a pair of women. Thin wrinkles creased the skin of the older of the pair. Her eyes were dark and her hair darker still. A magnificent dress of white covered her from shoulder to foot, and a crown adorned her brow. Graceful, regal, elegant. This could only have been the empress.

The other woman was younger, half her age. Her brow was not marked by the passing of time, yet her golden eyes shone with the intelligence of someone well beyond her years. Dark shadow ringed her eyes and only added to the allure of her long lashes. Her nose was narrow and her brows sharp. A necklace of orange and emerald beads hung at her throat, while her white dress was sleeveless. Her crown was made of finely linked silver strands from which more beads of green and orange were strung. Her hair fell down her back like a cloak of the richest ebony. She watched the two knights enter. Duran could see her eyes sparkle with curiosity. He tore his gaze away from the most beautiful woman he had ever seen.

The man atop the silver throne rose to his feet. His long cloak was violet and his tunic white. The crown atop his head was one that Duran had seen before upon the statue of Auris. This one was of silver, not stone. His neat hair was cut above his shoulders, while faint grey strands weaved through his dark beard. His cheeks and temple were lined, yet everything about the man said one thing: power.

Silence filled the hall as Dresige led the knights towards the throne. He swept his arm towards the emperor as all eyes turned to Duran and Kaladin.

"The King of Kings, His Imperial Majesty, Janus the First, Emperor of Aureia and High Lord of Berenithia."

Sir Kaladin and his apprentice knelt at the foot of the dais. They bowed low.

"My emperor," they said in unison.

Janus descended the dais towards the knights. "Rise," he instructed.

Duran rose to his full height beside his mentor. Janus looked Kaladin up and down with a frown. The Sword of Kil'kara stared over the emperor's shoulder as if he was greeting a superior officer. Janus' lips twitched and then his frown broke. The emperor's laugh echoed through the hall as he pulled his brother into a tight hug. Kaladin grinned, embracing the emperor. All thoughts of status and decorum were forgotten as the brothers reunited.

"Rejoice," Janus called, stepping back from Kaladin, "for my brother has returned home at last!"

The hall echoed with the thunder of cheers and applause.

"What is your name?" Janus' gaze moved to Duran.

"Duran, Your Grace," he replied. "Duran Cormac."

The emperor's brow rose in surprise as his ears caught the knight's accent.

"You're from the Northlands?"

"I am."

"How was your journey south?"

A slight frown tugged at Duran's brow. All watched him closely. The emperor, his family, the Arkin Garter, the nobles, ambassadors and aristocrats. He knew that all would judge his next words.

"It has been ten years since I made the crossing, Your Grace," Duran started. "But what I do remember of the journey was when I first saw your country … a sunrise to the night. Oceans of grass as far as the eye could see. A blue sky that stretched from horizon to horizon. Curtains of mountains and a sun-bathed land. Most of all, I remember the cold."

Chuckles ran through the throne room. Many would have thought it to be a jest, but it was the truth. Despite the sun and its warmth, compared to the Northlands it was as cold as winter.

Janus' lips twitched. "You are most welcome in my home and country, Sir Duran."

"Thank you, Your Grace," Duran replied.

Janus' eyes flicked over Duran's shoulder as a commotion came from the doorway. Five men strode into the room, drawing the eyes of the guards. Duran scanned the faces and made out the unmistakable features of a northern delegation. They wore the colours of the Aloys family.

"Forgive me," Janus said as he looked to his brother, "but I must leave you now. Affairs of state. Until we speak again, my hearth is your hearth. Sir Kaladin, Sir Duran."

"Your Grace," Sir Kaladin replied with a bow as Janus made towards the northerners.

"Your Grace," Duran said, dipping his head.

The two knights left the throne room and were escorted by the steward Dresige to their lavish quarters. No expense had been spared for the emperor's own brother and his protégé. They had separate rooms to sleep in, each bigger and grander than any Duran had ever seen before. The bed sheets were of the finest silk. Books filled the shelves that lined the walls, and the fire below the mantlepiece burned brightly. Servants had been sent to take care of their every need. They had also been afforded a small courtyard that was open to the sun.

The knights stowed their things before Kaladin called his

apprentice into the yard. The book that Duran had been reading was placed upon one of the small stone seats that ringed the yard and a blunted training sword was taken up instead. An older servant watched from the edge of the courtyard as the two knights stepped out into the grass within. Duran tested the ground as he circled his mentor. He felt the grip of the grass and earth. He felt it move, he felt its pull. Within a heartbeat Duran knew how to use it. Sunlight kissed steel. Air parted against blade. The yard echoed as the swords came together. Kaladin was near two decades older. Strength and the wisdom of years were his allies. Youth, speed and the mentorship of the greatest swordsman that Aureia had ever seen were Duran's. Ten years of training and discipline had forged Duran's body into a weapon. His mind was a library filled with the knowledge of battle. Feints, moves and countermoves. Each step had purpose. Each flick of the wrist and angle of the body was filled with intent. The yard became a canvas that was covered stroke by stroke with their skill. Duran could not feel the sun nor the beads of sweat that ran down his face. He had been trained to see through it all. He had been drilled so that he could fight in the depths of winter or the middle of a desert without pause. His footwork matched his head movement and the constantly changing stance of his body. He moved like water.

FIVE

The Northlands, Fiefdom of Cadiza

The gentle light of the dawn sun that crept through the canvas flaps of the wagon was anything but gentle to Naidra as she awoke. Pain lanced through her head. Wincing, she sat up and rubbed her throbbing temples. She'd drunk too much. She usually did. Naidra could still feel the effect of the alcohol as she glanced around the dim wagon. Thin beams of light cast shadows through the carriage. Empty wineskins lay abandoned. A pile of clothes lay at her feet while Leonardo was stretched out beneath a blanket at her side. Naidra's hair fell down her shoulders in a snowy avalanche as she rose to her feet and gathered up her shirt.

"They're very beautiful." Leonardo's voice came from behind. "Your tattoos."

He didn't just mean the right side of her face, for the canvas of black art spread down from her neck to her ankle. Naidra let him admire them for a moment before she pulled on her shirt. Each line had meaning. She remembered the rituals in which she had received them. As the years of her training had progressed, so did her tattoos.

"Thank you," Naidra replied. "I received them long ago."

"I have heard tale that elves can live throughout all the ages of the earth," Leonardo murmured, watching her curiously. "Is it true what they say?"

Naidra's lips twitched. "Of course." Humour lit her voice.

"And your markings. How long ago did you get them?"

"Almost thirty years."

Naidra's grin broadened. She could almost feel Leonardo's shocked eyes widen. She pulled the last of her clothes on, slipped through the wagon flaps and dropped down onto the ground below.

The earth crunched beneath her boots. The earlier risers of the performers wandered around the small grove. Some ate while others prepared the horses and wagons for travel. It was a long journey to Saragoza, and they would have to leave by midday if they wanted to make good time.

Naidra turned as she heard a splash by one of the wagons. Nevra shook her head as she pulled it from the watery depths of a barrel.

"That will sober you up quick," Nevra called.

The autieyar rolled her eyes but made her way over to the barrel. She plunged her head into the water. It was cold but for a few moments she felt nothing but serenity. Water cascaded all around as she pulled her head free. Wet hair clung to Naidra's face. She took a long breath.

Nevra nodded behind her sister. Leonardo had emerged from the wagon.

"I see you had an eventful evening," she goaded.

Naidra raised her eyebrows and then wrapped her arm around her sister's shoulder, steering them into the camp.

"I trust that you did too," Naidra replied. "Who was it this time? The lute player? The acrobat? The woman who–"

Her words halted as she felt something. She froze. Her eyes stared down the road.

"What woman who what?" Nevra laughed. She felt her younger sister stiffen. "What is it?"

"Riders," Naidra stated.

"We have to–" Nevra's words were cut off as a whistle rang through the camp.

A warning.

Naidra's eyes flicked across the encampment towards the alarm. Through the trees she could make out the first of the riders as a mounted company made their way down the road. They were armed and clad in chainmail. Cloaks fell down their backs and amulets bearing the sun and moon hung at their throats. The performers gathered and formed a line around the camp. Faces darkened. Arms were crossed and hands lowered near weapons. A greeting was called as the riders reached the performers. Naidra reached out with her gift. She could not see faces of the soldiers, but she could feel their emotions. They were cold yet determined. She could feel their gazes searching the faces of the performers; she could sense their eyes sweeping through the camp.

"They're looking for something," Naidra muttered. "It was not by chance that they stumbled across this camp."

"Soldiers?"

Naidra nodded.

"What are soldiers looking for so far in the wilderness?"

"I do not know, but I think it is probably time that we found out."

Naidra glanced at her sister and then started towards the gathering.

"Naidra," a voice hissed.

The elves turned to see Leonardo hasten towards them from across the camp. He looked worried, concerned even.

"Put your hoods up," Leonardo whispered as he reached them.

"Who are they?" Naidra asked, though she did as he said.

She tried to look past him to see the riders, but they were hidden by the wagons and performers with whom they were now speaking.

"They bear the colours of Gior Meridia," Leonardo told them. "Baron of Salaman."

Naidra froze and looked to her sister. They knew of the baron by deed as well as they knew him by title.

"Elf hunters," Nevra growled.

Their ears were covered and their white hair hidden, yet they were still elves. All it would take would be a second glance and those riders would come for them. Salaman. A fiefdom that regarded the elves with suspicion, fear and hate. Its soldiers had killed many of Naidra's people long before Gior Meridia had come into power, yet the baron had only fanned the flames. Nevra's hand gripped her dagger. Rage flashed across her eyes.

"There are too many," Naidra said quietly and placed a hand on her sister's wrist. "If we stand and fight, then some of these people may die."

"I know." Nevra grimaced. "If we leave, they will see us."

"You have to hide," Leonardo said. "Come with me."

Slowly he led them through the maze of wagons. Leonardo pulled back the canvas flaps on one and they clambered up inside. Nevra sat with her back against the wagon. She closed her eyes and let out a long breath. Naidra sat at her side, yet her eyes remained open, and her mind keenly focused.

"Thank you," Leonardo said gratefully as he joined them. "I can see how much you want to fight."

"The day is still young," Nevra replied. She pulled her dagger from its sheath and spun the knife around in her hands absently.

"Very far south for soldiers of Salaman," Leonardo said after a moment.

"They will be heading to Saragoza for the festival same as you," Nevra told him. "They are searching for something ... for someone. I would expect that they heard tell of my sister and I travelling through the villages. They are here for us."

"They will not have you," Leonardo said firmly.

Nevra's lips curled into a smile.

"They're leaving," Naidra said at last as she felt the riders continue on their way.

The canvas flaps were pulled open and one of the men thrust

his head inside. Lana's husband, the woman who the sisters had helped give birth.

"They were here for you," he confirmed. "Said that they had been on your trail for two days. They wanted information, but we take care of our own."

"Thank you." Naidra was sincere as she hopped out of the wagon. "You risked your life and those of your people to help us."

"You saved one of our own," he replied, waving away her words. "We cannot turn our back on good grace. It invites darkness. You are both always welcome at our fire."

Nevra glanced around the camp. Her eyes came to rest on the horses. Only two were not the heavy draft horses of the travelling performers.

"The horses," she said slowly as she realised. "If they were seen–"

"They will be seen as just horses," Leonardo told her. "You have nothing to fear."

"If they were seen, then those men" – Naidra thrust her arm towards the road as she spoke – "they will more likely than not have guessed that we are here. They will return and they will not be so kind."

"Then you should stay with us tonight," Lana's husband replied. "If they have seen nothing, then you will have a bed and hot meal. If they return, then we have numbers and will not be so easily cast aside. You are safe here. I will not allow you to ride to your deaths."

Naidra gave her sister a knowing glance. They did not know if those men were the only from Salaman here. They did not know if dozens or hundreds lay behind the next ridge.

"Alright," Nevra told him reluctantly. "One day. We will travel with you and stay the night. But then we must leave. We cannot linger for too long, nor can we endanger you."

"One day then," Lana's husband agreed. He turned back to the camp. "Make ready. Saragoza isn't coming any closer."

The camp vanished as swiftly as it had once been assembled.

Like the elves, the performers were nomadic. The wagons and carriages were loaded. It was not long before the caravan began their journey west. Some of the travellers walked, others drove or sat within the large wagons. Lana and her newborn were rugged up inside a carriage. Her husband led the column. Naidra and her sister rode beside the new mother in case they were needed. The elves watched the road, tree line and fields closely as they made their way across the countryside. This time Naidra's glaive was not strapped to her saddle. This time she held it tightly in her hand. The sun rose and fell as the miles vanished. They set up camp as the last rays of the dusk sun disappeared beyond the horizon. The elves broke bread and shared drink with their companions. They talked and laughed, but neither let down their guard. Gior Meridia's men were still out there. As the moon rose, the fires were put out and the performers made beds in sleeping rolls and inside the wagons. Thin wisps of smoke faded into the blackness.

Naidra found her sister standing sentinel at the edge of camp. Her eyes were locked to the east where they had last seen the riders. She held her glaive close.

"Do you feel it?" Naidra asked her.

"I do not have your power, but I feel it in my blood," Nevra replied. "Something draws near."

Naidra silently agreed. Her eyes washed across the dark land.

"I cannot feel them, but they're out there … somewhere."

She could feel it. Not with her gift, but in her heart, she knew it to be true.

"We have lingered here too long," Nevra said. "In my heart I know that Meridia's soldiers still hunt us."

"These are good people," Naidra added. "We cannot endanger them any longer."

"We must leave now."

The sisters crept back into the camp. They gathered their things, saddled their horses and rode away. They were never seen. They were never heard. The performers remained asleep and none the wiser. There was no time for goodbyes.

Naidra kicked her heels in. Canter turned into a gallop. The drumbeat of hooves turned into thunder. The horses accelerated. They surged northwards across the plain. They did not slow until the first light of dawn crept across the plains. They had travelled many miles in darkness without rest, and crossed into the fiefdom of Villzira, yet the nomads were used to it. They had been travelling on foot and in the saddle for decades. They pulled their hoods up as the sun washed across their faces. The road that they followed led through a forest. Trees arose on either side. Naidra felt it in the back of her head. Shadows drawing closer.

"Nevra," she called. "They're here."

The words had barely left her mouth when riders emerged on the road in front of them. Riders bearing the colours of Gior Meridia.

Naidra brought her horse to a halt as the humans approached. There were eight, all soldiers. Where the others were, she could not see, but she could feel them. Sixteen men. Sixteen swords. If they did not see the white hair and pointed ears, then the elves may yet pass freely.

"Light of the Twins be with you," one of the soldiers called out as they approached.

The sisters placed him as the captain.

"And with you, my friends," Nevra replied.

Her accent had shifted. No longer did she sound fluent in the common tongue. Now her words were slightly broken and slow as if she rarely spoke the language.

"I do not know your colours," Nevra continued.

"We serve Baron Gior Meridia of Salaman, my lady," the captain explained. "We are riding to Saragoza on his behalf. If I may, it is a dangerous time for you to be both so unattended."

"We are strangers to these lands," Nevra told him.

"And you carry steel?"

"We are Tariki," Nevra replied with just enough pride. "Carrying steel is our right."

The man offered a mirthless smile. Though the northerners had no quarrel with the Tariki, some of their ways were still considered too close to barbaric for many. Here women did not carry swords or spears. Here they did not fight. Naidra could only hope that the men before her had never met one from the snowbound lands.

"What brings you so far from your home?" the captain asked.

"I am a wanderer," Nevra said. "I belong to the world. We wished to travel the Northlands."

"And her?" The captain nodded towards Naidra.

"My sister. She does not speak your tongue."

"Forgive the intrusion," the captain said. "There are rumours from the villages. Talk of strange folk abroad."

Nevra frowned. "We have seen no one," she replied.

The captain's gaze darkened. Naidra felt his suspicion grow. He pursed his lips and glanced at his men.

"Unfortunate then that Tiago there," the captain nodded to the man at his side, "thinks that he saw you with a band of travelling performers not two days ago. I must admit that I had my doubts right up until I saw your horses. Horses that I saw with that caravan. You said that you had seen no one. A lie. I wonder, what other lies have you whispered?"

Naidra felt the presence of the men moving through the trees before they emerged on foot either side of the road.

"If you would dismount," the captain commanded.

Three of the soldiers raised bows towards them.

"Please." The captain gestured to the ground.

The elves dismounted slowly. Naidra's glaive was torn from her hand. The humans forced them away from their horses. Hands stayed atop swords. The bows were lowered yet arrows remained nocked. Sixteen men. Naidra's eyes scanned the trees searching for any advantage.

"This is good steel," the solder who had taken the glaive said as he ran his eyes across the blade.

"Now," the captain said, dismounting and striding towards them. "We track a pair of elves northward across the plains. Elves … those same creatures that not so very long ago murdered the lords of my land and killed many of my people."

They were going to be searched and found guilty. The fight was inescapable. The façade of not speaking the human tongue dissipated like smoke.

"Another time," Naidra replied. "Another lord. You would hold all elves accountable for the crimes of but a few?"

The captain flexed his weathered hand upon the hilt of his blade. Steel sang as he pulled it from its sheath.

"Remove your hood," he ordered.

Naidra stepped forwards and put herself between the captain and Nevra. She raised her hands to her hood. There was no turning back now. Lowering her hood, she let her white hair fall free. The distrust on the soldier's face morphed into malicious elation.

"Elf," he snarled and spat at her feet.

"*Human*," Naidra countered in the same snide tone.

She was not afraid.

The captain thrust his sword under her chin and forced her head up slightly.

"For what your kind did to my people, did to mine, I have a message," the captain growled. "Salaman sends its regards."

Naidra never looked away. Her eyes, fiercer than any storm. Her poise, unyielding, unbendable, unbreakable. She showed him anger. She showed him pride. Her jaw was squared. She did not budge as the captain raised his blade. Her fingers curled. A savage roar left the man's lips as the sword came down. Naidra could hear the murmuring in the wind. She reached deep within. She saw triumph in the captain's eyes. She saw victory. Her fists clenched. Her eyes ignited with blue light. The look of triumph on the captain's face evaporated as the sword stopped an inch from her face. His brow furrowed. Naidra gazed deep into his eyes as the confusion spread. Confusion turned into fear as chips appeared in the steel. Chips became splinters. Fear turned to horror, for the man could not move. He was stuck, frozen in time. Naidra could see his heart through his eyes. Shards of steel rained through the air as the sword shattered beneath the autieyar's might. Naidra tilted her head ever so slightly, her hands curled into talons. The soldier's eyes shone with terror as his feet slowly left the ground.

How many of her people had this man and his kind murdered?

Dozens?

Hundreds?

Rage flashed across her face. She stepped forwards, thrust an arm out and with a cry sent the captain flying through the air. His back slammed into a tree with a sickening crunch and then he crashed to the ground in a broken heap. Shouts echoed through the forest. Nevra's knife flashed across the throat of the man who held her sword. She snatched it from his hands before he fell in a pool of his own blood. Naidra's power flowed through her. Her teeth were bared, eyes shining like infernos of sapphire light. Soldiers flew backwards into tree and earth. The force of the magic shattered armour and the bone beneath. Nevra's sword moved like a steel whirlwind as she danced into the soldiers. She slew two before they could react. Naidra's arm shot forwards. Invisible fingers of magic latched around her glaive and tore it from a soldier's grasp, sending it flying through the air and into her outstretched hand. Instead of fleeing or running for her horse, Naidra charged the soldiers, leaping over the bodies of the men that her sister had slain, and soared into the air. Magic flowed through her. No human could move like this. No *elf* could move like this. The staff of her glaive knocked aside a sword as her boot smashed into the side of its bearer's head. The man crumpled but Naidra kept moving forwards. Her foot had not left the soldier's cheek when the sharp steel of her glaive drove deep into another soldier's neck. The unconscious man fell as the dying man toppled over. Naidra went down with them, narrowly avoiding a spear thrust. She rolled and drove up with all her might. She ducked and spun as the blade of the man on her left sliced towards her head. Rising, she caught the blow of a sword from the soldier to her right with the shaft of her glaive even as its steel sliced across the hamstring of the man on her left. He screamed as he fell. Naidra continued her spin as her shaft deflected the sword of the soldier on her right. The steel of the glaive came around, slicing up into the soldier's chin. Naidra leapt forwards. The glaive turned in her hands. She cut down a final man and path was opened.

The elves ran into the forest as the soldiers of Salaman charged, on foot and on horseback. They used the trees to cut their foe off and kept moving to stop the soldiers from surrounding them. Naidra spun her glaive like a whirlwind of steel and wood. The shaft deflected a blow and the blade opened her attacker's throat. The sisters had learnt to fight long ago. They had stood shoulder to shoulder for decades. They were masters of death. They picked off the soldiers one by one. Naidra cut a man down. More surged forwards. She killed the closest with her glaive, spun, flicked her wrists and caught the blow of the second. The magic aided her. She moved faster. She moved like an acrobat. Angles and forms that would never work for anyone else served her. None had seen her movements before. None had seen a glaive before. None that had not been born autieyar could have been prepared.

A third soldier charged at her back. Naidra slid under the man's sword, came up under his guard and smashed the wooden shaft into his jaw. The steel came around. It bit into his legs and sliced open his neck. Naidra stretched out an arm, called forth her power and raised a fallen spear from five paces. The magic launched the weapon through the air at a mounted soldier hurtling at Nevra, driving through his mail and gambeson beneath. The force of the blow carved a bloody furrow through the man's chest and erupted from his back. He fell ... and then there was silence.

Nevra twirled her sword. Red blood covered her face. Human blood. Naidra reached out with her gift. They were alone, save for the bodies strewn through the forest. Naidra took a step towards her sister. She staggered as pain lanced through her temple.

"Naidra?" Nevra cried.

"I'm alright." Naidra raised a hand to her throbbing head as Nevra reached her.

The older sister placed a hand on her shoulder to help steady her.

"It's nothing." Naidra took her sister's hand. "I am not hurt. It's just the gift."

Nevra stroked her sister's cheek. Naidra could see concern clouding her sister's eyes. It was the same worried look she had seen for four decades. It had not ended then; it would not end now.

"You need rest," Nevra instructed.

The aches that came when she used her gift were nothing to her. Everything had a price. If she had not used her power, then they would both be dead. Nevra would be dead. She had long ago been taught her limits, and that fight was far from them.

"I swore a vow to you." Naidra placed her sister's hand over her heart. "That what happened to father will not happen to me. I know what he was ... what he became."

Naidra shook her head to clear it as she started towards the road.

"There may be more of them," she said. "We have to go."

SIX

City of Aureia, The Aureian Empire

The silk sheets that lined his bed felt foreign. In the north, Duran been no more than a commoner, and in the Order, he was a soldier. A knight had no need of silk. To him the sheets were more uncomfortable than the hard earthen ground of the road. Duran rose before dawn as he always did. He clothed and armoured himself before he and Kaladin were shown to a small hall attached to their suite. Food was prepared by servants and placed upon a grand table. Duran could only raise his eyebrows at the delicacies that he could not name as they were laid out on the table before them. As the knights ate their fill, the doors to the hall opened. In walked Emperor Janus and his steward, Dresige Vesper. The knights rose to greet the leader of the empire. They bowed.

"My apologies that I could not greet you as you deserved yesterday," Janus called, striding across the room. "I am afraid that the time of warm welcomes may be coming to an end."

His expression was grave and his eyes tired. He had not slept long, if at all.

"Troubling news?" Kaladin asked.

"From far away." Janus nodded.

"The north?"

"Indeed," the emperor replied. "Each day more stories reach my ears. Whispers, rumours … I cannot make the truth of it."

Duran clasped his hands behind his back. "It has been many

years since I saw Adrestia and called the Northlands home," he said. "But in all that time, one thing has remained true. The barons are a rule unto themselves. They construct their own truths ... To them the real truth doesn't matter."

Janus looked at Duran thoughtfully.

"Then perhaps you can be the northern voice that I can rely upon."

"Your Grace?"

"I must admit that I did not come here for idle conversation," the emperor pressed on. "The barons have sent envoys to negotiate. I am to meet with them and hear what they have to say about the brewing storm. So, you will join me and lend your voice."

"You wish me to speak?" Duran asked with a frown.

He was a Knight of Kil'kara. Advising all from lowborn to wealthy lord was his job, yet his years of training had not prepared him for this. The imperial court.

"Indeed," Janus intoned. "Perhaps together we can uncover the truth."

The knights gathered their swords and followed the emperor from their quarters. It was not long before they found themselves in the same hall in which they had met Janus. The imperial throne room. Janus took his place atop his great chair. Empress Lysaea and the princess, Leona, stood at his left, while Dresige stood to his right. Duran scanned the room. Most were politicians. Magisters, lords and senators. Some were soldiers. All were Aureian. The doors opened and in walked men from the Northlands. Eight men in all. Their skin was tanned, their hair and eyes dark. Their clothing was loose and flowing, befitting those from the warm lands of the north. Long swords hung from their hips. Each man wore a different emblem, the head of the contingent bearing a thin banded crown and garb of orange. The fox was his symbol. He was the first to bow. He dropped to a knee as he lowered his head.

"Emperor Janus." His heavily accented voice rang through the hall.

The rest of the northmen bowed low in the wake of their leader.

"Rise," Janus called, motioning for the man to stand.

"Esteemed lords," the man bearing the fox symbol began, "my name is Lucen Alacala, baron of Linair. I take this first moment before you not to glorify myself or countrymen, but to honour our history." He gestured around the hall. "Many years ago our forefathers came together in peace. You showed us into the light of the gods and helped us become more. When the Delions sought to take your land, we stood shoulder to shoulder with our Aureian brothers and cast out the usurper. Together. Together we have ushered in a new era. An era of unity. An era of peace. Our friendship has kept war at bay for sixty years. The chaos that we once had to endure came to an end. Aureia. The Northlands. Proud nations united by blood."

Lucen tapped his heart as he let his words echo around the hall. The Aureians clapped. Duran watched the man closely as he joined in with the applause. The baron wore orange, but his tongue was silver. It was no wonder why the delegation had chosen him to be their spokesman, but what did Lucen Alacala want? This baron of Linair. When at last the applause died off, he continued.

"I come to you now not as a baron, or as a soldier, or a northerner, but as a man," Lucen said. "Elves and ruskalan are running rampart across our lands."

Though he tried to hide it, Duran could hear the anger in his voice. Lucen pointed towards one of his kinsmen, one who bore the colours of Salaman.

"Not eight years ago the baron of Salaman was murdered in his own bed by an elf," Lucen growled as he looked to the crowd. "The bloodshed did not end there. As the devils spread through the north, more and more fall to their barbarism and greed. Some openly take up arms. Others worm their way into courtrooms and positions of power only to betray us from within. Many have fallen, my own father among them. I come to you now, great king of kings, to propose a motion. To declare the elves and ruskalan enemies of us all."

Silence gripped the room.

"To declare them enemies of all is to declare war," Emperor Janus told Lucen.

"They have always lived in peace." Princess Leona spoke up. She stared down at the northerners, a slight furrow in her brow.

"They walk among us true enough, my lady," the Salaman ambassador said. "But I fear it is nothing but a disguise to bring chaos, calamity and death to us."

"You claim that they come to bring death to us, to humans," Leona continued. "There has never been any war between our race and theirs, yet you claim that they come to make war on us. What proof do you have?"

"They killed my lord," the Salaman ambassador said. "They killed my people. All of us here have lost family, friends and loved ones."

"And, as I hear, have you not been doing the same to them in all the years since?" Leona countered, watching him closely. "Now, if what you say is true and tensions have indeed begun to rise, could this not be the cause?"

That silenced the ambassador. Duran felt the beginnings of a smirk curl his lips. She was good. She was very good. Emperor Janus rose to his feet and walked down the dais.

"You come speaking words of murder, violence and conspiracy," he started. "Reports that I have heard before, yet always there are a great deal more that speak of the kindness and friendship of those you so condemn." The emperor looked to the Knights of Kil'kara and directed his next words to Duran. "Sir Duran Cormac of Adrestia, I would have you lend your voice to the council."

Duran felt the weight of dozens of eyes on him.

"Yes, Your Grace." He bowed to the emperor before striding out into the centre of the hall.

He looked to his countrymen, his mentor, the Aureians and the royal family. He had never been surrounded by so many politicians, least of all ones he didn't know.

"I stand before you as a Knight of Kil'kara, yet I was born Adrestian. Blood and bone, I am a northerner," Duran began. "Many years ago, my parents were taken when the pestilence came to Adrestia, and so I was raised by my father's parents. I was a blacksmith. A simple life. I learnt to forge swords without one day knowing that I would wield one. I was happy right up until the day that my grandparents were murdered by elves."

The knight felt an edge of pain enter his voice as he remembered that night ten years ago. The storm. His grandfather's blood upon his hands.

"The night that I lost the last of my family," he told the court. "I can feel the heat of the fire and the lash of the rain even now."

"You have our sympathy, brother," Lucen Alacala told him. "We all grieve for your loss."

Duran cast his mind back. He could remember more than just what had happened, but how he had felt. He remembered it all.

"When I held my grandfather in my arms, I felt anger … and rage," Duran admitted. "Perhaps, Baron, you and your men would say I had every right to hunt down the murderers and their kin. I didn't. What right did I have? Are we so very different? They love and hate, they dance and sing. I met many that came through Adrestia. Like us, there are good ones and bad ones. I have seen their darkness, yet also their light. Almost everyone in Adrestia would have died to the pestilence if it wasn't for the kindness of ruskalan and elves."

The young knight turned to his countrymen sadly. He could see the anger in their eyes. He had spoken his truth.

"You want to go to war?" Duran asked them.

"They brought the war to us," Baron Alacala hissed. "They hate us. They hate you – anyone who worships the Twins."

"I do not believe that," Duran countered. "For what if a human had killed Salaman's lord? Would you be so bent on destruction?"

Lucen Alacala shook his head sadly. "You may not want this war, you may not see it, but it is coming," he said. "The families stand against–"

"Caspin, Lintera, Pavila, Valcas, Assa." Emperor Janus cut him off. "Five families who trade with and readily support those you so condemn. There are more and you know that. Eight great houses there are in the Northlands and not *one* seeks elven blood."

"It is the influence of sorcery, Your Grace," the baron countered. "I have seen it."

"I have heard tale of the magic that those from Salvaar command, Lord Alacala," Emperor Janus said coolly. "What is that to me? Whether they have these gifts or not, they are not our enemy. No, my lord Alacala, I will not send my people into war, and I urge you to do the same."

"How can that be your decision?" the Salaman ambassador snarled. "After all that–"

"Peace, my friend." Baron Alacala cut his companion off before he turned his eyes to the court once again. "There will come a time when those creatures turn their full strength against us. I can only hope then that it is not too late."

He bowed low and his countrymen followed him towards the door. Suddenly he stopped and turned back.

"You may close your ears to the whispers of fate, my emperor, but they cannot be silenced."

His words echoed throughout the hall as the northerners left. A warning. But was it true, or the lie of a suspicious man?

The Aureians watched them leave. An uproar filled the hall as the doors closed behind the northern dignitaries. All it took was the thud of a spear upon the tiled floor for silence to return. The captain of the Arkin Garter stamped his spear upon the ground one last time before turning his gaze to Janus. The emperor had returned to his throne.

"My reign is the first in known memory free of wars in which we have fought," he said. "The first in which none of our people have been sent to slaughter. I will not do so over rumour and superstition."

That was the emperor's final word. He was unmoveable. It was not long before the northerners took their leave. The evening sun shone down upon Aureia when Duran made his way to the royal gardens. He had long since shed his armour; in its place he wore his midnight blue tunic and dark grey trousers. His sword, however, remained with him, as was befitting of a knight. The gardens stretched for near half a mile and were decorated with trees and flowers from all corners of the world. Ponds and small creeks flowed endlessly and broke up the green. Birds sang and flowers bloomed. A rare beauty in the midst of the great capital.

Duran lay upon an Aureian couch beneath a shaded pavilion. The couch – half bed and half chair – was as magnificently carved as anything in the palace. His sheathed blade sat upon a small wooden table, while his eyes were glued to the pages of the book in his hands.

"Of all the places I could find a knight, I did not expect the Imperial Gardens to be one of them." A woman's voice broke the silence.

He had not heard her approach. Duran recognised the voice before he saw the woman and hastened to his feet. He bowed.

"Princess Leona."

"Sir Duran Cormac, was it not?"

"Yes, my lady."

A pair of maids waited outside as Leona glided into the pavilion. Her light blue dress flowed like a river and left her arms and one of her shoulders bare. Her left hand was wrapped tightly around a book, and her right trailed across the table to where it came to rest upon Duran's blade.

"These gardens are my refuge from the whims of the court,"

Leona said. "These gardens are my peace." She ran her fingers across the crossguard as her eyes swam across the hilt. "This is a beautiful sword," she remarked. "Its creator is a true master of the craft."

When Leona looked at Duran, he could see no lie or jest in her eyes. She was sincere. Somehow, she knew about blades, or at least the forging of them.

"Thank you, my lady," Duran replied.

Whether by the pride in his voice or the gratitude in his eyes, she understood his meaning.

"You forged it?" she asked.

"My grandfather showed me how," Duran explained. "He taught me how to speak to the steel, and how to listen to it."

"He would be proud of you then, to know not only that you can create something so beautiful but have become so well versed in its use."

Duran smiled at the thought. "I truly hope so."

Leona turned to face him properly now. Curiosity sparkled in her amber eyes.

"How many men have you killed with such a blade? A hundred? A thousand?"

Duran was taken aback. Of all the things that he had expected the princess to say, of all the questions he had expected her to ask, this was one he had not been prepared for.

"As many men who tried to kill me," he said, unable to disguise the hint of irritation that crept into his voice.

"Forgive me, I do not mean to offend," Leona replied. "I have a curious mind. I only wish to know you."

Her words were as sincere as her expression. It was only for that reason that Duran answered her.

"I am a warrior, a knight, but a knight is more than the sum of the men he has killed," he said simply. "I have killed, yes, but perhaps a better question would be how many have I saved?"

Leona raised her eyebrows. "Indeed. I must admit I was curious that you stood as a shield before those who once wronged you."

"No, my lady, they did not wrong me," Duran replied. "Less than a handful caused me grief. Why should I turn my anger upon the rest? As I recall, it was you who suggested that those men who came all the way south might have brought their own misery upon themselves. I am inclined to agree."

"A peacemaker then?"

"As you say," Duran said with a shrug.

Humour danced through her eyes.

"Walk with me, sir knight," Leona said and gestured towards a path the led further into the gardens.

Duran gave her a nod. He buckled on his sword, gathered his book, and then the pair walked out of the pavilion and into the sunlight. A glance from the princess was all it took for the maids to remain behind.

"I noticed the book you carry," Leona said. "*The Works of Esmeray Vana.*"

She knew the book by less than a glance through the fingers that held it.

"You speak as though you know it."

"I do," she replied. "I have read it many times. I must admit that I am curious about a knight who has a fondness for poetry."

Duran chuckled. "There is more to this life than the sword," he told her. "These books, they open up new worlds, new ideas, new possibilities. They help you to see through the eyes of another."

"They paint the world in a riot of colour." Leona grinned. She glanced at Duran. "Adrestia is a small town, is it not?"

She spoke as if she knew the town in which he had been born and raised. No doubt she had read about it or been taught, though to remember such a small glint in a land of many thousands … She was wise beyond her years. Duran bit back a laugh, as he knew by now that he should not be surprised by Leona's intellect.

"It is, my lady."

"Who was it that taught you to read?"

"Kaladin," he replied. "He took me in long ago, taught me more than just the sword. He taught me to read, how to better myself."

"You speak highly of him."

"He is like a father to me," Duran replied.

He meant every word. The knight had given him everything and had helped forge him into the man he was today. Duran gestured to the book clasped in Leona's hand.

"You like to read too."

"Yes, yes I do." Leona gazed out into the gardens. "I like pages and the words within. History, journals, poems, all of it. I ... I even copy for the royal library."

Duran's eyes widened. Dozens, perhaps hundreds if not thousands, of the books within the palace had been inscribed by the princess. A rare talent.

"Truly?"

"Truly," she echoed. "Books, reading, writing ... It is my passion. I read and copy and write and let me tell you something."

A laugh slid through her lips. She gave him a mischievous look as she met his eyes.

"You cannot tell a soul. Sometimes when I copy and I see things that could be made better ... sometimes I improve."

Duran froze. He stared at the princess as she turned back to face him. If anyone found out, be they scholar, noble or priest, she would be thrown behind bars – or worse.

"That bothers you, does it?" she asked him.

"No, my lady." Duran grinned. "Forgive me, you are not what one expects."

Leona took a step towards the knight and looked him up and down.

"Neither are you," she said. "Blacksmith, knight, apprentice to the great Sword of Kil'kara and a lover of poetry and books. No, Sir Duran, you are not what one expects either."

"Duran, my lady. Duran will do," he said without thinking.

Perhaps it was an overstep. To share such familiarity with a noble he hardly knew could get him greeted by a tempered response or ill will.

"You are not one for titles or tradition, are you?" Leona stated with pursed lips.

"I grew up with soldiers, and before them a blacksmith, my lady," Duran replied. "I am not well acquainted with the rules of court. Apologies if I overstepped."

The princess tapped her book thoughtfully. There was no irritation, malice or annoyance in her eyes, only curiosity.

"My lady." A new voice rang through the gardens.

The pair turned to see a royal servant hasten towards them. He offered the princess a bow and extended a small roll of parchment; the kind that the Aureians attached to pigeons to send messages far away. Leona took the letter and glanced at Duran. She handed him her book before she flicked the parchment open. Her dark gaze scanned the contents.

"I'm on my way," Leona told the servant before she turned back to the knight. "Forgive me, the whims of the court."

They shared a smile as she echoed the very reason she had come to seek sanctuary in the gardens.

"Your book, my lady," Duran said and held it out.

"No," she replied. "It is yours to read. We both came here for a few moments away from a duty that we cannot seem to escape from. Perhaps when next we meet, we can discuss that book. In any case, Duran it is then."

She raised her brows mischievously.

"And in return I insist you call me Leona," the princess said as she made to leave. "Good day, Duran."

The knight glanced down at the book she had given him. *Elven*

Song, it was called. She wanted to learn more about the growing conflict in the north, more about his land. Duran watched her leave.

"Good day ... Leona."

SEVEN

The Northlands, Fiefdom of Ciras

A blanket of orange covered the land as dusk descended. The elves had ridden for miles after the slaughter of the Salaman soldiers. The bodies had been abandoned, unburied and unattended, left to rot in the sun. The crows would see to them soon enough. Such was the fate of murderers. The elven sisters had crossed through three fiefdoms during the day and were now so far north that any pursuit would have long since vanished. They found a clear place to make camp by a river and angled their horses towards it. They descended onto the bank. Naidra dismounted and led her mare over to the water. She stroked the horse's long neck, encouraging her mount to drink from the river. Naidra moved downstream and crouched by the water. Dried blood streaked around her fingers and across her skin. She could feel it on her face. She could smell it. Naidra scrubbed her hands clean and splashed water over her face. Red tears dripped from her cheeks into the river. She watched the tendrils of blood be claimed by the water as Nevra knelt beside her.

"How are you feeling?" Nevra started to clean herself.

"I'm alright," Naidra replied, staring out across the river. "The pain faded long ago."

She turned to her older sister and reached out. Naidra's fingers wrapped around Nevra's hand to stop her from cleaning for a moment. Nevra looked up at her.

"I know that you believe that this gift is part curse," Naidra said.

"I did not choose this power. I did not want it. In a different life I would not have it, but this is not a perfect world. Perhaps with you and me and this gift we can make it so."

Nevra squeezed her sister's hand.

"I believe you." She was sincere. "Forgive me, I just do not want to see you hurt."

"I know," Naidra replied quietly as she rose to her feet. She pulled her wineskin from her saddlebags and took a long draught. She had not been cut, hit or suffered so much as a scratch in the fight, yet the wine soothed the few aches she had. It warmed her throat and heated her spirit. "Here." She handed the wine to her sister.

Nevra gulped down a few mouthfuls before they made their way back up the riverbank. As nightfall descended, the elves set up camp by the river. A small fire was brought to life and their bedrolls stretched out alongside it. Together they sat by the fire, stars alight above them. They shared the wineskin until it was empty, and then they brought out another.

"We're in Ciras now," Nevra said. "Meridia's men have no cause to be here."

"They had no cause to be in Cadiza," Naidra countered. "Yet they were there all the same. They really hate us that much, don't they? Just because we're … different."

"The sheep follow the shepherd blindly," Nevra replied with a shrug. "The men of Salaman are no different."

Naidra smirked. Nevra handed her the wineskin again.

"They give as much a fight as sheep too." Naidra brought the wineskin to her lips.

Nevra laughed and slapped her sister's back.

"Just you wait," Nevra told her. "One day Salaman and all those humans will accept us. Perhaps Meridia will not be sat on his throne, but on that day, we will feast and dance and drink beneath a sea of stars."

She raised a hand to the heavens where the sky was silver. The firelight danced across Nevra's face as she lay back on her bedroll. Her hand wrapped around the silver orb on her necklace. She was happy. It was infectious. Naidra lay down and stared up at the starry sky. Her head spun from the alcohol.

"Nevra?

"Hmm?"

"I'm glad you're here."

"Always."

Naidra closed her eyes. Despite the bloodshed of the day, it was nights with the performers and nights like these, beneath the stars with her sister, that gave her hope. There was good in the world, and it was worth fighting for. She locked Nevra's words and the memory away as sleep took her.

Naidra's eyes flickered open as the wind whispered her name. The river, the fire and the campsite were gone. Her sister was gone. She rose to her feet slowly. Her eyes blazed blue. A forest had grown all around her. It was dark, wreathed in an aura of power. It was the Veil, the plains of the dead. The birthplace of magic. Naidra could feel it pull at her gift. She felt strong here. She felt free. Naidra felt the presence of another. Slowly, she turned to face the one clad in darkness. Dark robes covered his body. Pale hands reached up and pulled his hood back to reveal hair the colour of midnight. His face was thin and covered in black runes. His ears, like her, narrowed into points. The irises of his eyes were the opposite to her own. While hers were bluer than any sapphire and shone thanks to the magic of the Veil, his burned with ruby light. He was ruskalan.

"I heard your call," Naidra said, taking a step towards him. "I do not know your name, but I know who you are, ruskalan."

"Welcome, autieyar." The man approached and revealed his pointed teeth. "My name is Valmoar."

She could feel the strength radiating from him. He was old, very old. Perhaps he had lived for a millennium.

"I'm Naidra."

"The wind whispered and I felt your power through the Veil in the morning."

"We were attacked," Naidra explained.

"We?"

"My sister and I."

"I see," Valmoar replied.

Naidra extended her mind and reached out with her gift. It weaved through the ruskalan and travelled far beyond the Veil. She could feel the people he was with. She could see them.

"You are not alone either," Naidra stated. "The elves in your company I have always known about, for I can feel the presence of every one of my people around the world. Now I can see the ruskalan ... and something else."

"You are everything that I imagined you to be and so much more," Valmoar replied. "The other that you feel, his name is Raeghan. He is half-elf. A union of your kind and the humans."

Naidra's eyes widened. "A rare thing for one to share our blood and that of the humans," she said softly.

"There are few who do," Valmoar told her.

Naidra pursed her lips. "Few of your people ever leave sacred Salvaar, let alone in such numbers and travelling with elves," she said. "You have my interest. What business brings you so far into human lands?"

"We travel to Monocena," Valmoar explained, taking a step towards her. "Tell me, Daughter of Sylvaine, you say that you were attacked by humans. Do you bear their people ill will?"

Naidra frowned. The ruskalan were smart. Perhaps Valmoar could read the answer in her eyes before she spoke it, but she could not read him.

"No," she replied honestly. "The acts and words of but a handful are no way to judge an entire people. I have danced with them and sung with them. We trade and laugh and drink. A few soldiers from Salaman could not turn me from such beliefs."

"Then perhaps we can help one another."

Naidra gestured for him to continue.

"We travel to Monocena to meet with an envoy from Baron Mataro Aloys himself," Valmoar explained. "We wish to create trade routes between our people and theirs. It is my hope that this union will help to quell tensions between our races and show all that doubt that we can live and work together."

Hope bloomed in the ruskalan's eyes. Naidra saw how fervently he believed in his words.

"This dream is one that I share," she said. "I know Monocena. It is a farming town on the edge of Aloys lands. Why meet there and not in Sergova itself?"

Valmoar held up a hand and then knelt.

"Ah, but you see, trade is only a part of this arrangement." He ran his fingers through the earth. "The true gift is this."

The ruskalan stood and held up a handful of the soil.

"Land," he explained. "For too long our people have lived so very far away from the humans. Salvaar is our home, true enough, but what if we established a settlement here in the Northlands?"

"A village for elves and ruskalan?" Naidra said in surprise. "There has never been such a thing."

"Nor has there been a village for elves, ruskalan *and* humans," Valmoar countered. He held the earth out and watched the soil slide between his fingers. "Northern earth is far more rich than ours. We could grow crops and other food. We would not need to rely upon the hunt, trading and the humble offering that the great forest has to offer. Here is a place that we could settle. A place that we could grow old in peace. The baron believes the same and his offer is this: our people can build homes in Monocena, and his people will teach us their ways. How to till the ground, grow crops and make bread."

Valmoar spread his arms.

"You see, Naidra, this meeting offers countless possibilities for our people."

Naidra imagined it all: farms stretching horizon to horizon, elven houses and elven markets. An impossible future that suddenly did not seem so distant.

"This future is beautiful," she replied, unable to hide her grin. "Why did you call my name? What purpose do you have?"

"Myself and my ruskalan companions have rarely ventured beyond Salvaar," Valmoar said. "The elves among us little more than that. Raeghan offers a great opportunity to show unity. I for one cannot see a greater asset than the aid of those who have spent so long upon human lands. I would consider it a great blessing if you and your sister were to accompany us to Monocena and join us in leading our people into the light of a better world."

Naidra stared at the last of the earth as it slid through Valmoar's fingers. In all of her years, she had never been more certain of anything.

"We will come with you," she promised.

"The bridge at Yecala is half a day's ride north of you," the ruskalan said. "I will meet you there."

He faded into shadow and disappeared. Naidra was alone once again. She closed her eyes, and when she opened them, the first rays of the morning sun appeared upon the horizon. Thin wisps of smoke rose above the ashes where the fire had once been. Naidra rolled onto her side and looked to her sister. Nevra's gaze was fixed to the east where the sun had begun to emerge. She was at peace. Naidra's lips twitched into a smile as she pushed back the blanket of her bedroll and stood up.

"Nevra." She called her sister's name and extended an arm towards her.

"Mm?" Nevra rolled to face her and took Naidra's offered hand.

"Get on your feet." Naidra laughed and pulled her up.

"What is it?"

"We ride to Yecala."

"We do?"

Naidra nodded. "Valmoar of the ruskalan called me into the Veil last night," she explained. "He rides to Monocena to meet with a delegation from Mataro Aloys. They plan to open trade routes and create the first settlement for elves, ruskalan and humans."

Nevra stared at her in surprise. Like Naidra, she knew that such a thing had never been attempted let alone realised before. The very idea was some kind of fever dream … and yet the baron himself had agreed.

"Is such a thing possible?"

"The arrangements have been made," Naidra replied. "We are to meet Valmoar and his company in Yecala and from there ride east to Monocena."

Naidra snatched up her sword and buckled it around her waist. "Then the sooner we get to Yecala the better," she said.

Naidra could hear the joy in her sister's voice. She could see it in her eyes. Nevra had seen more than fifty summers and was still little more than a child among the elves, yet even she had heard of nothing like this. The sisters packed up their bedrolls, saddled their horses and were on the move within moments. They thundered north across the plain with purpose. The wide river stayed at their left as they raced from fiefdom to fiefdom. It was not long before they left Ciras behind and crossed into the realm of Lajera. The fiefdom spread for fifty miles and was filled with towns and villages. It was not long before Yecala came into sight. A small city that marked the edge of Lajera lands and bordered with those belonging to the great House of Aloys. A large bridge crossed the river between the two nations. A bridge that was filled with traders crossing from one side to the other, for the Aloys city of Otava was barely a mile from the crossing. A stone wall ringed Yecala though its gates were always open. Soldiers bearing the grey and white colours of the Lajera family stood atop the fortifications. Chimney smoke rose into the sky. Farmland spread around the city, while within was filled with bustling markets. The sisters rode into Yecala. The people did not stop or stare as the elves rode amongst them, for they did not seem to care. Stalls and vendors were everywhere. People traded and bartered. The city was loud and full with life.

They made their way to a large inn close to the massive bridge. They stabled their horses and made their way inside. Tables lined the bottom floor of the inn, and each was filled with patrons feasting and drinking. The light from the open shutters lit the room and a fire burned happily at the back. A waitress gracefully glided around the inn to supply the customers with drinks, while a bartender served more at the bar with a grin upon his wide face. It was loud and happy here. Naidra could feel the hum of energy. Despite the dozens of patrons, they were all human. Naidra glanced at her sister and with a shrug pushed back her hood, starting towards the bar. Laughter boomed from one of the tables as the elves reached the bar. As the bartender handed drinks to some customers, Nevra leaned her back against the counter.

"They will be here," Naidra stated.

"I know," Nevra replied.

"Good evening, ladies," the bartender called, welcoming them with a toothy grin. "If you're looking for rooms, we have some available. Warm beds, hot food."

"Thank you, but we do not anticipate a long stay," Nevra replied, eyes glinting mischievously, "But drink on the other hand …"

"Two pints and fill them to the brim," Naidra finished for her.

Within moments their pints were in their hands. The sisters knocked them together and then as one took a gulp. Nevra leaned against the counter, gaze sweeping the room. Aside from the occasional curious glance, they were ignored. The curiosity stemmed from the fact that these people would have seen few enough elves. She doubted that many would even know what a ruskalan was. Nevra took another sip, also surveying the room. The door opened and in walked a dark-haired man. His face was pale, runes marked his skin and his eyes were the colour of crimson. He was ruskalan, and he was not alone.

"Naidra." Nevra nudged her sister and nodded towards the newcomers.

The autieyar looked to the door as seven entered the inn. She recognised the leader from the Veil.

"Valmoar," she told her sister.

The other six wore hoods, yet their clothing alone set them apart. It was clear that they were from Salvaar – even a blind man could have seen it. Now heads were beginning to turn. Nevra glanced back at the bartender.

"Innkeeper," she called. "It would appear that we may be in need of your largest room. There are nine of us."

"Right this way," he replied.

Naidra caught Valmoar's eye and gestured for him to follow as the innkeeper led them up the steps, along the balcony and into one of the inn's many rooms. The fire was brought to life and three jugs of ale were placed on a wooden table. Eight beds filled the room, the most that any of the chambers had. It was only after the human left that the hoods were lowered. Including Valmoar, there were three ruskalan, shrouded in dark clothing and long cloaks. Blades adorned their belts and Valmoar's companions both had bows slung across their backs. Ruskalan were scholars and thinkers first and not known to be great warriors, yet these two clearly carried themselves as such. They all had the same red eyes, black hair and pale skin, though the runes tattooed upon their faces varied. Two men and one woman completed the ruskalan company. Valmoar's eyes darted from Naidra to her sister.

"Friends, sisters, I am glad you have come." He placed a fist over his heart. "I am Valmoar."

"Aedella," the woman said as she in turn placed her fist over her heart.

"Sarnai," chorused the third ruskalan.

The three elves were next. Their clothing was lighter than that of the ruskalan, yet they carried themselves more fiercely. Hair of snow and eyes bluer than any ocean. They bore no tattoos or markings upon their skin, for none were autieyar. Like Naidra and her sister, they were warriors and held a varying assortment of weapons. One kept his hood up and his hand stayed upon the hilt of his sword.

"Sivan," the first elf introduced himself.

"Cadoc," the second said before he gestured to the third, the one who kept his hood up. "This is my brother, Varde. He does not speak."

Varde glanced at the sisters and placed his hand over his breast. His eyes were fierce and there was a darkness to him that Naidra had never seen amongst elves before. That left the seventh member of the company.

"I am Raeghan," the young man said.

His ears were not as sharp as an elf's, nor were his eyes as blue. They were the colour of winter ice. His hair was a union of white and brown that appeared almost silver in the firelight.

"Son to an elven mother and a human father," Valmoar explained. "The embodiment of the northland that must emerge."

"One day," said Raeghan, "it is my hope that all kingdoms – elven, ruskalan and human – will be united as one. The idea of a single north, a whole north, needs to begin at Monocena."

"We here are scholars, traders, warriors and wanderers," Valmoar told the sisters. "We are gathered here today for one goal – peace. A true, lasting peace. We wish to show not only that we can coexist with the humans, but that we can work with them and live with them as well."

"When this deal with Aloys is agreed to, then it will only be a matter of time before even men such as Gior Meridia see us as fellow northerners," Aedella said. "When that happens, this future we seek will be certainly, if not inescapably, underway."

"So tonight, we rest here," Valmoar continued, pouring ale into nine cups. He lifted his own and gestured for the company to do the same. "Tomorrow, we ride to Monocena and our destiny."

As one the companions drank from their cups.

"It is also the Festival of Lineao tomorrow," Nevra added. "Aloys and his people will be celebrating."

"Come evening," Naidra told her, "so too will we."

EIGHT

City of Aureia, The Aureian Empire

"Perhaps you were the wise one," Emperor Janus said as he looked to his brother.

Kaladin glanced at Janus with raised eyebrows. They were alone in the throne room. No nobles, guards or members of the aristocracy could be found. Even the servants had been sent away. Kaladin watched his brother as the emperor stared at his throne.

"To turn down the throne in favour of a simple life," Janus continued. "Each day I feel the weight of the crown I bear. It grows heavier."

Kaladin shrugged. "I've never been one for formality or pontification, Janus," he replied. "I was never much good at politics."

"Yes, and you always spoke your mind no matter the consequences."

"I am just a simple soldier. The sword was my calling, the gods my destiny."

Janus shook his head with a snort. "You are not a simple man, Kaladin," he said. "You never were."

The emperor gestured for his brother to follow him, and the two men left the throne room.

"Tell me, what do you make of the conflict brewing in the north?" Janus asked as they walked.

Kaladin thought for a moment. His right hand stayed upon the hilt of his sword, his left resting atop his right. It is how he had always been for nearly fifty years. Ready for the fight. Ready to win it.

"Much has changed since I gave up my claim. Lands, titles … Delaureia," Kaladin told his brother simply. "I am an older man now. My skin is lined and my hair greying. Yes, I am older now than our father ever was. In all my years, one thing has remained the same, one thing unchanged by the wrath of time: the look of a man seeking a fight. Those northmen who came, whether provoked or not, seek blood. I do not know the mind of the north, but I know the mind of my pupil. The people up there do not want to fight … yet the lords of men are looking for one."

"So you believe that is inevitable?" Janus suggested, clasping his hands together. "That there will be war?"

"Perhaps," Kaladin replied. "Perhaps not. They are just *looking* for one. It may be inevitable unless someone puts a stop to it. You know politics better than I ever will. What would the northern barons have to gain by manipulating a war that would kill thousands of their own people?"

"A united north," Janus stated. "A human north. Every time northmen travel here, or send word, or ambassadors, I hear whisper of a nation called Medea."

"Medea?" Kaladin asked with a frown.

"Yes," Janus replied, stepping closer to his brother. "Medea. In the old tongue of our people, it means 'united'. Some of the barons believe that the north cannot be united while the elves live among them. Without the armies of Aureia and without our cardinal declaring a holy war, these barons will sow disloyalty and resentment towards the elves and ruskalan."

"The people of the north are not blind," Kaladin said, following his brother onto a balcony overlooking the palace gardens. "They will see it just as my student has seen it. I do not believe that the commoners would so easily take up arms against those who they have ever been friends with."

"Politics," Janus growled. "It's a devil's curse. The people are not blind, but those lords seeking violence are not fools. They will manoeuvre events and perhaps all it will take is a single push to spread chaos throughout the north."

"Make no mistake, war is coming," Kaladin told him. "It might not come in our lifetime, but it's coming."

"Then your student and my daughter may inherit a world gone mad."

The brothers looked down into the gardens. They could see Duran walking with Leona as they had been most evenings since the knights' arrival in Aureia.

"Though it would appear perhaps that my daughter will have already found a trusted advisor in Duran," Janus said. "In little more than two weeks, your student has already made a mark here in the palace."

"When I last saw your daughter, she was barely the height of my knee. Now look at her. She has grown into a fine woman. A true princess of Auriea."

"Twice as strong as her father and three times as wise," Janus told Kaladin. "Though as impulsive and with as little care for the aristocracy as her uncle."

"That may be why they have become such great friends in so short a time," Kaladin observed. "Duran is not a nobleman or knight of the realm or worse … a politician."

"They are both truth speakers." Janus leaned upon the ornate balustrade. "The time may come when their friendship will change the destiny of all."

"Why did you join the Order?"

Duran glanced at Leona as she spoke. His brow furrowed slightly.

"You are a warrior, true enough," she continued. "Yet it is clear that violence is not your calling."

"I did not become a knight to kill pagans if that is what you mean," Duran replied with a smirk. "No. I believe in honour. I believe in justice. I have been wronged, my family was wronged, everyone everywhere has been wronged in some way. There are many injustices in this world, and I wish to answer them with justice."

"Justice." Leona smiled. "Yes, the world could use more of that."

Duran heard the unmistakable hint of sadness in her voice.

"You speak as though you have been wronged."

The princess turned to face him and put her hand lightly on his arm. She looked up into his eyes as if she was trying to show him her meaning without saying the words.

"Duty is the death of many things," she told him quietly.

"How do you mean?"

"Being a princess is more than a title and the power that comes with it. It is a duty and one that I *will* fulfill … and that is the end of it."

"What is it that ails you?"

"Please do not ask me this."

Her eyes pleaded for him to not continue. Instead, Duran bit his lip and gazed around the grounds for a moment.

"As you wish."

Relief overcame Leona's face, and she slid her arm through his before pulling him down the path once more.

"There are some, much like the northern barons, who believe that the Order should only serve those of our faith," Leona said after a moment.

"Do not count me among them," Duran replied with a snort. "Kil'kara means *I am worthy*. I can think of nothing less worthy than to ignore the plights of many based upon their beliefs. If people are in need, then they are in need, and I will help."

"Noble words," Leona continued. "I wonder, what would you do when forced to choose between two causes? Both are just and good, yet with opposing ends. One for the good of the many, and one for the good of the few."

"I try to do what is right, for my gods and for the people," Duran stated. "I hope if I were to ever face such a choice that I would choose right."

"Areut talc cuun'ect," Leona said. "The words of your Order."

She said the words perfectly in the tongue of Ancient Aureia as if she had been born in that time. No doubt it was one of the many languages that she spoke fluently.

"Blood or immortality. Those are more than just words. They are a sacred vow. They are law."

"And do you believe them?" Leona asked. "Despite being a peacemaker?"

"I do," Duran replied sincerely. "Some believe the creed to mean to kill or be killed, yet to me it means something different altogether. It means being willing to lay down your life for what you believe in. It means fighting for a cause so just that if I died, then I would greet the Pale Horseman gladly, knowing that I have done right."

"And if you meet that end?"

"There are no words."

"I could think of a few." Leona turned to face him. "Cuun'etca hěy'læn."

Duran knew the meaning of the words, for like all knights, he was learned in the old tongue of the empire long before it rose from the dirt. The phrase stirred something in his beating heart. In his soul.

"Immortality in paradise?"

"Just so." She brushed her fingers across the petals of a flower. "Life is fleeting and as beautiful as a flower, yet the soul will know true freedom and true happiness … serenity. Forever."

"That is beautiful," Duran murmured. He looked into her eyes. "I will remember those words."

He had not yet noticed the shimmering flecks of golden light that danced through her brown eyes. Her gaze was like amber fire. Leona's lips twitched, a smile lighting up her face.

"Come with me," she said. "There is someone I would like you to meet."

Leona led him through the grounds and back into the palace. The vibrant colours of the gardens transitioned into stone. She took him deep into the depths of the halls. Leona knocked upon a simple wooden door and then led Duran inside. The knight's eyes widened as the grand room opened before him. There were no silks or finery, no thrones or lavish comforts. There were basic shelves and tables, desks and stools. Littered upon them were books and scrolls, vials and potions, metals and tools. There were wheels and measuring devices. Duran could hardly recognise any of it. The room was lit by torches and light that streamed through the open windows. There were maps across the walls and parchment covered with writing, drawings and symbols across the tables. There were things that looked like puzzles and others that almost looked like machines. A man stood amongst it all. His clothing was more vibrant than any noble, though his body was strong and hardy. His hair was well groomed and hung to his shoulders, and his beard was thick and brown. He turned to the newcomers as he heard them approach.

"Stefanos." Leona greeted him as a friend.

"Princess Leona," he replied with a toothy grin.

Instead of greeting her in the fashion befitting the nobility, or even in the Aureian way, he took her shoulders and placed a gentle kiss upon each cheek.

"Stefanos, I would like you to meet Duran Cormac."

The man took a step towards the knight and looked him up and down.

"A pleasure," Duran said, extending an arm.

Stefanos looked at the offered wrist and laughed. Instead of taking it, he pulled Duran into a tight hug. Hesitantly, Duran returned the embrace. Stefanos clapped the knight on the back and stepped back.

"So, you're the one who shares her love of books." Stefanos chuckled. "Good. Good."

Duran glanced at Leona. She had spoken of him then.

"Stefanos," Duran said. "That is not Aureian."

"No, no it is not," he replied. "My family and heritage are Delion."

Duran nearly shook his head but refrained from doing so. He should not be surprised by the friends that Leona had. Here in the palace, she was a rose among thorns. It only made sense that those she chose to spend her time with were the same.

"Now that is an oddment," Duran admitted. "A Delion in the heart of the imperial court."

"The fight between Delios and Aureia ended many years ago." Stefanos shrugged as he turned his eyes back to the gadgets upon his desk. "Yes, the empire killed and enslaved many of my people, but who started the war and who gave the empire the idea of slavery to begin with? Aureia merely adopted the practice as a revenge against those who sought to sow destruction upon these lands. Nothing more. What happened to my people was tragic, yet it was the great conqueror Nykalous Gaedhela and his children who saw to that."

The knight could not hide his surprise. It had barely been sixty years since the great war that had almost destroyed Aureia and in turn had led Delios to ruin. Few were left of Stefanos' kin. Those few who survived were scattered and divided.

"As you say," Duran replied, approaching the table and running his gaze across the map that Stefanos was marking. "What is this? I have seen no map nor drawing like this before."

"Ah, but it is the stars," Stefanos explained. "I watch them and read them, and they in turn reveal their secrets."

The Delion turned to a golden orb upon a stand. Around it was a pair of smaller orbs. Stefanos approached the device and placed a hand upon the large ball.

"This is our world," he explained. "Over the centuries many thousands of people have chartered its oceans and lands. What if I were to tell you that our world is only one of many, and that the stars and the sun and moon were not drawn here for the reason that our world is the centre of everything, but because that is how they were forged?"

Stefanos grinned as he looked to Duran and slowly moved the smaller orbs. They moved in a circle around the large ball.

"And that the sun and moon circle around like so, and not because of the gods' will?"

Duran frowned and placed both hands upon the table. The man had his curiosity.

"There are some who would call you mad," he said as he watched the Delion work. "Others would say that you betray the gods."

"I love the gods," Stefanos remarked heartily. "And for a reason beyond my understanding, they have granted me this mind. I see things where others do not."

Duran watched the Delion closely. He was an enigma that the knight could not solve. Stefanos spoke as though he loved his work. The map of the stars showed as much.

"When I look around, I see tools and stars and maps and machines," Duran said. "You see possibilities. What are you? Who are you?"

"He's an inventor," Leona answered.

"A what?"

Stefanos stepped back and spread his arms.

"I create things from which there is nothing," Stefanos exclaimed. "My eyes were opened long ago, and I have given my life to my craft. History, medicine, art, science … everything that is and everything that is not. When I first came to Aureia, I did so with nothing but my hands and my mind. I had *nothing*. Now, the emperor, in all his wisdom, has granted me his patronage. He pays me to pursue the unknown."

"And where has this unknown taken you?"

"Come with me." Stefanos beckoned for Duran and Leona to follow him deeper into his workshop.

Against the back wall there was a wooden mannequin garbed in a tunic, gambeson and a layer of steel plate armour. The cost of such a piece of metal would have been extremely high, for even few kings wore such armour. Stefanos gathered something up from one of his benches. It looked like a short bow attached sideways to a longer strip of wood in the shape of a cross.

"I call it a crossbow," Stefanos explained as he held the device aloft. "It holds more power than any longbow you will find."

"It is very small," Duran said doubtfully, examining the weapon.

"That is the beauty of it. Here, let me show you."

Stefanos heaved the string back to where it locked into place. He gathered up a half-sized arrow and slid it into the crossbow. Stefanos turned to face the suit of armour and pressed the end of the crossbow to his shoulder.

"I am told you were a blacksmith."

"I was," Duran replied.

"Then you will know how impossible it would be for an arrow to pierce such steel."

"Indeed." Duran crossed his arms.

The inventor aimed down the sight and pulled the trigger. Within a heartbeat the arrow had smashed through the steel and gambeson and dug deep into the wood behind. Duran's arms fell to his sides in disbelief.

"Impossible," he muttered and shot a glance at Leona.

The princess merely raised her eyebrows as humour danced in her gaze.

"Stefanos," Duran said and clapped the inventor on the back. "You're a genius."

"HA!" Stefanos boomed with laughter and offered a theatrical bow. "It has shorter range than a longbow and loads slower, true enough, yet it can reach near one hundred and fifty yards with accuracy. The arrow flies faster with greater impact. At close range it is unstoppable. And here is the real beautiful thing. It may take months to learn to use a longbow, years even to master it, yet the crossbow … any peasant in the field could use one to great effect with no training."

Stefanos handed the weapon to Duran and allowed the knight to examine it more closely. He ran his hands across the surface and tested it against his shoulder. The trigger made of steel was a simple union of wheel and lever. The wood was perfectly carved and showed the love Stefanos had for his craft. A true work of art.

"It is brilliant." Duran handed the crossbow back.

"A little more work and then before long they will be in every city in the empire," Stefanos replied.

"Tell him about your latest work," Leona called.

"You are certain?"

Leona nodded. "If there ever was someone to understand, it is Duran."

The inventor stared at the knight. His eyes revealed that he was coming to a decision about Duran. Duran met the look head on. Stefanos had piqued his interest long before he had revealed the crossbow.

"Alright," Stefanos said after a moment, making his choice. "You are from the Northlands. You will know about the elves and ruskalan."

"Elves I have met before," Duran told him. "The ruskalan, however, prefer to find solace and sanctuary in the trees of Salvaar."

"Indeed," Stefanos replied.

He pulled forth a large book, opening it upon a desk and flipping through the pages. Filled with drawings, annotations and symbols, it was clear that the book was Stefanos' own work.

"Aside from their unnaturally long lives, they are little different to us, yet that does not interest me," Stefanos continued, at last reaching the page he was looking for. "Their magic and where it comes from – now that interests me."

Duran's gaze was drawn to the pages. One side was covered in Stefanos' writing, the other was the sketch of an elven face. Half of the elf's features were covered in dark tattoos.

"They say that it is a gift from their spirits," Duran explained.

"Perhaps." Stefanos' eyes shone as he spoke. "But I believe something else entirely. I believe that their power is drawn from the mind. Little is known about the ruskalan, true enough. Some do not even believe them to be real. Elves, on the other hand, frequent the Northlands. Few enough have been granted this gift of the mind, and those that bear it are called autieyar."

"I have heard the word before," Duran admitted.

"I have studied the elves, I have studied Salvaar, and I have come to learn a great deal about them," Stefanos continued. "Their ways, their magic, their *language*. In their tongue, autieyar means *stormbringer*. Storms caress the land and can bring about new growth, or they can crash and destroy. The marking upon their face shows that they walk alone, for even their own people fear them and what they are capable of. Yet, like storms, they need them all the same."

"What you say may be true." Duran glanced from the page to the inventor. "An impressive theory if you can prove its veracity."

"Precisely," Stefanos said and turned towards a plant growing in a small pot. "And as a man of science – of curiosity – I feel the need to pursue this idea."

"Elvira," Leona explained as they all looked to the flowering plant. "It grows only in the harshest of climates. The Talismon Alps, far to the north upon the border of Larissa. An all but impassable mountain range of sand, stone and rock."

"When mixed correctly, elvira can induce its patient with a

temporary state of blurriness of the mind," Stefanos added. "It is my belief that such a state will briefly cut off the use of magic. At least until the effects of the plant wear off. But that is another story entirely."

"Well," Duran said, looking to the inventor. "When I next return north, you should come with me. Perhaps we can test this idea of yours."

"One day I should very much like to travel north. Not to just your land, but Tarik and beyond. I would like to explore the wide, wide world, and I shall if it is the gods' will."

"Perhaps one day we will see it together," Duran mused. "Visit Tarik and see the snowbound lands."

"Perhaps." Stefanos offered a toothy grin. "Now, forgive me, the great celebration for the Festival of Lineao is tomorrow and one must prepare. I hear that the emperor has planned a grand party."

"The emperor?" Leona questioned with raised eyebrows.

Stefanos laughed heartily. He kissed the princess' cheeks once again before he embraced the knight. Duran returned it fully this time. The man's enthusiasm was infectious.

Leona led the way from the inventor's workshop with a smile upon her lips.

"What do you make of Stefanos?" she asked.

"He is brilliant." Duran was breathless.

"Some would call him mad."

"He is that as well." Duran chuckled. "The world would be a much brighter place with more men like him."

"Indeed. The only thing he loves as much as his works are parties and celebrations," Leona told him humorously. She turned to face the knight. The green in her eyes danced. "Can you dance, Sir Duran?"

"I have never had the occasion," the knight conceded.

"Well then." Leona's mouth twitched. "Tomorrow at the festival, I shall teach you."

NINE

Road to Monocena, Fiefdom of Aloys

The company of elves and ruskalan stayed in Yecala for the night. They drank and celebrated their newfound alliance before they found their way to their beds. Even here among such a small gathering of those who all wanted to achieve the same goal, Naidra could feel the glances upon her. She could feel the suspicion and fright. Perhaps Valmoar had told them who she was – what she was. Perhaps he had not. All the same, they could all see her tattoos. The tattoos of an autieyar. The markings of one both revered and feared. Naidra had long since become accustomed to the glances and paid them little heed. Everyone with her was good and true and meant no ill. If the only thing she had to endure was sidelong glances, then she would.

The company rode out come sunrise. They crossed the great bridge as the dawn sun rose before them. Eight rode horses, while the elf Sivan drove a large wagon filled with goods from Salvaar. Pelts, carvings, gems and elven wine. The first of many such shipments. Valmoar called for the column to halt as the sun descended. They dismounted and started to make camp for the night. The last night before they would arrive in Monocena, before they would meet with the Aloys delegation and change the future for their people. Nevra watched as her sister walked out into the forest alone. Thanks to her gift she would always be different. She left to escape the looks of the rest of the company. The dark-haired ruskalan talked quietly amongst themselves at the far end of the camp as the elves gathered.

"Do they not join us?" Nevra asked her companions, nodding towards their leader and his people.

"You know the ruskalan." Cadoc sat back against the wheel of his wagon. "They walk their paths alone. Not much for conversation perhaps. They are the reason why we are here."

"They are all thinkers, true enough," added Sivan. "But Valmoar is different. He is a dreamer. Brought us together to change the world."

Varde, the silent elf, leapt back up into his saddle with the grace of one born to ride. He kicked his heels in and surged eastwards. In all the time that Nevra and her sister had been with the company, Varde had kept his hood up and said nothing. His hand had never left his sword and his gaze remained dark.

"Where does he go?" Nevra asked, eyes following his trail.

"My brother rides to make sure the road ahead is safe," Cadoc replied.

"We have been with you a day and a night and yet he has said nothing," Nevra mused.

"If you are asking, it is not a choice," Cadoc muttered.

"How do you mean?"

The man sighed as he watched his brother vanish down the road.

"It was not long after the baron of Salaman was killed that we found ourselves in his lands," Cadoc explained. "We used to be wanderers same as you. After Salaman's murder a bounty was placed upon elves. His people were angry and understandably so. We thought we could help them. We were wrong. So blinded by fear that they could not tell the difference between friend and foe. They could only see the white of our hair and the points of our ears. We were captured and they cut out my brother's tongue. A serving girl took pity and risked her life to free us. We escaped and found our way back to Salvaar. I did not see what they did to my brother, but I could hear his screams. Since that day he has dedicated his life to the sword and bow."

Nevra glanced into the woods where she had seen her sister vanish. She wondered what Naidra felt when she looked at Varde, what her power told her. Nevra at last recognised the look in Varde's eyes. It was the look of a tormented man.

"He may not be much for manners, but he is a good fighter," Sivan added from his place on the wagon.

"Good?" Cadoc smirked. "He's the best."

"I hope that I never have to see it with my own eyes," Nevra replied.

"But if you do, you'll be glad to have him," Cadoc continued.

Nevra looked to the man on the wagon. "Sivan, right?"

"Aye."

"What are you then?"

"Trader, craftsman, merchant. Call me what you like."

"And your part in this is coin?" Nevra asked curiously.

Sivan grinned and shook his head.

"No," he replied. "No, I have traded with the humans many times before. I travelled the fiefdoms from north to south along the border for years until one day it became readily apparent that things were changing. Tensions had begun to arise. Darkness was spreading across the land. Suspicious eyes followed me where the questions could not. Fights started between our people and theirs. Lies, murders … The land had become too treacherous even for a trader. It became too dangerous to travel with my family. My daughter. I returned home and remained in Salvaar ever since. But I remember the days when the humans greeted me with open arms and warm welcomes. I wish for those days to return. I wish to drink in every town in the Northlands without fear of a knife in the dark. I want a better future for my daughter. That is why I am here."

His story was dark, yet his eyes shone bright.

"It is true," Nevra said. "Times have changed. The men from Salaman patrol the south far from their own lands."

"South?" Cadoc frowned. "How far?"

"Cadiza and then they tracked us to Villzira."

"What were they doing there?" Sivan asked.

"They say they were heading for Saragoza for this festival of theirs." She bit her lip. "A lie perhaps. I do not know."

"They are getting bolder, true enough," Cadoc added. "We have our good friend Gior Meridia to thank for that."

"And his bounty," Nevra agreed. "It is no secret that elven blood commands a great price in Salaman. A shame for him that most humans do not share his ideals. Just days ago, a travelling band protected my sister and I from their wrath. They risked their lives for strangers."

"And it is in those people, and men such as Mataro Aloys, that we must place our faith now," Sivan said.

"You say that you were attacked, and that the travellers protected you." Cadoc gave Nevra a sidelong glance.

"Mmm?"

"You are a wanderer, one of the greatest warriors among our people," he continued. "Your sister is autieyar. I do not think that you needed protection."

Nevra snorted and gave him a smug look. She rolled her eyes and met his gaze.

"Well, Cadoc, we did not. Tanris rose from the Veil and now sixteen men lay dead upon the earth of Villzira."

Cadoc laughed. "Ha! You truly are a Daughter of Sylvaine."

"Quite the merry gathering you have here," Nevra stated as she looked around. "A ruskalan dreamer and his companions, a trader who knows the human ways and how to talk to them, one who shares their blood to unite us and two warriors."

"Soon to be the stuff of legend." Sivan chuckled.

Cadoc took a swig from his wineskin. "Perhaps one day they will make statues in our honour," the warrior said with a toothy grin.

"Perhaps one day they will," Nevra agreed and took a swig from her wineskin.

"We are merchants, fighters, dreamers and storytellers. Not much to the eyes of the world," Sivan gestured up to the silver stars, "but here we are kings."

Naidra watched the heavens from her perch in one of the trees. She leaned back against the thick trunk with crossed arms and her legs hanging to either side of a great branch. She watched the moon and the stars above as they danced through the dark, cloudless sky. Her ears pricked as she heard someone walking through the woods below. Naidra didn't look down, for her gift told her all she needed to know.

"I thought I would find you here," Raeghan called.

"In a tree?"

"No," the half-elf replied. "Beneath the stars."

At last Naidra looked to the boy as he started to clamber up the tree. She extended an arm and helped him up. Raeghan gave her a nod and sat beside her. His gaze turned to the heavens and for a moment they sat in silence.

"It is a great burden you carry." Raeghan's voice was quiet.

"Pardon me?"

Naidra's brow furrowed. She had to bite back the irritation that came crawling up her throat. Many tried to understand her.

"I know how you feel."

Naidra scoffed. "You know nothing of what I feel," she hissed through bared teeth.

"I see the way they look at you. One part adoration, one part fear. They revere your gift and connection to the spirits, yet they also fear it," Raeghan said simply. "You are elven, the same as them, but you will always be different. An outsider who walks her own path. To be autieyar is to be alone. I understand what it is like to have no place with your own people. I understand that burden."

A lump formed in Naidra's throat. She did not feel anger or rage at his words. She felt sorrow. She felt pain. She barely noticed the moisture that misted her eyes.

"How can you know that?" she whispered, unable to hide her sadness.

"Because I am a half-blood," Raeghan returned. "The first child born of the love of an elf and a human. I believe that the spirits have always guided down this path, and that this journey is fated. But let me tell you something: I too walk alone. Travelling through Salvaar and the Northlands has taught me one thing. I am too human for the elves and too elven for the humans. I do not have a place. It is my hope that this meeting can change that. That one day outsiders like you and I will have a home."

"Do you really believe that that is possible?"

"I do … I have to," Raeghan said. "There is good in this world, Naidra, we need only find it."

Naidra let out a long breath as she pondered the half-elf's words. He understood part of her, that was certain, yet he knew nothing of the rest.

"For my entire life I have been pushed aside just because I am … different," Naidra stated. "Perhaps you understand that, but know this: every day and every night I suffer with the knowledge that I am more powerful than anyone I know. I understand why they fear me. I understand that this gift is also a curse. I am the first autieyar to share this gift with a parent. My father was autieyar. He was good and kind until the magic took its toll. He lost his mind to the gift. He killed dozens of people, and when she tried to stop him, he killed my mother. He died with the knife of the woman he loved buried in his heart moments after he took her own. The destruction he caused before he fell … I have only heard the stories, yet I have seen the remains."

Naidra looked to Raeghan. She shivered, though not from the cold. She had been a baby when it had happened, but her sister had witnessed it all. Naidra had seen the horror in her eyes when her sister had deemed her old enough to learn the truth. It still haunted her.

"I understand why they fear those with unimaginable power, a power that can turn a good man into a monster. That is why all autieyar walk alone, away from their own kind. In all the time since, the only ones who have seen me, and who I really am, are those who do not know of this gift and Nevra … That is, until I met Valmoar."

Naidra could see Raeghan taking it all in. They were alike; they were not the same.

"Nevra. Has she always been by your side?" he asked.

The one person who had never treated her as an outcast. The one who had never abandoned her. The one she loved with her entire soul.

"Always," Naidra replied. "She is my sister, my confidant and my dearest friend. She is my keeper … I would say."

Naidra barely slept that night. She was restless. Her mind was filled with what could change in the days to come. Perhaps the fear and mystery that surrounded the autieyar would fade just as swiftly as that between the humans, elves and ruskalan. This dream of Valmoar's was something out of song and fairy tale, yet if they succeeded … the gateway to possibility would be flung wide open.

Varde did not return until the company had risen and were preparing the horses for travel.

"To Monocena!" Valmoar's voice echoed through the woods.

As one, they leapt up into their saddles and turned east once again. The sunlight swept across the lands as they rode. Earth churned beneath hoof. Manes streamed in the wind. The farmland came into sight first. It stretched far and wide from north to south, east to west. Houses and barns were scattered through the fields.

Farmers tended to their crops as the company rode by. Wheat grew so close to the road that they could touch it. Naidra extended a hand. The crop ran through her fingers and tickled her skin. She pulled a single stalk out and raised it to her lips. Nevra waved to one of the men and he waved back. Soon the fields and crops gave way to the village of Monocena. Barely two dozen wooden houses filled the township. The headman's manor sat at the centre of the town, the song of a hammer on an anvil ringing from a small blacksmith. A temple of the Twins was raised in the south and a large warehouse sat to the west. Monocena was quiet and small. A simple town. A peaceful town. Naidra exchanged a smile with her sister as they entered the village. Banners bearing the white tiger of Aloys were scattered through Monocena. The manor doors opened and out came the headman.

"Greetings, noble guests," he called. "I hope that your journey was kind."

"It was," Valmoar told the headman.

The ruskalan dismounted and greeted him with an extended arm. The northerner took it and gripped it tight.

"Monocena welcomes you all," the headman said happily, spreading his arms.

"We look forward to working with you," Valmoar replied.

"Come." The headman gestured towards the western warehouse. "Traders and ambassadors from Sergova have just arrived. They are waiting for you."

Valmoar and the headman talked as the company followed them towards the warehouse. For a trade deal to be arranged, where best to make it than inside one of the very buildings that would one day store the goods? They dismounted and tied their horses to the outside of the shed. Sivan pulled the rug back from across his wagon and revealed everything that he had brought. Pelts and skins from animals native only to Salvaar, carvings and jewels, trinkets and rare stones, medicine and other brews.

"Here," Sivan called, beckoning his companions.

As Valmoar followed the human inside, the rest of the company gathered up armfuls of the Salvaari goods. Sivan handed Naidra a huge bundle of pelts. She held it tight, nudged her sister and then side by side they entered the warehouse. It was huge, as tall as four people, and filled with crates and barrels, hay and farming tools the likes of which none of the Salvaari had ever seen. Naidra placed the bundle of pelts on top of a wooden crate.

"I will help your man," the headman called as he made for the door again.

Valmoar gave him a nod.

"Well," the ruskalan leader said as his companions gathered. "Here we are, my friends. Before the day is done, we will have achieved what many believe to be impossible."

An icy shard of pain lanced through Naidra's mind. She grimaced as it hit her hard. She curled a shivering hand into a fist and closed her eyes. The blue of her iris flashed as she called upon her gift. She felt the presence of humans and something more. Something darker. Her eyes flew open, and her gaze shot to the doors as she recognised the pain that she felt. As autieyar she was connected to every elf.

"I'm sorry," the headman's voice called through the doorway.

"Sorry?" Nevra muttered as the man's running footsteps could be heard.

Sivan stumbled through the doors. His hands were clutched to his chest. White blood leaked through his fingers. His eyes glazed over. He crashed to the floor, dead before he hit the ground.

"Sivan!" Cadoc shouted. He rushed to the fallen elf's side.

Naidra turned to her sister and met her eyes.

"Soldiers," the autieyar rasped. "Dozens of them."

"Dear spirits," Raeghan murmured as he looked out of the warehouse doors.

Cadoc closed Sivan's eyes and followed the half-elf's gaze as the rest of the company joined him. Soldiers filled the village. Far more than a town such as Monocena could have produced. There might have been near a hundred. Bows were raised towards the warehouse. Raeghan leapt backwards and slammed the doors shut as bows sang. Three arrows slammed into the wood where he had just been.

"We are betrayed," Aedella hissed, unslinging her own bow.

"Why would they do such a thing?" Sarnai snarled, following Aedella's lead. "They have no honour."

"This was a trap," Nevra added. "The whole time this talk of peace was a lie."

"It does not matter why they betrayed us," Cadoc spat. "Only that they did."

"Naidra, we need numbers," Valmoar said.

"I can sense one hundred, perhaps more."

War cries thundered through the village.

"They're surrounding us," Nevra called as she peered through the cracks in the walls. "We're trapped."

Swords and spears slammed into shields as the humans added to their cries. One by one, the elves and ruskalan armed themselves. Valmoar drew his sword. Aedella and Sarnai nocked arrows in their bows. Varde and Cadoc did the same. Naidra's glaive was with her horse outside of the warehouse, but she still had her magic. Nevra pulled forth her blade.

"I should have seen this," Naidra hissed. "I should have felt it. I was blind."

"We need to think." Sarnai glanced at his fellow ruskalan.

"They won't give us time to think," Valmoar replied, watching the humans move. "They are coming."

Chants came from the road leading to the warehouse as the humans made their approach.

"I am sorry that I brought you to this, my friends," Valmoar growled. He adjusted his grip upon his sword, beating it upon his breast. "This is where we hold them!"

The chants became a roar.

"TANRIS! RISE FROM THE VEIL!"

The humans closed in. The thundering charge began.

"DESCEND UPON THESE LANDS!"

Valmoar heaved the doors open. Arrows spewed forth from the defenders' bows. Humans fell beneath the storm of steel. Varde tossed his bow aside, drew his sword and shield and stepped forwards to stand shoulder to shoulder with Nevra and Valmoar. The arrows broke the charge and when the humans arrived, they were drawn out and scattered. They fell easily to the swords that awaited them. Blood wet steel and rained through the air. Naidra stared out the doorway. Amongst the houses surged the horde of soldiers. A horde broken only by the buildings and a tree.

A tree.

It grew by the path that led to the warehouse. Naidra extended a hand and reached out with her gift. Her eyes blazed with blue fire. Magic ran through the wood as she searched for weakness. There was none, so she made her own. Naidra's outstretched fingers curled. Bark shattered around the bottom of the trunk. Her teeth were made bare. Her hand twisted as her magic flowed through the breaking wood. Naidra cried, swinging her arm back. A great crack sounded, and the massive tree came down across the path, crushing those beneath it. Human screams filled the air. The attack halted. Naidra took a deep breath as the first of the pain started to hit. A cry came from the human ranks, and they surged forwards once again, arriving in full force. Only the narrow doorway stopped them from overwhelming the defenders, but they could not hold for long. Red blood was joined by white and black as elf and ruskalan were cut. Naidra's eyes darted around the warehouse. An arrow sank deep into Aedella's shoulder. She stumbled backwards. With a savage scream, she snapped the shaft of her bow and took up her sword. Naidra's eyes locked on the hay.

"Raeghan," she cried. "We need fire!"

The boy obeyed without question. He leapt towards the pile of elven trade goods and snatched up a precious stone. He ran to the hay, drew his knife and sliced it into the stone.

Naidra turned her gaze to the doors as her companions were slowly driven back. Sarnai fell, a spear pierced through his heart. The red irises of the ruskalan faded into grey as his life was taken.

"Quickly!" Naidra pleaded.

Raeghan worked faster and faster. Sparks danced on the rock and flew into the hay. It smouldered and smoked and then flame roared to life. Naidra watched as the fire spread through the huge stack. She took a long breath. Her eyes ignited once again as she reached out with her magic. Her gift caressed the growing flames. She could feel the power of the fire as its heat kissed her face. The fire grew. It licked at the roof of the warehouse. Naidra centred herself as her magic reached deep into the flame.

"NEVRA!" she bellowed.

Nevra glanced over her shoulder and saw the flames.

"BACK!" she shouted, moving away from the doors. "BACK!"

The elves and ruskalan stood aside. The humans roared in triumph. Naidra roared and flung an arm towards the doors. The flames surged forwards, obeying her without question. The tongue of fire spewed through the entrance. Screams of nightmare were barely audible over the sound of roaring flame. Humans were ignited wherever Naidra directed the fire, their bodies disintegrating into ash beneath the wrath of magic and flame. She was its master. It roiled and flared. The humans fled. Naidra fell to a knee. A moat of fire ringed the warehouse and forced the attackers away. Agony tore through her mind. She held the fire in place and fought for control. A howl left her lips as she forced the flames to dissipate into smoke. Within moments the fire was gone, in and out of the warehouse. Everything was silent. The stench of thick smoke filled Monocena. Wood was scorched and burnt. Ashes covered the blackened ground. Wood, plant and flesh – nothing had been spared. Naidra's eyes flickered and the blue light faded from them. Her hair was singed, her face covered in ash. A trickle of white blood ran from her nose. Her beathing was laboured and rasping. All she could feel was pain.

"Naidra," Nevra murmured, kneeling beside her.

Naidra barely had the strength to meet her sister's gaze. She couldn't even feel the eyes of her companions as they stared at her.

"They have retreated for now," Valmoar called. He closed the warehouse doors. "They know an autieyar is here and will not try again soon. But they are still out there. They are not defeated. We have been given a second chance."

The locking bar was set into place and only then did the elves and ruskalan find places to rest. They were bruised and battered, covered in ash and the blood of friend and foe alike.

Like the humans, they were not beaten.

Shivers ran through Naidra's body as her sister helped her back to a crate. She slumped against it and closed her eyes. Her head spun and she could barely think, such was the pain. Nevra crouched before her sister and gently cupped her cheeks, wiping away the blood with her thumb. Naidra took a rattling breath and looked into her sister's eyes. Nevra said nothing. She didn't have to. Her touch alone was enough.

"I think … we might have made a mistake … leaving Salvaar," Naidra managed and offered as much of a smile as she could bear.

Nevra tenderly stroked her sister's cheek.

"We will get out of here," Nevra promised. "We will find a way. I will make a way."

TEN

City of Aureia, The Aureian Empire

Duran's dark hair was neatly tied back into a small bun and his face was cleanly washed. The shirt and trousers that he was garbed in were finer than any he had worn before. The shirt was deep green and embellished with silver lining. The trousers were brown, a shade lighter than his boots. His belt was snug around his waist and unencumbered by sword or knife. He felt naked, exposed, without his steel. The silk that caressed his skin was uncomfortable after a lifetime of the rough clothing of a peasant and then the garb of a soldier.

Duran joined Kaladin in the courtyard of their quarters. Duran raised his eyebrows at his mentor, spread his arms and slowly spun in a circle. Kaladin gave him an approving look before his lips curled into a smile.

"You look as uncomfortable as I first did in those things," he said with a growl of a chuckle.

"Give me chainmail and I will gladly wear it," Duran told him seriously.

"We would not need minstrels as you graced the hall with your dancing. The sound would be enough."

"We would not need a jester then either."

Kaladin laughed and clapped Duran on the back.

"Well, you had best get used to these ordeals," he said. "There may be many more in your future."

"Lord have mercy."

Kaladin beckoned his apprentice towards one of the tables. "Here." He gestured towards a pair of masks.

One was green and silver to match Duran's clothing, the other blue and silver to match Kaladin's. Duran picked up his mask. The silver of the brow and nose faded into the varying shades of green that ringed the eyes and ran beneath them. Small carved embellishments covered the mask, while the lacing that would bind it to his head was as emerald as the green that surrounded the eyes. It would cover his nose, half of his cheeks and his brow, making him all but invisible to the throng of people who would all be wearing such things. Duran placed his over his face and fastened the lacing. Kaladin did the same, and together they made their way to the palace gardens.

The corridors were packed with hundreds of guests. Nobles, knights, visiting dignitaries and ambassadors. For one night while the Festival of Lineao was celebrated, all were made equal. The streets, inns and taverns beyond the palace would be filled. No one would sleep tonight. Song, dance and revelry would consume even the most reserved of men. The knights wound their way through the throngs of finely clad and masked partygoers. Many were drinking. Some were already drunk. The only people not richly clothed or wearing masks were the stone-faced men of the Arkin Garter. They were the emperor's elite guard and their duty this night was to be the palace's sacred sentinels. No soldiers were as loyal as the Valkir guardsmen.

The stone walls and corridors gave way to the lush grass, green trees and vibrant plants of the emperor's gardens. People in their hundreds started to gather before one of the pavilions. Kaladin led Duran and soon they found themselves at the front of the growing crowd. Hundreds became a thousand. Horns blared and silence filled the gardens. All watched the pavilion expectantly as a single man separated himself from the pack and climbed the wooden steps. The man gave a sweeping bow as claps and cheers resounded. He held aloft a single hand, silencing the crowd. He was no more finely clad than any of them; indeed, until he had stood alone, he had been invisible.

"Welcome," Emperor Janus called, spreading his arms and revealing himself. "Today is a day of happiness, a day of equality, where one's birth or title does not divide but unites! In years gone by, I and my predecessors would have stood among you, none would have given a speech and instead revelled in the anonymity that this night provides."

His words gripped them all by more than their ears and eyes, but also by their hearts. The swell of the crowd stilled in the wake of the break from tradition.

"I stand before you humbled on this great occasion, surrounded by my noble people and friends from distant lands who have travelled for countless miles across plain, desert and ocean to be here this day. Today marks the turning of the year, and what a year it has been! The Silver Tower has been completed. Our friendship with King Siaed will see Larissan wine flow in every tavern. We even brokered a treaty with the mighty Valkir so that our coast may be secured for years to come! And last … my own brother has returned home!"

The people roared. Duran glanced at his mentor as he clapped. The mask hid much but he knew Kaladin well. He could tell what filled his mentor. Pride.

"Tomorrow marks the beginning of the twenty-fifth year of my reign," Janus declared. "Twenty-five years as emperor. There are some that would say that alone is a blessing, but I would say that the true blessing is living and working with you all to create a better world. Twenty-five years of peace … I wonder what blessings the next year will bring."

Emperor Janus lifted an arm to the heavens. Flaming lines streaked into the sky. They thundered, and then the darkness of

night exploded with colour. Blue, red, green, yellow – a rainbow
in the night. Duran's jaw dropped as he watched the change again
and again as more and more explosions rocked the city. The great
cheer started in the palace and rolled down onto the streets. Tens
of thousands of voices rose in unison. Kaladin gave his apprentice
a wink.

Fireworks.

Just as he had once said.

When the last of the colour had died in the skies, the knights
made their way back inside and towards the great hall. Minstrels
played boisterously. Tables covered in food from every corner of
the world and golden jugs filled with drink lined the walls, while
the centre of the chamber was reserved for dancing. Dozens of
nobles filled the floor. They spun and twirled to the rhythm of the
music as it flowed. No eyes lingered upon the knights. The gazes
of respect and admiration were gone. Here they were invisible. A
roar of a laugh reached Duran's ears, a laugh that he recognised.
He stifled a grin as he saw a man that could only be Stefanos
surrounded by lords and ladies. They were listening to the inventor
intently as he told a story that, even without hearing it, Duran
could tell was embellished beyond reason. Stefanos' mask and
garb were as vibrant as a rainbow. He was born for great occasions
such as these. Kaladin poured himself a cup of wine, took a long
draught and nudged his apprentice.

"I must find my brother. I will see you later."

"And what about me?"

Kaladin chortled and spread his arms as he backed away.

"Enjoy the party."

Duran bit back a chuckle and shook his head as his mentor
vanished into the voracious crowd. His eyes flicked around the
room. The laughter, warmth, free-flowing drink and tightly
packed room almost reminded him of the barracks in Rovira.
The soldiers were crude, true enough, yet here in the palace

there was far more debauchery. He took up a cup and poured himself a drink.

"You won't be needing that," a woman's voice called.

A voice he knew as well as his own. A voice that he had grown to admire and care for. Duran turned to face its owner. If he didn't recognise her voice, he would have recognised her eyes even amidst such a crowd. The green flames in her hazel eyes danced in the light. They were soothing and fierce, the colour of autumn.

"Is that so?" Duran replied as he took Leona in.

Her dress was simple and red and left her right shoulder and arm bare. A short sleeve hung to near her left elbow. Thin bands of gold ran around the end of the sleeve, bottom of the dress and single-shouldered neckline. The gown hugged her body tenderly like the kisses of a fire. A cuff of the same gold wrapped around the bicep of her bare right arm and a pair of rings adorned her fingers. A common ruby pendant hung at her throat, while her mask was as crimson and gold as her gown. Leona's rich hair hung in dark waves that tumbled down her shoulders and back.

"You look beautiful," Duran said.

Perhaps he overstepped. He did not care. With a smile that could paint sunshine, Leona stepped towards him and reached out a hand. She gently took his cup. Her eyes never left his.

"I believe you owe me a dance," Leona whispered, leaning past Duran and placing his cup upon the table, forgotten.

"I suppose I do."

Her eyes shone. "Take my hand."

Her skin was soft to his touch, yet she was not delicate. She was strong and filled with purpose as she led him into the middle of the hall. Duran could not stop his smile as they joined the dance. It was true, he had never danced before, yet he knew footwork and he knew grace and for now that would do. He could see the humour in Leona's eyes as she took the lead. Tonight, she was free of the burden of being a princess just as his chains of knighthood had disappeared. Tonight, she was like anyone else. Tonight, she was free. Duran could see it in her smile, in the way that she laughed and moved. Her body spoke it, even though half her face was hidden by a mask. They were in step. Their eyes never left each other. The dancers, the music, the party … all of it dissolved, leaving just the two of them. Paradise.

The night was late, but they had not felt the passing of time when at last, hand in hand, they left the hall. The forgotten crowd seemed to part around them, until it too vanished into nothing. The night air was cool to their warm skin as they walked into a quieter section of the palace far away from the drink and celebration.

"Dancing. You're a fast learner," Leona said.

There was a joy in her voice that she had not had before this night. Freedom suited her well.

"I had a good teacher."

"Only good?" Leona chortled and turned on him.

Duran pursed his lips as he stared into her eyes. He offered a shrug.

"Perhaps."

"*Perhaps?*" Leona ran a thumb across his hand as she spoke. "You mock me."

"I would not dream of it."

Leona stepped in close without looking away. She gently placed a hand on his chest.

"You insult a princess of Auriea."

"Is that so?"

"I wonder what the emperor would do if he heard of such a slight."

"I have heard he has a great temper."

Leona stopped and for a second looked away. She chewed the inside of her lip. Duran could see her mind working in her eyes. Leona looked back. The humour in her eyes was gone, replaced with true seriousness.

"Duran. I have a name for myself here. I have a title and all of the shackles that come with it. I do not know what the gods have in store, but I want you with me."

Duran could see her lips tremble as she spoke the words. She knew what she was asking, that his words would either be a refusal or a promise. He was a Knight of Kil'kara who had a duty to his brothers and the people. What he decided now could change every vow he once swore. Duran looked down. His heart slowed as he took her hands and held them tight. He lifted them and, in his soul, he knew he had only one choice.

"Then I will be with you," he whispered.

Leona's gaze softened. She leaned in and pressed her forehead into his. He closed his eyes. He knew how much his words meant to her. Now she would know how much she meant to him. Slowly his eyes flickered open and something drew his gaze away from Leona. Around the corner of the hallway was the tip of a spear. His face hardened as his years of training resurfaced.

"What is it?" Leona asked as the knight drew away and took a step down the corridor.

Duran did not reply, for his focus was fixed keenly upon the fallen spear. He heard Leona follow. Duran halted as he rounded the corner. A soldier lay on the stone floor. His blood pooled from a wound in the side of his neck. He was of the Arkin Garter. Duran knelt beside the body and gently closed the dead man's eyes.

"He's gone," Duran said quietly, eyes sweeping the hallway.

Leona placed a hand on his shoulder. "No sign of a struggle," she said.

"There was none." Duran analysed the hallway and then the cut. "This is a knife wound. The blow was precise and strong. He had no time to react. We are not alone."

"An attack as such at a festival … This is a message."

Duran nodded. A message to the empire.

✦ ✦ ✦

Kaladin sat at one of the long tables as he shared a drink with his brother. The music was growing louder. Empress Lysaea laughed. Dresige Vesper raised a cup towards the emperor's table. They all returned the gesture. The dancing was quickening. Kaladin's brow furrowed behind his mask. He cut off his brother with a raised hand as his eyes scanned the hall.

"Kaladin?" Janus questioned.

Kaladin saw them moving. They were clothed and masked in the same finery as all present, but their hoods and cloaks revealed them. Kaladin had seen them through the night individually, yet now they started to gather. Some made for the doors. Some lined the pillars. Kaladin rose to his feet, hands balling into fists. They were positioned near many of the Arkin Garter. As the music rose, the cloaks fell away. Swords were unsheathed.

"NO!" Kaladin roared.

Screams filled the hall as the swords were plunged into flesh. Soldiers fell. The music stopped. Shocked eyes stared … and then the blades were turned upon the crowd. Kaladin leapt past his brother as one of the attacker's came from behind with a knife. He was the Sword of Kil'kara. He saw it all. Kaladin took the attacker by surprise. His hand latched around the attacker's wrist. He twisted it hard and drove the dagger back into its bearer's throat. The man made no sound as he fell. His clothes were not stained red as his blood flowed. They were stained white. Kaladin stared at the dying man in disbelief. He tore the attacker's mask from his face and ripped his hood back. White hair.

He was an elf.

They all were.

"PROTECT THE EMPEROR!" Dresige Vesper cried.

"We have to warn–"

Leona's voice was cut off as a horn blasted. Screams filled the air and the clash of steel followed.

"Duran, my father …"

Duran turned and gripped Leona's arm as she made towards the hall. Towards the fighting.

"No," he insisted. "Your father is protected. The Garter is with him. Your nobles are with him. Kaladin is with him. We do not know how many have come. We cannot go that way. An attack at the heart of the palace is an attack against your family. I have to protect you. We cannot stay here."

Leona gritted her teeth. She understood.

"This way," she told him.

Duran snatched up the fallen guard's spear and followed Leona as she started running away from the fighting. Kaladin was the greatest warrior Aureia had ever seen. Whoever attacked the palace was in for a very rude awakening when they crossed blades with him. Leona was a princess, untrained in the arts of war. She had no blade, so tonight he would be her sword. She was the only thing that mattered. Shouts and screams erupted all around them. Duran saw flickers of fighting down the corridors. He did not know how many attackers there were. Perhaps dozens. They were masked and clothed like everyone else. It would have been easy to infiltrate the castle on such a night. A cry in a foreign tongue went up. They had been seen.

"RUN!" Duran shouted as two of the attackers surged towards them.

Leona needed no further instruction. Shouts and screams filled the hallways as the pair fled into corridors bustling with Aureians. Duran glanced over his shoulder as the footsteps closed in. Two masked men rounded the corner with bloody swords in their hands. Leona ran as fast as her dress would allow. The two men quickened their pace. Duran turned. His spear came up. The sword aimed at his head was deflected to the side by the spear's wooden shaft. They would have thought him just another noble. He was not. He was apprentice to the Sword of Kil'kara. The blade of Duran's spear came around and sliced through the man's soft throat. White blood cascaded through the air.

White blood.

Duran thrust his spear at the second attacker. The man leapt to the side and countered. Duran blocked once, twice, three times. His feet moved on instinct. His form was perfect. The spear spun in his hands. The shaft knocked aside his assailant's sword. The spear's blade sliced through the flesh of the man's thigh. The spear came around as Duran moved and then steel tasted blood once more as it sliced through the mask and across the man's face. The mask, cloven in two, fell to the ground as the dying man did. White blood stained the stone and ivory hair fell free.

Duran stared at the *woman* who lay before him. Eyes bluer than the ocean faded to grey.

Elves.

The sound of footsteps brought him back to the present. Shouts came from further down the corridor as more elves charged towards the princess and the one who had killed their kin. Duran turned and raced down the hallway. Elves came from every direction. They cut down all in their path and painted the stone red. Duran leapt bodies as they ran. An elf surged forwards from a side corridor with a cry upon his lips. He was too close for Duran to get between him and Leona. Duran launched his spear. Flamelight danced across the steel tip moments before it drove through the elf's heart. The man screamed as the force of the spear spun him and sent him crashing to the ground. Duran risked a glance over his shoulder as he ran. Their pursuers were too close for him to retrieve his spear.

"HERE!" Leona shouted.

She heaved open a door. Together they leapt inside. Duran shoved his shoulder back into the door as Leona slammed the lock closed. Not a moment too soon. The door shuddered as the elves reached it.

"Elves," Duran growled.

"Elves?" Leona's eyes widened in horror. "What are they doing here?"

"I do not know."

Duran surveyed the room. A large bed sat at the far end. Shelves of books lined the walls and cupboards and desks filled with finery were everywhere. The chambers of a lady with higher standing than a noblewoman. These were Leona's rooms. The door thudded. Duran's eyes darted around the chamber.

"I need a weapon."

Thud.

Leona pulled open one of her drawers.

"Take this," she said and handed him a kukri.

Thud.

Duran drew the blade without question. The Delion knife was as long as his forearm and angled down in a vicious curve. The steel was razor sharp and finely honed. The door shuddered. Something snapped in the lock. Duran held his right arm back to shield Leona, his left holding the kukri tight. The bed was at their side and would narrow the elven attack.

Thud.

"Stay behind me," Duran ordered.

His eyes hardened. His breathing slowed. His body was loose. The kukri was light in his hand. Leona was at his back. Whatever came through the door would not make it to her and live. The door flew inwards as the lock shattered. The first two elves raced inside, their blue eyes blazing with hunger. They saw their cornered prey and charged. Duran strode forwards to meet them. Steel rang as the kukri intercepted a sword aimed at his head. Duran lashed out and kicked the desk chair at his side into the path of the second elf. It smashed into the man's shins and sent his attack wildly to the side. Duran leaned aside from the first elf's thrust. The sword nicked Duran's shirt but not his skin. Duran slammed his arm down on the flat of the blade even as he countered. The elf couldn't move. His companion and the bed trapped him. The kukri drove up into chin and brains beyond. Duran heaved the blade free as blood watered his face. His free hand snatched up the sword just in time to intercept the second elf's blade. Duran narrowly deflected the blow that darted towards his face. The steel grazed his cheek as he pivoted and countered. Once more the kukri tasted blood as it sank into the elf's chest.

Kaladin roared as his sword took an elven head from elven shoulders. The body crashed to the ground to join the dead.

"ON ME!" Kaladin bellowed.

Eight men of the Arkin Garter stood with him and a dozen more armed nobles. Dresige Vesper held a sword close. They were all that stood between the emperor, his empress and the horde of elves before them. Men fell as the attackers pressed forwards. Guards and nobles alike. They fought for their lives, they fought for their gods, they fought for their emperor and they died for him in droves. The ranks of guards and nobles thinned. Kaladin killed again and again and again. His body was a canvas of white and red. A blade sliced his arm. The blood of an ally washed across his face. Kaladin killed the elf before him. They were well trained. Even the Garter had few answers, but still the Valkir guardsmen held. The emperor joined his people as they fought to their last. He fought to defend them. He fought to defend his wife.

"TO THE DOORS!" he cried.

The Valkir roared and marched as one, their shields locked in an unbreakable wall. Kaladin gathered a shield from the dead and led them forwards. The elves fought back hard. They had no shields.

The Garter did. They had no armour. The Garter did. Another foe would have fallen long ago, but these were no mere warriors. They were elves; when they lost ground, blood was the only currency they accepted in exchange. They surrounded the wall of shields as the defenders fell one by one. A gap in the wall opened. An elf screamed and leapt forth. Blue eyes flashed hungrily. The steel of his blade glistened as it drove towards Janus. There was no escaping it. Dresige Vesper, Steward of Auriea, leapt in front of his emperor, in front of his friend. The elven blade sank into his heart. Aureian steel found a home in the elf's breast in return. Dresige roared in defiance as the elf crashed to the stone. The steward fell to his knees, his blood watering the ground.

Kaladin bellowed as he slew the elves to defend his family. Janus fought at his shoulder. They would not be so easily swept aside. The elves came from every side as the shield wall became a ring. The empress was at the centre and the armed nobles filled the gaps. Few remained. A Valkir chant came from the doors – a dozen men of the Arkin Garter appeared. They crashed into the back of the elven formation. Blow by blow, the tide turned. Blow by blow, they forced the elves back. For every elf killed, three of the defenders were slain. The number of Aureians and Valkir began to overwhelm the elves.

"FORWARD!" Kaladin roared as he cut an attacker down.

The defenders charged. One by one, the last of the elves were slaughtered. One by one, they fell to the blades of those who they fought to destroy. Steel slid between ribs and tore through hearts as Kaladin slew the last elf standing. As the man's body hit the ground, Kaladin's gaze darted around. Three guardsmen and half a dozen nobles remained. The sounds of fighting rang from the corridors.

"Bar the doors," Kaladin commanded.

He ignored the deep cut in his arm as he glanced from his brother to the empress who sheltered behind the guard. Blood leaked down Janus' leg, but he was alive. They both were. A shout echoed through the hall. Kaladin turned as the men closest to the doors were hurled aside like leaves in the wind.

A single man entered. A mask fell from his fingers.

His hair was white as snow, his eyes shone like sapphires. Half his face was covered in spiralling black tattoos. The closest of the Valkir charged. He raised his axe as a vicious war cry left his lips. The elf did not even look at the guard. He turned his hand slightly. The Valkir flew backwards through the air, striking a stone pillar hard. The bones in his back shattered.

Fear filled the room.

The elf had magic.

The elf was autieyar.

An elf screamed as Duran's sword found a home in her chest. Blood dripped from Duran's cheek as he kicked the dying elf down. Six others lay scattered around the chamber. He kept himself between them and Leona as he fought. Every time they tried to flank him, he moved. Every time they came at him, he killed them. He deflected a blade, slew its bearer and stepped forwards. Kukri and sword obeyed him as he flowed like water. A blade sliced his shoulder, another his side. Duran bellowed as he fought back. He would not fall. He would not die. He spun between the elves. His sword drove deep into one's body. A fist hammered into his face. Another elf leapt upon him. His hand was torn from his sword. Duran crashed down onto his back, air forced from his lungs. The hot breath of an elf filled his senses. A hand found his throat. Duran stared into the elf's hate-filled eyes. He thrust up with his kukri, but the elf blocked the blow with his wrist. Duran's head rang as a fist smashed it into the floor. His vision flickered. He roared and heaved. The elf fell to the side and Duran leapt on top. The kukri came down hard. The elf raised his arms to block the blow, catching the knife. Duran shouted as he drove down with all his might. Steel bit into flesh. Blood flowed. The elf gasped, air fleeing from his lips. His eyes turned to silver glass as life left his body. Duran started to rise. Something heavy slammed into his back. The knight fell, pain lancing through his body. Everything screamed. Duran snarled as he fought to rise. The blade of a spear narrowly missed his face as Duran threw himself to the side. Steel grated upon stone. The wooden shaft cracked into his cheek. Duran spun back and rolled to face his attacker. The elf raised his spear. There was no escape. Duran raised his kukri in defiance and roared. The elf brought the spear down.

The torches and candles flickered out as the autieyar walked among what remained of the humans. Darkness took the room. The smoke was as thick in the air as the blood was on the ground. Kaladin held his sword tight. A pair of nobles charged the elven sorcerer. He swatted them aside like they were nothing. Their crumpled bodies hit the stone floor. The thud echoed through the hall as the elf approached. He did not even glance at the lifeless bodies as he strode by. Kaladin stepped between the autieyar and his brother. He levelled his sword.

"KIL'KARA!"

The words had barely left his lips when the elf thrust out his arms. The nobles and Arkin Garter were cast aside. Kaladin was cast aside. The air caressed his body as it welcomed him. He slammed into the hard stone wall and crashed to the ground. The bones of his left wrist shattered. He struggled to breathe. The autieyar extended a hand and a spear rose from the ground, hovering beside the elf.

"Emperor of heretics," the autieyar snarled, locking eyes with Janus.

Janus held the autieyar's gaze.

"King of nothing."

Janus looked to his wife. He said nothing, for his eyes alone held meaning. Kaladin tried to rise. He failed. His body would not obey him. The spear flew higher as the elf approached, its blade angled towards Janus.

"Lord of no one."

Janus spread his arms. He held his sword and he held it tight. This was the day he died, and he would die as an emperor of Aureia. The elf raised his arm. Air whistled and there was a thud. The elf staggered, revealing an arrow pierced deep in the back of his shoulder. A bellow ripped through the autieyar as he fell to a knee. The elf turned towards the doors.

Stefanos of Delios stood alone, his crossbow aimed at the elf. He was covered in the red blood of his slain companions.

The elf's blue eyes flashed. He thrust an arm towards Stefanos. His cry echoed as his spear shook. Then it fell and bounced upon the stone. The blazing light left the autieyar's eyes. Horror contorted his face. His magic had *gone*.

"SEIZE HIM!" Janus shouted.

Kaladin heaved himself to his feet. The Arkin Garter rose. Kaladin stumbled towards the elf. His teeth were bared against the pain. The elf cried out, snatching a knife from his belt.

"NO!"

The words had barely left Kaladin's lips before the elf took his own life.

Duran thrust his kukri forth. A last show of defiance as the spear descended. Triumph lit up the elf's eyes and then a sword tore through his back. The spear fell from the elf's nerveless fingers. He tried to will himself to stand. Leona's face appeared over his shoulder as she forced the blade deeper. The elf crumpled and Leona pulled the sword free with a gasp. She stared at the steel covered in white blood. The blade rang as it bounced upon the ground. Leona's eyes were wide, her face pale. Duran did not tear his gaze from the princess as he rose to his feet. A tremble shook her body. The sounds of fighting had stopped. No more elves were in sight. The battle was over.

A Valkir cry of victory echoed through the castle.

The cry of the Arkin Garter. Duran dropped the kukri, his pain forgotten. Leona collapsed into his arms. She pressed her head into the crook of his neck as he held her. The blood that covered them both did not matter now. He closed his eyes.

They had won.

ELEVEN

Village of Monocena, Fiefdom of Aloys

Nevra gripped her arm ring as she gazed around the warehouse. Her face was bloodied and blackened by ash. Everything smelt charred or singed. Even the air was burnt. Cadoc knelt beside the bodies of Sarnai and Sivan. Their eyes, now grey and lifeless, were closed. Cadoc placed weapons upon their chests and wrapped their hands around the steel. He was gentle and gave them nothing but respect. Varde stood at the doors, a silent sentinel. An arrow was nocked in his powerful bow as he gazed out through the thin cracks in the wood. Night had fallen hours ago and Sylvaine's moon shone high above. Aedella sat against the wheel of a wagon, her sword at her side, shirt unlaced and drawn back from her shoulder. Black blood stained her pale skin. The broken end of an arrow shaft protruded from her flesh. The steel-bladed tip was hidden within her. Valmoar crouched before her, staring into her eyes as he tenderly reached out and took hold of the arrow. Aedella gave him a nod and squared her jaw. The ruskalan leader did not look away as he slowly pushed the arrow free. Aedella barely grunted as her blood flowed from the wound. Placing the broken shaft to the side, Valmoar drew his dagger. In a single move he sliced it across the flesh of his palm. Valmoar pressed his bloody palm to Aedella's shoulder and gripped it tight. The red of his eyes blazed – he was calling upon his gift. Aedella grimaced, her steady breaths turning into laboured pants as the magic of the ruskalan blood coursed through her, working its magic. Skin and flesh stitched itself back together. Piece by piece, she became whole once again. Aedella gripped Valmoar's arm gratefully, and the leader stepped back. The wound was gone. Neither cut nor scar remained on her perfect skin. Aedella laced up her shirt. Nevra glanced down at her own wound. The sleeve of her right arm was sliced open above her bicep. Dried blood stuck to her skin and covered the cut beneath. She gathered up a rag and started to bind her wound. Ruskalan blood had no effect on elves. Elven blood had no healing properties.

Valmoar and Aedella joined Cadoc by their fallen friends.

"Fathers, brothers, sons," Valmoar began in Salvaari as he looked to the dead.

His words were strong, filled with deep sadness. Varde turned away from the doors. Nevra stopped her work. Naidra and Raeghan watched on in sorrow.

"Even in death you are victorious. Your names will never be forgotten. Honour, loyalty and courage. You answered the call when many would not. Farewell, my brothers. The spirits fly with you. May you find peace in the Veil."

They stood in silence as Valmoar's words faded. Elves were bound together. Ruskalan were bound together. They all felt the same pain. They left the dead to their peace. Nevra continued to wrap her wound once more.

"Let me help you," Naidra said quietly.

Her strides were weak and her eyes tired. She was exhausted. Her mind frayed.

"No," Nevra replied, tying off the bandage. "You need rest."

"I am strong enough."

Nevra gave her sister half a smile and reached out a hand. She stroked Naidra's jaw.

"I know," she said simply. "It's just a scratch."

Naidra bit her lip. "I didn't see it, Nev," she said. "I think I did not see it because I did not want to."

The pain in her words broke Nevra's heart.

"This is not your fault." Nevra's tone was heavy. "Mataro Aloys was a man we trusted. We believed that he shared our dream, but he did not. The fault does not lie with you or I; it lies with the baron and his schemes."

She took Naidra's hand and placed it over her heart.

"You saved our lives and for now that will do."

They exchanged a smile.

"We must plan," Valmoar called.

All eyes went to their leader.

"What do we know?" he asked.

"They have us surrounded and have over a hundred men," Aedella answered. "Torches line the warehouse and they have left our horses. Bait."

"Any attempt to reach them will be met by arrows," Cadoc added.

"So, we must find another solution," Valmoar said.

"We could create a way out, slip out the back unnoticed using the dark," Raeghan suggested.

"No," Nevra said. "The torches. You would not make it five paces."

"We need the horses," Aedella said. "Any attempt to flee on foot would see us caught before we escaped Monocena."

"We need a diversion," Valmoar stated. "We need something to draw them away while we get to the horses. It is the only way."

"I can do that," Naidra offered.

"No," Nevra countered.

"If I can—"

"No!" Nevra cut her off, her voice sharp and loud.

"You're afraid," Naidra shot back and shook her head.

"Yes! I am afraid. You have given enough. You cannot give anymore."

"Nevra—"

"I KNOW YOU ARE STRONG!" Nevra shouted. "You are the strongest person I have ever met! Our father was strong. He pushed too much and when the gift claimed him ... I was there. I saw it. Innocents dead. Our *mother* dead. Every night I see them. Every night I feel their blood. Yes, I am afraid. I am afraid that you will die saving us. I am afraid that even if you do not a part of you will die anyway."

Nevra could not stop the tears from rolling down her cheeks. She could not stop the shakes that ran through her body.

"I lost them. I cannot lose you too."

"You won't," Naidra swore as she took her sister's head in her hand.

"You cannot do this," Cadoc growled. "If you awaken that power, you will destroy us."

"And what are you going to do about it?" Naidra snapped and stepped towards him. She bodied him backwards and thrust her head forwards. "What are you going to do?" she asked again.

Cadoc's hand fell to his sword. His blade was half drawn when Valmoar shoved his way between them.

"Enough," he snarled.

"And what would you have us do?" Cadoc questioned, shoving his sword back in its sheath. He did not look away from Naidra. "Watch as her power kills us all?"

"Cadoc is right," Aedella agreed. "It is too dangerous."

"You mean *I* am too dangerous," Naidra replied.

"Watch your tongue." Nevra glared at Aedella.

"She is not." Raeghan stepped to Naidra's side.

"You are not completely human yet, are you?" Cadoc seethed. "For all we know, if it was you who–"

"ENOUGH!" Valmoar shouted.

He drew his sword and drove it into the ground.

"Whether you are ruskalan, elven or half it matters not," Valmoar cried, sweeping his gaze to each in turn. "Everybody here is on the same side. Now, the only way out is those horses and the only way to reach them is diversion. Aedella, can you shoot?"

She nodded and rolled her arrow-struck shoulder back.

"Good," Valmoar continued. "Then tomorrow, at dawn, you will light every house in this village ablaze. In the chaos, as the soldiers move to save this place, we will escape. Now, if there is no further argument, I will take first watch."

He gave each of them a withering glare before he snatched up his sword and strode away. Nevra watched Cadoc and Aedella with baleful eyes. Tension ran deep in the air.

"We should all get some rest," Nevra said.

No other words were spoken as one by one the companions scattered around the warehouse. Nevra glanced at Varde who still stood stationed at the doors. His eyes were glued to Aedella's back and his hand gripped the hilt of his sword. He exchanged a glance with Nevra before he let the blade go. They all found their own places to rest. Nevra curled up beside her sister. She took Naidra's hand.

"It will work," Nevra said.

She didn't know whether she said if for her own sake or for Naidra's.

"It will work."

The moon passed its peak and all too soon Varde was waking them all from their slumber. His watch had been the last. Darkness still shrouded Monocena. The sky was cloudy and starless. Dawn was on the verge of breaking. The companions said nothing as they gathered up their weapons and made ready. Some offered prayers to the spirits, others tested the edge of their blades. Aedella approached the sisters. Her red eyes went from face to face. She offered a smile and extended her arm towards Naidra.

"Forgive me," Aedella said. "I was wrong to doubt. That is my shame. Sarnai was my cousin."

Naidra took her arm and returned the smile.

"There is nothing to forgive," the autieyar told her.

Nevra took the offered arm in turn.

"Shoot straight," she said.

Aedella nodded and turned to the rest of the company, clasping their arms in turn. When she reached Valmoar, she pressed her forehead to his. She took a breath and then, using a rope, began her ascent up the beams to the warehouse roof. They watched as she found a place on a ledge and cut a section of thatch from the roof. She made a hole and pulled out half a dozen arrows. Aedella wound the steel tips in oil-soaked cloth and placed her bow upon the warehouse roof. She turned a pair of flint stones upon the thatch she had gathered. They held their breath as Aedella brought a fire to life. The first rays of the dawn sun had emerged when she clambered up onto the roof. As one, the company drew sword and bow. Naidra pressed her head into her sister's. She gave a savage grin. They were elves. They were warriors. Valmoar eased the locking bar from its place. Aedella reached down through the hole and stuck her first arrow into the flames. Within moments the cloth ignited. The soft flights of the arrow caressed her cheek as she rose to her full height. Aedella took a breath. The bow sang. The arrow flew through the air. It sank into the thatching of another roof. There was nothing … and then the first tendrils of smoke materialised. The fire had not yet emerged when Aedella shot another arrow. The roof of the first house began to burn as smoke rose from the second.

The first shouts went up.

Aedella ran across the roof of the warehouse. Her arrows found their targets without fail. Shouts became screams as the villagers realised what was happening. Bells pealed. Smoke filled the air. Soldiers ran all around. Buckets were gathered from wells. Water was thrown upon the burning buildings to no avail. The company exchanged glances and held their weapons tight. It was working. Fire ran through Naidra's blood. She spared a glance up towards

Aedella. Soldiers with bows were shooting back now. Arrows hissed through the air. Aedella did not stop moving. She could not stop moving. Soldiers fell as her steel-tipped arrows found their marks. The thatch she had used to start her fire blazed. Tongues of flames licked the roof of the warehouse hungrily. It began to spread. Aedella was trapped.

"GO!" she shouted from above.

Valmoar heaved the doors open and led the way outside. Soldiers and townspeople were everywhere. Some fled while others turned buckets of water upon the village. Houses burned. The headman's manner was aflame. Fire raged and plumes of smoke turned the dawn sky grey. The rising sun was all but hidden by the dark mist. Two guards stood by the doors. Guards who were taken by surprise. Guards who fell to Cadoc's sword. Few soldiers were close, and they were scattered. Varde's arrows took another, and Nevra's blade a fourth. Two more leapt the railings of a fence and charged. They fell to Aedella's bow.

"GO!" she cried again.

They neared the horses. More soldiers appeared. Valmoar and Cadoc slew them where they stood. A scream came from behind. Naidra turned and saw Raeghan fall. His eyes faded as he collapsed, a pair of arrows protruding from his back.

"RAEGHAN!" Naidra cried as her friend's lifeless body crashed to the ground.

Varde's bow sang as he killed one of the archers. Aedella's arrow claimed the second. Shouts filled the air, signalling they had been seen. Soldiers surged forwards. Aedella leapt from the roof as arrows rained down. She hit the ground with a roll and sprinted to join her companions.

Cadoc engaged the soldiers closest to the horses. He was a warrior, trained from birth. The humans fell to his sword. Valmoar, Naidra, Nevra and Varde took separate fights as they moved. They worked in unison, but they were few. Too few. Naidra cut a man down, spun, took a second soldier's head and turned just in time to see a third hurl a spear towards her. She had no time to react. No time to think. Magic leapt from her fingers and knocked the spear aside. Naidra fell back into the mud. The heat of the flames kissed her cheeks. Smoke filled her lungs. Humans fell as the elves and ruskalan fought. An arrow drove into Varde's arm. His bow slipped from his fingers as he tore free his sword. Nevra cried out as a spear sliced her side. Aedella slew her attacker. Soldiers poured forth from everywhere. Naidra started to rise. The soldiers charged. Valmoar reached the horses.

Sivan.

Naidra reached deep inside.

Sarnai.

She found the magic. Her eyes blazed blue.

Raeghan.

Naidra's fingers curled.

She refused to let her sister die. She *refused.* The first of the humans reached them. The song of steel began. Agony tore through her mind like a blade. It burned like flame. The wind whipped. Wisps of air glowed white, streaming around her. Her arms were outstretched as she started to spin. The wisps grew stronger. They became currents. The white light burned. Naidra could barely feel anything as she gave in to the magic. The streams surged outwards. They moved in between her fighting companions. Naidra's eyes burned brighter than ever before. The magic shot forth, slicing through armour and flesh as if it was nothing. Human blood fell like rain. Naidra spun, her feet and arms moving at the will of the magic. Fallen weapons flew through the air and drove into soldiers. A sword was raised as a soldier charged. Fire roared from the warehouse roof. A plume shot forth and slammed the human to the ground, his body aflame, his shrieks grotesque. The white light sliced through the air. Flames from the houses roared and spewed down upon the humans. The screams of the dying were overcome by the screams of fear. A blast of white light surged along Naidra's arm as the humans tried to rally. Four men were taken by it. The light wrapped around them and tore them to pieces. White cracks emerged in Naidra's blue eyes. Fire fell like hail. Those few not killed by the magic fell to the swords of elf and ruskalan. Naidra directed the light and tore Cadoc in two. The elf's bloody body crashed to the ground. The magic gripped her mind. They became as one. Humans were torn from their lives. Aedella was next. The light slew her where she stood. The magic ringed Naidra as she continued to spin, channelling around her in waves. She was autieyar. She was a stormbringer. The waves of light weaved together as they slew the humans. Her arms raised higher. The magic flowed faster. It streamed and grew, wrapped around her like a veil. Light curled around her arms. The pain took her. A scream tore through Naidra. She fell to her knees as the scream carried to the heavens. The magic roared. A wave of light surged from her. Men ran. Too late. The light sliced through them. Those too slow to run fell with cries upon their lips. The heat of the light charred flesh and stopped blood from washing away the earth. Naidra's gazed flickered as the pain engulfed her, and then she saw black.

Nevra stared in horror as silence fell upon Monocena. The light was gone and the magic with it. The only life left within the village were the four foreigners covered in dust, soot and blood. Ash fell all around. Dozens of bodies were strewn through the streets, most barely recognisable as bodies. Varde stared in horror at his brother's lifeless form. Nevra dropped her sword and fell to her knees beside her sister, her own wounds forgotten. All she cared about was Naidra. Her sister had given too much barely a day ago. Now she had given far more. Nevra silently prayed. She begged. She pleaded.

"Naidra," Nevra called.

She brushed hair from Naidra's face and caressed her cheeks. Naidra was breathing. Barely.

"Naidra," she called again.

The autieyar's eyes flickered open. Terror gripped Nevra as she met her sister's weak gaze. The blue of Naidra's eyes was broken. Webs of white ran through her irises like cracks. Nevra froze, fear driving through her heart. Despite the heat of the fire, her body chilled. She was as cold as winter ice. She had seen those eyes before.

She had seen them in their father.

TWELVE

The palace was quiet in the morning. Dozens had been killed in the attack. Servants, nobles, soldiers and knights. Dresige, his friend and confidante. None had been spared the wrath of elven blades. The emperor watched on coldly as the linen-wrapped bodies of his people were placed upon great pyres and set ablaze. He held his amulet to the Twins tightly as he watched them burn. Janus had always believed in peace. His words and decisions had kept the shadow of war at bay for decades. A peacemaker, that was what they called him. Now he wasn't so sure. While hundreds left, Janus stayed by the pyres until the last of the flames died. They had all come to his home for the festival, for the celebration to bring in the year. A time of rebirth and healing blackened to a time of death. His wife never left his side. A cold, burning anger threatened to consume the emperor. Ash and dust. That was all that remained of his people.

Soldiers stood at every corner of the palace. The gates and bridge were closed to the world. Any seeking entrance to the castle were searched under the watchful eyes of the Arkin Garter. Janus wore his sword as he made his way through the palace, a pair of the Garter accompanying him. They were his shadows. Who knew if elves still patrolled the corridors and halls. Janus' left hand stayed clamped upon the hilt of his longsword, while his right held a short arrow. The weapon that had saved them all. He found the door to

Stefanos' workshop open and he walked inside. For many months, years even, he had always been humoured by the creations upon the inventor's desks and shelves. He had since grown to see them as what they were: brilliant. Janus approached one of the tables and sifted through an open book. It was from the Northlands, filled with writings and images of the elves and ruskalan.

"Lord Emperor." Stefanos bowed as he greeted Janus. "Forgive me, I did not see you enter." The Delion appeared from the depths of his workshop as flamboyantly dressed as always.

"You've been studying the elves," Janus stated.

"Yes, my lord."

"What do you make of them?"

"I would say that they are not so very different from us," Stefanos replied. "The elves are impulsive where the ruskalan are patient. Two sides of our nature."

"And yet they are not human."

"No, my lord, they are not."

Janus flicked through the pages until he came across the image of a tattooed elf. He saw in the sketch the same face that he saw in the elf last night.

"I must admit that I had always been sceptical about the rumoured magic of the elven sorcerers," Janus admitted. "Even in the north no one truly knows. Yet I have seen it now with my own eyes. Power that goes beyond crowns or armies, beyond titles or thrones. True power."

"They are called autieyar."

"Autieyar," Janus said slowly as he learnt the word.

"In their tongue it means stormbringer," Stefanos explained. "You see, they believe their gifts come from their spirits, that they themselves were born from Sylvaine's tears."

"And the ruskalan?"

"Less is known about them, my lord. They tend not to stray far from Salvaar. But what I have read and heard tells that they are the children of Tanris, the spirit of death. That they were born of his blood. They carry magical gifts like the elves; however, it lives in all of them. Only a handful of elves are blessed with their power."

"Yet the rest are great warriors."

"Indeed, they are, my lord."

Janus placed the short arrow on the desk next to the book. He looked to the inventor.

"Forty-six people died last night," the emperor said coldly. "Forty-six of our people. At a celebration. They died defending the castle. Died defending my family. Died defending *me*. I will not forget that. Nor will I forget the one man who was able to defeat the autieyar. Your arrow somehow took the elf's power. However did you do it?"

Stefanos approached the desk and took up the book. He flicked through the pages and then after a moment put it down before the emperor.

"Here," Stefanos said, thrusting a finger towards his own writing. "When I first uncovered the mystery of their magic, I was inspired. How could such people be blessed with these abilities? What purpose would they serve? I am a man of science and the pursuit of the unknown calls to me. I asked myself, what made the elves and ruskalan so different from you or I that they could control such wonders? They bleed like us; they are made of flesh and bone like us. That left me with two ideas. These gifts could come from the blood, or from the mind. It seemed only fitting that I would start with the mind, for the mind is curious and it opens up so many possibilities."

Stefanos flicked to another page filled with his writing and drawings. He gestured to a series of plants.

"From there my questions only grew. If this magic was indeed connected to the mind, how could I ascertain that truth? In my searchings I stumbled across elvira."

"The weed that grows deep in the mountains near the Silver Tower?" Janus questioned, recognising the name.

"You know it?"

"When I journeyed to the Tower to oversee the construction of the Azaria's Rose, I met many Larissan travellers," Janus explained. "They would use this weed in a tea to enter some kind of dream state."

Stefanos nodded. "They do indeed," he replied. "However, when left raw, an extract from elvira can dampen the mind, not enhance it, as the Larissans would try. It seemed only fitting that if the elven magic did indeed come from the mind, elvira would be the perfect counter to it. It moves fast in the bloodstream and within moments attacks the mind. A temporary haze, I would say. Until last night I had not had the opportunity to test my idea."

Janus paused. He looked into the Delion's eyes and picked up the arrow. He ran a finger across the tip.

"So that concoction that you placed upon the arrow was a guess?"

"Yes, my lord."

Janus glanced at the bladed tip. "And yet it saved us all," he said quietly. The emperor gathered a large coin purse from his belt and tossed it to the inventor. "For your research," Janus explained. "I would have you look into this further."

Stefanos offered a low bow. "I am your humble servant."

"You are much more than that," Janus told him as he placed a hand upon the inventor's shoulder and gripped it tight. "There is a storm gathering and I plan to be ready before it breaks."

Janus had not even made it to the doors before Stefanos called after him.

"Lord Emperor. My research. It has proven to cut off magic for a moment. You do not plan to use it as a weapon, do you?"

Janus sighed and did not look back.

"I *pray* it never comes to that," he answered honestly.

Cool wind caressed the emperor's cheeks as he gazed out from his balcony. Azaria's moon lit up the heavens and silver stars danced in the sky. Even the breeze could not take away the warmth of summer. Janus let out a long breath as he scanned his city. His home. He had been born here. He had given his life to Aureia, to his people, to his family, his country and to his gods. Diplomacy had been his greatest tool. With it he had kept war at bay for decades.

Was that time coming to an end?

Janus' hands clenched upon the railing. He turned his eyes to the moon and clutched his amulet.

"What is it that you want from me?" he asked Azaria softly.

The emperor stared at the moon.

"Do not drive yourself mad trying to comprehend her will," Empress Lysaea murmured.

Janus could not even manage a smile as he turned to see his wife. Her dark hair was unbound, and she wore no adornments. Her silk shift hung gracefully from her body and her arms were bare. She was as beautiful as the day they had met nearly thirty years ago. Lysaea reached out tenderly as she approached and took his hand.

"This is not the end," she comforted him.

Janus stroked his wife's arm and nuzzled her brow.

"It seems that everything we have built is on the edge of a knife," he muttered. "This peace that I have made is threatened. The nobles gather in five days. Magisters gather. The cardinal will arrive to usher in the new year and when he learns of what has transpired here ... I know what they will all say. Lysaea—"

She cut him off by placing a finger upon his lips.

"Your path is laid at your feet," Lysaea whispered. "It may be hidden but you will find it. Trust in the gods."

Her compassion warmed the ice in his heart that had grown from the attack.

"I trust in them," he told the woman he loved. "I trust in you."

✦ ✦ ✦

"Not dead yet, I see," Kaladin called as he approached.

Duran grinned, pushing himself from the physician's bed and pulling on his shirt. His injuries had been stitched and patched by the palace's best.

"Cuts and bruises," Duran replied with a chuckle. "Nothing more. The physician says I will live."

Kaladin extended a hand and cupped his apprentice's chin. He tilted his head as if examining the cut on Duran's cheek. He offered a whistle at what was barely more than a scratch.

"Ugly."

"Like its owner." Duran slapped the hand away.

Kaladin held out the young knight's sword. Duran took his blade as the pair exchanged a nod.

"You fought well," Kaladin said sincerely. "If not for you, then the princess would be dead and we would be at war."

"All because of your training."

"I'm proud of you."

Duran froze and was unable to stop the smile from etching itself upon his lips. It meant more to him than anything.

"There is to be an assembly in a matter of days," Kaladin stated as they left the hospital.

"What do you think they will decide?"

"I do not know," Kaladin replied. "Many will call for blood, but my brother–"

"Is a peacemaker," Duran finished for him. "Janus is a great man with a good heart. Whatever decision he makes will be the right one, I am sure of it."

"It is not his heart that makes me nervous," Kaladin said. "Many are already calling for blood."

"Not all elves are the same," Duran emphasised.

"I know that. But the nobles here, few have ever been to the

Northlands, and do you really believe that those who did went anywhere except the palaces of lords? No, Duran, this attack changes everything. With the pressure of the Aureian nobility and the words of the northern barons that clammer for war … I fear for Aureia. I fear for my brother."

"What of the cardinal?" Duran suggested. "He will arrive in a few days to bless Aureia and celebrate the new year."

Kaladin shook his head slowly. He stopped and turned to face his apprentice.

"I don't think anyone will be celebrating," Kaladin said. "Cardinal Octavan is an honourable and just man. The gods' chosen voice. His words carry weight beyond those of kings and emperors. We have no say in the matter. Few in the assembly will. It will come down to my brother and the cardinal and how the words of others sway them. I know what my brother thinks, what he believes … but of the cardinal's decision? Only the gods know."

Duran could see the slight tensing of Kaladin's jaw. He could see how his mentor gripped the pommel of his sword slightly harder than usual. For the first time that Duran had ever seen, Kaladin seemed unsure.

"Sir Duran."

Both men looked down the corridor as a servant approached.

"What is it?" Duran asked.

"Princess Leona awaits."

"I'm on my way."

The manservant led Duran out from the stone walls of the castle and into the gardens beyond. It was night and the air cool. None walked within the greenery or took refuge in the pavilions. The pale light of the moon washed everything in greys. It was silent, peaceful, serene. Leona waited in the pavilion where they had first met over a month ago.

"My lady." Duran offered a bow.

She returned the nod and glanced at the servant.

"Thank you, Palin, you may go."

"Your Grace." The servant bowed and vanished back down the garden paths.

Leona watched Duran curiously for a moment.

"You've made quite the name for yourself," she said.

"So I am told," Duran replied with a shrug. "Men will speak while they have tongues to speak."

"The First Knight they call you now."

"I was not the first nor the only to stand against the attack."

"No, but you fought alone."

"I did not."

"I have never killed before." The words rushed from Leona. "I know that I had no choice but there is a feeling that I cannot shake. Almost guilt, in a way."

Duran placed a hand on her arm to comfort her. He looked into her eyes and gave her a smile.

"It is no easy thing to take a life. There has never been someone as kind or gentle as you. You have a good heart. Nothing will ever change that."

The despair in her eyes faded. Duran could see her body relaxing. Together they looked out across the gardens. Duran felt the weight of last night's attack fall from his shoulders. Here he was at ease.

"Thank you," Leona said.

"What for?"

"For your friendship. For your courage."

Her words were whispers as she looked away from the beauty of the gardens and to the man beside her. Leona's hands found his.

"Thank you for saving my life." She looked into his eyes. "Duran, I am a princess of Aureia. Bound to my title. Bound to my duty. But I am decided. I choose you."

Duran raised a tender hand to her cheek. He brushed a lock of stray hair back from her face. Leona nuzzled into his palm and Duran kissed her. He did not care that it was forbidden. He did not care that she was expected to marry royalty. In this moment the only thing that mattered was her. Those were the words his heart spoke, the words etched upon his soul as he tasted the joy on her lips. All that he could feel was her.

In that moment, he was hers.

In that moment, she was his.

THIRTEEN

Village of Monocena, Fiefdom of Aloys

Valmoar helped Nevra pull her unconscious sister into the saddle before he too mounted up. Nevra held her sister tight as she took in the destruction. The air was thick with ash and dust; it was hard to breathe. Flames roared as the village was engulfed. The humans had fled.

Naidra's power had saved them, but at what cost?

An innocent village, townspeople who had done no wrong.

Cadoc. Aedella. Both slain by her sister's hand.

Had her mind too been claimed?

Nevra kicked her heels in and the three horses galloped from Monocena. They had no choice but to leave their own dead, no choice but to abandon them to the flames. Her eyes stung and her throat screamed when at last they rode from the smoky embrace of the village. There was a great roar. Nevra turned as the riders brought their horses to a halt. They all watched as the warehouse collapsed beneath the weight of the fire. That was all that remained of their dream. They had come here for peace and had found only treachery and dishonour. Their friends and companions were dead. Tears rolled down Nevra's cheeks as a piece of her heart broke. Her wounds ached but she had no time to wash away the blood let alone stitch herself back together. Valmoar, Varde and Nevra, battered, bruised, covered in ash and stinking of smoke, turned their horses and rode north.

The miles vanished beneath the heartbeat of hooves. They did not stop. They did not slow. Still, Naidra did not wake. Still, only her sister's arms kept her from falling. Dark clouds gathered overhead and the rains began. It was heavy, a summer storm.

The riders stayed clear of the roads. They had better chance of fading into invisibility if they weren't seen. If any pursuit followed them, perhaps they would follow the roads. Perhaps. The storm darkened the sky, and it grew darker still as the sun set. Without a word Nevra brought her horse to a halt. The rain lashed her cheeks and made her clothes heavy. She could feel her exhaustion. Nevra checked her sister's breathing. It was shallow but still there. She was alive at least. Valmoar turned in his saddle and then he and Varde returned to Nevra's side.

"How is she?" Valmoar called.

"Alive."

"We do not know if we are being followed," the ruskalan cried over the wrath of the storm. "We have to keep moving."

"Valmoar, she needs rest," Nevra snapped.

"We cannot—"

"We need to rest!" Nevra shouted.

With a grimace she turned her horse to the side and pulled up the hem of her soaked shirt with her icy fingers. Her unpatched wound was gruesome. It ached and burned. Nevra did not care for herself, but perhaps if their leader saw the injury, he would rethink. Valmoar looked at the wound. He could see the pain in Nevra's eyes. His gaze flicked to Varde who cradled his left arm. The silent warrior said nothing, instead nodding into the distance. Small glints of light could be seen through the dark. A farmstead, no more than five or six houses. Valmoar ground his sharp teeth. The elves were not going to compromise. Finally, he gave a nod. As one, the companions spurred their horses onwards. As one, they angled towards the farmstead.

Thunder roared and lightning danced angrily through the

heavens when they reached the first of the wooden buildings. Water and mud splashed as Valmoar's boots kissed the ground. He gathered up his reins and approached the doors of what appeared to be a barn. Nevra and Varde watched the surrounds closely with peeled eyes. People lived here, that much was certain. They would be in their beds. Nevra prayed that she and her friends would be long gone before the humans discovered their presence. Valmoar pushed back the locking bar and led the way inside. Nevra dismounted with a grunt. She had been so focused on her sister that she had not realised how much pain she was in. Varde too grimaced as he dropped from his saddle. They followed Valmoar and led their horses inside the dark barn. The only light was from the all but hidden moon and the streaks of lightning. Valmoar closed the doors behind them. It was quieter in here, warmer.

Something rustled in the darkness.

Steel rang as Nevra tore her sword free. Varde levelled his blade and Valmoar slowly drew his own. The wooden floorboards creaked. Nevra took a slow step forwards. Her heart raced.

A goat bleated as it emerged from the shadows. The companions stared in stunned silence before a chuckle escaped Nevra's lips.

She cleaned her wound with the contents of her wineskin and Valmoar went to work with a needle and thread. Slowly, agonisingly, he stitched the torn flesh back together. Nevra had been lucky, the spear had done little more than tear through skin and muscle. The ruskalan tied the wound off, cutting the excess thread with a knife. As Valmoar placed a comforting hand on her shoulder, Nevra offered him a grateful smile, heaving herself to her feet. Varde grunted as he bound his arm tight. The arrow had done damage to flesh, muscle and bone, yet the warrior was as strong as any. His face showed no pain. His expression was as cold and dark as it always was. His gaze burned with rage as he turned it upon Naidra. The woman who had slaughtered his brother. Varde drew his knife. Nevra saw his face. She saw the steel. Nevra leapt in front of Varde, breaking his stride towards the sleeping autieyar.

"Please ... don't," Nevra begged.

Varde ignored her words, his eyes locked on Naidra as he shoved Nevra back. Nevra drew her sword. She levelled the blade at Varde. He was injured, unable to use an arm. The steel rested against his neck.

"Do not make me do this," Nevra pleaded. "She did not mean to kill him."

Varde snorted. Nevra knew as well as he that if Naidra had not called forth her magic then they would have escaped. They had reached the horses. He took another step. A trickle of blood ran down his neck as Nevra's sword nicked his skin. She did not budge. Varde stared at her in disbelief. He shook his head and bared his teeth before striding away. Varde swung himself back up into his saddle and rode back out into the storm. Valmoar shut the doors behind the rider as Nevra raced to her sister.

"He will not be coming back unless he brings murder with him," Valmoar muttered. "Not after Naidra killed his brother."

"Cadoc ... Aedella ... I do not know what to think anymore. She did not mean to ... she did not mean to."

Tears rolled down Nevra's cheeks as she knelt beside her sleeping sister. Naidra lay upon a bed of straw with a rug pulled up over her body. She had not woken yet. She had barely stirred. Her skin was pale from exhaustion. The magic had nearly killed her. Nevra placed the back of her fingers upon her sister's cheek.

"She feels like ice," she murmured, worry threading through every fibre of her being.

Naidra's chest barely rose and fell.

"It will pass," Valmoar said.

"Will it?" Nevra whispered as she stroked her sister's cheek. "I've seen it before."

"She is strong."

"I know. She is the strongest person I have ever met."

Valmoar gestured further back into the barn. Nevra gave her sister a last glance before she rose to her feet and walked towards Valmoar. Her sister did not need to be disturbed. She needed sleep.

"We should discuss what happened in Monocena," Valmoar stated.

"We were betrayed, and a lot of people died," Nevra growled. "What else needs to be spoken?"

"Everything. What happened in Monocena has changed the world."

"In what way?"

"Mataro Aloys was supposed to be different. A man of peace. A man who believed in honour. A man we could build a better future with. Everything that he told us, everything that he whispered, all of it was a lie."

Nevra bared her teeth and shook her head.

"Do you know something?" she hissed. "After what they did to our friends, after what they did to my sister … I am *enraged*." She could barely keep the anger from her voice as it broke.

"Then are we agreed?" Valmoar continued.

"What do you propose?"

"It was not Mataro Aloys alone who deceived us. It was the people of Monocena as well. People we trusted and opened our arms to, only for them to sink a knife into our backs. What they did cannot go unpunished. It cannot go unanswered."

Nevra paused. "They lost many people," she replied.

"That is not enough, not to me." Valmoar was fierce. "We offered peace, and they killed us. Monocena was only the beginning. It will happen time and time and time again without end. Not unless we answer."

"You speak of revenge."

"I speak of justice."

"Vengeance and justice are not the same thing," Nevra warned.

Valmoar shook his head in disbelief. "No, they are not," he countered. "But would you let the man who betrayed and murdered your friends go unpunished? Would you let the man who spilt your blood and nearly killed your sister go unpunished?"

"No," Nevra admitted angrily.

Her fists were clenched. She met Valmoar's crimson eyes. He was as enraged as her. His dream had been snuffed out like a candle.

"We were this close," Valmoar hissed, holding his thumb and finger an inch apart. "This close to everything we had ever dreamt and fought for. Now it is nothing. Now we *have* nothing. All of my life, and all of your life, we have been seen as little more than animals by them and now we know that that is true. I intend to strike back. What I want to know, Nevra, is are you with me?"

He held out an arm, eyes boring into hers. Nevra chanced a look at her sister. Only the spirits knew if she would live, and even if she did, she would be changed. That made her blood boil. Mataro Aloys would answer for his crimes.

Nevra turned back to the ruskalan and took his arm in a tight grip. She had made her decision a long time ago.

"I am with you," she vowed.

"When your sister wakes, we will return to Salvaar and from there–"

A gasp cut through the air.

A long breath of air was taken.

Naidra awoke.

Nevra looked to her sister. She still looked half dead. The tenderness of the past vanished the moment Naidra opened her eyes. In her sister Nevra saw their father surrounded by the bodies of those he had murdered. She saw the death of her mother, the death of so many at his hand. In Naidra's eyes she saw Aedella and Cadoc. Naidra smiled at her sister. The smile faltered as she saw the burning anger in Nevra's face.

"Nevra," Naidra murmured.

"We had reached the horses," Nevra growled, stepping towards her sister. "Why … why did you do that?"

"I wanted to save you."

"Save us?" Nevra snapped. She shook her head in disbelief. "WE WERE ABOUT TO ESCAPE!"

"I–" Naidra's voice wavered.

"I TOLD YOU NOT TO USE YOUR MAGIC!"

"Nevra, please." Naidra's voice trembled.

She was weak, exhausted beyond understanding. She was scared, afraid of what had happened and what she had become. Naidra reached out a hand towards her sister. She needed her, now more than ever. Nevra flinched, turned to avoid the blow that never came. She did not notice that her hand had curled into a fist. She could see the heartbreak in Naidra's eyes.

"Cadoc and Aedella are dead because of you," Nevra snarled. "Varde is gone because of you … because of *you*."

Tears formed in Naidra's eyes. "I did not want this."

"YET YOU MADE IT SO," Nevra shouted. "You made it so …"

The doors flew open.

Swords leapt into hands as Nevra and Valmoar turned on the intruder. An old man stood silhouetted in the doorway with a pitchfork in hand. Beside him, a younger man held a hatchet. There were four others, all similarly armed with farm equipment. Their faces betrayed their anger. They were strong and weathered from a lifetime of farming.

"Salvaari," one of the company hissed.

"We heard shouting," the younger man growled. "Who are you?"

Nevra inwardly winced. She had lost control. They had been found because of her. The man's eyes were suspicious. He glanced at the steel and adjusted his grip upon the axe. Nevra sheathed her blade and tried to make eye contact. She offered a smile.

"My name is Nevra," she told them. "We came seeking sanctuary from the storm."

"You break into our home like ghosts in the night," the older man said sternly.

Nevra pointed to her sister. Even in the darkness only a blind man couldn't see that she was in a bad way.

"My sister is wounded," Nevra told them. "We needed somewhere to rest. I-I feared out there she may die."

"I can see blood on your clothes," the older man stated.

"We were attacked on the road," Valmoar replied. He held up his empty palms. "We do not want trouble."

"Your actions speak otherwise."

"Please," Nevra pleaded. "Please let us stay this one night. We will leave with the dawn sun."

"Father?" the younger of the two looked to the older.

The old man snorted as he ran his stern gaze across the intruders. "One night," he told them. "Then you leave."

"Thank you," Nevra replied gratefully.

Hooves splashed in the mud as a horse galloped into the farmstead. The farmers turned as the horse slowed to a canter. The younger man raced out into the rain and held up his hands. He called out with a calming voice and when the horse slowed enough, he took its reins. The horse was not alone. A man lay upon its back with arrows riddled through his body. Nevra's eyes widened in horror.

It was Varde.

"No," Nevra cried and without thought raced past the farmers towards her friend.

Rain lashed her face. Mud splashed over her boots. Nevra eased Varde from the saddle. She lowered him to the ground and held him close. His unseeing eyes were grey. His clothing was soaked in blood. He was dead. Nevra looked to Valmoar as he reached her.

"They have found us."

The words had barely left Nevra's mouth when riders appeared from the blackness. A dozen of them. Helmets covered their heads and armour their bodies. They held spears and shields. Two carried bows. Nevra closed Varde's eyes and rose beside Valmoar. Her hand fell to her sword. The farmers gathered. More people emerged from the houses. Women.

"Farmer," one of the soldiers called out. "Do you know who it is you shelter?"

"We have only just found them, sir," the old farmer called back.

"They," the soldier gestured towards Nevra and Valmoar, "attacked Monocena. Slaughtered many of its people. We are here to see justice upon them."

Nevra glanced at the farmers. Their indifferent expressions turned to rage and hatred. This place was not so far from Monocena. Perhaps they had friends and family there.

"Justice?" Nevra snarled. "You know *nothing* of justice."

The soldier pulled a coin purse from his belt and tossed it to the farmer.

"I apologise for the intrusion. We will disturb you no longer."

"Go on, do your duty," the farmer replied, leading his men away.

The soldier raised his arm and the spear along with it. Nevra drew her sword. Valmoar drew his.

"Kill them," the soldier commanded.

Nevra turned and ran. Valmoar stayed at her side. The rain grew. The winds howled. Soldiers roared as they charged after the Salvaari. Nevra's side ached. The storm darkened her hair. The splashing of mud turned into the thud of wood as they ran into the barn. The soldiers dismounted and surged after them with sword, shield and spear in hand. Nevra ducked as a spear thrust towards her. She slid under the soldier's arm and came up far from his shield. Her sword found a home in the soldier's neck. He fell with a scream. Valmoar leapt at the second man, driving him back into the wall of the barn. They struggled and fought. Valmoar used his blade to trap the human's sword and shield. He bared his fangs and stared into the soldier's eyes. His gaze lit up red. It took only a moment. Valmoar stepped back as another human came at his side. Valmoar deflected the spear and took another step back. The spearman charged straight into the sword of the first man. Valmoar's magic was strong. He controlled the first soldier with his mind. The spearman's eyes widened as blood spilled from his lips. The first soldier swung his sword and took his own ally's head moments before Valmoar took his own.

Nevra took the steps to the wooden balcony three at a time. She turned, blocked a soldier's sword with her own and kicked out. Her boot connected heavily with the soldier's face, shattering his nose and causing him to topple backwards. More came. Nevra used barrels, stacks of hay and crates to avoid her foes. Dust kicked up as the soldiers moved against her. Nevra deflected a sword, ducked a second and sliced her own across an exposed throat. Before the man could even fall, she leapt from the balcony down onto the floor of the barn. She leapt aside from a spear, barrelling out into the rain. She barely had time to lean back as a bow sang, an arrow springing forth, slicing through the storm. Nevra raised an arm as she moved. The steel arrow tip nicked the side of her neck. Her blood ran hot. She snatched up her dagger and launched it back at the archer. He raised his bow to deflect the knife. Nevra charged into him. Her sword bit into the wooden bow and the hand that held it. Her blade sliced his cheek and she kicked him into the mud. An exhale fled her as she lowered her sword to his neck. He tried to flee across the ground on his back. His hands scrabbled at the mud. Fear shone in his eyes. Nevra thrust forwards. Hooves thundered and then she was flying. Her sword vanished from her fingers and she hit the ground hard, mud washing over her as she rolled. Her vision blurred, her head rang, her body burned with pain. Nevra took a long croaking breath. She struggled to rise. The butt of a spear crashed into her side and sent her back down into the mud. It was all she could feel, all she could taste. It ran through her fingers, ran through her hair. Gasping, she reached for her sword. The spear slammed into the side of her head and flipped Nevra onto her back. She could barely breathe. Her lungs wouldn't obey. She could hardly see. Nevra fought to rise, heaving herself back onto her hands and knees. A heavy boot connected with her side. She screamed as it hit her fresh wound. Nevra crashed down, her hands gripping her side. She could feel the blood beneath her fingers – her wound had ripped open.

A cry of despair filled the streets as a ring of steel surrounded Valmoar. He spun everywhere to keep the ring of spears at bay. His clothing was pierced, and he bled from a dozen wounds.

The blade of a spear lowered to Nevra's chest. She met the eyes of her foe. Hatred. It was all she could see in his gaze. She was unarmed, her body a canvas of blood and bruise. Her clothes and face were covered in mud. She could not fight him; instead, she gazed at him defiantly. She dared him with her eyes. His hands adjusted their grip. He raised the spear. A cry left his lips.

Then he flew. Nevra could only watched as the soldier's body smashed into the wall of a house so hard that every bone in his body shattered. Shouts filled the farmstead as Naidra appeared from the barn. Her eyes blazed, her hands clawed like talons. Rings of light surrounded her as she tore soldiers down. Her hair lashed through the air. It was the opening Valmoar needed. He attacked.

The distraction was their only hope.

Nevra fought back the pain as she forced herself to rise. Her hands found a spear in the mud and she started towards her sister. Soldiers came from everywhere, on foot and on horseback. They fell to Valmoar's sword. They fell to Nevra's spear. They fell to Naidra's magic.

Nevra could only stop and stare as Naidra cut through them like they were nothing. The humans were pieces on a gameboard, and she was their master, a god toying with them. Blood trailed from

Naidra's mouth and nose. A drop streaked down from her cheek as it spilled from the corner of her eye like a tear. Fear clutched at Nevra. Her sister was going to kill herself to save them. She fought harder. Her spear moved quicker. Fear drove her forwards. Fear kept at bay the pain. She slew the last man that stood between her and Naidra. Now only the ground separated them. Nevra pressed a hand to her side in an attempt to stem the bleeding. She bit back a grimace. A streak of light shot past her. Nevra glanced back as it wrapped around a farmer and tore him in half before vanishing. Her eyes flew back to Naidra, and she could see her sister controlling the light. Now she wasn't only aiming it at their attackers. Now more than soldiers fell.

"NAIDRA!" Nevra shouted.

The light moved at its master's command. Farmers were ripped from their lives without mercy. Screams filled the air as the women could only watch. Naidra turned on them.

"NAIDRA!" Nevra bellowed again, horror gripping her, rooting her to the ground.

She could only watch as her sister directed her magic at the women. Her eyes were so blue they were almost white. The farmers and their women tried to flee but Naidra stopped them. They were innocent. They had done no wrong. Naidra tore them to pieces like an animal. A savage smile curled her lips – the magic had taken her. The women screamed for mercy but none came. Their burnt and broken bodies littered the ground. The last of the cries echoed through the farmstead … and then there was silence.

Nevra forced herself to move. She *had* to move. She had to save her sister. Naidra was all she could think about, all she could see. She was blind to all else. Nevra barely heard the splash. Steel whistled past her head as she swivelled. She deflected the hammer with her spear. The shaft came around and smashed into the farmer's head. Everything turned light. Then they were flying. Nevra glimpsed her sister through the light as the magic threw them back. She smashed into the side of the warehouse and crumpled into the mud. Air fled her lungs. The spear fell from her nerveless fingers. Her stomach ignited like fire. Blood flowed through her shirt. She tried to move. Her vision danced and then faded.

The last thing she saw was her sister directing the storm of light.

Valmoar cut a soldier down and spun back expecting a second, but there was no one. His eyes swept the farm as humans were slain. Men and women, soldiers and farmers. The magic of the autieyar was a curse. Naidra had gone too far at Monocena, pushed too far. The magic took its toll, consumed her. Her face was pale and without emotion. Valmoar could only watch as Nevra was lifted from the ground and thrown by the magic that flowed from Naidra. He saw her fall into a lifeless crumple. A rasping breath fled Naidra's lips. Blood streaked down her cheeks from her eyes. It spewed from her mouth as she fell. She crashed to the mud. Valmoar roared and charged across the road. His sword moved freely as he leapt between the final two soldiers. Steel sang, felling two soldiers. Valmoar stared around wildly.

Only the lash of the rain greeted him.

Only the howl of the wind.

He dropped to his knees beside Naidra and felt for a pulse. It was weak. Very weak. She was in the spirits' hands now. Valmoar whistled. His horse cantered from the barn into the storm. The ruskalan gave a final glance at Nevra. She lay still, surrounded by the bodies of humans. With a growl, Valmoar heaved Naidra up into his saddle. He swung himself up behind her and gathered the reins of a second horse. He wrapped an arm around Naidra's waist and then with a yell kicked his heels in.

FOURTEEN

Fiefdom of Aloys

The lashing wind and biting rain covered their tracks as they fled north. The churned mud was washed away and all trace of Valmoar and Naidra was washed with it. They left the storm far behind as they raced across the plains. Valmoar held Naidra tight as she rocked unconsciously in the saddle. His anger burned cold. It was the rage of an ancient dragon that had at last begun to stir. A rage that, in the darkness, whispered to him. It called his name. His wounds meant nothing, only his purpose, his resolve. Dawn was not far off when Valmoar slowed the horses and made for a nearby woodland. He glanced at the rising sun and turned his gaze south towards the farmstead. Towards Monocena. They would be safe here. If there was a second pursuit from Monocena, then they would have no reason to be this far north. They would have had no reason to reach the farmstead, and even if they did, the storm had taken their tracks.

Valmoar rode deep into the forest before he at last dismounted. He gently lowered Naidra down to the ground. Her face was as white as winter ice. Her pulse fluttered and her chest barely rose. The only part of her that showed life was her lips. They moved; whispered words so quiet that Valmoar could not make them out. The ruskalan tied the horses off and unfurled a bedroll. He shifted Naidra onto it and wrapped her in woolly blankets that had been kept dry by his saddle bags. Crouching, Valmoar felt her cheek.

She was even colder than she looked. Valmoar pursed his lips and without hesitation brought a fire to life. It was worth the risk.

Only then did he see to his own wounds. It was a thing well known that a ruskalan could not heal themselves with their own blood, and he had no companions to aid him. Instead, he pulled his shirt from his body and washed away the black blood with the contents of his wineskin. Cuts covered his chest, arms and the back of his shoulder. The flames heated the steel blade of his knife while he cleaned himself. When the last of the blood was gone, he turned the burning steel upon himself. Fire crackled and skin melted, sealing his wounds closed. Barely a groan left his lips. He bared his fanged teeth against the pain as he closed the cuts one by one. Once sealed, he gathered up his shirt and pulled it back on. Valmoar glanced at Naidra and took his place by the fire. She was still asleep. She still muttered beneath her breath. Valmoar pulled his sword from its sheath and ran his keen eyes across the steel. Dents and furrows ran along the blade from the last few days. He took a whetstone from a pouch and slowly worked it along the edge of the steel. The blade began to reform.

Naidra cried out as she awoke.

Her eyes flashed open as she sat bolt upright. Valmoar dropped his sword and leapt to her side. Naidra raised a hand to her temples. She had never felt such pain in her life. Every movement, no matter how small, sent tendrils of fire lancing through her mind. Every sound, every last thought, *burned*. She grimaced. Voices clouded her mind. She could not make out the words, for they were as faint as the quietest whisper, yet she could hear the song of the tongue of Salvaar. The language of her people. Her gaze flickered around the forest as she tried to find the source of the voices. There was none and it terrified her.

"It's alright," Valmoar said softly. "You're safe."

She looked at him with wild eyes. Eyes that were blue but cracked with white.

"I can hear voices," Naidra muttered as she winced. "In the wind … in my dreams."

"We are alone," Valmoar replied quietly.

Her eyes searched the empty forest. She was confused. Adrift. She wrapped the blankets around herself as she sat up.

"Here." Valmoar extended his wineskin.

Naidra hardly had the strength to take it. She screwed her eyes up and winced as pain rolled through her. Her head rang like a bell. She was missing something. Her head screamed. Naidra groaned, fighting for control. The whispers grew in number and volume. They consumed her. Her breathing grew short through her bared teeth. Her heart pounded. She felt agitated. There was too much in her head, the voices too loud. She could not hear, could not think.

"Stop talking," Naidra hissed, hands shaking.

The voices echoed as they grew into an unintelligible clammer. Her breathing grew faster. She started to pant. Her fists curled.

"STOP TALKING!" Naidra shouted.

Her voice shook the forest. The fire flickered. The voices vanished like smoke. Then she realised, realised what was missing.

"Naidra." Valmoar called her name.

She didn't answer. She couldn't.

"Naidra," he said again.

At last, she looked to him as her racing heart slowed to a pulse.

"No one is here," he told her softly.

"I cannot feel anything," Naidra whispered.

"How do you mean?"

"I cannot feel the birds in the trees or the foxes on the ground. I cannot feel you … I cannot feel my people … I cannot feel the Veil."

She felt as if she had lost a limb.

"The connection to life is who I am." She barely managed a whisper. "I am afraid. Alone. Adrift."

"You nearly died twice," Valmoar said. "You need to rest. In time it will return, I am sure of it."

"No this is different. My connection is washed away as if it never existed. Half of who I am is suddenly … gone."

The absence of her connection to the Veil echoed within her. Naidra knew in her heart that it was never coming back. She was drained, empty.

"And your magic?" Valmoar asked.

Naidra had her doubts. Tentatively, she cupped her hands together. She reached deep inside herself. She could hear the whispers again. Perhaps they were remnants of her lost connection. Her eyes flashed and she opened her hands, revealing a tiny flame dancing upon her palm. Relief seeped into her as she watched the fire burn. If nothing else, she at least had her gift.

"There were more than soldiers at the farm," Valmoar said after a moment. "Why did you kill those people?"

Naidra did not look away from her flame and did not hesitate as she replied, "Because they were nothing."

"Nothing?"

She stared into the fire as it danced. It was as if she could see part of herself in it.

"Aloys betrayed us," Naidra said. "Monocena betrayed us. In time those people would have betrayed us too. If we were human, then our skill as warriors and healers would be revered, but because we are of the old blood we are the enemy. It is us or them."

"All of them?"

"Any who do not see that are our foes."

"Do you not care that–"

"Why should I?" Naidra snarled, snapping her fist shut.

The fire died, smothered by her hand. All she felt was anger and pain. She winced as she at last looked up. Naidra gazed around the clearing. Horror gripped her. Memories of Monocena came back.

"Aedella ... Cadoc," she murmured.

Valmoar nodded.

"I-I only wanted to help."

Tears rolled down her cheeks. She had killed her friends. Slaughtered them with her magic. Her jaw trembled. She needed her sister. She needed Nevra. Naidra froze as her eyes saw the horses. Two horses, hers and Valmoar's. Panic clawed at her chest.

"Where's my sister?"

Valmoar paused. Naidra could see the look in his eye.

"Where is she?" Naidra pressed, her heart cracking.

"She fell."

The cracks of Naidra's heart grew larger and then it shattered. The voices rose in unison. They tried to overpower her.

"You lie," she hissed.

"I do not."

"YOU LIE!"

Naidra leapt to her feet as the wind sang around her. Her eyes flashed. The fire blew out. Rage fuelled her as she reached out with her mind. She willed her gift to work, she willed her connection to return. All that she found were the voices in her own mind. The voices grew loud again. Naidra gripped her head. The memories came back. She saw her sister thrown into the warehouse wall.

"She's dead." Valmoar rose to his feet.

Naidra staggered as if struck. She fell to her knees, exhaustion hitting her, tears flowing freely. She could not feel her sister. She could feel nothing. She was alone, abandoned.

Her sister. Her closest friend. Nevra had been her life, her heart. Now she was gone. Killed. By Naidra's hand.

"My heart is broken," Naidra managed between sobs.

Valmoar placed a hand on her shoulder. It did nothing to comfort the pieces of her shattered heart. She had killed her friends. She had killed her sister. Nevra had been right to fear her.

"Mine aches for your loss," Valmoar murmured.

"I have destroyed us."

"No, this was not your doing. It was the humans. Why?" Valmoar asked the wind. "Because they are afraid of us. Because we are different. They are right. They are right to fear us. Monocena was supposed to be a display of their power. Instead, they received a glimpse of ours. For too long we have lived in the shadows of shame and fear. For too long we have been forced into the darkness. I say no more. No more hiding. No more suffering. Never again. I can *never* forgive what they have done to us. The lives they have taken. The graves they have filled. Our future is not peace; they do not really want it. They were once our friends. Not anymore."

Naidra met his eyes. She could see the dragon of rage moving within. She felt it stir in herself.

"We will kill them," Valmoar told her. "You understand that? We will kill them."

Naidra could only nod. She had killed her sister. She had killed Cadoc and Aedella.

She could only hear the screams as people died all around her. She was terrified. She was helpless. Her sister killed everyone. The guilty. The innocent … and she smiled.

Silence.

The screams stopped. Light flared.

Mud filled Nevra's senses. She could not move. Blood covered her body as it streamed from her stomach. She could not speak; she could not shout or cry out. She could see Naidra watching her.

Light assaulted Nevra's eyes as she came to. Her eyes flickered, adjusting. She winced. Her body ached. The searing light faded, and a room materialised around her. She was in a small bed with thick woollen blankets pulled over her body. The room had almost no adornments and was made of simple wood. A peasant's home. A *human* home. Her hair hung around her face like an ivory curtain. Nevra raised a hand to her cheek and felt that her shallow wound had been stitched back together. So had the side of her neck.

Her stomach screamed.

She remembered the magic. She remembered falling. Then she was here. Nevra fought against her protesting body as she forced the covers back. Bandages were wrapped around her stomach, torso and right shoulder like a makeshift shirt. They were bound tight. A dull burn came from her abdomen. Nevra could feel the stiches there as well. She frowned, staring around the room with confused eyes. After Monocena and the farmstead, this was the last place she had expected to be, wherever this was.

Unless it was a trap.

She had to leave. She had to get out. With a groan, Nevra heaved her legs from the bed. She wore her own trousers but that was all. Where the rest of her clothes were, where her sword and horse were, she did not know. Her bare feet touched the wooden flooring. It wasn't cold. The Northlands rarely were. Nevra tried to stand, and her legs barely took her weight. They felt weak. *She* felt weak. She staggered and clutched at the bed posts. Her body singed, every nerve on fire. She breathed through gritted teeth as she struggled across the room. She nearly fell and only the back of a chair saved her.

"You'll open your wounds," a lady snapped.

Nevra froze, glancing up towards the voice. A middle-aged woman watched her with a frown and pursed lips. Her hands were on her hips. Like the room, she had no adornments. Her dress was as common as the house they were in.

"Where am I?" Nevra managed.

"Arutilla." The northern woman's accent was heavy. "A mile northwest of the farm you were found in."

Nevra knew the town. She had visited it once before many years ago. Her legs began to shake. Spirits, she was weak. She had trained with the sword every day for years – her body was strong and lean, yet now even walking felt impossible.

"Here." The lady approached.

Without waiting for permission, she wrapped Nevra's arm around her shoulders and her own around the elf's waist. She half carried Nevra back to the bed. The elf took a long breath as she slumped back upon the headrest. She closed her eyes.

"How did I get here?" Nevra asked.

"My husband found you half dead in the mud," the woman replied.

"I know the people there," a man's voice added.

Nevra opened her eyes. Like the woman's, his dark hair was greying. His face was weathered and his body strong.

"Finally awake I see," he continued.

"How long have I been asleep?"

"Three days," the woman said. "We feared you might not wake up. Your wounds were grievous but your will to live strong."

Three days? Three days since Varde had been killed. Three days since her sister had …

Nevra needed to get back to her sister. She needed to save her from herself.

"Thank you," Nevra told them gratefully. "Your kindness will not be forgotten."

The man sat up in the chair and faced her. He leaned his elbows on his knees. His face was sad.

"They were good people," he said after a moment. "I searched the wreckage, but you alone survived."

Disbelief hit her hard. This man had no reason to lie. She could see the truth clear as glass in his eyes. Something inside Nevra broke at his words. *She had been the only survivor.* Naidra and Valmoar had been killed. In her last moments before she had fallen, Nevra had known true fear. She had been shaken to her core by what she had seen. She was terrified *of* her sister. Nevra had seen the beast in her glowing eyes. She had seen the monster. A monster with a passion for blood regardless of whose it was. None had lived. Defenceless women and farmers. If Nevra had kept her wits, this would not have happened.

"I had hoped that you might be able to give me answers to what happened there," the man continued. "Some were killed by sword and bow, but others … I'm not sure. I have never seen such wounds before. Farmers. Women. What attacked you?"

Nevra's eyes welled as she remembered Naidra turning the magic upon the farmers and their families. On Cadoc and Aedella. On her. Now her sister was dead. She was dead. Nevra did not know what to think.

Nevra had failed her sister. It shattered her soul. Nevra had *sworn* to protect her. Naidra was the Snowflame. Nevra was the Flamekeeper. Her sister's keeper. She had told Naidra that she would always be there to watch over her. She had told her that no monster was going to hurt her. All of it had been a lie. Nevra could not bear to meet the old man's eye as she replied.

"A monster."

FIFTEEN

City of Auriea, The Aureian Empire

The sand in the courtyard crunched and shifted beneath Duran's light steps. His movements were slow and precise. Every step, every motion, every breath was relaxed. Steel cut through the air at his command as he weaved through the motions of tarkaras. His body was centred, his mind loose. He could think clearly. He could see clearly.

"Good," Kaladin commented, admiring his pupil's form.

The Sword of Kil'kara made his way around the courtyard slowly as he watched Duran go through the motions.

"The swordsong is the divine union of man and steel, yet it has many melodies," Kaladin said. "Your Kyras is perfect. Show me your Aiyla."

Duran's form changed without a thought. He had no need to think about his movements. The slow and methodical moves became faster, swifter, but no less certain. His muscles stretched as he gracefully turned the steel. Nothing was as perfect or beautiful as tarkaras.

"Good," Kaladin said again. "A bird came this morning along with the dawn. A paid agent of the imperial court within the house of Baron Mataro Aloys sent word that one of his villages had been attacked and all but destroyed by a company of elves and ruskalan. Dozens dead. Whether this was the act of a small group seeking some kind of glory or something larger at play, I do not know.

The northern delegation has been made aware of the attack and will no doubt cry out for justice. War should not be the answer, not yet. Not until the culprits have been caught and truth made known. The northerners will be blind to this and on their own seek vengeance, as is their right. There are dark days ahead."

All of this Duran heard as he moved his sword. All of it he heard as he sang the swordsong. He did not react to his mentor's words. There were no distractions. To be distracted in a fight was to die.

"Hold now," Kaladin said at last.

Duran's final stroke sliced through the wind. He held his poise, locked in the perfect extension of muscle, flesh and steel. Duran slid his feet back across the sand and flicked his sword before lowering it.

"I cannot believe that the elves would do something so foolish, not after attacking Aureia," Duran remarked. "This cannot be a coincidence. One maybe, but to try and assassinate the emperor of the greatest nation in the world and to sunder a town that belongs to one of the strongest northern families … Some of them want war too."

"But how many?"

"Now that is the question," Duran agreed. "No one knows how many elves there are, how many ruskalan there are. For all we know there could be legion within Salvaar. If someone wants to start a fight between us, it may be hard to stop."

"And if this fight does come to us, then we must be ready," Kaladin replied. "Not just the emperor and kings and barons, but we knights as well. Now, come with me."

Kaladin gestured towards the doors. He led his pupil further from the palace and deep into the gardens beyond. He had not brought Duran here for idle chatter or to enjoy the flowers and peace. Instead, he took Duran to the edge of the gardens where vines spread all around. There was no path, and none would have thought to walk so far into the darkness. Kaladin gathered up a torch from where it hung on a stone post and sparked its end to life with a flintstone. Without a word, Kaladin descended down what appeared be a slope into the blackness. The slope became a tunnel and from there a cavern opened up. Fire sparked as Kaladin strode around the circular hall and lit torches with his own. The hall was round and the stone walls marked with Tariki symbols.

A large circle surrounded the chamber on the stone floor. A smaller circle, half the size, was drawn within. A third was smaller still, while a fourth, joined to the third, completed the design. The last was barely big enough for a single person to stand within. Other lines, all straight, yet carved from every angle, cut across the circles.

"What is this place?" Duran asked. "I recognise it as a hall of training, but why is a Tariki wheel carved in the heart of the palace?"

"When my mentor served as advisor to my father, he had this place built," Kaladin explained. "He was Tariki, the first ever within the Order of Kil'kara. Tell me, what is the purpose of the Tariki wheel?"

"A diagram drawn in the sands or on stone to show various attacks, defences and movements," Duran responded. "It is used for training until the dimensions and angles of the wheel become ingrained in the mind and muscles of the warrior and he no longer needs to think in order to step or strike."

"When you were first introduced to the wheel, you were but a boy." Kaladin gestured to the larger circle. "For fifteen years these circles have been your life."

The Sword of Kil'kara tapped his blade into the second ring.

"As your skill with the blade grew and your mastery increased, you progressed to a smaller circle. Only the greatest warriors in all of Tarik can master three wheels as you have."

Kaladin tapped the third ring. He was close now, barely a pace away. At last, he gestured to the fourth and final ring.

"It is time that you learnt the fourth."

Horns blared and cheers filled the streets of Aureia. Tens of thousands filled the streets as the entire population of the city emerged. Soldiers, traders, crafters, men, women and children – it mattered not. They all lined the cobblestone. Duran and his mentor watched from the walls of the palace as a great column approached. Riders atop white horses came first, their silver chainmail dancing beneath the light of the sun. Bracers, greaves and pauldrons of the finest steel adorned their arms and legs. Magnificent helmets crested with ivory plumes sat atop their heads. Brilliant white cloaks trimmed in silver hung from their shoulders. Their surcoats were ivory and the gorgets at their necks embellished with the sun and moon; amulets bearing the same hung from their throats. Round shields with the symbol of their gods were slung across their backs and long spears were clasped in their hands. White banners blew in the midday breeze from their lances as they rode through the city. The cardinal's guard. Elite soldiers not so very different from the Order of Kil'kara. They lived and bled for their faith.

Then came the carriage, led and drawn by a pair of white horses. It was ivory and silver, the same as the men who guarded it. The curtains were pulled back, and if Duran peered close enough, he could see an arm waving to the crowd from within. Kaladin clapped his pupil on the shoulder and the pair descended into the courtyard below. Nobles ringed the yard around the statue of Auris. Emperor Janus, his wife and daughter took prominence upon the steps that led to the palace itself. Ambassadors and visiting dignitaries from all across the world gathered, as did the high priest of the city. Kaladin and Duran, their armour polished to perfection, joined the ranks of the aristocracy. The men of the Arkin Garter lined the great bridge as an honour guard for the white-clad procession. The ten white-clad horsemen arrived first. They formed a circle in the courtyard. Their faces were weathered and beardless, but their eyes were full of pride. Then came the wagon in all its silver glory. The wheels stopped turning and the wagon stopped with them. The driver leapt down from his station and reached for the wooden door.

"His Holiness, Cardinal Octavan of Rovira," cried one of the guards as the man himself descended from the carriage.

Emperor Janus was the first to bow, falling to a knee and lowering his head in deference. The cardinal was the only man in the entire world whom the emperor knelt to. Soldier and noble alike followed his lead. White robes brushed cobblestone as the cardinal approached the kneeling emperor.

"All rise," a kindly voice called.

Duran glanced up as he rose. He had seen the cardinal in person before, yet most, if not all, gathered here had not. Octavan's face was lined with his years. His head was bald and his jaw strong. Octavan had once been a soldier before the gods had chosen him to be their voice on this earth. Though his eyes were kind and his smile genuine, only a fool would have mistaken those for weakness. A younger man, barely a few years older than Duran, walked at the cardinal's back. He wore the robes of a priest and carried a sceptre in his hand.

"Cardinal Octavan." Janus greeted him with open arms. "Welcome to Aureia."

"The light of the Twins shines bright upon your great city and its noble people, Emperor Janus," Octavan replied.

Janus reached out and took the cardinal's proffered hand. He placed a kiss upon Octavan's ring.

"Empress Lysaea, as radiant as ever," the cardinal told Janus' wife.

"Your Holiness, Aureia is made warmer by your arrival," Lysaea replied.

"And Princess Leona, you are your mother's image," Octavan said, turning to her. "Tell me, how goes your translation of the Fiodine into the common tongue?"

"Well, Your Holiness," Leona replied. "Soon all will be able to know the words of the gods."

"Greatness takes time, and your work is of utmost importance," Octavan said with a smile. "I thank you for your dedication and skill."

"Thank you."

"It is my hope that the written word of our gods will flow through Aureia, and perhaps even the whole world one day. If it is the gods' will," Octavan stated before turning to address the gathered few. "Rovira is, and will always be, the sister of Aureia. The new year is a time of fellowship and rebirth, yet you have all suffered. Allow me to offer my sincere condolences for our beloved friends taken so cruelly. To lose such great people at such a sacred occasion must have been a terrible blow to you, as it is to all of Aureia."

Janus paused and took a breath. Duran could see a flicker of anger dance across the emperor's face. Not at the cardinal and his words, but at the deaths of his people. He had loved them; he would have died for any of them and now he had been given an almost impossible decision.

"Thank you, Your Holiness," Janus replied. "What happened inside of these walls was a terrible tragedy."

"Know that their souls have found peace in the eternal heavens," Octavan said. "As the gods chosen voice, I give you my solemn word that this attack, waged not warrior to warrior but waged on innocent men and women, will not go unanswered. The gods are with you. They will not abandon you."

Octavan's eyes searched the crowd as the people cheered. They came to rest upon the two Knights of Kil'kara. They stood clad in their brilliant armour with their helmets tucked under their arms. Octavan gestured for them to follow as Janus and his family led the cardinal and his procession into the palace. Kaladin nudged Duran, signalling they were to follow.

The cardinal and his guard were taken to their quarters, what was almost an entire wing of the palace. Rooms given only to visiting kings and queens now serving a higher purpose. Only once the royal family and their household staff left did the knights make their presence known. Duran exchanged a glance with Leona as they passed. The princess offered him a smile and then was gone.

"Sir Kaladin Galad and Sir Duran Cormac." Octavan greeted the knights as he motioned for them to come close. "My brothers in faith."

"Cardinal Octavan." Kaladin offered a bow.

"Your Holiness," Duran added, following suit.

"You do not need to bow, my friends." Octavan shook his head. "Rovira has missed you both. The Pale Horseman scours the Northlands and now I hear has ridden into the heart of the south. There are dark days coming and the world will need men like you and I to bring it back into the light."

"Then you have a plan?" Kaladin asked.

"I do, but first I need more information," Octavan replied. "Kaladin … tell me everything."

The knights stayed with the cardinal and his staff for hours, and then when at last the sun began to set, they were summoned to the royal court.

Dozens gathered there. The emperor, his nobles, the Magister of Auriea, delegations from across the empire, Northlands ambassadors, the cardinal and the Knights of Kil'kara. The hall was silenced when, at a gesture from the emperor, the captain of the Arkin Garter stamped the butt of his spear upon the stone.

"Welcome all," Emperor Janus called. "Nobles of the empire, friends and allies from distant lands. We are gathered here to discuss the threat in the Northlands. I would call to the floor Baron Lucen Alacala of Linair to plead his case."

The baron stepped out into the open floor. He offered a bow to the emperor.

"Thank you, Emperor Janus," Lucen said before he turned to

address the gathering. "Many of you know me, some have heard my words. I am the baron of Linair, a bountiful land not so very far from the Salvaar border. It tears at my heart to have been so long absent my lands, yet for my people I fear it must be so. Little over a month ago, I addressed many of you here in this very room. You had your doubts then and a part of me understands, for you have not seen the things I have seen, heard the things I have heard. I warned you. I warned you all about what these *people* are capable of, yet you wanted to hold the peace. An honourable thing to save countless lives, yet there is no going back from this now. An attack came. Forty-seven people lie dead. Your people and my own. At a *festival*."

The last words were spoken as a growl.

"And that was not all," Lucen continued. "Word came from the north, from Baron Aloys himself, for there was another attack. Houses and livelihoods burned to the ground in Monocena. Dozens dead, thanks to the will of Salvaar."

"May I remind you, Baron, that we do not know if the attacks are related," Emperor Janus said. "Nor do we know if this was the work of a splinter group trying to spread discord and start a war."

"The war has already begun," Lucen snapped. "It did not end at Monocena. A farming settlement was destroyed as well. Women. Farmers. A slaughter. I will not let the murder of so many go unanswered, I will not."

"Then what do you plan to do?" Janus asked him. "Lead thousands into a war that you do not know you can win? None of us here know the numbers of the elves. None of us know their ways."

"I do not care for their ways," another of the northerners snarled. "I do not care for their spirits or the forests they call home. I only care for the blood of our people spilt, the graveyards they have filled."

Some of the Aureians in the crowd voiced their approval.

"Baron Mataro Aloys is mustering his army," Lucen told them. "Baron Gior Meridia is mustering his army. I have sent word to do the same … and there are more. War is upon us whether you will join us or not. The elves and other creatures of darkness are tearing the Northlands apart. Join us, Emperor Janus, fight with us, and I swear that these attacks on your home and family will never happen again."

Janus clasped his hands behind his noble back as he approached the northern delegation.

"I refuse to believe that war is the only way," he said. "The gods have taught us peace and how to be merciful. What are we if we do not show that now? If we negotiate, perhaps we can find another solution."

"*Negotiate.*" Lucen nearly spat the word. "These people cannot be reasoned with. They kill absent cause. They slither into our homes and turn good people against each other, away from the gods. Durandail, the Father of all Fathers, is a warrior. He would not stand idle while his people were butchered."

"No, my son, he would not," Cardinal Octavan called.

All turned to the cardinal as he at last spoke.

"And we will not be idle today," Octavan continued, turning his gaze to Lucen. "What of your countrymen who have chosen to take up arms with the Salvaari? Word has reached my ears that they learn the Salvaari language and some bow to the spirits."

"They are heathen," Lucen replied. "Little better than the elves."

"But they are in fact human?"

"Yes. They look like us and talk like us, but they are more akin to those they so revere," Lucen said. He turned to address the gathering again. "None of us wants war but it is the only way."

Cardinal Octavan's hand went to his amulet of the Twins.

"It is my responsibility as the Twins' holy servant to watch over their children, be they Aureian or northerner or any other," he said. "Before war is decided, then we must ascertain the truth, for it is the truth that seems to have been long forgotten. A lost relic in a distant memory. It must be found again. If war is to be decided, then we must know with absolute certainty who it is we are fighting. *What* it is we are fighting. And so, I propose a compromise. An inquisition must be held. I will assemble the faithful. Seven will be chosen. Seven who will place the truth over obedience to a baron, over obedience to king and emperor. They will serve as inquisitors upon the Holy Tribunal of Rovira. They will ride north with men beholden to no crown or title and scour the north for the truth. Every baron must answer, every headman, every priest. Let no man claim ignorance. Let no man make excuse. If these ungodly roots twist as deeply as you say, then we must uncover them. All those guilty will be brought to justice."

Duran glanced around the room. He had expected war or negotiation. This was an entirely different outcome altogether. It was neither one nor the other, but something in the middle. How the north would react to such an undertaking he could only guess.

"If this is indeed your will, then I will follow whatever verdict is decided," Emperor Janus said calmly.

"And if it is war?" Lucen asked him.

"Then it is war," Janus told the baron.

They were in agreement. The choice had been made. The compromise. This was not war and nor was it peace, but it could result in either. Only the truth would know.

"We are decided then," the cardinal said. "The inquisition has begun."

PART TWO

REBIRTH

SIXTEEN

Despite the black blood that ran through her veins, Aerlyia wore a dress from the Northlands and she wore it well. Even on the darkest day of winter, the northern sun burned hot, and the garment left little to the imagination. Her arms and fingers were wrapped in jewels; more yet hung at her slender throat. Dark runes were etched across her face. Her thick hair was curled and pulled into a bun, the latest northern fashion. Her skin was fair to the humans' tan. Her eyes were blood red to the humans' brown. Her ears were sharp and theirs rounded. Aerlyia did not care. She had no shame, only pride.

The man at her side stepped forwards as cries rang through the town square. He wore a golden band upon his brow, and his clothing was the embroidered finery that only one born into nobility could hope to possess. Baron Arcos Jarez raised an arm to silence the braying horde. Drums sounded. An executioner garbed in the white of the Pale Horseman stepped onto the raised platform, a large axe grasped in his weathered hands. A pair of soldiers dragged a woman clothed in rags up behind him. Her wrists were rubbed raw from the rope that bound them. There were no tears darkening her eyes, only heartbreak and pain. She stood proud before the executioner's block. The drums stopped.

"I did not do it, husband." Her voice was loud, dignified. "I am no traitor to Jarez."

Baron Arcos gave a single nod and the woman, his wife, was thrust to her knees. The soldiers drove her head into the block. They held her fast. They held her steady. The executioner raised his axe.

Silence veiled the yard.

Steel sliced through air.

Ravens cried out.

The crowd cheered as the woman's head rolled.

Aerlyia's heart raced as red blood flowed. The hint of a smile slid across her lips. Her plan was sound, as it always had been. Whispers in the right ears. Words spoken in the dark. Rumours of treachery and dishonour. A lowcut dress. Now the people of Jarez would bow to her will.

A man took her arm as they turned away from the roaring crowd. Baron Arcos Jarez's touch was as gentle as it always had been.

It was not long before they were married. It was not long before a crown sat upon her head. It was not long before Arcos Jarez swore a vow to Tanris while Aerlyia looked on. He knelt in darkness amongst the trees as blood spilt from the palm of his hand wet a Salvaari arm ring. The ruskalan walked around him whispering in her mother tongue. Arcos spoke Tanris' name as he cast aside the gods of his forefathers.

All of Jarez belonged to Aerlyia just as its baron did.

A servant from the House of Jarez met with a black-cloaked man in the dead of night. No words were spoken, no secrets uttered. A single letter was passed from hand to hand, and then the servant was gone.

Aerlyia, the Lady of Jarez, kissed the baron deeply. His hazel gaze melted into the ruby of her eyes. His gentle touch traced the runes on her face, the points of her ears, her hips. The doors of their room crashed open. Soldiers stormed inside. Soldiers bearing the sun and moon of the Twins. Aerlyia's eyes flashed. Arcos bellowed. A cry flew from behind the ruskalan's fanged teeth as she was torn from her bed. She tried to fight back. They had armour, while she wore nothing but a thin shift. They had swords and spears and shields. She had nothing but her bare hands. She met the eyes of one. He turned on his brothers, but it was not enough. The heavy pommel of a sword cracked into the back of her skull.

Baron Arcos Jarez was dragged into the temple and thrown at the mercy of an inquisitor. Beneath the stone eyes of Durandail and Azaria he confessed. The judgement was swift and without mercy. Before the midday sun, the baron and lady of Jarez swung from the gallows to the roar of the crowd.

Treason.

Murder.

Heresy.

All charges punishable by death.

Fontara. A wealthy fiefdom a few days south of Salaman. The great city of Ciraneia rose as its capital. Tens of thousands called it home. Market stalls often packed the busy city streets, streets that were now cleared. Vast crowds stood to either ride of the cobblestone road. The overwatching balconies were overflowing. All watched and cheered the line of soldiers as it marched through Ciraneia. Soldiers bearing the colours of Salaman. The colours of Gior Meridia. A new alliance had been forged between the fiefdoms and to seal it Meridia had offered the hand of his cousin to Fontara's baron. She rode in the heart of the column at her newly betrothed's side, smiling and waving. The cheers grew louder. In a matter of days, Gior Meridia would join them. In a matter of days, the wedding would unite the fiefdoms.

Sunlight glinted on steel as arrows rained down. They sliced through wind, muscle and flesh. Cheers turned into cries and shouts. Valeria Meridia and Baron Fontara were thrown from their bellowing horses. Blood wet the ground. Men raised their shields, but it was too late. Valeria gave a final breath.

Soldiers flooded the streets. Thousands of them. No house went unsearched, no alley unchecked. It was not long before they found the assassins. Not long before they cornered them. The killers fought. They fought hard. They fought well. Three soldiers fell before the masked assassins joined them in death.

Spears painted the alley white with blood.

The blood of elves.

The streets of Palanza were filled as they always were. A trading city to the far north, often called a sister capital to Sorovia in the fiefdom of Bailon. Overseen by the watchful eye of the baron's younger brother, Mathias Bailon, Palanza had grown strong, and it had grown fast. The markets operated every day. Goods from across the known world passed easily from hand to hand. It was a maze of life that even those who had been born in the city could get lost in. Men and woman from all corners of the Northlands filled Palanza – some had even made the journey from Annora, the empire and beyond.

Five Salvaari walked amongst the humans down one of the bustling alleys. Four elves, the fifth a ruskalan. They traded gold for goods. They drank and laughed and cast all else from concern. Adarlan wrapped an arm around Azura's shoulders.

His wife's shoulders.

Larein, at the front of the company, turned to face them. His blue eyes danced in the sunlight and a joke was upon his lips. An arm wrapped around his chest and he cried out. Blood wet steel as a knife was driven through his back and deep into his heart. Adarlan shouted and leapt forwards. Too late. Air was driven from his lungs, an unseen dagger plunged into his side. He turned with a shout. His fist connected heavily with his attacker's jaw, his knife following and tearing through the human's throat. His furious eyes searched the crowd. He stepped towards the man who had slain Larein but staggered, jolting forwards. Blood soaked through his shirt. He fell to a knee as more and more assailants emerged. There was no fight. It was over in moments. One by one, the Salvaari fell to the repeated blows of human daggers.

Harkan the Firstborn stood alone amidst the trees. He could hear the spirits in the wind. He could hear them in the earth. They were angry. A dozen of his people were with him yet scattered through the woods. They watched him now with eyes of red. All had crossed into the Northlands with a sole purpose. It had been decided and they had agreed. The ruskalan stared from the trees as Harkan was joined by three men. Three barons.

From his robes the Firstborn pulled three arm rings.

In turn the barons took them.

In turn they placed the steel around their wrists.

Thud.

Carrillo's fist connected heavily and dropped Emiliano to a knee. The crowd cheered. Ale flowed. Smoke created a haze through the tavern that stank of sweat. Men and women ringed the two combatants, passing coin from hand to hand. Gambling. Games. The life of the working class in the Northlands. Emiliano had bet a sizeable amount on himself to win. He spat a drop of blood down onto the tavern floor and rose to his feet. The cheers grew into a roar. His wrapped hands curled into fists. A bead of sweat dripped from his chin, splashing onto his bare chest and streaking down across his skin. Dancing lightly on the balls of his feet, he swayed back from Carrillo's fist. Knuckles missed his jaw by a hair. Emiliano came up under. His uppercut split Carrillo's guard. A right cross followed. Carrillo staggered. A left hook to the body drove the air from his lungs and brought his guard crashing down. A second cross followed and sent Carrillo to the ground. Emiliano dropped to the floor and raised a fist to finish the fight. Carrillo met his eyes and gave a bloody grin before he raised two fingers.

The symbol of surrender.

It was over.

Emiliano took Carrillo's hand and heaved his opponent to his feet. This was sport to hone and sharpen and win coin. They were friends. Emiliano extended a hand. A heavy purse of gold was tossed into it. The man who passed the coin grinned and clapped a hand on Emiliano's back.

"Food for winter." Fernan laughed.

"Drink more likely," Emiliano replied.

"I will try," a deeply accented voice called.

All eyes went to the white-haired man who stepped forwards. His hands were not wrapped, and he wore a shirt, but only a fool would not recognise the man for what he was. An elf. A blooded warrior. Here in Genilabra they were allowed to travel. It was not Salaman here. Still, the stories had reached them. Still, they were forced to deal with the arrogance of the Salvaari. Elves were stronger. They were faster. Born for the kill. Emiliano knew it. They all did.

"Don't," Fernan implored his brother.

Emiliano shoved the coin purse into his brother's hands and gave the elf a single nod. Instead of cheers there was nothing, no sound but that of feet upon the wooden floor. A man offered the elf wraps for his hands. The Salvaari merely shook his head and moved into the circle. Emiliano bounced on the balls of his feet once again. A bell rang to start the fight. The elf moved towards him. Emiliano danced forwards, feinting. The elf remained motionless. Emiliano threw again. This time it was real.

A single blow was all it took. The elf slid to the side and threw a vicious uppercut. Emiliano crumpled to the ground. Darkness took him.

Fernan Peralez stared at his fallen brother as the elf walked past Emiliano. The Salvaari ignored his opponent and instead reached out a hand towards Fernan.

"I believe that belongs to me." He motioned to the coin purse.

Fernan barely felt the gold be torn from his hands as his eyes stayed upon his motionless brother. The Salvaari left the tavern as Fernan fell to Emiliano's side. Blood dribbled from his lips. Already, bruising was appearing across his face. He was hurt. He was hurt bad.

Summer rain fell upon the village of Genilabra. Silver moonlight danced through the muddy streets. Fernan Peralez leaned against a tavern's wall as his weary eyes went to the glass bottle in his hand. His breath stank of alcohol. He was enraged. Fernan pulled the cork free and took a long draught of ale. His gaze swept to the man crossing the street. His hood was up, but still Fernan could see the tips of white hair. He recognised the clothing. He had been waiting for it. Fernan passed the bottle of ale to a companion and pulled his own hood up, crossing into the rain. Each step took him closer to the elf. His right arm wrapped around the elf's shoulder. His left hand drove a knife up hard into the Salvaari's back.

The elf had no time to cry out.

His eyes glazed over as he crashed into the mud. Blood ran through the watery ground. Fernan snatched the coin purse from the corpse's belt.

The unicorn banner of Granadix flew high above the nobleman's carriage. Mounted knights surrounded the baron and his wife as they travelled through their land to visit one of their border villages. Granadix had known peace for a long time and the baron maintained it despite the rising tension across the land. The inquisition had not yet reached Granadix and even when it did, he had no secrets to hide. The road came alive with the song of bows. Man and horse screamed. The baron looked to his wife, horror paling her face. He pulled back the curtain as riders emerged from every side. The last of the knights fell to sword and spear.

Warriors awash with crimson war paint surrounded the carriage.

Warriors with white hair and blue eyes.

The baron and his wife were torn from the carriage and thrown into the mud. They were stripped of their possessions. Every ring. Every necklace. Every jewel and every ounce of coin. The elves were not gentle as they thrust the lord and lady to their knees. The wet blade of a bloody knife was pressed to the baron's throat. Its bearer knelt before him.

"Heretic," the elf Callan growled, pressing the steel against the baron's amulet of the Twins.

The blows came hard and swift.

Light left the lady's eyes as she watched their murderers vanish into darkness.

"Go!" Headman Pedros urged. "Leave now!"

The elven man and woman fled through the back doors of Pedros' hall. The headman slammed them without hesitation and drove the locking bar into its place. Not a moment too soon. Soldiers flooded the hall. They surrounded the headman and his family and encircled them with a ring of spears. Pedros stood tall and proud. One of the soldiers stared at the headman's arm ring and spat at his feet.

"You are not the inquisition," Pedros told him.

"You are a heathen and a traitor," the soldier countered.

Rough hands seized the headman. They seized his wife and brother.

All three were hung from the gallows in the village of Algelance. All were human. All wore Salvaari arm rings.

As day turned to night, the bodies grew in number. Dozens were slaughtered in Algelance. Men and women. Soldier and serf. Rain mixed their blood into the earth. A ruskalan man stepped up onto the raised dais of the gallows. The black markings of his people were stained by red. It streaked across his skin and dripped down onto the wood below. His crimson eyes never left the unseeing gaze of Headman Pedros. The ruskalan placed a fist over his heart and bowed his head in respect. Pedros and his family had saved Salvaari lives and had paid with their own.

The three were cut down from the gallows and burnt in the Salvaari way.

The slaughtered dozens were dragged into the town square where a great tree stood. One by one, they were stripped of their clothes. One by one, they were strung from the thick branches.

"The baron will not see you, Inquisitor," the white-garbed soldier said. "There are rumours that a demon stands at his side. Whispers in his ear."

"A Salvaari in a northern court is no crime," replied the inquisitor. "We must try again. The world must know the truth."

The soldier of the inquisition bowed.

He returned in a matter of days. His *head* returned. A rider bearing the colours of the baron of Marelva tossed the bloody trophy at the inquisitor's camp. The mounted soldier stared at the inquisitor and his men before he turned and galloped back to his master's city.

It was not long before the armies of the inquisition reached Marelva's capital.

The inquisitor grasped his amulet tightly as he unleashed the hounds of war. Cavalry surged forth across the plain. The city was large, but it had no walls, no defences save the men who called it home. Against the armies of faith, they had no hope. The inquisitor's men cut through their defenders. Soldiers were slain. Homes were burned.

The baron and his red-eyed advisor swung from the gallows by sundown.

The baron of Karcera leapt between Gior Meridia and the elven girl who knelt before him. Her lips were bloody and broken. Her skin was battered, bruised and scarred. Tears stained her pale cheeks.

"That is enough!" Santiago Karcera gripped the arm of the man who was about to strike the girl.

Steel rang as swords were drawn. Surprise turned into rage as Gior Meridia tore his arm free. Karcera ignored his fellow baron and instead wrapped his cloak around the elven girl. He paid no heed to the steel that surrounded him. Every Salaman soldier waited upon the order from their baron. Men belonging to four other houses waited for the same. Men from Fontara whose barons had been assassinated. Men from half a dozen other houses. Many had sworn to fight alongside Meridia as he took to the warpath. Santiago Karcera helped the girl to her feet and gently led her towards the courtroom doors.

"Take one more step and you have chosen," Gior Meridia thundered.

Karcera took that step as his own guard joined him.

"Santiago Karcera, you are henceforth banished from the land west of the Arwan River," Meridia shouted after him. "Your lands forfeit. Your title stripped. All who follow you are our foes."

The baron of Karcera ignored him as he and his people left the hall of Meridia. They took their horses and rode hard. It was not long before the soldiers of Salaman emerged at the border. It was not long before Gior Meridia and his allies attacked. The people of Karcera were pushed back to the river. The elf Santiago had saved fought at his side. The Arwan was stained red. The muddy banks became a slurry of death. Nearly a thousand had joined the baron in banishment. Soldiers. Nobles. Farmers. Little over a hundred soldiers held the line side by side with the menfolk of Karcera as the women, children and elderly fled across the waters. They took wagons and carriages and as many livestock as they could. Most had barely more than they could carry. The line faltered beneath the weight of the Salaman alliance. Santiago Karcera roared and thrust his blade towards the heavens as he urged his soldiers on. He lost count of the men he had killed. He could kill a hundred and it would not halt the defeat that was encroaching. His boots slid back into the river. Water lapped at his knees. Still, he fought.

Suddenly the weight eased. Horns sounded and the army of the alliance pulled back. Arrows flew across the river. A line of riders charged into the ranks of Salaman.

Elves.

Ruskalan.

The Salvaari had come.

The alliance fractured and ran. Santiago Karcera could sense the rage within Gior Meridia as he was forced to call the retreat. Mud fell from his boots as the baron made his way up onto the eastern bank of the Arwan. Many of his people had died to reach Salvaar. Many had given their lives to defend those who had done no wrong and committed no crime. Santiago dragged the body of a soldier from the river and knelt by the fallen man's side. The soldier breathed, yet every breath was a struggle. The she-elf Alora placed a gentle hand on the baron's shoulder. Santiago looked up at her. She gave him a thin smile before her gaze moved towards a dark-clad man, approaching them from the shadows. He held a spear and his eyes shone crimson.

"Harkan," Alora murmured in reverence, bowing her head.

The Firstborn approached Santiago and extended a hand to the kneeling baron.

"Come with me ... brother."

Santiago took the arm as he rose to his feet, gripping it tight.

The elves and ruskalan led the humans into Salvaar. They found them food and drink, gave them sanctuary and welcomed them *home*. Santiago slid his knife across the palm of his hand. He curled his fingers into a fist and squeezed. Crimson tears dripped down onto the arm ring beneath. He closed his eyes and slid the bloody band onto his wrist.

"Salvaari," Harkan told the baron as he stared at the ring.

A vow.

A pact with the spirits.

Raigath.

Months passed beneath the sacred trees of Salvaar. Villages emerged. The elves and ruskalan taught the humans their ways and gave them a new home. In turn the humans swore to stand alongside them. More and more humans crossed the river, turning hundreds into thousands. They came rich and they came poor. Some joined with their own free will, others were cast from their land. Eight tribes had already formed beneath the banners of the greatest barons.

Delegations of each of the eight came together with elves and ruskalan when Santiago, newly crowned chief of the Káli, relinquished his northern name and became Ivar. They came together when he took Alora as his bride.

SEVENTEEN

Village of Vallgena, Fiefdom of Tolgoza

Silver moonlight shone down upon the village of Vallgena. The air was still warm, as it always was in the Northlands. Rain and heat, that was all they knew. Nevra stumbled through the tavern as she raised a glass bottle of wine to her lips. Half of it ran down her throat, the other ran down her chin and shirt. Her hair was wild and unbound, half brown from dirt and dust. Her dark-ringed blue eyes were glossy and adrift. She could not focus, let alone think. Her body, covered in sweat, stank like the stables. She could not remember last night; in fact, she couldn't remember when she had last bathed and could hardly find the will to complete such a task anymore. Scars remained etched upon her flesh from Monocena and the farm. They had healed along ago, but the memories remained, with only the wine keeping them at bay. The people around her laughed and sang. Wine and ale flowed freely. The tavern was filled to the brim, unlike the cups of the clientele. The last drop of wine fell. Nevra stared at the empty bottle in dismay and then thumped it on a nearby table.

"Nevra," one of the men called. "Would you like another?"

Nevra lifted her heavy head. She could barely make out a face through the blur.

"I would," she managed, staggering towards the voice.

Another bottle was shoved into her hands. She fumbled with it and reached for the stopper, pulling it free. The bottle found her eager lips.

"Haven't you drowned your sorrows yet?" another voice called.

The people around her roared with laughter. At least, she thought they did.

"What was that?" Nevra slurred, swinging back towards the voice.

"I lost my brother in battle," the man replied.

"We have *all* lost someone. Friends, family. In battle, to sickness, to time," another chimed in.

There was a ring of them now. They were angry. Nevra took another mouthful. Sorrow turned into rage as she drank.

"Look at yourself," called a third. He pushed past her. "Three years wasting away over a sister. What makes you so special?"

Her punch was wild, but it was hard and strong as it struck the man firmly in the jaw. Nevra could only see blurs and shadows, but it was enough. She had seen her father become a monster and kill her mother. The glass bottle in her hand shattered as it struck another of the men. She had seen her friends die one by one at the hands of a traitor. Nevra hit a third before the first blow was returned. It hit her hard in the jaw. She returned the blow in kind. Her sister too had become a monster before she had died. Blood, sweat and wine rained through the tavern as she fought. Men fell. Punches landed. Nevra smashed her head into a man's nose. It shattered. Blood covered her face. She could taste it. Hands grabbed her from behind and threw her into a post. Pain rolled through her shoulder. She turned, swung back and hit nothing but air. A fist found her cheek and she was thrown to the ground. Her lips split. Perhaps her nose was broken. A boot found her side. She did not care if they killed her. Part of her wanted them to. Her blood dripped upon the wooden floor; it was all she could smell, all she could taste. She barely tried to rise. She did not have it in her. Not anymore. Nevra gasped for breath. This was the end.

A shout cut through the air. Flamelight danced along the blade of a sword. The blows stopped. Nevra felt herself being picked up. She was floating. Then there was nothing but darkness.

Weathered fingers roughly clamped over Nevra's mouth and ripped her from her sleep. Her eyes flew open as the hand smothered her gasp. Her head ached from the alcohol; her body ached from the punches and kicks. She was in her own bed, though how she got there, Nevra did not know. It was still night, but despite the blackness, she could make out the man's face. Piercing brown eyes, a short beard covering his jaw and dark hair brushing his shoulders. He was young, barely over twenty summers. He was dressed in a loose shirt and trousers, like any northerner, and a longsword hung at his hip.

"Andreas," Nevra groaned as she raised a hand to her pounding head.

"You won't be sleeping any longer, Nevra." He spoke urgently, taking hold of her arm and pulling her from her bed. "Come, we must go now."

Nevra staggered to her feet as Andreas led her across the room.

"What is going on?" Nevra asked.

Andreas turned to face her. There was a hidden plea in his eyes.

"The inquisition is here. People have talked. They are coming."

Nevra felt her face pale. Her blood chilled. Her eyes darted around the room. She was an elf under the protection of Headman Otto, yet the inquisitors were harbingers of the truth. They would discover that she had been at Monocena three years ago and when they did, she would at last find rest at the gallows. Nevra knew in her heart why people had betrayed her. She was not so popular here.

"Come," Andreas continued, making for the door. "We must hurry."

Footsteps came from outside of the room. Nevra stared at her friend. They both ducked behind the door as it opened. Two men walked inside – soldiers clad in the white of the inquisition.

They crossed to the bed, their backs to Nevra and Andreas. Nevra ignored Andreas' pleading gestures as she stepped forwards. Her feet were light upon the ground. She edged towards the soldiers and only when they turned did she leap at them. She snatched the knife from the first man's belt and opened his throat. Without hesitating she stepped past and shoved the second soldier hard into the wall of the room. Her left hand covered his mouth, her right thrust the dagger up under his chin.

"Are you looking for me?" Nevra growled as she drove the blade in deep.

He tried to shout behind her hand. His cries turned into a tide of blood and his struggles ceased. Nevra watched the light leave his eyes and felt nothing as she stepped back and allowed the dead man's body to crumple to the floor.

"Nevra," Andreas called.

Nevra wiped the knife clean and gathered up the soldier's swordbelt. She buckled it to her waist and the pair finally fled. Horses waited for them at the back of the inn. They were saddled for a long ride. Andreas had been prepared.

"We must make for Salvaar." Andreas leapt into his saddle. "They won't follow us there."

Nevra heaved herself up onto her own horse.

"Will I ever see Otto again?" she asked.

"No." Andreas' jaw clenched. "Tonight, he makes his sacrifice."

Deep pain filled his voice. Shouts and running footsteps echoed. Soldiers were coming. Nevra's horse shifted under her as it heard the sounds.

"Now ride," Andreas hissed.

As one they kicked their heels in. The horses surged forwards. Cobblestone sang beneath hooves.

"HALT!" A shout ripped through the air.

A spear thrust towards Andreas. He grabbed the shaft and tore it from its bearer's hand. The soldier was left behind as the horses accelerated into a gallop. Andreas cast the spear aside and the darkness enveloped them.

The door to the manor study opened and three men walked inside. Two were soldiers. They wore bracers, greaves and gorgets of steel over chainmail and gambesons. White cloaks hung at their backs, helmets sat upon their heads, swords were belted at their waists and amulets of the Twins sat at their throats. Religious mercenaries who would never betray their faith or those who paid them. The third man wore the garment of a priest. His clothing had no embellishment and nor did his medallion. The inquisitors had been chosen from only the most faithful. Men who cared nothing for position or riches. Headman Otto rose from his seat.

"Welcome to my home, Inquisitor Renzo." Otto greeted the priest.

"Light of the gods be with you, Headman," Renzo replied.

"Please." Otto gestured to the seat opposite.

Renzo bowed respectfully and took the chair. They sat across from each other.

"How goes your inquiry?" Otto asked.

"Tell me, Lord Otto, what is the purpose of a headman or baron?" Renzo replied.

"To protect his people."

"Yes, good. These last years, my colleagues and I have searched far and wide, from west to east in search of the most sacred of things: truth. Truth in a world where it does not matter. Truth in a world that forgot its meaning a long time ago."

"What have you discovered, Father?"

"The roots of treason run deep. Heresy, murder, corruption. For decades you have lived in a land torn apart from within but soon the inquisition will purge it of this disease. Sinners hide in plain sight, even within your walls, Lord Otto. And so today, we will wash Vallgena clean by the light of the gods."

"How can I help?"

Renzo stared at Otto with shrewd eyes. The two soldiers had their hands placed upon their swords. There were many more outside.

"I hear rumour that you harbour an elf within your walls," Renzo told him. "An elf who they say was at Monocena three years ago. If you shelter a murderer, that would be quite unfortunate."

"I shelter no one."

The doors opened once again and in walked a third soldier. In his hands he clasped a sheathed sword. An elven sword. He placed it on the table between the inquisitor and the headman.

"Two men dead. Riders fled into the night," the soldier said.

Renzo ran his gaze over the sword between them, looking up to meet Otto's eyes. A moment of silence passed as the two men stared at one another, willing the other to break it first.

"Elven steel," Renzo stated, holding Otto's gaze. "Curious that such a blade would be found inside your house even as you say that there are no elves in Vallgena. Even as two of my men are now dead. To lie is a sin, Lord Otto, yet why would you keep an elf secret unless you know what she has done and what I will do if we catch her? Where is she?"

Otto's stare hardened. He squared his proud jaw.

"You will not find her."

Renzo rose to his feet and gestured to the old lord.

"Arrest him."

The night sky was moonless. The air was warm and the wind quiet. Torches were the only light in Monocena. The town was silent apart from footsteps of the few sentries who patrolled the city streets. All of this she saw as she approached, wreathed in black clothing, a glaive held tightly in her right hand. A soldier saw her and called out. He saw the white hair adorned with beads and braids. His cry was silenced as steel sliced through the air and tasted blood. More shadows emerged from the darkness, all clothed in black, all carrying steel. Her eyes, blue and cracked with white, swept the streets. Naidra snatched up a torch from its holding and tossed it through the shutters of a house. Screams filled Monocena. Sentries fell in droves. Flames spread as the attackers set fire to house, temple, tavern and stables.

Footsteps.

Naidra whirled around. A human charged at her. Her glaive deflected his hammer and opened his throat. He wore the garb of a blacksmith. He was no soldier nor warrior. Naidra did not care. She snatched up the smithy torch and cast it inside the man's house, not sparing a thought for who was inside. More and more people fell to the raiders as they marched through the city like ghosts. Blue and red eyes saw everything. None could escape them. Horses galloped through the streets as mounted elves made their presence known. Shadows danced – Monocena was illuminated by fire. Three years ago, some of the city had burnt. Now it all would. Naidra increased her pace, walking alone. She had purpose here. One that the humans could not stop. Her glaive tasted blood twice more as soldiers charged her. She could hear the wind talking to her, whispering in her ears. An elf cut down a man and then turned his eyes to a woman at his feet. He made to strike.

He hesitated.

The woman cried out and fled. The air crackled. Light wrapped around Naidra's arm and she directed it forwards. The woman barely made it five steps before the light tore her in half. Naidra ignored her; instead, her venomous gaze went to the elf who had hesitated. Her eyes showed her disdain. They all but called the elf a coward for sparing the woman.

Naidra turned back and continued on her way. The headman's manor loomed ahead. The doors fell open before her and she crossed the threshold, scanning the room. There were no soldiers or servants. Only two stood within the room: the headman and his wife. They were in their bedclothes. Naidra recognised the headman. The same man who had killed Sivan and betrayed them all. Cadoc, Varde, Raeghan, Aedella, Sarnai. Nevra. Her sister. They were all dead because of him, because of Mataro Aloys and because of her. The blood of her sister, of Cadoc and Aedella, was on her hands, yet the man before her had forced it to be so. Naidra remembered it all as she stared across the room at the headman. She could see the fear in his eyes. The red blood of his people covered her glaive and face. Naidra's fingers tightened upon the handle of her weapon. The voices in her head spoke louder. She touched her gift.

"You spoke to soldiers three years ago," Naidra said, memories crashing through her mind. "To men who hate my kind. About what you believe we are ... what we can do."

She reached for her magic.

"Do you want to know what I am?" she asked. "Think of the person that you love most in your life. Now they will know what it is to lose someone they love. As you did to me."

Naidra extended her arm. Magic flowed through her, wrapping around the headman. She watched as his eyes bulged and his hands went to his throat. Air fled his body as the magic ripped it from his lungs. He tried to breathe – he couldn't. The headman fell to his knees. His wife screamed. Naidra's fist curled. The headman's body crashed to the ground. She watched the corpse, a hint of a smirk contorting her lips.

Naidra struck.

Light blazed, the woman cried out ... and then there was silence. The headman's wife lay dead upon the ground beside her husband. Blood dripped from her lips. Naidra's eyes ignited as she watched them. The flickering flames from candle and fireplace roared and then swarmed around the room. Wood, thatch and curtain were set alight. Naidra gripped her glaive tight as she left the manor. Monocena burned from north to south. No building had escaped Salvaari wrath. By morning this place would be nothing but ash.

EIGHTEEN

City of Kamlan-Tor, Kingdom of Laeoflaed, Annora

"Make way for Princess Leona, Daughter to the King of Kings and Lady of the Silver Court," Captain Arne of the Arkin Garter announced before he stepped aside with a bow.

Through the open doors of the Kamlan-Tor palace court, she emerged. A flowing dress of a dozen shades of violet brushed the stone as she glided into the throne room. Her dark hair was pulled back into a single thick braid that tumbled down to her lower back. Glimmering rings adorned her ears and fingers. A band of silver sat atop her brow. She was dignified and proud, the very image of grace. Four steps behind her walked Duran. A magnificent cloak of midnight blue hung from his shoulders and his armour shone in the light. His left hand rested atop the hilt of his sword. His eyes swept the room and took in the faces of dozens of noblemen; they were a long way from Aureia. The rules and ways of the Annoran kingdoms were all but foreign to him. He did not trust these people – he had no reason to.

"You are most welcome in my city and my kingdom, Princess Leona." King Esmond of Laeoflaed greeted his guests. "Though I must admit, I was expecting to meet with the emperor himself."

There was a challenge in his eyes and in his voice, as if the presence of Leona was an insult. He was a king in his own court, arrogance was his right.

"My humble apologies, King Esmond." Leona addressed him

directly. "The emperor remains in Aureia at this very moment and is meeting with the rulers of Larissa, the last descendants of the Gaedhela line. As you no doubt are aware, he is also overseeing an inquisition in the north, fighting for the most sacred of things: truth. That is why the emperor is not here, *King* … Esmond."

The slight pause between the words was enough to counter yet not directly insult the Annoran. Janus was an emperor. He was *the* emperor. He was not to be summoned to a distant land at a foreign king's behest.

"I am the voice of Auriea," Leona continued. "A decision made by myself is a decision made by my country."

Esmond tapped the armrest of his throne, watching Leona carefully. She was playing the game well and no doubt he had never been spoken to by a princess with such authority before.

"Tell me, Princess Leona, why is your father meeting with our enemy?" Esmond asked. "It is no secret that the mountains between Laeoflaed and Larissa are watered with blood."

There was an irritated edge in his voice, though whether it was at Leona's words or her father's dealings, Duran wasn't sure.

"Bloodshed, King Esmond, and the ending of it."

"Many have suffered at the hands of Delios and the Gaedhela bloodline," Esmond continued. "Your lands were plundered, and your people made slaves. Tens of thousands died because of Nykalous and his children. That was over sixty years ago now, yet the shadow remains."

"Does it really?" Leona questioned.

"Indeed, it does," Esmond said. "The shadow of Delios is vast. It remains in the form of King Elias. It remains in the form of the aristocracy of Larissa, where the blood of Delios survived. I am forced to wonder now whether these attacks upon my sovereignty and my people are but the beginnings of a second Delion invasion."

"If you are indeed forced to believe that, then I will remind you that all of the Gaedhela bloodlines have died out, bar one." Leona approached the throne. "That there are fewer than one hundred Delions yet remaining in the whole world. I will remind you that barely sixty years have passed since Nykalous and his children conquered my lands, enslaved my people and slaughtered untold thousands. I know people who lived through those shadows, King Esmond. My grandfather Emperor Laeon was there. He told me stories of the great heroism of his people. You will recognise of course, King Esmond, that I understand your fears of an invasion, fears of a Delion empire reborn from the ashes."

Leona stopped barely ten feet from the ruler of Laeoflaed. There was no acquiescence in her. She did not know how. Duran, only paces behind Leona, kept his gaze upon the king. He was trying to play the part of the innocent, the part of the victim. He thought that the foreign princess would know nothing about the political climate so far from her palace. He was mistaken.

"You are at war with the desert clans, not Larissa," Leona countered. "Not with King Elias and the throne."

"If that is so, then why does King Elias allow the clans to cross the mountains, lay waste to our towns and slaughter our people?" one of the nobles cried out.

"We make war on our enemies and they in turn make war on us, my lord," Duran answered in Leona's stead. "This fight you have with the clans is not so very one-sided as you would have us believe."

"We did not start this fight."

"I did not say that you did, lord." Duran turned to King Esmond. "Lord King, I understand the retaliations against the desert clans for what they have done. I understand that it is not just your right but your responsibility to fight back and defend your people. The most important element of a strong kingdom is trust. Without it, a kingdom falls."

"Laeoflaed is strong, King Esmond," Leona added. "You have made it strong. It is my father's deepest wish that you remain so, and that you prosper."

Esmond glanced from the princess to the knight and back.

"I take it then that you have an answer to the proposal I sent the Imperial Court?"

"I do," Leona replied. "You asked that the emperor come here to forge an alliance against Larissa. I can offer you far more."

King Esmond tapped the armrest of his throne once again.

"You have my attention."

"A coin has been cast in the north," the princess stated. "We do not know which way it will land, only that it *will* land. The future of the north, perhaps even the whole world, rests upon how it falls. With so much at stake, none of us can afford disunity. None of us can afford bickering and endless debates. Emperor Janus meets with King Elias for a great many reasons, it is true, but one of them is peace. For Elias to create a union with Aureia, he must create a pact to end the fight with Laeoflaed. He will agree."

Esmond rose from his throne and stepped towards her. "How can you be certain?"

"He has no choice," Leona explained with a shrug. "He cannot stand against the might of both Laeoflaed and Aureia. King Elias will put the clans in check and then and only then will he have his alliance. After all, why have enemies when you can have friends?"

"You are wise beyond your years, Princess Leona."

"War is evil," Leona replied. "You know this. All of us here know this. War will only leave this world worse than it was when we found it. We will not do that. We will build a better one so that when we leave, it is a far grander place than we found it."

Leona's dress swayed as she glided towards the king.

"You will respect the integrity of the alliance between Aureia and Larissa," Leona said. "No more raiding across the mountains. No more burning the sands beyond."

"Even if—"

"No more."

Leona extended her arm. She was not scared or intimidated by a king. It took the nobles of Laeoflaed by surprise. It took Esmond by surprise. Leona was in charge here and they all knew it. At last Esmond nodded. He took her arm and clasped it tight.

"No more," he said.

The deal was made. Laeoflaed would stand shoulder to shoulder with the empire. Peace between Annora and Larissa had been forged in but a few words.

The Aureian delegation stayed in Kamlan-Tor that night. They feasted with King Esmond and his nobles and celebrated their newfound alliance. They left come morning. There were no carriages or wagons for the long journey home. There was no luxury or embellished finery. No nobles or members of the Aureian elite. Captain Arne and a dozen men of the Arkin Garter rode with Sir Duran, Princess Leona and her maid, Evangeline. The ride south would take over a month, yet there were enough towns and villages in both Laeoflaed and Aureia to see them back to the imperial palace with a bed each night. That was the only comfort Leona needed. She refused to be treated as more than the soldiers that accompanied her.

Days, weeks and miles passed in the blink of an eye. The earth sang beneath the hooves of the horses as they raced across the green fields. Eilia emerged before them. An Aureian town barely a day's ride north from the capital. To the east rose mighty mountains, while to the west ran open plains. The sun had started to lower in the sky when they arrived at the town. With silver they paid for warm food and beds for the night. The orange light of dusk settled over Eilia when Duran stripped himself of his armour and made his way to the stables. He entered the stall with his stallion, found a brush and slowly slid it across the horse's dark pelt. Duran looked the stallion in the eye as he worked.

"We've travelled a long way these last three years, you and I," Duran murmured softly. "I wonder, where will we be in the next?"

"Only the gods know that," Leona called as she walked into the stables.

Duran glanced up and saw her grin.

"The gods," she continued, "and perhaps my father."

Duran chuckled. Entering the pen, Leona gave him a smile before she extended a gentle hand and slowly stroked the stallion's powerful neck.

"When I first arrived at the palace, I never once thought I would end up becoming an ambassador," Duran said.

"Do you regret it?"

"Do I regret it?" Duran replied. "Three years, most spent in the saddle, forging peace … No, there is nothing to regret."

Leona's hand brushed Duran's. Without hesitation she took it and stepped in close. Duran met her gaze. The gaze he had fallen in love with long ago. The green flecks in Leona's eyes shone bright as she leaned close.

"We could be seen," Duran said, though he did not pull away.

"The guard are loyal. They will not speak."

"Your maid …" Duran smiled.

"She will not," Leona murmured, her lips tickling his. "We return home tomorrow. They will make us hide … I do not care who sees us tonight."

Emperor Janus did not look up as Kaladin entered his study. The knight watched his brother put quill to paper in silence for a moment before he closed the door behind him. Shelves of scrolls and books lined the walls. Janus had always sought knowledge as a child and that had not changed. Ink dried as the emperor shaped words on the parchment. Janus put the quill aside, folded the paper into a letter and sealed it with his ring. At last, he looked up and extended the letter towards the only other man in the room, the emperor's body slave.

"You have your orders," Janus said.

"Yes, Lord Emperor," the man replied, taking the letter and making his way from the room.

The slave bowed to Kaladin on his way past. The door shut at his back and the brothers were alone.

"I have sent word to my son in Tarik," Janus answered Kaladin's unspoken question.

"What has it been?" Kaladin asked. "Seven years? Eight?"

"Nearly eight to the day," Janus replied, gesturing to the seat opposite.

"Eight long years," the knight muttered as he took the seat. He grasped the jug on the table and poured the contents into the cups beside it.

"He will be nearly twenty-four summers now." Janus took an offered cup. "Ilarion writes to me often. He speaks of his studies in science, philosophy, politics, art, culture, swordsmanship – all of it. In a matter of weeks, perhaps a month, the inquisitors will return to Rovira. The tribunal will make its decision. Will we have peace or war? I do not know, but I will be ready. It is time for my son and heir to return home."

"May the gods speed him on his way," Kaladin replied. He took a sip of wine. "With peace at last established between Larissa and Laeoflaed, all eyes will be fixed upon the north."

Janus tapped his cup upon the desk. For the first time that Kaladin had known him, Janus looked unsure.

"I have heard stories," Janus said after a moment. "Terrible stories. We both know that the houses are fighting amongst each other. Many are in open rebellion. There have been arrests, trials … Many barons have been put to the sword by the inquisition. I ask myself: Did I make the right decision?"

"What you did stopped a war." Kaladin was firm.

"Stopped it, or delayed it?" Janus replied. "You say that I stopped a war, but I know you. What does your heart tell you?"

Kaladin tapped his cup with a finger, letting silence take hold for a moment.

"There is going to be a war," Kaladin finally replied. "I don't know when, I don't know who will be fighting, but war is coming for the north. Which barons choose to raise arms and for which side, that remains to be seen. The size of this war will rest upon decisions made in the coming weeks and months. The barons' decisions, the tribunal's decisions, your decisions. Whichever way the stroke falls, I will follow you."

"What if my decision does not align with that of Rovira, with the cardinal and your Order?"

Kaladin paused. He had given his life to the Order of Kil'kara. He had honoured every vow he had ever sworn. If Janus defied the holy seal, then he would be forced to choose between loyalty to his family or loyalty to his vow. Kaladin met his brother's eyes.

The doors opened.

Knight and emperor turned as a man of the Arkin Garter strode inside. He bowed.

"Forgive me, Lord Emperor," the soldier said. "Men have arrived from the Northlands."

Janus frowned. They were expecting no one.

"Which house?" Janus asked.

"None of them."

"What do you mean?"

"They come from Salvaar."

Janus froze. The guard had said men, not elves or ruskalan.

"Gather the council," the emperor commanded.

Kaladin and Janus hastened from the emperor's study. Men of the Garter and servants hurried around the palace. Every available lord was called to the throne room. Empress Lysaea joined them. She took her husband's arm as they strode through the ornate doors. Nobles and men of the Garter bowed as the royal family made their way to their thrones. The captain of the Arkin Garter took his place at his emperor's right hand. Kaladin took his place at Lysaea's left. The emperor and empress had barely sat down when the throne room doors boomed open once again.

Four entered. Their faces were weathered, and they looked exhausted. A stunned silence entered the throne room as the northerners strode through their midst. Though they bore the same dark eyes and rich skin of their northern kin, that was where the resemblance ended. The loose, flowy garments, that left much skin exposed and were beloved by the north, were gone. Their hair was longer and untamed. Beads adorned a thin braid that hung beside the leader's face. He wore a shirt of mail over his tunic, and black fur ran beneath his greaves and bracers. A dark wolf pelt fell from his shoulders as a cloak. No amulet or medallion bearing the symbol of his forefathers hung at his throat; instead, an arm ring was wrapped around his wrist. War paint as black as night was drawn across his face and neck – across all of their faces. It was only then that Kaladin realised one of the northerners was a woman. She did not wear a dress and was instead clad in the same garb as her kinfolk. The garb of a warrior. Two glanced around the throne room with wide eyes. Any man could tell that they were not used to the rules and grandeur of the nobility. Perhaps they had been farmers. The fourth was an elf. A she-elf. Her white hair hung down her back in an ivory waterfall. The four stopped and looked towards the emperor. The leader bowed and his companions followed his lead. Janus watched them curiously and slowly dropped his head in reply.

"Greetings, Lord Emperor," the leader said. "Please forgive our lack of manners. The ways of the south are unknown to us."

"Welcome to Aureia," Janus offered.

"My name is Ivar."

"Ivar? That is not a name from the north."

"It is not a name from the fiefdoms," Ivar corrected darkly. "There they called me Santiago. And then they cast us aside, scattered us to the wind. Why would I keep such a name?"

If Kaladin harboured any doubts about Ivar's provenance, his words gave him away. He spoke well but lacked the decorum or tongue of one used to the halls of power. Perhaps he had been absent them a long time.

"I am told you are from Salvaar," Janus stated.

Ivar snorted. "I come bearing a message from the blood of Tanris," he answered, ignoring the question.

"The last time a message came from Salvaar, a lot of people died in the hall," Janus countered.

"Then allow me to offer my sincere condolences on the untimely death of *all* who died here," Ivar replied firmly. "Elf and Aureian."

Shouts echoed. Tempers flared. Hands fell to swords. Many had died. Family. Friends. Janus rose to his feet.

"PEACE!" he thundered.

The Arkin Garter stepped forwards. The cries of anger died down, yet the rage was still alight in the eyes of those who had shouted. Janus' gaze swept the room and finally came to rest upon the Salvaari.

"I warn you, Ivar, choose your words with care," Janus commanded. He left his throne, striding down the dais towards the northerners.

Ivar did not back down, did not look away. He met the glare head on as Janus stopped mere feet from him.

"A terrible blow it must have been to *your* people," Ivar continued.

"Enough platitudes," Janus snarled. "Deliver your message."

At last Ivar looked away. He circled the space in front of the dais, the Arkin Garter watching his movements. His words were directed towards every person in the room.

"The petty squabbles of barons and fiefdoms mean nothing," Ivar began. "The fights between kings and lords mean nothing. There is only one war that matters, and it is coming. None in the north can stop it. None in the north want to stop it. That power lies with you and you alone, Emperor. In order to prevent the effusion of blood, you are invited to attend negotiations."

"Negotiations?" Empress Lysaea asked. "To what end?"

"To end this war before it ever begins," Ivar replied. "Many of the great families have accepted invitations. Perhaps they can make a difference, but none hold the power of your empire. None in the north have ever had that kind of power, enough that whatever your decision no baron will have the power to refuse. That is why I am here. That is why I have been sent."

"If I were to consider this proposal, I would like first to know who I am dealing with," Janus replied thoughtfully. "As you are aware, the inquisition is not yet complete. The truth. Once it has been illuminated, that is the side I will take. I do not even know the name of the one who has so graciously sent this offer and yet remains in the shadows."

"He is ruskalan. The blood of Tanris. Two months hence, these negotiations will take place in Alvillia." Ivar locked eyes with the emperor. "If you truly are a man of peace, you will be there."

Ivar pulled a twisted ring of silver from his wrist, an arm ring that Janus had only seen on the arms of the elves and ruskalan who had attacked the palace.

"Deliver this to Alvillia," Ivar told the emperor. "This peace can only begin with your nod. Two months hence."

Stone rang as the arm ring hit the ground.

The words had barely left Ivar's mouth before he turned and strode from the court, his companions at his back. Janus watched them leave. He clasped his hands as the doors closed.

Voices rose around him as the arguments began.

It was only after the doors had shut that Janus knelt and retrieved the ring. The iron was well crafted, and its ends were carved into the image of snakes. Janus knew little of the ways of the Salvaari.

Perhaps this was a religious symbol. Perhaps it meant something deeper to them.

"This is a trick," one of the nobles roared. "A ruse that they may take the life of our beloved emperor. They attacked here once. They failed. This negotiation is their best chance of slaying Emperor Janus."

"Lord Alseige is right," another cried. "What if they are leading us to our deaths?"

"We cannot trust them, we've all heard the reports," yelled a third. "Towns and villages put to the sword."

"We do not know what is true! Perhaps they truly wish to end this war."

"That man Ivar–"

"Is a man committed," Emperor Janus called as he rose to his full height again. "He is not placing his hope in this peace as much as he wishes for it. He is resolved to fight and die. That is why his manner was what it was, nothing more."

"They sent northerners here in place of their own people to show us that they are not alone in this fight," Kaladin stated plainly. "To show us that even the women take up arms against their foes."

"Godless, like the one who commands them," one of the nobles suggested.

"What do we know of Alvillia?" Empress Lysaea asked. "I have not heard of it."

"It is a farming town in the fiefdom of Canaeric, Empress," the Delion, Stefanos, answered. "Baron Florenzo Canaeric has traded with the elves in the past."

"When last I heard, Canaeric is yet to pick a side," Janus stated.

"None of us is truly neutral, Lord Emperor," Stefanos replied. "Florenzo will reveal his intentions soon enough."

"Hosting these talks is intention enough," Empress Lysaea added. "Whatever their reasonings, be they selfish or selfless, every family who attends the negotiation wants peace, else they would simply fight. They have seen their share of loss and have had enough of it."

"It is true, they could truly wish for peace," Lord Alseige said, looking to the emperor. "Or perhaps the stories we have heard are true. They hate our gods. They have already attacked us once absent cause. As soon as you arrive in Alvillia, they will slit your throat."

"There is no proof of that," Stefanos countered.

"There is no proof that they want peace."

"It is a gamble," Janus told them. "Only the gods know which way the dice will fall."

"Ivar said two moons." Kaladin spoke up. "If we were to attend these negotiations, then we must leave within a matter of days. The inquisition is also nearing its end. In a few weeks, perhaps a month, we may well have the tribunal's decision. We do not know if there will be peace or war. This result that we have all sworn to uphold will be decided upon before any delegation arrives in Alvillia."

"And again, it is a risk," Janus replied.

Kaladin paused as he looked to his brother.

"You are decided then?" he asked.

"Thirty years," Janus said. "It has been thirty years since our nation has known war. Since our people have died upon the battlefield. For the past three we have helped forge peace across the land. I think we should at least hear what the pagans have to say."

Kaladin tapped the pommel of his sword. "Well, if that's your decision, then you cannot go."

"I am the emperor."

"Exactly," Kaladin replied. "If peace is not the intention, then they could kill you, and even if it is, there are those among the Salvaari who could be emboldened. Your death could unite more than just the pagans. The war that followed ... that war could change the world."

"We must maintain the peace," Janus countered.

"We will," Kaladin told him. "A Delaureia *will* be travelling to Alvillia … and they won't be going alone."

NINETEEN

Fiefdom of Aloys, The Northlands

Naidra sat alone upon the thick branch of a great yew tree. She leaned back into the embrace of the trunk. Her eyes were closed, yet her ears open. She could hear the wind as it weaved through her hair. She could hear the voices that plagued her day and night. It had been a long time since they had first begun, but now Naidra could understand them. The voices grew louder; they were many. She was floating in a void of sound. She could not hear the rustling of leaves in the trees, nor the sound of footsteps in the undergrowth.

"Naidra!"

The autieyar's eyes burst open as she was torn from the void. The voices were still there, but they had quietened. She glanced down from her seat as a man walked forwards. Callan, his name was. A warrior of great skill. Two dozen elves and a handful of ruskalan were gathered in the woods. The company she had ridden with from Salvaar months ago. They were warriors, fighters, yet fewer than there had been when they had left their homeland. Naidra leaned back and allowed herself to fall backwards from the branch. She rotated in the air and landed on her feet. Her glaive leaned against the side of the yew. Naidra bit her lip, clasped her hands behind her back and strutted towards the elven man who had called her name.

She could see the anger in his eyes. It only amused her.

"What is it?" Naidra asked.

"We must return to Salvaar," Callan told her.

"Must we?" Naidra cocked her head.

"We run low on supplies."

"Then we will take them from the humans."

"We have been fighting for months," Callan replied. "Many of our people lie dead in human lands. We need supplies. We need more men."

Naidra snorted and pushed past Callan. Her eyes swept the woods. A chuckle broke her lips as the rest of the company watched on.

"Is something funny?" Callan said disdainfully.

Naidra did not even bother to turn to face him as she replied. The laugh turned into a grin.

"It is amusing that you of all people ask to return home after what happened in Monocena."

"What do you mean?"

"I saw you step back from that woman, the human girl, and let her live," Naidra replied, at last turning to face Callan. "It is clear to me now that you have no stomach for this. You are a coward."

Silence filled the woods as the elves and ruskalan stared. To accuse a man as renowned as Callan of cowardice in front of his people was a great insult, yet to Naidra it was true, and she *only* spoke the truth. Rage flashed through Callan's eyes. He took a step towards her, the anger in his eyes teeming with venom.

"A coward?" he hissed. "I have fought in every fight from here to Salvaar."

The amusement in Naidra's eyes only enraged him further. She met his gaze.

"We keep moving." Naidra held her chin high.

Callan stood his ground.

"You are not the leader here, Naidra," he replied.

Naidra watched Callan closely. She could see the doubt in his face, yet something within pushed him.

"Is that so, coward?" she goaded.

"You may have wormed your way into your position with magic, but in my eyes, without it you are nothing."

Naidra laughed. "In the eyes of a coward? For that is what you are, Callan. I once thought you were a great warrior, but great warriors do not hesitate in battle or run from a fight. Poems will be sung about your cowardice. I will pay to have them written."

Callan's gaze hardened. His hand twitched near his blade. He made to speak but all that came from his lips was a gasp as the air was driven from his lungs. White blood followed. Surprise widened his eyes and his knees buckled. The blow had been fast. He'd had no time to react. Naidra pulled her knife free from his heart. Ivory stained steel. The smirk never left her face as Callan crashed to the ground at her feet. Naidra glanced around the woods as the warrior's eyes glazed over. The elves and ruskalan watched on, staring in horror, in fear. None raised a finger. The white shards in her eyes glimmered.

"If any of you wish to go, betray the spirits and show the whole world that you are a coward, you can leave now," Naidra told them all. "I will not. Not after what they have taken from me. Not after what they have taken from us all. Now, if there is no further argument, we will continue tomorrow."

Naidra left before any could protest. She gathered up her glaive and walked out into the woods alone.

Alone … She was never alone.

The voices in her head came rushing in. The camp was far behind when Naidra slumped to the ground. She clutched at her head as the voices whispered to her. Now she could understand them.

They don't care what you lost.

"I didn't lose anything."

She abandoned you the same as they will.

"I remember her telling me father was dangerous," Naidra snarled. "That he had to be killed."

Who knows what she told the dark about you.

"She feared what I would become – and she was right."

She could not see you for who you are.

Remember how she looked at you last.

Nevra's face flashed before her. Her face from the farm. In her eyes there was horror.

"She would have *caged* me like an *animal!*"

A monster.

That is why you killed her.

"I–"

They're going to turn against you.

They all fear you.

"They are cowards."

Everyone betrays you. Prepare for it.

"I am! Did you not see me kill him?"

They move against you.

"QUIET!"

The voices vanished. Naidra panted, leaning back onto the cool ground. A relieved smile curled her lips. She sat up, took a breath, placed her glaive upon her lap and ran a whetstone over the steel. The weapon had known much battle in recent days. Naidra had long since lost count of how many she had killed with it. Humans, elves, ruskalan – she did not even care. She heard the hooves of a horse echo through the earth.

"Naidra," an all too familiar voice called.

Naidra grinned and leapt to her feet. The man pushed back his dark hood, revealing his face. Valmoar stood before her. He had been gone for some time.

"Monocena burned," he said.

Naidra nodded happily.

"The whole town slaughtered."

"Yes."

"Callan dead."

"Yes." Naidra laughed.

"Callan dead," he repeated angrily.

"Yes."

"They are not happy," Valmoar growled, gesturing back towards the camp.

"I will never be what they want," Naidra told him. The low growl in her voice was as constant a companion as the voices in her head. "He was a coward," she continued.

"What happened?"

"They already told you."

"I am not asking them."

There was anger in his eyes, in his voice, yet he wanted to hear what she had to say. He always did. He was the *only* one who did.

"He hesitated in battle, showed his heart. He grows tired of this, what we do here. Perhaps he should have stayed home." Naidra halted, a step away from the ruskalan. "He would have betrayed us all."

"That is not certain," Valmoar replied.

"He decided long ago that he would rather me dead than at his side," Naidra said with a shrug.

Valmoar rubbed his temples. "What have you done?"

Naidra reached into her pouch and pulled forth a ring bearing the mark of the lion. The ring that had once adorned the finger of Monocena's headman. She handed it to Valmoar.

"The doors to Aloys are open and a coward is dead," she affirmed.

Valmoar glanced at the ring, at Naidra and then the ring once again.

"Welcome back." Naidra wrapped her arms around her friend.

He was more than a friend. In the years that had followed the betrayal, he had grown into a mentor, a protector and a father. Valmoar smiled and returned the hug.

"I am proud of you," he told her. "You have come a long way, but you need to be more careful."

Naidra raised a hand. Her eyes flashed and a glowing blue

butterfly appeared in her palm. Valmoar grabbed her wrist to bring her back to the present.

"Seven days I have been gone and everything has changed. I need to know that I can rely on you." His expression softened but passion lay in his words. "I am doing this for our people. The elves and ruskalan deserve more than scraps. Even Callan."

"You can rely on me," Naidra murmured.

"I know," he told her sincerely. "This war has only just begun. Our allies amongst the humans are marshalling an army."

"These alliances have made Salvaar weak," Naidra growled. "The spirits will not stand for those who would call our land *home.*"

"The inquisition, though not yet complete, has done its work," Valmoar continued. "You know this. Some of the fiefdoms have expelled our people, others have risen against us. There will be a war and there is no telling how big it will become. Harkan believes that we need their help."

"Harkan is a fool if he believes that he can trust them."

"Then we are of like mind, but nonetheless it is so," Valmoar replied. "Harkan has forbidden the killing of any human who does not raise arms against us."

"Then we cannot attack their towns and cities."

"Precisely. And if we cannot attack their towns and cities, then we cannot win this war."

Naidra chewed the inside of her lip, eyes narrowing. "We came here to fight back against injustice and to defend ourselves from the hatred of the humans," Naidra told him.

"And yet it is humans that Harkan has sent to the heart of the empire to make peace."

Naidra stared at Valmoar. She could not believe what she was hearing. The firstborn son of Tanris had started forging alliances with the humans years ago, but this was something else entirely.

"If Harkan seeks peace, then he betrays us."

"Everyone betrays us, Naidra. The humans and now Harkan. You have become my daughter. It is only us now."

"I will not walk back into the shadows and surrender to those who wish us purged from these lands."

"Nor would I, but we need to be careful," Valmoar said. "Talks have been arranged between our people and the humans at Alvillia in two months' time. Five of the great houses will be there. Aureia will be there. Harkan believes that this war can be resolved before it truly begins. We must tread carefully or be washed away by the seas of progress, rather than directing them."

Nevra and Andreas rode for a day and night until they found refuge in the village of Alusia. It was small and as of yet too far east to have been touched by the inquisition. Darkness shrouded the land when they made their way behind the town walls. Nevra kept her hood up to hide her ears and hair. Who knew if there were enemies here, who knew if there were spies of the inquisition. They were not questioned by the gate guard, nor stopped by any soldiers. Alusia was at peace. Nevra and Andreas stabled their horses and bought a room at the inn. They found a table at the back of the tavern and the innkeeper filled their cups before ambling back to the bar.

"Innkeeper," Nevra called. She pulled a coin from her purse and tossed it to him. "Leave the bottle."

"My lady." He dipped his head, shuffling back and placing the bottle on the table.

Andreas watched him leave and then turned his eyes to Nevra.

"We need to talk about what comes next," he said.

Nevra sighed. She rose to her feet, gathered up the bottle and started to walk away.

"Tomorrow," was all she said.

Nevra found refuge in the alcohol. She found sanctuary. She had lost everything and had no purpose. The drink at least kept the nightmares at bay.

Nevra awoke with a gasp as water splashed over her face. She raised a hand to her pounding head as light assaulted her eyes.

"You're a sorry sight," Andreas called, pity all over his face.

She lay in a bed of straw inside the tavern's stables. The stench of horses was almost as thick as that of the alcohol on her breath and clothing. Water dripped down from her unbound hair. Her loose shirt was soaked.

"What do you want?" she grumbled, reaching for her wineskin.

Nevra patted her belt in search for it, but it wasn't there. She glanced back at the human as she heard the distinct sound of wine cascading down onto the floor of dirt and straw and dung. She watched it fall with a sigh. Nevra could see that it was midday. She rarely saw morning light these days.

"That is cruel," Nevra growled as she at last sat up.

"We must leave by midday," Andreas said.

Nevra pushed a stray lock of straw-tangled hair from her face. She offered a nod and made to rise. Freezing water splashed across her face and body again as Andreas emptied the bucket on her.

"Damn it, Andreas, I heard you," Nevra cursed.

"First you must bathe." He tossed the empty bucket aside. "You stink."

With a sneer and a roll of her eyes, she went to do as she was bid. The water in the tavern tub was cold but it would do. With a thick brush she scrubbed a week's worth of dirt, sweat and grime from her skin. It took longer still to remove it from her once white hair. Slowly the ivory colour returned. The waters that cascaded down her skin turned the bath brown. It was hard for her to rise from the bath, the act alone exhausting her. Nevra cleaned herself with a towel and wrapped it around her body as she crossed the bathhouse. Her attention was taken by a glass bottle. It sat on a table beside a pair of cups. She did not know if it was wine or ale. She did not care. It would give her strength. Nevra ignored the cups, snatched up the bottle, removed its lid and raised it to her lips. She tasted the wine as it rolled down her throat. It was only then that she noticed that her clothes had been taken from the bench upon which she had left them.

"Looking for these?" Andreas called as he approached.

He held her shirt and trousers, and then without hesitation, he tossed them into the fire.

"What are you doing?" Nevra shot, placing the bottle down and leaning on the table. "Can you not leave me alone?"

She was exhausted and felt as if a great weight was dragging behind her. Always dragging.

"It is my job," he replied, shrugging.

With that, Andreas deposited a pile of new clothing on another of the benches.

"I did not ask you to be here," she snapped back. "If you will not leave me be, then go."

"Otto died for you," Andreas snarled and thrust a finger towards her. "For you!"

"I know that."

"No, you don't," Andreas growled. "You know nothing of his sacrifice. You know nothing of what he gave up just to have you live in his home. Three years. Three long years since you arrived at his doors. Do you remember that day?"

"I do," Nevra replied. "Isabella and Tomas Ricard brought me there to recover from my wounds."

"You stayed and remained as Otto's ward long after the memories of your wounds faded," Andreas continued. "He did his best to protect you and give you sanctuary despite the fact that his lands border with those of Mataro Aloys. Despite the fact that Aloys is at war with your people."

Nevra glanced at him sadly. She understood.

"And he has my undying gratitude for that," she told him honestly.

"He never wanted your thanks," Andreas said. "I merely wish for you to understand. You came to Vallgena a wanderer, a great warrior. What have you become? A drunken girl who spends her time fighting, clowning and whoring."

It was true, spirits, it was true. It shamed her yet it was all she could do to escape the past. All she could do to bring herself comfort.

"Andreas, I–"

"I am not judging you," Andreas said. "I know that you suffered a great deal. Lost friends. A sister. I am also not a fool. You were at Monocena and that farm – the very reason why Baron Aloys brings war to your kind. If he had looked, *truly* looked, he would have found you, and if he did, Otto would either have had to give you up or watch as both Vallgena and Tolgoza burned. You and your past are secret, and because you are secret, you were safe. But now war has come to us. Now Otto is dead. I had hoped that his sacrifice and the arrival of the inquisition would spark a fire in you, but once again you return to your drink. Shame on you."

Nevra slumped on the bench in despair. His words stung, but what right did he have to them? She had lost everything.

"I keep seeing them," she said quietly. "That day."

Andreas folded his arms. "What really happened in Monocena?"

The ghosts of her past flashed before her eyes. All of them had died. The elves, the ruskalan, all of them.

"We were betrayed," Nevra told him. "A lot of good people died … friends. We were about to escape and then – it doesn't matter."

"Doesn't it?"

"Andreas. Why have you come?"

"It was Lord Otto's last command, and you are my friend," he said. He gestured to the pile of clean clothes. "We have a long ride ahead of us."

Freshly clothed and washed, Nevra followed Andreas back into the stables. They mounted their horses and once again set off. They rode at a pace through plains, fields and woods. It was nearly dusk when they saw the thick smoke rising to the south.

"Smoke," Nevra said as they brought their horses to a halt.

"Less than a day's ride," Andreas replied. "Aloys lands. That is no forest fire. It is a town."

"What town?"

Andreas glanced at her. His jaw was clenched, and his eyes held something new. He did not want to speak.

"What town?" Nevra repeated.

"Monocena."

TWENTY

"You are my voice. You are my will. You are my blood. It must be you who goes to Alvillia."

Leona could see the pain in her father's face as the words left his mouth. He looked exhausted, both her parents did. They had not slept. Leona glanced from her mother to her father. The three stood alone in the throne room. No nobles. No knights. No servants or slaves. Only the Delaureia family. For Leona the answer was easy. She had made up her mind years ago.

"I understand why you fear," Leona comforted. "I understand what is at stake. I understand the risk, but if there is a chance for peace, a chance to end the fighting, then we have to at least try."

"I am sorry that I must ask you to do this." Janus took his daughter's hand. "I am sorry that this burden must fall to you. I am sorry for everything."

"I am the princess of Aureia. This is my duty. This is my test."

"Lions came here not so long ago to start a war," Lysaea murmured sadly. "And now we must send you into their den to end one."

"Our people have known much war," Leona replied. "Too much. Delios taught us that. The history of Aureia is written in blood. We cannot shed our past like a snake sheds its skin. We must continue the fight for peace."

Leona hugged her father and hugged him tight. Her mother's arms wrapped around them both.

✦ ✦ ✦

Sunlight danced upon steel as Duran weaved his sword through the summer air. It glinted and glistened as the knight slid effortlessly from move to move. His balance was perfect, his form the same. He could *feel* everything. The sword in his hand, the gentle breeze in the wind, the hard ground underfoot. He saw it all, he felt it all, but his mind was empty, weightless. Duran's feet slid across the stone. He turned. His blade came up.

Steel rang.

Sword hit sword.

Duran stared at Kaladin for a moment as his mentor appeared. A grin broke his lips. Kaladin laughed and tapped his blade onto Duran's.

"Welcome back, Cormac," Kaladin said, sheathing his sword.

Duran returned his blade to its scabbard and then embraced his friend and mentor. Laeoflaed and back had been over a three-month journey on horseback.

"How was King Esmond?"

"Agreeable … after a time," Duran replied with a chuckle. "The Larissans?"

"The same." Kaladin shrugged. "King Elias is sending a company of mounted men south to keep the desert clans in line until such a time as he can unite his kingdom under the lotus banner."

"And now all eyes turn to the north."

Kaladin did not reply. Duran could see it in his eyes now as before: the Sword of Kil'kara was unsure.

"Something has changed," Duran stated.

"We travel north."

"North?"

"Janus has been invited to oversee negotiations between a number of the houses and the people of Salvaar, be they elf, ruskalan or human," Kaladin explained.

"Invited by whom?"

"The messenger would not say," Kaladin replied. "Only that this may be the only chance for peace. Whatever Aureia decides could swing the balance."

Duran remembered the attack on the emperor as clear as day. Dozens dead. Rivers of blood across the tiles and stone floors of the palace.

"He did not say?" Duran's suspicion grew.

"No, he did not."

"Then what if it's a trap?"

"We are entering a dark game, Duran," Kaladin said. "Dark games are godless."

"If Janus is killed, then the peace between kingdoms we have fought so hard to establish will fall."

"The emperor will not be travelling north."

Duran frowned. "If the emperor will not be attending the negotiations, then how will Aureia have a say?"

"I did not say that the House of Delaureia would not travel to the Northlands."

His blood chilled. His heart raced. For a moment breath left him.

"No," Duran snapped. "We cannot send Leona into such danger!"

"Duran–"

"Even if she makes it through the fighting and reaches the negotiations alive, there is no telling what could be waiting for her."

"Listen to me."

"They attacked us here," Duran snarled and thrust an arm towards the castle.

"Listen to me."

"Out there" – Duran pointed north – "there are no walls. No armies. No guards. Out there is Old Religion territory."

"LISTEN!" Kaladin snapped. "Leona has made her decision. I suggest you do too."

Duran ground his teeth. He knew in his heart, in his very soul, that she would not have run from this. She would not have run from her duty.

"Then if that is her choice, I will go with her."

"And you will not be alone," Kaladin vowed. "I will go. Captain Arne and a complement of the Arkin Garter will go. We will keep her safe. That is my oath."

Duran curled his fists as he fought to compose himself. He turned away from his mentor, closed his eyes and took a breath. He needed to think.

"You love her, don't you?"

Duran froze. The words hit him harder than the fear of Leona riding into the north.

"I am not blind," Kaladin continued slowly. "I have tried to be. I will not pretend any longer that I cannot see it."

"Have you spoken those words to anyone else?" Duran asked.

The fear he felt now was greater than before. If anyone found out … if Janus found out …

"No," Kaladin swore. "But you must be careful. She is the princess of the greatest empire this world has ever seen. She is subject to the traditions and expectations of her people. You know that."

Kaladin spoke true. In time it would be expected that Leona marry for the good of her people. A knight was far below her station.

"Many would not deem it wise," Kaladin warned.

"I do not care for the opinion of those who rose to power because of the wealth and position of their forefathers," Duran replied.

"Think, Duran." Kaladin thrust a finger towards his student. "If they find out – if the emperor finds out – this is not going to end the way you think."

"Then tell them," Duran snapped back.

"Duran, I am on your side. You may not have my name, you may not have my blood, but we are family, you and I."

Duran sighed. "I know," he muttered.

When he looked at Kaladin, he saw more than a mentor and a friend. He saw a father.

"For as much as you love her, so do I," Kaladin continued softly. "She is my niece. If there was anything more I could do to keep her safe, I would do it. Right now, the emperor may well be about to sow unrest between the empire and our faith, for if Janus comes to a verdict different to the tribunal, then our world may fall. If the inquisition chooses the path of war and the empire the path of peace, it will mean choosing between loyalty to an emperor, a homeland, and loyalty to the gods. Ask yourself this, for it will be paramount in the days to come: How far would you go for your country? How far would you go for your family? How far would you go for your faith?"

It was not a question but a statement. It was the truth.

Duran closed his eyes. He took a long pause, controlling his breathing.

"Above all else, she must be kept safe," Duran said. He turned and made for the doors. "For that we will need more than just the Arkin Garter."

Duran was more than just good with the sword; he was great. This journey would require more than his blade and that of his mentor. Duran knew the north. He knew about the people, about their ways. He knew almost nothing about the elves and ruskalan. Duran never looked back as he crossed through the corridors and stone paths of the palace. He reached a wooden door, knocked three times and then entered.

"Duran Cormac of the Northlands," a voice boomed.

Stefanos of Delios pulled Duran into an embrace with a laugh.

"Welcome home, my friend," Stefanos said.

The inventor had barely aged a day in the three years since they had met. His hair and beard were still long and his garment was as flamboyant as ever. A red hat embellished with a long feather sat atop his head. The only thing that the years had changed was that now Stefanos wore an amulet of the Twins at his throat.

Duran clapped his friend on the shoulder. "And what a welcome it has been," Duran muttered, running a hand through his hair.

"Alvillia and the negotiations change many things," Stefanos replied.

"You know then?"

"I was there when it was decided."

Duran ran his eyes across the papers scattered across the tables. He glanced up at his friend.

"This world gets stranger every day," Stefanos continued. "It was not an elf or ruskalan that came to make this pact. The messenger was as human as you and I."

"They form alliances," Duran said.

"There are some northerners who now call Salvaar home," Stefanos stated.

"I know. It started some time ago."

"The men who came, they were dressed in pelts ... skins. They wore arm rings, skin awash with dark paint. They have not just found homes beneath the trees of Salvaar, they have taken their spirits, their ways, their beliefs. All of it."

"The world is shifting beneath our feet." Duran looked to the wall where a crossbow hung upon a rack.

It was so very different to the first crossbow that Stefanos had shown him. Before it had been little more than wood, rope and some small bits of steel. Now it was beautiful. Markings were etched into the wood. The long trigger had been refined and slightly curved. The limbs, once wooden, were now made of steel. Like the stock, the limbs were etched with beautiful designs. This was more than just a weapon, a tool; it was a labour of love.

"It changes and we must change with it," Stefanos added, following Duran's gaze. The inventor gestured towards the crossbow. "The next evolution in my design. See the limbs? The metal has replaced the wood. It adds power. Enough even to penetrate mail. A thing of beauty, is it not?"

"Yes," Duran agreed. "You're an artisan, my friend. When will it be ready?"

"It is ready now," Stefanos told him and waved a hand. "I plan to present it to the emperor in two days at the anniversary of his patronage."

Duran nodded slowly, staring at the weapon. The crossbow was far more than a tool capable of cutting through chainmail. It was but a glimpse of what Stefanos was capable of. True greatness.

"Stefanos, I must ask something of you."

"Ask away and if I can give it to you, I will."

"I am to travel north with Princess Leona," Duran said. "Whether these negotiations are real or not, she will need protection. More than any number of Arkin Garter. The Northlands are at war, the fiefdoms treacherous. The sword is all I have ever known, and if the gods ask it of me, I will gladly lay down my life for her. This journey needs more than just swords and steel and horses. If it is to succeed, then it will need the knowledge locked away in that head of yours."

Stefanos was silent for a moment. His hand rose to his amulet of the sun and moon.

"The emperor's cause is as noble as it is just," Stefanos said. "He wishes to bring friendship to the Northlands, but I fear he may well soon realise that an emperor has no friends. Only followers and foes. What he is doing here, going against the cardinal, the tribunal, the inquisition and the gods … it will not go unnoticed. You know that. How could you not know that?"

"I know," Duran replied. "Everything sits upon the edge of a knife. Which way it falls … that is for the gods to decide. I understand what I am asking of you. You know more about the elves and ruskalan than anyone. You know their spirits and their ways. You have a way to even the odds."

Both men glanced towards the inventor's table, towards vials and plants, towards the liquid that had stopped the autieyar in the palace. If one attacked them out there in the Northlands, there would be no stopping it.

"The autieyar," Stefanos murmured. "Janus asked me to research elvira after the attack. I have done my duty, refined the brew into something far more potent. I had hoped never to use it again."

"Please," Duran continued. "Will you do this for your emperor? Will you help to bring his daughter home?"

"I won't do it for Janus," Stefanos said. "I won't do it for his empire. I'll do it for you."

A great weight fell from Duran's shoulders as he looked to his friend.

"Then you'll come?"

"Aye," Stefanos replied sincerely. "I will follow you."

Duran held out an arm. Stefanos took it and held it tight.

"We ride at dawn," Duran told him.

The knight left the inventor to allow him to prepare for the journey that would take many months to complete. One night was all they had left. Duran had long since removed his armour when he made his way to the temple. His garment was the simple blue and black of the order. Torches burned and kept at bay the darkness of night. Silver moonlight shone through the stained-glass window at the far end of the temple. Rays danced across the image of the sun and moon before they cast down upon the statues below. Carved from simple stone as they always were, the images of the Twins looked as real as any man. A gentle smile caressed Azaria's lips. Her hood was pulled up over her hair and her hands were spread as if offering something to any who approached. Durandail stood proud, clad in armour and with a spear firmly held in his grasp.

Duran stared up into the face of his namesake. His fingers curled around his medallion and he knelt upon the stone.

"Durandail, Father of all Fathers, grant me the strength of the sun until my journey is complete. Azaria, Lady of Silver, light my way with the moon until my journey is complete." Duran closed his eyes. His words changed into Ancient Aureian. "I *swear* the sacred oath that I shall render unconditional obedience to the gods. I will set aside the deeds of darkness and put on the armour of light. I shall honour the man and honour my faith. I shall give all glory to the gods, and whenever they deem it, as a loyal servant, I will surrender my life for this oath."

A warm breeze kissed his cheek, travelling down his back. A single tear seemed to spill from the stone gaze of Durandail. The gods had made their decision.

Morning came around all too soon. Duran pulled on his armour, polished to perfection. It glistened in the sunlight as the company rode for the palace docks. The cloak of deep sapphire hung low. The sun emblazoned upon his shield shone bright as it sat upon his back. Proud crests of blue stood tall upon the silver helmet that he carried beneath his arm. A finely honed sword hung at his hip. Brighter than all was the medallion at his throat.

At his side rode Kaladin. The Sword of Kil'kara's cloak was trimmed in white and a pauldron of steel was strapped to his left shoulder. Behind the knights were two dozen men of the Arkin Garter. Their hair and beards were long, their armour and cloaks silver and violet. At the head of the column rode Stefanos, clad in his flamboyant clothes and feathered cap, and Princess Leona. Her dress was the deep purple of Auriea, and a kukri was strapped to the back of her belt. It had last tasted blood three years ago. Only the gods knew if it would again.

The nobility and their household staff lined the docks to bid farewell to the travellers, their expressions mixed. Some wanted peace, others war. The imperial family waited by the ramp that led up onto the great galleon that awaited the company. The Griffin's Grace floated in the waters of the Silver River. With four thick masts and a length of close to one hundred feet, the galleon was the pride of the royal navy. A griffin with spread wings flew as the ship's figurehead. Sailors stood upon the deck and hung in the rigging.

Goodbyes were said between father and daughter, and mother and daughter as the emperor and empress bid their princess farewell. There were no tears nor sombre goodbyes. None knew if they would ever meet again. This was Leona's duty. There was no place for grief, not when so much hung in the balance. Horns blared as the gangplank was pulled up onto the ship. The sails unfurled and the Griffin's Grace was underway. Tens of thousands of Aureians lined the banks of the great river as the only chance for peace was sent into the greatest of dangers. Duran glanced onto the quarterdeck. Leona stood beside the captain as he manned the helm. The princess alone was the beacon her people needed. She was all of their hopes and wishes for a better future.

The companions stowed their belongings and then gathered in the captain's cabin. The two knights, Leona and Stefanos were joined by Arne of the Arkin Garter.

"We follow the Silver River to the Lupentine," Sir Kaladin explained, running his hand across the vast map drawn upon the table in the centre of the cabin. "From there we track north to Palen-Tor. Once we make port, it will take near on ten days and nights hard ride to reach Alvillia. We have all heard the stories about what is transpiring in the north but make no mistake: we have no idea what is waiting for us."

TWENTY-ONE

City of Monocena, Fiefdom of Aloys, The Northlands

Ash crunched underfoot. Thick smoke hung in the air like a dark blanket. Every stone was charred, every piece of timber scorched and burnt. Even the bodies that lay scattered throughout the ruins of Monocena were blackened. The only sound that broke the crunch of the ash underfoot was the occasional splash as Nevra walked through the destruction. The splash of blood. Men, women, children – none had been spared. Nevra kept her hood up to hide her hair and pointed ears, slowly walking through Monocena. Memories filled her mind, memories of a lifetime ago. The dream of friendship and unity. The deaths of her friends … of Naidra. Her sister. Monocena had known so much death. Too much. Even here, well beyond the frontier of the conflict, the city and its people had not been safe. Nevra searched through the wreckage. Her blue eyes locked upon a blackened doll. She knelt and gently picked the child's toy up. Nevra had barely raised it from the ground when the doll crumbled into ash.

Even the children.

Few enough had escaped the wrath of steel and fire. Some stared aimlessly from where they sat against the remains of their homes. Some wandered with blank eyes. A soldier in blackened armour and with a bloodied bandage wrapped around his head talked with Andreas. Nevra's companion wanted information.

Who could have done this?

Nevra's eyes drifted to the body of a fallen soldier. His body was burned but nothing could hide the cut across his throat. Her mind pieced together the scene as she approached the corpse. The angle of his body, where he lay, the divots in the muddy ground. The soldier had been charging at a foe. Nevra knelt again, this time her gaze turning to the earth. Brushing her fingers against the ground, she read the distance between soldier and his killer. Something long had killed him. A spear, perhaps a glaive.

Nevra kept moving. The forge of a blacksmith still stood in the remnants of a smithy. The blacksmith's body lay face down, his hammer mere inches from his fingers. He had tried to fight back, yet the same one who had killed the soldier had claimed his life. Nevra cast her mind back as she pieced together the fight. The weight of the attacker's footsteps, the weapons used … This was the work of elves. Hoofprints began to churn the earth. Two bodies lay before Nevra in the street, slain by the ghost she was following. The weapon was a glaive, that much was certain. Then she saw it. Through the fog of memories that Monocena spoke to her, the one she was following stopped. Further down the street, the earth was disturbed. The signs of someone kneeling in the mud, of someone standing above them. The kneeling person had risen and fled. The attacker had *let* them go. Then Nevra saw the body face down in the mud. She had been killed as she had run.

Not killed.

Butchered.

Her body had been torn in half. No sword had cut her, no spear or axe had touched her. Charred clothing and burnt flesh told the story. *Magic.* Nevra's heart pounded. Her face paled. The one who had done this, the one who had led the attack, was autieyar. She remembered her father. She remembered Naidra. She remembered what they were capable of. Dozens dead. Ice ran down her spine as she remembered being cast down by her sister. The thudding in her chest was all she could hear as she watched the ghost turn towards the headman's manor …

"Nevra." Andreas' voice ripped Nevra from her dream.

Slowly Nevra took a breath, tearing her eyes from the ruined manor and turning towards her friend.

"Elves," Naidra rasped.

Andreas nodded. "There was no warning," he said. "They came from the blackness. They wore dark clothing. Few survived. They say hair of snow blazed in the wind like white fire."

"Why would they have come here?" Nevra asked as she stared around the destruction. "Monocena is well beyond the frontier."

"They would have come in strength and numbers," Andreas added. "It would have taken more than a handful to do this to such a place."

"Not if they had an autieyar. Not if they had magic."

"Magic does not exist."

"No." Nevra's tone was heavy. "You have not seen it."

"Superstition, nothing more."

"They brought magic with them," Nevra growled, fighting back the trembles that threatened to consume her. "One they call autieyar."

She thrust an arm towards the woman torn in two.

"No blade, no sword, no spear could have done that."

Andreas made to reply and then stopped. He stared over Nevra's shoulder.

"Riders," he said.

Nevra spun to face them. The riders dismounted at the edge of Monocena and started down the charred streets. Shining armour, banners that flew high. Their garb was golden. Each and all were marked with the same white symbol. A lion.

"Aloys," Nevra snarled.

One of the soldiers removed his helmet. His armour was finer and more grandiose than the rest; his golden cloak was trimmed in ivory. A long sidesword hung from his hip. This man had to be from the family that had brought death to hers. The burning fingers of rage wrapped around Nevra's heart as she stared towards the soldiers. She moved, blood splashing beneath her boots. Ash crumbled.

"Nevra," Andreas hissed. "Nevra, don't!"

Too late. Nevra was blind to everything but the soldiers she charged at. The soldiers spread throughout Monocena as they helped the survivors and searched the wreckage for more. The nobleman knelt beside one of the wounded, his back to Nevra. This man's family had set the wheel in motion that had taken everything from her. Her pace quickened. The betrayal of Aloys. Here, in this town. Nevra began to run. Andreas shouted. Her hand wrapped around her sword's hilt. The nobleman turned towards the thundering footsteps. Light danced across steel – Nevra tore her blade free. The nobleman's eyes widened, his hand falling to his sword as he started to rise. He was too slow. Nevra's blade drove forwards. A snarl left her lips. Time slowed.

An unseen shield smashed into her side and threw Nevra to the ground. Pain lanced through her left arm. Ash filled her nose and mouth. Nevra rolled across the ground, snatched up her fallen sword, turned and thrust. Steel rang and the shield deflected the blow. Nevra leapt to her feet. Shouts echoed through Monocena, along with the song of sword meeting sword. Nevra countered but again met nothing but shield. The nobleman drew his sword and moved to his guard's side, soldiers swarming. They surrounded her with spear and shield. Nevra turned this way and that. Her feet kept moving, her head on a swivel. Her sword stayed up. Spears were levelled. There was no escape from the wall of steel. The nobleman had but to give the command, say the words, and her life would be forfeit. Nevra did not care.

Why would she care?

The command never came.

"Drop your weapon," the nobleman called instead.

Nevra glared at the man. She did not move. She did not lower her sword.

"DO IT NOW!"

"STOP!" Andreas cried, leaping towards them.

The nobleman glanced at the unarmed man as he raised his hands to show that they were empty.

"Please stop," Andreas begged. "She does not know what she is doing."

"Seems to me that your friend knows exactly what she is doing," the lord replied.

"She's drunk and in pain," Andreas pleaded.

"I am not," Nevra snapped.

The nobleman narrowed his eyes, gaze flitting from Andreas to Nevra.

"My name is Solan Aloys, son of Baron Mataro. Hand over your sword and remove your hood," he said. "Then we will talk like civilised people. I will honour this new peace today."

Nevra did not move an inch. The nobleman extended a hand.

"Your sword."

Nevra shot him a withering glare. Aloys had so greatly wronged her, yet there was no fight here, only death. She took a breath. Andreas was right. She squared her jaw and slowly passed her sword to the lord. The nobleman ran his eyes over the steel.

"Hood off," he commanded. "Let us move on."

He would see that she was an elf. If he did, her life may well be forfeit anyway.

"Hood!"

Nevra did not look away from him. She raised her hands to her hood and pushed it back. A mane of white riddled with beads and braids fell free. Gasps echoed from human throats. Grips tightened upon spears. Nevra never tore her gaze from the eyes of the lord. Her life was in his hands now. She could see the war being fought within his eyes. Her people had killed so many. Her people had sundered a town. His town.

"You should not be here," the lord said.

"And yet here I am."

"Your people …" True pain entered the lord's voice. "Look at what they have done!"

Nevra stared at him. All of the rage. All of the anger. All of the agony. It all poured free.

"You father betrayed and murdered my friends!" she shouted. "MY SISTER!"

Nevra's hands balled into fists. She stepped towards the baron's son and cold steel touched her throat as a soldier held her back. Nevra fought against her emotions as they spilled forth.

"What do you mean?" Solan hissed.

"Peace talks. Three years ago," Nevra spat, waving her arm around. "In this very place. An ambush planted by the *noble* Mataro Aloys. I alone survived."

"Peace talks?"

"Do you not recall?" Nevra scoffed. "Let me remind you. Elves and ruskalan were supposed to live here with your people. Trade ideas. Teach each other. We were supposed to find friendship here. Instead, there was nothing but blood."

Solan tapped Nevra's sword.

"I will admit I have heard rumours about these negotiations," Solan conceded. "But *only* from your people. I am sorry, but I am afraid that my father never received such an invitation."

"No, that cannot be!" Nevra cried in disbelief.

She searched Solan's face for lies but she could see none. He *had* to be lying. Even if he wasn't, then perhaps his father had not told him.

"What have you heard?" Andreas said, sidling through the ring of soldiers.

"Then, as now, I came to Monocena," Solan replied. "I spoke to the headman myself. He spoke of murder, that your people killed a man and when confronted turned to steel."

"A lie," Nevra murmured. "That is a lie."

She felt as if she had been hit by a mighty blow. Her mind was shattered.

"And now?" Andreas asked. "Who did this?"

"The survivors all say the same thing over and over again," Solan told him. "A woman. An elf. Eyes a sea of blue with shards of white. Tattoos mark half her face."

Eyes a sea of blue with shards of white.

A broken autieyar. One who had reason to slip behind enemy lines. One who had reason to make straight for the headman's manor.

It cannot be.

"The people speak of magic," Solan continued. "Perhaps they were turned in the night. Fear deceives the mind. I do not know. This woman saw no difference between armed soldier and unarmed serf and with her own hand slew both."

Nevra stared at the bloodied and ashen ground. Her head swam.

Was it Naidra?

Was her sister alive?

It tore at her.

"The gods grace you with fortune this day," Solan Aloys declared. He handed Nevra's sword back to her. "Keep your lives. After what your people did here, the only reason I spare you is because I am soon to ride to these peace talks with your people at Alvillia."

"Peace?" Nevra asked.

Solan nodded. "Not all wish for blood," he replied. "Go now and keep your hood up. These lands are treacherous."

Naidra joined Valmoar as they made their way back to their

companions. There were thirty of them in all. Thirty who had heard Valmoar's words and had followed him far from their homes and into battle.

"She is still here?" called one of the elves as they approached.

"Indeed, she is," Valmoar replied.

"Naidra is a threat to everything we have created," the elf snapped. "Everything that we are."

"Her own sister knew she was dangerous," cried a second. "Nevra feared what she would become … and she was right."

"Naidra is the only reason that you were able to take Monocena," Valmoar countered. "The only reason that so many of you still live in this fight."

Erdan stepped forwards. His hand tightly grasped a spear.

"She killed Callan," he said. "One of our own, and not for the first time. How many more of us must die so that the *iristysi* has a place."

Iristysi. The Salvaari word for Broken One. A title given to those outcast by all. A condemnation to live alone until death. A curse.

Naidra gave him a mirthless smile. She strode towards Erdan and shoved her face towards his.

"What did you say to me?" Naidra growled.

"I spoke the truth."

The flames of the fire flared.

Alone.

The very thing thrust upon Naidra when she had been barely thirteen years old. She roared. Her fist connected heavily with Erdan's jaw. Shouts filled the woodland. Erdan stumbled backwards as Naidra's second blow landed. Blood flowed as Erdan struck back … then the magic caught him. It held him fast, slowly drove him to his knees. Naidra drew her dagger. The elves surged forwards with swords in hand to save their friend. Naidra drove her blade towards them. Fingers wrapped around her wrist. Valmoar heaved Naidra aside and then leapt between her and the elves.

"ENOUGH!" he roared, eyes blazing.

The fire dissipated, and smoke trailed through the woods. Naidra's knuckles were white around the grip of the dagger, lips drawn back in a soundless snarl. White blood streaked from her nose. Erdan glared back. He spat blood to the side as he was helped to his feet.

"Haven't enough of us died already?" Valmoar pleaded.

"She is *not* one of us," Erdan countered, thrusting a finger towards Naidra.

Naidra drove towards him again. She did not care that so many stood against her. Again, Valmoar stepped between them.

"She is as elven as any of you!" Valmoar cried. "Yet you spurn her, cast her aside, call her iristysi. Shame on you. We, all of us, came here for a single purpose: to avenge the killings of our people. Some of you lost friends, others brothers or sons, mothers or daughters. Naidra lost a sister, yet her fire still burns. Do yours?"

"Where you lead, we follow," Erdan replied. "That was our vow. But does our vow mean being blind to one among us who would so readily kill another?"

"You who have always spurned her and treated her as something less?" Valmoar countered. "Why? Why do we fight each other? The enemy isn't in this camp. The enemy is out there. The colour of your blood means nothing to me, but it matters to them, those who will not stop until every last one of us is dead."

Valmoar looked from face to face. From autieyar to warrior. From elf to ruskalan.

"The Firstborn of Tanris has made his will known," Valmoar continued. "In a matter of weeks, a delegation of our people will meet with the humans at Alvillia."

"To what end?" Erdan asked.

"Peace," Valmoar replied. "Many of the great families will be there. The empire. Others. It is Harkan's desire that to avoid the deaths of untold thousands, a deal has to be made. Whatever happens at Alvillia, whether we have peace or war, no blood is to be shed before that day."

"Harkan cannot believe that–"

"Harkan has made his will known and we will honour it," Valmoar interrupted. "For now, our purpose here is done. For now, Monocena *must* be the last. For now, our crusade has come to an end."

"No, that cannot be," Naidra snarled. "Not after what they have taken from us."

"I hate everything she stands for," Erdan snapped as he gestured towards the autieyar. "Yet on this we share mind."

"The decision has been made," Valmoar countered.

"Then what of us?" another of the elves asked.

"Erdan will lead you home."

"And you?"

"Here I must remain. The time has come, my brothers and sisters, for us to at last part ways."

Naidra stared at him. For years Valmoar had been all she had. A friend and mentor. The only one who hadn't cast her aside.

"You're leaving?" she asked him.

"The spirits guide me to walk a different path," Valmoar replied. "I cannot return to Salvaar. Not yet."

Erdan gestured towards Naidra. "She killed Callan. She nearly killed *me*. Now you want me to watch her and deliver her safely to sacred Salvaar?"

Naidra's eyes flickered with light, but she held her power back. She could hear the faint whispers gathering all around her.

"No," Valmoar told him. "For the spirits have called her name too. They granted Naidra her gift. The granted it for a reason, a reason that will soon be revealed. Can you not hear their voices in the wind? You only need to open your mind and listen. It is written that a time of change will come at the autumn solstice."

Naidra's eyes widened. Autumn was already upon them; the leaves were starting to change.

"The spirits guide you, my brother," Erdan replied. "May they show you the way as you showed us."

Smoke drifted through the woods as the last of the fires were extinguished. Bedrolls were gathered and horses were saddled. The white-haired elves and their black-haired brethren mounted up. The journey east was long and full of dangers, yet it was the path home. They were few in number, less than there had been when they had first begun their crusade. Many looked back in final goodbye. For three years they had fought and bled with Valmoar and Naidra. That was a bond not easily broken.

"It's not right," Naidra hissed as the warriors vanished into the woods. "Peace with the Northlands is a fantasy."

"It is the way."

"Even after everything they have taken, everything we have lost?" Naidra seethed. "No ... I do not forget, nor do I forgive. Nearly three hundred years ago, they took our spirts, warped and mutilated them and said they were theirs. They believe themselves to be redeemers, saviours ... but they are heretics and murderers."

"You remember everything, don't you?" Valmoar asked.

"Everything that you taught, it never left."

"I don't trust these humans," Valmoar said. "We will obey the will of the Firstborn but that does not mean we are to be blind. I ride for Alvillia – we ride for Alvillia. We were betrayed, you and I, and that betrayal made us stronger. The emissaries that Harkan sends, they must be kept safe. The Firstborn's will *must* be honoured."

TWENTY-TWO

Coast Of Aureia, The Lupentine Sea

The sky was clear and the breeze gentle. The Lupentine caressed the Griffin's Grace with tender waves as the wind pushed the flagship north.

"Look there," the helmsman called as he gestured towards a vast Aureian city emerging upon the coast. "Valentia."

"The northern border," Duran said.

On the horizon he could see the mountains just beyond Valentia, the gateway into the Kingdom of Laeoflaed.

"And to the east, far beyond the horizon, Nesoi and the lands of the Valkir," Arne of the Arkin Garter mentioned.

"I have never travelled to the Isles, nor seen the halls of your people," Duran admitted.

Arne wrapped an arm around Duran's shoulder and thrust an arm to the east. "The crackle of the fire," he said. "Singing, dancing, great stories. Those are the sounds of home."

"I would like to hear them some day." Duran grinned at Arne's enthusiasm.

"One day you will, Duran Cormac," Arne told him. "One day you will."

"We will have a story of our own to share."

"What kind of story?"

"One of victory," Duran said.

"I truly hope so." Arne laughed.

Duran left the helm and made his way across the decks to the prow of the Griffin's Grace. Stefanos stood at the front of the great vessel. In his hand was clutched a cylinder of gold rings and red-stained wood. In his eyes was the same spark of curiosity that Duran had noticed when they first met three years ago. The inventor's fingers moved as he turned the item over and over. He spun the gold rings.

"What is that?" Duran asked as he approached.

"A cryptex," Stefanos replied.

"Looks Tariki."

"It is," Stefanos said. "A puzzle invented by those from the far north. There is a hidden way to unlock the cryptex and discover whatever it is that waits inside."

"It holds something inside?"

"Indeed," Stefanos explained. "Perhaps it could be a new design, perhaps a map to untold fortune."

"But what if it is empty and you waste so much time on a game?"

Stefanos held the cryptex aloft. "Ah, but what lies inside means nothing to me. It is the challenge and the idea of such a puzzle that intrigues. Do you understand?"

Duran looked at the inventor inquisitively for a moment. "Yes," he said. "Yes, I think I do. That path upon which we now find ourselves mirrors the turning of the rings of a cryptex. What lies at the end of this path, this journey, only the gods know."

"Yes, good, the knight understands," Stefanos replied with a chuckle. "Warrior, scholar, priest – you are all of these things, Duran Cormac."

"And yet what are titles but words absent value?" Duran asked. "The name of one who achieves great deeds is worth far more respect than a title."

"Just so," Stefanos stated. "Your mind is open and only when it is open can you truly see. I have had a vision."

"What did you see?"

"Mountains that reach for the heavens. A green valley as far as the eye could see. Great walls taller than you can imagine, a temple shining in the light of stained glass. Beacons burning with red flame. Above it all, the sun and moon embraced. A haven. A haven of the gods. Duran, I saw them clear as glass."

"You saw the gods?"

Stefanos nodded. His eyes shone as words flowed from his lips.

"I could feel their presence," he explained. "They gestured for me to follow. I walked the city streets. Paved with cobble and filled with market stalls. Knights gathered all around. Knights and maija. This city was not Rovira nor any other fortress of your Order. I asked the gods where was this beautiful city, and the Lady of Silver replied with a single word. Kilgareth."

"Kilgareth?"

"The Tower of Worth."

"I have never heard of such a place."

"Nor have I, for it does not exist," Stefanos murmured as he remembered. "Duran, I believe this is a sign. A purpose for which I was put on this earth. This city … I must be the one to build it."

"I have never known you to be a godly man before."

"They now show me the way," Stefanos replied. "Azaria's words guide me. I have never been more certain. When we return, I will make for Rovira, say the words and pledge myself to her teachings."

Duran paused. He had grown to know Stefanos well these last few years and now counted the inventor as one of his closest friends. Despite every conversation they had shared, despite the long hours they had spent together in Stefanos' dusty workshop, Duran had not expected his friend to seek to join the Order of Kil'kara.

"You wish to become maija?" Duran asked his friend.

"I do. I believe that I was shown this vision for a reason, and I am committed. The gods … they guide me as they guide you."

"Another month nearly gone already," Emperor Janus said quietly. He heard his wife's gentle footsteps approaching behind him.

He stood in the gardens and for a long time had been alone with his thoughts. Autumn had painted the trees in brilliant shades of red, orange and yellow. Janus watched the leaves as they drifted down from their canopies and floated towards the grass. In a matter of weeks, the middle of autumn would be upon them. In a matter of weeks, his daughter would arrive at Alvillia in pursuit of peace.

Was it a fool's dream?

Perhaps, but he had to at least try. It had been decades since the empire had last known war – since before Janus had taken his crown. That was the way he intended to keep it, but if war was decided upon, then he would be ready.

"They have assembled, my love," Lysaea said as she reached Janus.

He felt her arm entwine with his own. Janus looked to his wife and gave her a smile. No words needed to be spoken, for she could see into his heart. She knew his fears, his hopes and dreams.

"Then it begins," Janus replied.

Together they made their way into the palace. Together they made their way through the halls and corridors. With each step they grew further into their roles as emperor and empress. With each step they prepared for everything that awaited them. The doors of the throne room opened, and they strode inside, the sea of nobles parting to allow the emperor and empress to their thrones. As one, they turned and sat. As one, they stared down across the ocean of people. Most were Aureian, yet the few visiting dignitaries that still remained in the capital had made an appearance. Larissans. Northerners. The passage between the nobility remained open as a trio walked into the hall. Two were dressed in armour and wore cloaks of pure white. Before them strode their leader. Before them walked a man clad in the ivory garb of a priest. His amulet was silver, and he clutched a wooden staff in his right hand. His eyes were fierce, and his face weathered by time. The sea of nobles closed behind the holy trio as they reached the dais beneath the thrones. The priest stepped forwards. His staff tapped upon the marble floor.

"Most noble emperor." He greeted Janus, bowing his head. "By the gods' grace."

"Welcome to Auriea, Father Valdemar," Janus replied. "Your reputation as a judge and a scholar precedes you."

Valdemar's hand flexed upon his staff as he stared up at the thrones.

"It has been three years since the winds of the heavens carried me north," he said. "It has been three years since I was anointed by the holy powers as an inquisitor. Every soul is subject to a higher power and there is no higher power than that of the gods. When I first set out from Rovira three years ago, I did so with a single purpose: to discover what for so long had been hidden. To discover the truth. There was no knowing what I would find there, who would greet me. Perhaps the whispers of darkness, which so many fear, or perhaps nothing but the good grace of peace and harmony. This is why I had come so far. To find clarity."

The words that flowed from his smooth Aureian tongue were spoken with strength and pride. He spoke like a man seasoned beyond his years and one who had found his purpose.

"What was it that you found, Inquisitor?" Janus asked the priest. "What secrets were revealed in the north?"

"Shadows spread from the dark heart of the Northlands. Many have heard the stories, but few truly see. In time all darkness has come forth. Chaos, calamity and death grip the land. Roving bands of those not native to the north have plunged the fiefdoms into chaos. Murder, deceit, treason. The devils of Salvaar have spilled into the gods' land and now seek it for themselves. Many have secreted themselves into the homes and hearths of good towns and cities. There they ply their dark trade. Some slithered their way into the beds of the god-appointed nobility. A wave of murder has swept the land, and many have been caught … even a northern baron! This deceit did not end there. Words of poison have turned men from oaths. They corrupt and defile. Indeed, some of the fiefdoms were all but under pagan rule. These dark forces of Salvaar kill without cause. They kill without reason. Towns and cities burnt … All those souls lost. I have seen things, my brothers and sisters, with my own eyes," Valdemar hissed. "Temples aflame. Priests left as carrion in their very own courtyards. Others I saw hung from trees, some with symbols carved into their flesh. These people do not discriminate. The Fiodine tells us to let the wrath of the gods fall upon the heathen who desecrate the holy places of their land, and we are the wrath of the gods. By the order of the inquisition, we held trials. By the order of the inquisition, we served as judges and many did we judge guilty. By the order of the inquisition, we removed those barons from power who had fallen to the darkness of the Salvaari devils. By the order of the inquisition, we found a most unholy truth that had corrupted the heart of the Northlands. That the nation rests upon the edge of a knife. That if this corruption spreads much further, then the north will fall. Many thousands will perish. The fate of this country rests in the hands of those who believe, in the hands of those who *truly* believe. Do we let them stand alone? Do we stand idle as the Northlands are consumed?"

Father Valdemar lightly tapped his staff upon the marble floor, emphasising his sermon. There was no sound in the hall but that of his voice. There was no movement. There was nothing but the gravitas of the message he brought from Rovira.

"I returned to Rovira once our findings were complete. The Tribunal gathered and I fell to my knees before the cardinal. I wept … I cried like a baby. He looked down upon me and he said, *Don't be afraid. The gods are here.* The vote was cast. The Salvaari will die. The inquisition calls upon the armies of faith to assemble and march upon the Northlands. We will strip them of what they have plundered. We will answer their injustice with the wrath of the gods, for by the gods' word we are told to show no mercy to nonbelievers, to devils and heathen. The cardinal had a vision and in that vision he saw all the dead bodies of the wicked lying in the streets of great cities, upon the northern fields and upon the banks of the mighty Arwan."

Valdemar stared up at the emperor and empress. He took three steps up the stairs of the dais and looked towards he who sat upon the Silver Throne.

"Oh, greatest of emperors, what say you?" Father Valdemar called. "Will the Silver Army take up arms for its faith? Will you march north?"

Janus looked down upon the sea of faces. He remembered the bloodshed that had taken place in his palace three years ago. Now as then he could hear the sound of war drums in his head. Now as then he could feel the current dragging at him, the inescapable pull of war. A tide of ruin. A tide of death that would be remembered for all time. He would be its architect. In a few weeks, it would be the winter solstice. In a few weeks … Alvillia. He could already feel the encroaching chill, but was it from the ever-nearing winter, or was it from the theatre of war?

"All of my life," he started, "every command I have given, every law I have written, every act – all have been in the pursuit of peace. Peace to prevent the deaths of untold thousands. It is for this dream that I have sent a delegation north. A delegation that rides to meet with the Salvaari."

Not a single breath could be heard as Father Valdemar stared at Janus.

"The Tribunal's word is absolute. As of this moment, we are at war," Valdemar declared. "There is no compromise."

"Compromise?" Janus said coolly. "A word often insisted upon yet one that I have learnt differently than most. I realise that this dream of mine will take a long time to come to fruition. I realise that I may not live to see it come to be, for the road is long and shrouded in shadow." Janus paused. "But I will travel down it nonetheless. *That* is my compromise."

"Then you turn your back on your church, you turn your back on your country and you turn your back on your gods," Valdemar countered. "Make no mistake, my lord emperor, neither the gods nor the kingdoms of man will forget your decision."

A man stepped forth, a northerner, who bore the colours of House Bailon. The sigil of a bear was emblazoned upon his shirt and cloak.

"With all due respect, you swore to uphold the decision of the inquisition, the verdict agreed upon by the Tribunal," he growled. "My lord, Baron Estevan Bailon, agreed to these peace talks in Alvillia when you vowed that you would cede to the Tribunal's decision. He agreed because the House of Bailon stands among the greatest in the north. Any decision made that impacts the land beyond the Eretrian will have his mark upon it. The baron in this moment rides for Alvillia. You swore that–"

"I did, Lord Gonzalo." Janus cut him off. "Before the Salvaari sent their own delegation into my court seeking peace. Many of them do not want this war."

"Tell that to the thousands of souls taken by their hands," Gonzalo hissed. "How many more must die for you to understand?"

"We don't have the right to decide that future."

"The right?" Gonzalo snarled. "We have the responsibility! Lord Emperor, you have always been a staunch defender of our faith. Show the people your power now, show them that you are not willing to let my country be destroyed. Stand with us! You are a dreamer, a visionary, just as my lord is. Medea. A dream of his own. A dream of a northland not divided by countless families. Countless fiefdoms. Bloodshed. Help us forge the united land of

Medea and I swear this debt will be honoured to you and your family now and for all time."

Janus motioned for his wife to rise. She did so and took his hand.

"My word is final. What happens in Alvillia will decide everything. The fate of thousands now rests upon that small village in the north."

With that Janus descended from the dais with the empress at his side. They strode through the parting crowd and out into the palace. It all now rested upon Leona.

Would they have peace or war?

"Soon we will disembark," Kaladin told the assembled few in the captain's cabin. "Palen-Tor is a city of great magnificence, but we cannot stay there. When we dock, we make for the northern gate and ride hard for the Eretrian. Few will know of our presence and that is how I would like to keep it. Even in Aethela there are those who would not hesitate to seek profit if they knew that the princess of Aureia walked among them."

"I can take care of myself, uncle," Leona replied. She reached down and pulled her kukri free from its sheath upon her boot.

A smirk spread across Duran's lips as he watched her. A wit sharper than any steel and bravery to match. Leona would stare death itself in the face and tell it to try its hardest.

"All the same," Kaladin replied. "I would rather ride to Alvillia and back before anyone knows that you have reached Annora."

"You carry Delion steel," Stefanos stated as he glanced at the kukri. Its pommel was as beautiful as the steel itself, carved into the snarling faces of lion, goat and viper.

"The blade that belonged to Alessandra Gaedhela herself," Leona explained, admiring as the light kissed the metal. "The inscription on the steel reads, *'Where the storm rages, the loyalty of one is proven'*."

"A fitting proverb for the last of the Chimera's children," Kaladin added.

"Her blade, how did you come by it?" Arne of the Arkin Garter asked.

"My ancestor took it from her hand after she died," Leona answered.

"He wasn't the one to kill her?"

"No, she took her own life before she could be captured and killed. She took her own life with this blade so that her blood would not be taken by Aureia. Vesperan allowed her to hold her blade until she breathed her last. A final show of respect to a great adversary."

"You speak as though you admire her," Stefanos said.

"Alessandra saw her father's death and then watched her family tear itself apart, yet still she remained true to the ideals of Nykalous. She remained loyal to her father, to her people and her country despite being asked for more when she had no more to give. She stood in the palace of Delios alone while her enemy closed in around her and her city burned. While Delios fell. A thousand times she could have surrendered. A thousand times she could have laid down her arms and vanished from the pages of history, never to be seen again. Alessandra did not. I can think of nothing more worthy of admiration."

Kaladin raised his eyebrows. "I have heard tale that she was as heartless as the sea," he said.

"Well perhaps those who are heartless once loved too much," Leona replied. She paused and glanced at Duran, before she continued. "Delios and Aureia were enemies because of time. Nothing more."

"What happened to Delios was a tragedy," Stefanos murmured. "A tragedy that they brought upon themselves. A cruel fate that an entire civilisation was to be washed away to give Aureia its freedom."

"And so did the tears of Delios fall," Duran said at last. "A history that we cannot repeat."

He looked to Leona, and she gave him a nod. Delios and Auriea, a tale of two empires. A war that had destroyed an entire people. It was no different to this conflict in the north.

A shout came from above deck. The cry of landfall.

"Palen-Tor," Kaladin told them. "We have arrived."

The company divided throughout the hold of the Aureian vessel. Everything bearing the symbols of Kil'kara and Aureia was stripped. In place of the garb of the Arkin Garter, the Valkir wore plain armour of mail and steel. Duran and his mentor removed their surcoats emblazed with the sigil of their creed. Their armour was plain and without embellishment; the blue cloaks upon their backs would give nothing away. To Annora and the Northlands they would be seen as naught but simple soldiers.

TWENTY-THREE

Fiefdom of Aloys, The Northlands

"NAIDRA!"

Nevra's shout echoed through the farm. The autieyar's hair flew around her in a storm of white. Eyes a blue inferno cracked with ivory shards. Blood streaked from her nose, from her lips that were curled back into a savage smile. Fear gripped Nevra. Charred and ruined bodies littered the muddy road. Soldiers. Farmers. Women. Screams fled the lips of the dying. Tears of blood leaked from the corners of Naidra's eyes. Steel rang as Nevra caught a farmer's hammer. Rained lashed her face. Ice froze her body.

Light flashed.

Light summoned by Naidra.

She hit the warehouse hard. A wound opened upon her chest. She crumpled into the mud, her vision fading to black.

Nevra awoke with a gasp, her skin glistening with sweat. Her heart raced and her eyes were wide. She trembled as the memory ran through her mind. Nevra could see her sister's face, a face she had known for decades yet barely recognised. Cradling her head in her hands, Nevra fought to steady her breathing and still the pounding of her heart. The beginnings of tears dampened her eyes.

"Nevra?" Andreas called from across the camp.

Nevra hastily wiped her eyes with the back of her arm and reached for her wine flask.

"It's nothing," she answered.

Nevra closed her eyes as the cool wine ran down her throat. This is why she drank, why she needed to drink …

"No, it's not." Andreas watched her. "Every night it is the same. I have never known someone to be so restless. Tell me, do you truly sleep?"

Nevra took a breath. The wineskin was half empty.

"What is it to you?" she snapped venomously.

"You are my friend."

Nevra snorted and took another gulp of wine.

"Enough of this," Andreas snarled and leapt to his feet. "You are not the only one who has lived and lost. I have followed you from Vallgena with nothing but the clothes on my back. I gave up everything for you – for Otto. Otto died for *you*! For you! Tonight, I want the truth. What cruel thing happened that turned you into *this*? Or are you really no more than the heartless husk of a woman eager to die?"

"You really cared for Otto, didn't you?" Nevra growled.

Andreas shook his head in disgust and turned away. "He was my father." His words were quiet, barely more than a whisper.

"Your father?"

Nevra stared at her friend. Her blood chilled.

"I am a bastard, Nevra of Salvaar," Andreas snapped. "The bastard son of a wealthy lord. In any other city, in any other land, I would have been cast aside, murdered or left with nothing. He took me in. Gave me a home … a family. And now his blood is on your hands. And what do you do? Drink. Drown yourself in pity. Enough. Give me the truth this night or I will leave at dawn."

Nevra could only stare at him. She felt empty. She felt alone, adrift. If Andreas left, then she would have no one. Perhaps she deserved it. What he said was true, Otto *had* died for her … because of her.

"You can't leave," Nevra murmured as she at last gave in to Andreas' request. "The truth is that I have barely slept in years and when I do my dreams are dark and cold. Every night I see their faces. I see my parents. My father, his blue eyes shattered with white, my mother's knife driven into his heart. My mother … slain by my father's hand. By magic. The thing that corrupted his mind and poisoned his soul. I watched him die long before the knife took his breath. Long before he killed so many people … women … children. He became a monster before my eyes. The same evil took my sister and there was nothing I could do. I was her sister. I was supposed to protect her and there was nothing I could do!"

Sobs broke her trembling voice.

"I saw the corruption take her at Monocena. I saw her kill so many … enemies … friends. I should have told her that I would never leave her side. That I would never abandon her. I swore her that oath so many years ago, but I betrayed it. I betrayed her. I betrayed my sister. My word means nothing, not even a whisper. She would have felt my heart and seen the look in my eye. My sister *died* believing that I hated her. My sister died believing herself to be alone."

Nevra bit down on the inside of her cheek. She could not still her trembling body.

"Even after she lost herself, even after she struck me … I still loved her. I still loved her."

"And that is why you attacked Aloys?"

"Aloys betrayed us, and that betrayal pushed her too far. Everything that happened. Valmoar. Aedella. Sarnai. Sivan. Cadoc. Varde. Reaghan–" Nevra struggled and then at last said her sister's name. "Naidra. All lost because of Aloys, because of their treachery. I would see the House of Aloys fall for what they did to us."

"And what if what he said was true?" Andreas asked. "The baron's son, Solan Aloys. That there was no deception. That there was no agreed peace."

"I know what happened. What Solan Aloys said was a lie. A lie!"

"But what if it wasn't? What if there is something more at play?" Andreas urged.

"There isn't – there can't be."

Andreas paused. He let Nevra's words fade into silence. Nevra stared out into the darkness as she drank more wine.

"These negotiations in Alvillia," Andreas said after a moment. "After what happened to Monocena ... I can't imagine that there will be peace."

Nevra didn't reply. She knew he was right. The Aloys delegation at least would be readily opposed to whatever peace offerings her people would suggest.

"Solan said that the people spoke of magic. I cannot imagine such a thing."

"Pray that you never see it," Nevra murmured and then she froze.

She remembered Solan Aloys' words.

A woman. An elf. Eyes a sea of blue with shards of white. Tattoos mark half her face.

"What cruel fate drove my people to travel so far behind enemy lines to strike at a town of little significance?" Nevra said. "What reason did they have to burn it to ash? I searched when we were there, found a trail. The autieyar ... she killed without cause or reason. Corrupted by what made her strong."

Nevra raised her wineskin to her lips. She made to drink – and stopped. Andreas watched her. Eyes red from tears, heartbroken and purpose gone.

"Vengeance," she whispered.

Nevra's eyes danced. They couldn't fix on anything. Her mind searched. She had never seen her sister's body, only heard tell that she was dead.

"I can't go home," Nevra said after a moment.

"We cannot stay here, Nevra," Andreas replied. "We go to Salvaar."

"I don't go to Salvaar," Nevra commanded.

Andreas snorted in anger. "What will you do?" Andreas growled. "Chase after this fantasy as if it is true?"

"I have to try."

"Hope is a dangerous thing. A loose thread that can pull you apart."

"Then leave."

Andreas shook his head and ran a hand through his hair. Nevra could see the rage in his eyes. The turmoil. He had lost his home because of her. He had lost his father. Taking her to Salvaar was Otto's last command.

"I will not ask you to come with me," Nevra offered.

"Of course I'm coming!" Andreas bellowed. "I can't let you go on your own. You'll get killed!"

Relief flooded Nevra's chest as she stared up at her friend. Andreas gathered his sword and strode away. He needed time but would be with her by sunrise. No words of thanks would ever be enough, so she said none. Instead, Nevra looked down at her wineskin, clenched her jaw and cast it aside.

No sleep was had that night. Nevra stoked the fire and stared into the crimson flames. Her mind flooded with images of her sister. How she used to sing with her, dance with her. Two halves of the same whole.

The sun rose all too soon. They mounted up and did not head east. Instead, they turned their horses back the way they had come. Back towards Monocena. Back to the beginning. Nevra kept her hood up as they rode. She kept it up when they reached the outskirts of the town, mud splashing beneath her feet as she led her horse by the reins. Tracks led away from the battle into nearby woodlands, and from there it became difficult. Nevra knew that if you looked close enough, then the truth would reveal itself. Her eyes scanned the ground, they scanned the trees and searched the wind itself. Elves were born of the wild. They were a part of the earth. She could see things that most could not. She could find signs from nothing.

"Any sign left behind has long since dissipated like smoke," Andreas said as he scoured the earth.

"My people are like ghosts," Nevra told him. "If they do not want to be found, then they will not be found. Only the children of the spirits could ever hope to find their tracks."

Nevra let the reins of her horse fall and walked towards a tree. The bark was rough to her touch. She closed her eyes and pressed an ear to the trunk. The heartbeat of the forest, she could hear it clear as anything. It traversed well beyond the borders of sacred Salvaar. She could feel its pull in her blood, in her soul. Nevra's eyes flicked open, her gaze drawn towards an overhanging branch. In her mind she could see it. Someone had been sitting high up in the tree and had dropped backwards from their perch. Only those native to Salvaar would know such comfort in the woods to do such a thing. Slowly it all revealed itself. The company of elves and ruskalan. Nevra's head swivelled as she walked beneath the trees. She could see where her people had stood. Not so far from where they had camped, she found a hint of ash upon the ground. It was hidden amongst fallen leaves and earth. Little more than a few pieces of grey upon the land. The rest would have been scattered by the wind.

"Ash," Nevra murmured, running her fingers through the grey dust.

"The fire that made it must have been old for so little to remain," Andreas said. "Why risk such a thing while so close to Monocena?"

"To burn the dead," Nevra muttered, her eyes following the wisp of a trail neatly written out before her.

"None died in the attack."

"The autieyar will have killed one of their own."

"And you know this how?"

"My mind is open to the wind, the trees, the earth itself. My blood is that of Sylvaine and she guides me," Nevra replied. "They have parted ways. It would seem that my people at last split from the iristysi."

"Iristysi?"

Nevra ignored him as she searched the ground.

"Most ride east. A lesser number, two, ride *north*."

Nevra found more questions than answers as she read the signs.

Why would someone stay with the iristysi?

Why would so many follow one to begin with?

"We have to keep moving." Nevra heaved herself back up into her saddle.

Plains, rivers and woodland flew by as the companions galloped north through human lands. They ate and drank in the saddle, only stopping to look for tracks and sleep. Like those they pursued, they stayed clear of roads and trails. This was a time of war and soldiers of every house would be on watch. The roads would be filled with warriors and bandits, and if even one caught sight of Nevra's white hair, then she would have to fight. Beneath the trees of a forest, Nevra knelt as she continued her search for tracks. She read the signs. Disturbed ground. A thread of cloth hung from a branch. Nevra plucked the strand and ran her keen eyes across it.

"Elven," she murmured. "We cannot be far behind."

"How far?"

"A few days perhaps. No more than that."

A woman's scream echoed through the forest. Shouts followed. Nevra glanced at Andreas. There was no thought, no discussion. She was an elf. Elves acted. Nevra gathered up her reins and leapt back up into her saddle. She kicked her heels in and surged towards the scream. They broke the tree line and thundered into fields of grass. An earthen road opened up before them. It intersected with another in the shape of a cross. Beside the intersection was a great tree. The heart of autumn had ripped most of the leaves from its branches, while those few that remained were the colour of flame.

Nevra's breath was torn from her lungs as she brought her mount to a halt.

"What kind of hell is this?" Andreas murmured from her side.

Bodies hung from the tree. Six of them. Their hands had been tied behind their backs before they had been strung up by their necks, necks that were now broken. There were men and women. None wore armour. None were soldiers.

"A warning," Nevra whispered.

She had seen it before but not so far from—

A woman screamed. Nevra's eyes narrowed. Beneath the hanging tree, she could see a pair of men. One held the woman tight and then threw her to the ground. She tried to rise, tried to run. The second man knocked her down and drove a heavy boot into her side. She cried out as a rough hand took her by the hair and dragged her towards the tree. She kicked and bit, yet the grip was unbreakable. A rope hit her. A noose. She screamed as it was tightened around her neck. Tears flooded her cheeks. Her cries died off as her head was wrenched back and she could see the bodies hanging above her. The rope was thrown up over a branch. A fist drove the air from her lungs. She managed to pull away, her feet scrabbling on the earth. She made it two steps before her head was again wrenched back. The noose tightened around her throat and then she crashed to the ground. The woman clawed at the earth as she was dragged towards the tree by the rope.

Hooves thundered upon the road. Nevra leapt from her saddle, her boots thudding upon the soil long before her horse came to a halt. Nevra's hand fell to her sword.

"Let the girl go," she commanded.

One of the men heaved the woman to her feet and held her tight. They both stared towards Nevra. They were beardless and their hair hung wild and free. If the bodies in the tree had not given their homeland away, then their white locks did.

Elves.

Only those native to sacred Salvaar would create a hanging tree. A warning to all that there was no fear here.

"And why would we do that?" the first elf said.

Nevra pulled her hood back. A slight frown broke the man's brow as he saw her ivory hair. She thrust an arm towards the tree.

"These people are not soldiers," she growled.

"They are the enemy."

"The enemy?" Nevra snapped, taking a step towards them. "Can you not see that this is why they turn against us? This cruelty."

"They took our gods, forced us back across the river and now hunt us like animals and you would have us what? Show mercy? No. We will show these people the same mercy that they have shown us."

"Did you not hear the lady, friend?" Andreas called from atop his horse. "She said to let the girl go."

The elf stared at Andreas. Dark hair. Dark eyes. A rich accent. *Human.*

"You travel with one of them," he snarled.

Steel flashed as Nevra drew her blade ever so slightly. Andreas slid from his saddle.

"Please don't make me do this," Nevra said.

The elf snorted. He gave Nevra a contemptuous look and took a step towards Andreas. Nevra stepped in his path. Sunlight danced upon her half-drawn sword. She met the elf's eyes and shook her head slowly.

"You would side with the humans against your own kind?" he said, lips pulled back in a snarl.

"We are responsible for killing innocents and burning cities!" Nevra cried. "I cannot – I will not let this happen again."

A breath of cool air caressed Nevra's cheek. For years she had been asleep, dead to the song of the world, the song of Sylvaine. She felt life stir inside her again. A great weight fell from her shoulders. She could finally breathe.

"Then may Tanris welcome you home," the elf replied.

He glanced back at his companion and gave a single nod. The second elf tossed the human woman aside and drew blade. The first turned back. His throat opened as Nevra's dagger drove home. White blood flew through the air and the first elf fell, his sapphire eyes fading to grey. She had never killed one of her own people before. It tore at her soul, but it had to be done. Nevra pulled her sword free. A roar left the second elf's lips as he charged. Steel rang beneath the hanging tree. Nevra blocked with sword and knife. Once, twice. The man's crossguard connected heavily with her face. Nevra staggered back. She hadn't fought in years, not sober at least and certainly not with a sword. She felt slower; her timing was off. Tears of red blood splashed as the elf opened Andreas' cheek. Nevra leapt to his defence but her dagger was torn from her grasp. The elf clad in armour was a born warrior who had known nothing but war for three years. He pulled his own knife free as he fought against two. Steel opened Nevra's sword arm. A kick sent Andreas back, but they did not give ground. Nevra gathered up her fallen dagger as she circled her foe. Her weapon was long, the length of her forearm. Nevra chanced a glance at the blood dripping down from her bicep. Her eyes flicked back to the warrior as she wiped the flat of her knife across the wound and in a single move licked the blood from her blade. As wild as the forest. As deadly. There was no fear in her. She levelled sword and dagger as Andreas approached the elf from behind. Before the warrior could move to create space, Nevra attacked. Fire warmed her veins. With each move she felt freer. The warrior turned and deflected Andreas' blade. His knife took Nevra's and then her sword opened his leg. The man dropped to a knee as the companions attacked in unison. Sword and knife were torn from his grasp. A pommel cracked into his temple and steel was driven into his neck. Nevra watched him fall and felt great sorrow.

"Nevra?" Andreas murmured as he saw her face pale.

"I have never killed my own people before," Nevra replied. She turned to face her friend. "But I fear that this will not be the last time. We must do what we can to survive this nightmare that has been created. See to the girl."

Andreas nodded, wiping his sword clean of blood. He sheathed it at his hip and then approached the battered and bruised woman as she cowered at the base of the tree. He gently reached out a hand and gave her a smile.

"Come with me," he said softly.

Lip trembling, she took his hand. Andreas led her slowly towards the horses in time to see Nevra pull her hood up and lower the dead elf's chainmail shirt over her head. His vest came next, followed by his sword belt and her own dagger. An elf needed elven steel. Nevra pushed the hood back to reveal her ivory hair and pointed ears.

"My name is Nevra," she said as she looked to the woman. "We are not all like them. I am truly sorry for what they have done."

TWENTY-FOUR

The Great North Road, City of Ilham, Kingdom of Aethela

Seven days had passed when the river arose before the Aureian delegation. It spread from horizon to horizon, from east to west. Second only to the Silver River itself, the great stream that split Annora from the Northlands was as vast as the stories foretold. An Aethelan city sat upon its bank. Stone walls wrapped around the township and castle beyond.

"The Eretrian and the city of Ilham," Duran announced as the company slowed to a halt. "Gateway to the Northlands."

"I have never been this far north," Captain Arne said, staring towards the river city.

"None of us have," Leona added. "We will soon find out if it is true what they say."

Duran glanced at his companions. "You southerners had best be glad that it is soon to be mid-autumn," he said with a grin. "Else I fear the heat would turn you to dust."

"Or shrivelled and angry like you," Kaladin countered, riding past.

Duran shook his head and laughed.

"Tonight, we will find rest here," Leona instructed. "Tomorrow, we will begin our journey through the Northlands. Be on your guard; we have no idea what is waiting for us."

Farmers watched from the fields around Ilham as the armoured company rode towards the city gates. The knights did not wear their knightly regalia. Though they wore cloaks of deep blue, they did not wear their surcoats embellished with the sun and moon. The men of the Arkin Garter wore chainmail in place of their garb of silver and violet. Leona kept the hood of her long cloak up. To the eye, they would appear as nothing more than soldiers. Aethelan guards with spears in their hands and shields on their backs made way to the gatehouse.

"Hold there," one called as they approached.

Duran brought his horse to a halt and gestured for the company to follow suit.

"Light of the Twins be with you, my brother." Duran greeted the Aethelan captain.

The captain chewed on a strand of wheat, running his keen gaze over the company. "You lot on the run?" he asked.

"No," Duran replied with a shake of his head.

"Look like you're on the run. What business brings you to Ilham?"

"Will stay one night. No more. My men and I heard there was a fight brewing. I wanted to return home and defend my people."

"Where are you from?"

"Adrestia, sir."

"I see," the soldier said slowly. "There are dark days coming and the woodland devils come with them. Even here we have heard the stories. Monsters hunting in the night. Men and women hung from trees. You cross that bridge," he nodded towards the north where the great river crossing stood on the far side of Ilham, "and you will be walking into that hell."

"That is our road."

"Then may the gods be with you on your journey."

He stood aside and gestured into Ilham. Duran dipped his head before he clicked his tongue and urged his horse forwards into the city. As the biggest crossing between Aethela and the Northlands, Ilham had grown large, and it had grown fast. The only cities that could rival it in the three kingdoms would have been their capitals of Palen-Tor, Kamlan-Tor and Toron-Tor. Ilham was a great trading hub between north and south. Market stalls filled every street while performers played their trade at every corner. For as many Annorans called Ilham home, almost as many northerners did the same. The dark eyes, black hair and rich accents were everywhere. As the sun set, the company stabled their horses before they found rooms and food at an inn.

Leona slowly turned the Salvaari arm ring over in her hands. The twisting metal was so very different to anything crafted in the forges of home. It was simple, almost primitive, yet held great meaning. It was this ring, such a small thing, that the peace would be built around.

If it wasn't a lie.

The thought had plagued Leona since the moment she had left Aureia. It could all be a trick to plunge the whole world into darkness.

"They will be there, my lady," Duran told her from across the table.

Leona turned her gaze to the knight. She could read his eyes, his heart. He wanted to do more than offer those words. He wanted to take her hand, hold her tight and convince her of them. He couldn't. Not with so many watching. Leona offered him a smile and pulled the ring around her wrist to keep it safe. Kaladin joined the company at the table.

"They say that the conflict hasn't reached this far south yet," he said. "But it is only a matter of time. They say that the darkness of Salvaar spreads across the land and consumes all. Towns and villages destroyed. People hung from trees. Annorans have already crossed the border to help the northerners. The storm is coming and only at Alvillia can it be stopped."

"And we are mere days away from it," Captain Arne added.

"Every story that I have heard seems more fantastical than the last. I wonder, how can such things be real?"

"There are many things in this world that are a mystery, my friend," Stefanos told him. "Things that go beyond our understanding. Only when the shadows have been illuminated may we gain the knowledge to uncover these mysteries."

"You speak in riddles." Arne chuckled.

Stefanos shrugged. "Perhaps that is what it will take to make these new discoveries," he replied.

The princess rose to her feet. "I would like to pray and then sleep," she told the company. "We have a long road ahead. Sir Duran, will you accompany me to the temple?"

"As you wish, my lady."

Duran clapped his mentor on the shoulder and without a word followed Leona out into the streets of Ilham. Torches and lanterns covered the city in orange light. Despite the moon high above, the roads were still filled with traders and those who called Ilham home. Leona took Duran's arm as they made their way to one of the city's temples. A garden of autumn trees surrounded the holy sanctuary. Leaves of fire covered the grounds, some still fluttering down from the branches. Duran placed a gentle hand over Leona's as they entered the temple. Pillars of stone held the arched roof high. A great sun and moon symbol was chiselled into the stone tiles beneath their feet and the windows were of stained glass in every colour. At the far end of the temple stood idols of the gods carved so beautifully that they appeared real. Leona took her arm back, her hand reaching for her amulet.

They knelt before the gods. Duran closed his eyes and bowed his head. Azaria and Durandail had guided him down this path. Their will divined the journeys of all. Duran had followed their teachings as a child and as a knight he served them, yet it was Leona's words that broke the silence. They were quiet but filled with strength.

"Eternal Mother, be with me now in my time of need. Lead me by the hand so that I may guide others in your name. Empower me with your light. Show me the way that I may bring peace to your kingdom. Exalted Father, Lord of Truth, guide my mind so that I may conquer the enemy that is war. Strengthen my resolve that I may bring peace to your kingdom. And Pale Horseman, Herald of the End, hold back your crows and keep at bay the demons that I may bring peace to your kingdom."

The echo of her words faded. Duran opened his eyes and looked up at the gods. His gods.

"Find the light," he said. "And the shadow will not find you."

They rose together. Duran looked back at the cold stone faces as they left.

What did they think of this journey north? What had they foreseen?

Instead of returning to the inn, Leona led Duran into the temple gardens. The knight took her hand as they walked. Leona smiled and stopped moving. She looked down as their fingers entwined, before she pursed her lips and met his eyes. There was something in her gaze, a sudden sadness.

"Duran ... we need to talk about what will happen when we return home."

The knight frowned, not understanding her sorrow.

"What will happen when we return home?"

Leona sighed but fought to keep their gazes locked.

"I was born into politics and for my entire life I have lived and breathed it. Where we travel now will change not just nations but the lives of all within them. Perhaps none more so than the nobility. To forge a lasting peace, deals will need to be made, just as if we go to war, alliances will need to be forged."

Leona took his arm. Her eyes pleaded for him to understand.

"Oaths will be sworn," she told him. "Kingdoms will be given away in coin. Marriages."

Duran froze, his joy chilling into an icy dread. He stared down at her as at last he realised what she was saying.

"No. No that cannot be," Duran growled.

"Duran. My father would sacrifice everything to ensure peace, and if peace cannot be obtained, then he will do what he must to ensure victory." She looked as though she was fighting back tears. She looked as if her heart was splintering into one thousand pieces. "Either way, my hand will be offered. I must uphold the expectations of my people … of my father."

"Expectations?" Duran muttered in anguish. "Leona–"

"I do not want this," she begged.

She held his hand and she held it tight. She did not look away. She couldn't. Neither of them could. Duran squared his jaw as pain rolled through him. He loved her. He always had. Now here, on the verge of achieving their dream, he would be forced to let her go.

"What do you want?" he said at last.

"What I want is *you*," Leona cried in desperation.

She shook her head, as if to shake away the turmoil, and slammed her eyes shut as tears spilled over onto her cheeks.

"I cannot bear to think what will happen when we return," Leona continued. "I wish that the moon could be stopped in the sky so that this moment, this time with you, would last forever."

Duran stepped towards her. He reached out a gentle hand and turned her chin. Staring into her dark eyes, he brushed away a tear. He felt her pain, her agony.

"Will you marry me?" he asked, unable to ignore his heart any longer.

"What?" Leona breathed.

Her eyes were wide. Her lips trembled and the beginnings of a smile broke free.

"A long time ago I was told that a man should use his mind but *always* listen to his heart," Duran said softly. "Leona, I will love you all my life and when I die, I will still love you."

The princess tried to fight against the emotion within. She couldn't. It was there in the tensing of her jaw and the furrow of her brow. Her face was a canvas and the pain as clear as an artist's paint.

"You know what they will say."

"I do not care what they will say."

"When we return home, you know what they will do," Leona pressed. "Duran, I love you, but I will not see you led away in chains or worse."

"But you would see us turn from this?"

"If it means that it saves your life, then yes!"

"Then we run," Duran tried.

"Where would we go?"

"I don't know."

Leona forced back tears. Anger surged through Duran. Anger at the world for forcing this upon them. He turned away from Leona. His hand curled. It took all of his will to not drive it into one of the trees.

"Then we run."

Her voice was little more than a whisper. Duran's rage dissipated like smoke. He looked to her and could see the hope emerging behind her wet eyes.

"We get married," she told him. "We forge this peace … and then we run."

"Where?" It was all Duran could say.

"Tarik … Larissa, the Isles, it does not matter. A hovel by the sea with nothing but sheep to huddle with at night to keep warm. It does not matter to me. Duran, I love you. I love you."

Leona pressed her forehead to Duran's.

"It must be tonight," Duran told her. "What tomorrow brings, we do not know. We may not get another chance."

"Tonight then," Leona agreed.

The moon had almost reached its peak when its silver light shone down through the stained glass of the temple. It was empty save for the priest who stood before them. The knight wore nothing grander than his travel-stained armour. The princess, a simple dress that she had worn that day. Neither cared. Tonight was for them. Nothing else mattered. Nothing ever had. Duran held her soft hands and looked deep into her eyes. He could see into her soul, and she into his. They spoke together and their words were as one.

"By the power of the gods brought from the heavens, may you love me. As the sun follows its course, may you follow me. As light to the eye, as joy to the heart, may your presence be with me. I will be the shield at your back and sword at your side and we will remain forever more as one."

The priest drew forth a pair of simple rings. They were silver, free of embellishment. A devotion of love, not wealth. Duran took a band and slid it onto Leona's finger.

"May Azaria's moon bring you peace and serenity," the priest said.

Leona took the other and slid it onto Duran's. The priest took their hands.

"May Durandail's sun grant you warmth and light and today may the spirit of love find a dwelling place in your hearts."

Duran's heart raced as he kissed Leona. His dearest friend. His eternal confidant. His love. His *wife*. Delaureia was she no longer.

Leona Cormac.

That was her name now. They were one heart. One soul. Even if they lost everything in the coming days, that would be enough.

There was no wedding night. They had already been gone for perhaps too long and any longer would have aroused too much suspicion. No one could know. Not until after Alvillia. Not until peace had been won. Duran pulled his amulet from his neck as he sat upon the edge of his bed. He unclasped it and slid his wedding band down the thin silver chain. He kissed the ring and then hid it beneath his shirt. His hand did not stray from it as he at last drifted to sleep.

The sun rose and the travellers rose with it. They gathered their armour and left on horseback. Everywhere they looked, the fiery leaves of trees in the heart of autumn fell. They drifted gently through the morning breeze as the company crossed Ilham bridge, nearly eighty paces long and fifteen wide of hardy oak and solid stone. Duran could only stare as the Northlands opened up before him. This land had not been home to him for eighteen years now.

Could he still claim it as his own?

Who would greet him?

The steel of the Salvaari, as he feared?

Or nothing but the falling leaves of autumn?

Duran brought his horse to a halt. His companions continued at a walk past him. He dismounted and knelt upon the earth. With one hand he held his reins, with the other he trailed his fingers through the soil. Northern soil. Duran took a handful and watched as it slid through his grasp.

"Home," the knight murmured.

They rode for miles. They rode fast. The less time that they spent in the wild the better. These lands were treacherous. They saw refugees hastening south to get away from their own country. All carried the same story: the Salvaari were coming. Elves, ruskalan and the men who served them. Thousands had already died and there was no true war yet.

Only with the going down of the sun would the company find rest, whether it be in the beds of a village or beneath the trees in the wilderness. Moonlight glistened upon steel as Duran and Kaladin moved through the forms of tarkaras in perfect unison.

Side by side.

The swordsong in all its deadly beauty. Blade moved in harmony with the body. To both men, steel and flesh were the same. Hilt was bone. Crossguard was tissue. Pommel was sinew. Edge was blood. Their form was perfect. They flowed like water.

Each day was the same. They crossed plains and rivers, fields and hills. Villages, towns and cities. Soldiers and refugees. The further north they travelled, the worse it became. They were challenged at every corner by warriors; not a day went by without the threat of conflict. In time they saw bodies hung from trees. The attacks, they had been told, had greatly lessened since the negotiations had been announced, yet those who disapproved openly sought blood.

Human, Salvaari – it did not matter.

A day out from Alvillia they changed out of their travel-stained clothing and into garments befitting their roles, which had been stored in saddle bags. The Arkin Garter once more wore their violet cloaks over their finely wrought cuirasses of the highest quality. Once more Leona appeared as a princess. Once more Duran dressed himself as a Knight of Kil'kara. A surcoat of dark blue sat atop mail, while bracers, greaves and pauldrons of steel were strapped to his body. Duran strapped on his sword and pulled his cloak over his shoulders. Before he could reach for his helmet, a rough hand lashed out and tore his amulet from where it hid.

"What is that?" Kaladin growled as he saw the ring. He turned his angry eyes on Duran. "That is what I think it is, is it not?"

Duran shoved his mentor's hand away. Kaladin's keen gaze had seen what had been visible for only a moment.

"Do you have any idea what you have done?" Kaladin hissed.

"Listened to my heart, is that such a bad thing? Love is not the death of duty."

"Duty?" Kaladin replied incredulously. He glanced around to make sure they were alone. "Duran, can you hear yourself? Do you know what they will do when they find out?"

"They say we don't have a choice in life," Duran countered. "We do have a choice. Whatever happens, I will not lose her."

Kaladin scoffed. "What has happened is not just personal between you. It is political."

"She is not a possession!"

"You defy everything we stand for as knights. You defy why we are here! What you have done forces her from her family. It forces you from your oath. But you did not think about that, did you? You speak of the heart, yet you know nothing of the pain that this will cause."

"I do not care."

"One day you might," Kaladin shot back. "Listen to me and listen well. If we are successful and all that we hope for comes true, that will not change the fact that you will both be banished. Never to return on pain of death. She will never see her family again. Your children will grow up not knowing where they came from. That is the price if we herald victory in Alvillia. If we do not, then any chance to forge alliances in this war will be gone. You are young, so you never saw it. You were born far in the north, so you would have heard nothing. You know *nothing* of war. My father, Janus' father, raised us on tales of Delios. He was the *last* of his line. He saw his family slaughtered like dogs. Fields so thick with blood that they became lakes. Towns and cities ripped to their foundations and entire populations put to the sword. Hundreds of thousands dead. You weren't there, but there are those who remember. They remember the sacrifice that so many gave so that Aureia may be free. Preventing another great war is Janus' life work. He would give up anything so that such a tragedy does not occur, that the Northlands do not suffer the same fate as Aureia and Delios. That is his agony. That is what you threaten to destroy."

Duran took a breath. His mentor's words came from love. He spoke his truth as he always did. It was no secret that the Delaureia line had suffered greatly beneath the heel of Delios. It was no secret that their country had almost been destroyed.

"I know," Duran said quietly. "I know. But I love her. After Alvillia, we are going to run."

Kaladin's eyes softened as he looked at his pupil. Both knew what that meant. Leona would be torn from her family just as Duran would be torn from his own. He would never see Kaladin again. He would never see the towers in Rovira or his brothers-in-arms. All of that would be taken from him. His title would be stripped, and his name tarnished.

"Duran, I love you like a son, but I fear you have made a grave mistake."

The young knight looked to his mentor. To his friend. His father.

"I am sorry that I must ask this of you," Duran started desperately. "But please, will you help us?"

He could think of nothing else to say. Perhaps there was nothing else but a single plea. Duran knew what he was asking of Kaladin, but he had no choice. He was the Sword of Kil'kara. He had a duty to his Order. He had duty to his brother, to his family.

"Aye, lad," Kaladin told him. "That I will."

TWENTY-FIVE

Village of Cordojar, Fiefdom of Gonaelric, The Northlands

Sunlight crept through the canopy of the forest as the riders made their way west. They had followed the road from the hanging tree into a large woodland. The wind carried the sound of a gentle river as the forest thinned. A small wooden bridge appeared and not far beyond arose the village of Cordojar. Wisps of smoke wafted over the rooftops of two dozen small houses. There was a temple in the centre, while farmland surrounded the small northern town. Nevra stared at the humble village. It was peaceful and had never known the suffering of war. She brought her horse to a halt and ran a gentle hand down the mare's powerful neck.

"We can go no further," Nevra told the woman they had saved. "You are safe now. I am sorry for everything that you have endured. Know that it will not be forgotten."

"Thank you," Sibil replied gratefully. "May the light of the gods be with you always."

"May the spirits fly with you," Nevra said, placing a hand over her heart.

"Go now," Andreas bid the girl. "And stay safe. It is probably best that you forget us."

"I will never forget," Sibil stated before she offered a smile in farewell and continued towards Cordojar.

Nevra watched as the girl vanished into the village.

"It is a good thing that you did," Andreas said.

"I have never killed my own people before," Nevra replied without looking at her friend. "But evil is evil, no matter the colour your blood."

At last, she clicked her tongue and turned her horse back towards the path.

"We must go," she said. "The trail cannot grow cold, or this will have been for nothing."

"No," Andreas replied. "What you did will always count for something."

Nevra paused. His words stirred something in her, a feeling long forgotten.

Pride.

"I'm glad you're here," Nevra said.

She kicked her heels in and the two companions surged east. They rode hard. They did not stop or look back. The sun lowered in the sky, yet Nevra urged them faster still. The orange light of the falling sun cast shadows across the land, across the hanging tree as they galloped back into the forest. Every moment that they delayed gave the trail more time to fade into nothing. Nevra leapt from her saddle. Leaves crunched beneath her feet as her blue eyes searched the undergrowth. She knelt atop the cold earth and placed a hand against the ground. She listened to the wind, to the trees and soil. The secrets of the past could be revealed if she but looked close enough. Beneath the going down of the sun, Nevra found the trail.

"They turn north-east," she said.

"How do you know?"

"It is in my blood," Nevra replied. She rose to her feet and followed the trail as it revealed itself. "I was a wanderer."

"And what is that?"

"One who explores the wide, wide world," Nevra explained. "A healer. Historian. Linguist. All these things and more."

"Is that how you learnt to fight?"

"I learnt steel and I learnt it well. To survive out there, I had to learn to be more than just good. I had to learn to be great. As you can tell, I am a little out of practice."

Andreas shook his head and scoffed. "I have never seen anyone move like that before."

"The warrior at the tree should not have been able to touch me. I need to be better. I *must* be better, for the one who leaves the trail we find ourselves upon is a far greater foe than any other."

"The autieyar?"

Nevra paused and turned to face her friend.

"Death itself," she replied. "As a wanderer, I can see that which is hidden. I can read signs in the wind, hear the song of the trees all around. I can feel it."

Andreas stopped in his tracks. "I have known you for years, yet you are a mystery to me," he stated as he at last began to realise that he did not know her at all. "Before Vallgena, why did you not return to your homeland when you had the chance?"

"Above all else, a wanderer is destined to walk the lands alone."

"But you weren't alone."

Nevra froze.

She did not look back at her friend as she replied, "Not until my heart was torn from my chest."

Silence crept into the woods as the last of the sunlight faded.

"You're afraid," Andreas said quietly.

Still Nevra did not look back. She did not want him to see her eyes, her face, in case they told him even more truths. Perhaps he had already guessed them. She wondered if he knew that she feared. At last, Nevra glanced over her shoulder. She gave a single nod.

Andreas was right. She was afraid.

They travelled until the last of the sun disappeared beyond the horizon. Darkness cloaked the land. Wind gently caressed the falling leaves.

"We rest for a few hours," Nevra said, dismounting.

"What if we lose the trail in the dark?"

"No, I can see." Nevra crouched and pulled forth a flintstone.

Andreas could only shake his head as the elf tendered a flame and brought a fire to life. Nevra sat back against the trunk of an oak, leaning her head against the bark and closing her eyes. She took a long breath. For the first time in years, she could feel freedom once again. The shackles of her past would forever bind her, but it was here amongst the trees and stars that she felt truly free.

"You are right," Nevra said after a moment. "For years we have been friends, yet it has become readily apparent that you know so little about me. While I have told you the truth, I have not told you all of it."

"You do not owe me anything," Andreas replied, taking a seat opposite her.

Nevra smirked as she glanced at him through the flames.

"For so long I have lived in darkness and not cared who I hurt, yet … yet you followed me. Left your home and family to travel with someone you hardly know."

"You are my friend," he said simply.

"I have come to realise that I did not give you the same respect you gave me, and for that I am sorry," Nevra replied. "Perhaps my truth will go some way in repaying this debt to you."

Andreas said nothing. He watched her in silence so that she could speak.

"You know where I come from, what I am, what I once was," Nevra started. "All these things you know, and you are right. I am afraid. Hope is like fire. It can warm or it can destroy. You see, Andreas, I am afraid of the autieyar we now track. Only a fool would not be. More than anything though I am afraid of possibilities. This is a ghost that we are chasing. The people at Monocena spoke of an iristysi. An autieyar corrupted by the magic that they wield, consumed by it until nothing remains but darkness. That in turn begs the question: Who travels with one so condemned? In my culture, autieyar are feared as they are respected … But iristysi – they are monsters. Elves driven to madness by their gift. They will torture. Kill. Without conscience. Without mercy. That is why they are branded iristysi. *Outcasts.* To be hunted so that they will not bring untold death to this plain."

Andreas stared at her. He could see the pain in her eyes as clear as a summer sky.

"Are they truly feared so?"

Nevra could only nod.

"Yet the one we pursue is not alone," Andreas said.

"No, she is not," Nevra murmured. "That is what concerns me. Many warriors sacked Monocena, and even after that, one remained at the iristysi's side. Who rides with her? Whose will divines that warriors gladly follow this iristysi? What compels them to travel with her even after she has killed one of their own? There must be a cause hidden in the shadows and all we have to do is illuminate it. Madness is what drove a blade between elf and autieyar. Madness. Madness and fear. Ask yourself, what do you know of fear? Do you know where it was born? Who first uttered the word? In recent years, I have learnt the word well and so I will tell you what I fear now. Perhaps this autieyar is nothing but a faceless warmonger intent on killing innocents and destroying cities. A ghost. A harbinger of death. But what I fear more strongly is a fool's hope. A hope for family."

"Your sister?"

"And that is what makes this evil even worse." Nevra looked into the fire. She felt her anger stir within, ignited like the flames before her. "You see, Andreas, I do not care for what happened to Monocena. I would have gladly given my own life to see its headman dead for his betrayal and see his house fall. But what is done is done. I cannot change the past any more than I can stop the sun from setting. What I fear, what I truly fear, is that Naidra is alive. For if she is alive, then she knows that I am as well."

"How would she know that?"

"Her gift. An autieyar has a strong connection to the Veil. A connection strong enough that she can sense every elf no matter their provenance. She could feel me, know where I am in this moment. And if she can feel me and yet does what she does, then she is lost."

"And you want to save her."

"Or die trying." Nevra chuckled as she looked up. "As I said, a fool's hope."

"No." Andreas was serious. "You are no fool. There is a fire burning inside you more real than the one before us."

"I have at last learnt how to breathe again."

The sun had not yet risen when they mounted up once again and set off through the woods. Miles vanished beneath the beat of horses' hooves. The north wind lashed at them, yet even in the heart of autumn, the heat warmed their bones. Beneath the falling leaves Nevra saw it written on the earth so neatly before her. So clear was it that she could see from horseback.

"Their pace has quickened. They turn west."

"West? What lies to the west?"

It made little sense.

Why come this far only to journey further into human lands?

Nevra closed her eyes as she read the map drawn in her mind. She could picture towns and villages, fiefdoms and forests. Her eyes shot open. Her heart near stopped as she stared at Andreas.

"Alvillia," she breathed.

Horror chilled her blood as she remembered Solan Aloys' words.

"What business would they have in …" Andreas trailed off as realisation dawned on him. "The negotiations."

"We go to Alvillia," Nevra commanded, turning her horse.

No more words. No more delay. She kicked her heels in.

Naidra closed her eyes as she spun her glaive, moonlight kissing steel, dancing off its edges. She closed her eyes and opened herself to the will of the spirits. From the moment she had been taken by the autieyar as a child, she had learnt the weapon, learnt to turn it into an extension of her body. Whispers caressed her ears, whispers that told her of the deep dark. Whispers that spoke to her soul. They spoke to her in her dreams, in the dead of night. They spoke to her in brightest day. There was always sound. Endless.

"Feel the Veil," Valmoar called as he watched her move. "Feel its power coursing through your veins. Feel it, don't try to command it."

The glaive spun faster. Muscles loosened and tightened, obeying her will without thought. Naidra could feel the gift given to her from beyond the other plain. A gift from the spirits. Human, elf, ruskalan – it mattered not. She was a god to them. Her form was perfect, her poise stronger than any stone. The earth thudded as the haft of the glaive bit into the soil. Eyes of blue and white opened.

"Perfect," Valmoar commended.

Naidra turned her gaze to the clear skies. To her there was no difference between day and night. She could see it all the same. Naidra gazed at the moon and felt her blood boil.

"The spirits watch," she said. "We stand under their unyielding gaze, and they are angry. Though the Veil has been shut to me, I see it very clearly."

"What is happening here is beyond us," Valmoar said. "It goes beyond blood and bone. This is a war for the heart of this Plain."

"The Firstborn is wrong," Naidra growled. "Peace with the humans is a lie, for that is how they see us. When the humans look at us, they see darkness. Darkness and lies. They do not fear the spirits. What do they know of them? Of their ways? They know nothing."

Valmoar walked to Naidra's side. Together they stared out from the tree line across the plains of the Northlands.

"What does your heart tell you?" Valmoar asked.

"While the elves learnt steel and the ruskalan spread their whispers through the land, the humans stole our gods. Twisted them. Mutilated them. Said they were theirs. Now the humans declare war on us in their name, allowing those who so willingly hunt us to cross the river, to wear our arm rings and learn the ways of the spirits ... I can think of nothing worse. The humans are demons. The Dark Ones returned to make slaves of us."

"Such hatred," Valmoar stated.

"I am the wrath of the Veil."

"You believe Harkan's faith to be misplaced?"

"He must have been deceived. Peace is a lie. There can be no peace. It was you who taught me to fix my eyes on what I believe and not what I see. I believe this with all my heart."

Valmoar took a slow breath.

"Our hearts are as one. The humans should never have been allowed to cross the river. Did we not learn from our mistakes centuries ago with the Idrisians who have abandoned us? The time of the Wolf of Black and White is done. Over a thousand years I have walked this Plain, and I have seen all. Darkness and light. Balance. Elves and ruskalan – we are the eyes of the spirits."

"You cannot control loyalty," Naidra said. "A truth I learnt when I was a child. Monocena, that farm, even my own people. My sister ... I saw her eyes. Her truth. I would *never* be what she wanted."

"It is only us."

In her heart Naidra knew it to be true. The voices often spoke to her. The *fear* in her sister's gaze. In time she would have betrayed her too.

"It is only us," Naidra agreed softly. "You are the only one who does not look at me as if I am a monster."

"I made you safe. You are my daughter," Valmoar said simply. "We are family."

"One heart. One mind. One soul," Naidra vowed. "From this day until the end of days."

"Until the end of days." Valmoar reached out a gentle hand and stroked her cheek with the back of his fingers.

Red eyes met blue. Naidra could see the pride in his gaze. She could feel it.

"The world is wrong about you. One day they will see. We will show them. And it will start at the city they call Alvillia."

Naidra turned her gaze westward across the plain. The lights of Alvillia could be seen from miles away. They were close now, so close.

"Harkan is blind to this deception," Naidra murmured, eyes locked on the city.

Valmoar circled Naidra. The white moonlight kissed his pale skin and shadows danced around his face, weaving through his dark tattoos. His eyes, the colour of blood, swam across Naidra.

"The spirits voice is the wind." Valmoar's voice was a low hum. "The storm. The earthquake. The flood. We are their voice."

His fangs were made bare. There was true belief in his words. True rage.

"The emissaries of the Firstborn must be kept safe," Valmoar continued with his musical voice. "There can be no treachery here. I will ride to meet with them."

"I will be at your side."

"No," Valmoar commanded.

"I will protect you as you have protected me for so long."

"If this is betrayal and my fate is to die in Alvillia, then so be it," Valmoar countered. "But you must live. You must take this tale and deliver it to our people. To Harkan."

"I have lost my connection to the Veil. He may not listen."

"Then you will make him listen!" Valmoar bid her fiercely. "Are you Naidra, sorceress of the Veil? The Veil helped you to control the power, to focus it. It was never the source of your strength. The true source lies here."

Valmoar curled his hand into a fist and placed it over her heart. "Now hold me like a daughter."

Naidra wrapped her arms around Valmoar and held him tight. He was the only man she had ever known as a father. The only family she had. Now he was going to ride into danger alone. It tore at her. Valmoar held her back and placed a gentle kiss upon her brow. He lifted her chin and gave her a single nod before he started towards his horse.

"I'm not as strong as you," Naidra called.

Valmoar paused as he took hold of his reins.

"No," he said. "You're stronger."

TWENTY-SIX

Road to Alvillia, Fiefdom of Canaeric, The Northlands

They saddled their horses as the first rays of the morning sun caressed the land. The company had crossed into the fiefdom of Canaeric barely a day ago. Baron Florenzo's lands were small, barely more than two towns and a handful of smaller villages, yet he was neutral in this fight. Florenzo had openly worked with Bailon to the north, Aloys to the south and Salvaar to the east for years. It would be in Alvillia, this town built around the harvesting and storage of grain, that the fate of the Northlands would be decided. The fire was put out and the camp hastily disassembled. Packs were strapped, horses saddled and bedrolls gathered. Duran slung his shield bearing the sun of Durandail across his back. He placed a foot in the stirrup and then a hand grabbed his wrist. The knight turned to see Stefanos standing at his side.

"We cannot know what awaits us," the inventor said, extending a fist.

A vial hung from his fingers upon a thin leather cord. Duran knew what it was. Poison crafted for a single purpose, to sever the magic of an autieyar.

"Take it," Stefanos bid the knight.

Tentatively Duran reached out a hand. The inventor lowered the vial into Duran's palm and wrapped his hands around the knight's.

"Pray you never have to use it," Stefanos urged.

Duran nodded and gripped the vial tight. Stefanos let his hand go. The knight stared down at the vial in his hand as the inventor clapped him on the shoulder and turned back towards his own horse. At last Duran placed the leather cord around his neck. The vial hung at his throat. Such a small thing that could change the world. He pulled himself up into his saddle with the rest of the company.

"To Alvillia," Leona cried.

As one, the riders kicked their heels in and started the ride north.

To Alvillia.

To peace.

Endless farmland wrapped around Alvillia, spreading from horizon to horizon. Northern famers toiled beneath the burning sun. Soldiers bearing the horse banner of Canaeric stood at the gate and atop the town walls. Travellers and wagons filled the road. It was not long before the company was seen. Farmers stopped their work and stared. Travellers watched them go by. None would have ever seen the armour of the Order or that of the Arkin Garter. None would have seen a woman, one who carried herself with the pride and grace of a princess, clad in such a dress. Valkir and Aureians now rode amongst those who had seen naught but their own people. The great silver griffin of the south flew above the company. Banners carried by the Garter blew in the autumn breeze. Kaladin and Captain Arne were at the head of the column, flanked by a pair of the royal guard. Then came Princess Leona followed by Duran and Stefanos. Behind them the rest of the Garter rode tall.

Three mounted men garbed in the red and black of Canaeric met them at the gates. Two were knights clad in steel. The third wore the flowy gown of a wealthy lord. The aristocrat offered a bow as the southern delegation arrived.

"Baron Florenzo Canaeric, at your service." The lord introduced himself. "Welcome to Alvillia, Princess Leona. You are most welcome in my city and my lands."

"Your fiefdom is as beautiful as its people, Baron Florenzo," Leona replied with a graceful smile.

Florenzo took her hand and placed a kiss upon it.

"The northern delegations are gathering at the amphitheatre." He gestured further into the town. "Please."

Baron Florenzo led the way at Leona's side. A handful of his men joined the company as it rode through Alvillia. Still the people watched on with wide eyes as the Aureian riders ventured further into the town. Strong men with long beards from across the seas. Olive-skinned Aureians with unheard accents. None could believe it, and Duran could see it in their eyes.

The cheers started.

They echoed through Alvillia and rose into a thunder. Duran chuckled as he saw what started the roar. Leona. While the Arkin Garter rode tall and proud, showing no emotion, their princess openly smiled and waved to the townspeople. If another were to have done the same, it would have diminished the crown upon her head, yet with how she did it, how she showed her heart, it only elevated her. Leona's radiant smile grew when a young woman handed her a flower as the company rode by. The princess only had the time to nod her thanks before the girl was gone.

Before them rose the amphitheatre of Alvillia. From the outside it appeared as no more than a tall, curved wall of stone with tunnels that led deep into its heart. Finely carved steps led up to the tunnels, while stone pillars surrounded the grand structure. Soldiers bearing the horse of Canaeric stood at each of the many tunnels.

"You may bring three companions, my princess," Baron Florenzo told Leona as he dismounted. "No more."

Leona paused for a moment as she turned her gaze to her people.

"Three it is," she said simply. "Sir Kaladin. Stefanos. Captain Arne. If you would join me?"

"Lady," the three men chorused, moving to her side.

Leona gave Duran a knowing look. He knew why he could not follow. Though it tore at him to stay, Duran knew that his mentor, the guardsman and the inventor were the right choices. Kaladin was wise, he was experienced, and he was the emperor's brother. He understood both the soldier and the nobility. Arne was a simple man who came from poverty and cared nothing for politics. A Valkir guard assigned to protect the princess with his life and remove all else from concern. Stefanos was neither warrior nor aristocrat. He could watch, listen and give a voice that one born into wealth or steel never could.

Princess Leona slowly turned the blue flower in her hands before she turned to the tunnel and followed the baron inside. The guards at the amphitheatre entrance took the weapons from her companions. Arne grasped his griffin standard firmly. Duran watched them leave. His hand tightened upon his sword in anticipation.

Torches lit the dark corridor. The echoes of boots upon stone rang through the tunnel. Sunlight bloomed at the end. Kaladin's hand curled into a fist as he stared dead ahead. He wished for his blade but knew why he could not have it. Keen eyes peered out from behind his helmet.

Were there enemies hidden beyond the end of the tunnel?

Was there nothing but the wind?

Kaladin was the Sword of Kil'kara. If an army waited at the other side, he was ready. Day broke through the darkness of the stone corridor. Light illuminated what lay beyond. There were soldiers but they were few. Dozens of men stood in the heart of the great amphitheatre. They were old. They were young. They were tall. They were short. Some were poor; others showed off their wealth with magnificent rings and jewels. Some wore steel, others fine clothes, the thousand colours of the Northlands fiefdoms emblazoned upon their garb. The amphitheatre was a massive semi-circle. The seats that rose to the heavens on three of the sides were empty, while the wall that soared behind the stage merged with a house of stone. A backstage for actors and orators. Inside the stage was a large ring of simple wooden chairs broken only by large stone pillars. Flags and banners ran around the edge of the stage. Shafts were driven into the earth and the sunlight washed over the sigils. Kaladin eyed the banners. Whether a baron, his family or a representative had made the journey, many had come.

The viper of Caspin.

The wolf of Monares.

The bear of Bailon.

The lion of Aloys.

The flying horse of Granjaen.

The tiger of Reyna.

The boar of Luarco.

The stag of Salazar.

The eight great houses of the Northlands were here, be they neutral, fighting for the north or fighting against it. The men from Luarco and Monares stood aside with representatives of a number of the smaller houses. They had chosen to ally themselves with Salvaar years ago and wore the arm rings to prove it. Granjaen, Caspin, Reyna and Salazar were all neutral. Bailon and Aloys … they pushed for war. All of this Kaladin knew. All of this Leona knew.

Eyes flew to the Aureian contingent as Captain Arne planted the griffin banner.

"Make way for the High Princess Leona Delaureia," Arne cried proudly.

Heads bowed in deference. Some eyes did not. Kaladin was no fool. He could see the kingdoms that lay behind those gazes. The barons owned small tracts of land, a few dozen miles at best. The entire south belonged to Leona and her family.

All sound left the amphitheatre. Idle chatter stopped. So quiet was it that Kaladin could almost hear the heartbeats of the northerners. Footsteps echoed. Four emerged from another tunnel; two of the party were human. They wore pelts and skins in place of northern garment. Black warpaint covered their faces and the hair upon brow and jaw was long. Some kind of white grease had been used to slick their long manes back. Silver arm rings adorned their wrists. These were men who had left their homeland and crossed the river. These were men who had given themselves to Salvaar.

But they were just men.

Kaladin could not help his stare as he watched the other two from the east. Both had pale skin, pointed ears and sharp jaws. That was where the similarity ended. Thick black hair adorned with beads and knotted in a thick braid fell down the right side of the woman's head. Dark runes marked her face. Her eyes were as red as rubies and blazed with intelligence. Her teeth were hidden behind her lips, yet Kaladin knew that they were fanged. Unlike other women, she did not wear a dress, but boots lined with bear fur covered her feet and trousers her legs. An embroidered wrap crisscrossed her chest leaving much of her midriff and shoulders bare. A band wrapped around her right bicep and leather wrapped around her wrists. Her arm ring glinted in the sunlight. A necklace of wolf's teeth hung at her throat.

She was ruskalan.

The man's skin was marred by no runes or tattoos. His white hair tumbled behind his shoulders, while a small braid hung before his left ear. Blue eyes danced with sapphire light. He was tall and broad, a man who had spent many lifetimes dedicated to steel. A cloak trimmed in fur hung at his back and his sleeveless chainmail shirt shone silver. The corded muscles of his arms were covered in a web of scars. Steel bracers wrapped around his forearms. Unlike the ruskalan, the elf wore no embellishment save his arm ring. He was a simple soldier.

Thud.

Thud.

Thud.

The stone stage echoed as wooden staffs cracked against it. Florenzo Canaeric stood in the centre of the circle of chairs. Four of his staff-wielding soldiers surrounded him.

"Friends. Brothers and sisters," the baron began, gesturing towards the chairs. "Please join me."

The other barons and leaders found their places. The companions of each group stood behind their liege lords to complete the ring.

"We gather here in the city of Alvillia to discuss the future of our land," Florenzo continued. "Its people – all people. As we await the final decision of the tribunal in Rovira, we come together to shape the future of the Northlands. Will there be peace or war? That is what we must decide."

With that, Baron Florenzo took his seat and joined the ring.

"Peace?" one of the barons muttered. "What peace can there be?"

"I am sure that you do not desire the shedding of blood, Baron Meridia," called another.

Baron Gior Meridia of Salaman rose to his feet. Kaladin knew his name well. Years before the inquisition, Meridia and his people had hunted the natives of Salvaar. Gior looked to the man who had countered him.

"Blood has already been shed, Baron Monares," he said. "It has been shed for generations. You may have forgotten, but we of Salaman remember well. There can be no peace while *they*," Gior thrust an arm towards the Salvaari delegation, "haunt our land and kill our people."

The elven man leapt to his feet.

"Do you expect us to stand idle against an enemy who has hunted us for decades?" he snarled. "We will not."

"It is a thing well known that the soldiers of Salaman openly cross into other fiefdoms at but a whisper that even *one* Salvaari is there," Baron Luarco added. "You speak as though the Salvaari should allow themselves to be killed without purpose. Why should they? Would any of us?"

Gior Meridia snorted and glared venomously towards the elf. "What is your name?" he asked.

"Envar," the elf replied.

Gior smiled contemptuously at the name. "Your people meddle in our affairs," the baron snarled. "Break our laws. The blood of thousands has washed the land between the Arwan and the Eretrian, between your river and ours. The inquisition has shown us enough."

"The inquisition is not yet complete, Baron Meridia," Princess Leona called. "And it will not be until the decision of the tribunal reaches us here."

"As you say, my princess." The baron's tone suggested anything but.

Solan Aloys took to the floor. He offered Leona a bow.

"Forgive Baron Meridia, Your Highness, this fight has affected Salaman far longer than any other," Solan said graciously. "What the baron suggests is that the inquisition has merely revealed the heart of this land. A nation tearing itself apart. Eighteen barons have been executed." Solan gestured towards those barons who had sided with Salvaar. "Some are in open rebellion. Not to mention those who have sought a new home across the river."

"They came to us seeking sanctuary after you pushed them from their land." The ruskalan woman spoke up.

"Their lords were found guilty of treason and when confronted they turned upon their own people," Gior Meridia countered. "They are traitors to their land."

"Is that why Salaman steel stretches from Meridia to Palanza?" the woman shot back.

"My people aid all those who need our protection. It is our god-given duty."

"And do they command you to butcher unarmed travellers upon the road?"

"Aeslin is right," Baron Luarco agreed. "Many of her people have been slaughtered for the crime of wandering the land."

"Then what of Monocena?" Solan Aloys growled. "A city destroyed mere days after my father agreed to these peace talks."

"There is light and dark in us all," Aeslin replied. "There are those among my people who seek war, it is true; however, Harkan brands all who break this peace traitors. Those who attacked your city will be dealt with. We will make amends as we hope that in time you will for every elven and every ruskalan life taken absent cause."

"An entire city," Solan hissed.

Mathias Bailon stepped forwards. He glanced from Solan Aloys to Aeslin and her companions.

"Where is Harkan?" he asked.

"He is not here," Envar told the baron.

"Where is he?"

"The Firstborn is in Salvaar."

"A puzzle then, that one who wishes for peace would not bring his voice to these negotiations. Negotiations that he himself asked for."

Whispers ran through the circle of nobles.

"Lord Bailon speaks true," the Baron of Granjaen added, turning towards Aeslin. "I am the last Granjaen, the last of an old and powerful house. I answered these summons to protect my people and I expected this commitment to have been answered in kind by the man who sent word."

Aeslin gave him a cool smile.

"With the deepest respect, noble baron, many of you here are not the lords of your land," she started. "Many of you come as sons and brothers, ambassadors sent in place of your own liege. Harkan *is* Salvaar. Not only the first of his kind but the leader of all peoples beyond the Arwan. For him to venture so far into the heart of the Northlands surrounded by many who wish him dead – no, in Salvaar he remains. But make no mistake, I stand as Salvaar's body and voice. If we decide upon war here, then there will be war. If we decide upon peace, then there will be peace."

Princess Leona took a step towards the Salvaari delegation.

"Peace comes with agreements," she told the assembly. "With terms. Name them."

Aeslin met the princess' eyes and noddled slowly.

"Very well. All Salvaari are to be free to walk human lands absent the threat of persecution, imprisonment or death. We are to be free to hunt and dance and live heartily. To worship our spirits. In turn we will abide by your laws and traditions. There will be no more fighting. No more killing. No more stealing, reaving and raping. No more."

Kaladin let his eyes wander the amphitheatre. Many of the barons were nodding. Many of those neutral, enough of the great houses to keep the rest in check. Even Gior Meridia. All Leona had to do was raise her voice, accept the terms on behalf of the emperor and peace would be theirs. It could not be that simple. It should not be that simple.

After years of bloodshed, this is all it would take?

Kaladin watched as voices in agreement began to rise. One by one, the barons decided. Even some of those who had declared against Salvaar were starting to turn. Perhaps the whisper he had heard held truth after all. Perhaps none of them wanted war.

"The gods teach us to be merciful. They teach us forgiveness," Leona addressed the Salvaari. "On behalf of my people, I forgive those who shed blood in the hall of my family three years ago. I say let us have peace. Let us move on and usher in a new future. Together."

She paused a moment, and a smile graced her lips.

"Together," she said in Salvaari.

Kaladin's eyes widened. He could see shock run through the circle of barons and nobility. A foreign princess knew at least a single word in Salvaari. Kaladin chuckled and shook his head. Even after all these years, his niece still surprised him. Anger burned across the face of Gior Meridia and his followers but there was nothing they could do. Against the might of the north, the might of Aureia, they were *powerless*.

"In payment of the lives of his people stolen, Harkan has one final demand."

Aeslin's words echoed through the stage. The voices of the nobles died off. The mood fell. Leona's smile faltered.

"Name it," she commanded.

Aeslin strode further into the circle.

"A gift of land," the ruskalan said. "Land once promised to us. Land for farming, for building. Land west of the river."

Kaladin closed his eyes. Just like that, everything shattered.

"Is this a jest?" Solan Aloys snarled.

"I assure you not."

"It belongs to us."

"There may be some hardship," the elf Envar told them. "A lesson learnt and a new dawn on the horizon."

Gior Meridia strode to Solan's side. "Oh, I see," he sneered contemptuously. "This is why you are here. Not for peace but to take that which belongs to us."

"We are here because enough blood has been shed," Aeslin replied.

"Please," Leona told the Salvaari. "Consider the best option for your people."

"You want our land. Absolutely not," Mathias Bailon called loudly. "If you want peace, let us make peace, but you will not have one inch of the Northlands."

Roars followed. Men leapt to their feet. Shouts thundered from every throat.

"I wish you to understand that we have a large military force that will defend our border," Solan Aloys continued.

"No one wants war," Aeslin said.

"No? You just want land. *Our* land!" Gior Meridia shouted.

"If you continue on your present course, you will be leading our people to their deaths," the baron of Granjaen cried. "Do not do this."

Aeslin met his eyes, defiance flashing across her face.

"If war is the only way path, then so be it," she declared. "If I am to die, then it will be beneath a sea of stars drenched in the blood of my enemies."

"Lady Aeslin, perhaps we can find another solution," Leona called over the raised voices. She did not plead. She did not beg. She was *the* princess of Aureia. "Another road that we may take. What if … what if I were to offer you land. My own land. That of Aureia."

Again, there was silence.

Again, it was caused by the princess of Aureia.

She was her father's will, yet perhaps here she had overstepped. Kaladin knew it. He knew that Leona knew it. She was too smart not to.

"There would be enough for what you need. More. We could show you how to build, how to farm, how to sail. Whatever your needs, the empire will provide."

"And you could guarantee this?"

"You have my word."

Aeslin paused. She stared into Leona's eyes. Red eyes met brown. Neither looked away. Neither gave ground.

"Perhaps then we can come to an agreement."

Leona at last turned to the barons.

"What say you?" she asked.

The baron of Granjaen was the first to speak. "Granjaen is with you."

"Canaeric."

"Salazar."

"Caspin."

"Reyna."

One by one, lords and ambassadors called the names of their fiefdoms. One by one, they agreed.

"Monares."

"Luarco."

"Bailon," Mathias said at last.

"And you, Aloys?" Leona asked, turning to the ambassador of the last great house.

Solan squared his jaw as he glared at Envar and Aeslin. Monocena had been put to the sword in recent days. So many dead. Kaladin could see the war in his eyes, in his heart and soul. After a moment, he slowly nodded.

"Aloys."

"You cannot seriously–" Gior Meridia started angrily.

"This is not a debate." Princess Leona cut him off.

Meridia thrust an arm at the Salvaari. "They assassinated my sister! The baron of Fontara. Nearly drove Salaman to ruin!" Meridia roared at her. "My sister!"

"Do not raise your voice to me, sir," Leona ordered as her own rose in turn. "I am not a helpless child. I command the hurricane. I command the earth beneath your feet. Let it be heard and known that *any* attack upon Salvaari, be they human, elven or ruskalan, is a direct attack upon the empire."

"You would remove the choice from my hands?"

"I am sorry, but there *is* no choice."

Gior Meridia ground his teeth. He glared at the princess of Aureia. There was nothing he could do but nod. If he took up arms against the Salvaari, then he would have to contend with both Aureia and the full might of the Northlands. No one had that kind of power. At his nod, the princess turned back to the Salvaari.

"You have your answer," Leona told Aeslin. "The rest falls upon your word."

The ruskalan extended an arm to the princess.

"I must traverse the Plain and send word to Salvaar," she said. "If there is no argument, we will meet here tomorrow before the sun arises. Our peace will begin with the new dawn."

Leona took Aeslin's arm and grasped it tight.

The deal was made.

TWENTY-SEVEN

Road to Alvillia, Fiefdom of Canaeric, The Northlands

The silver light of the moon blazed through the heavens. It caressed the trees and kissed the earth. It danced upon the flowing muscles of horses as they thundered down the road towards Alvillia. Gallop slowed to canter. Canter slowed to a walk. Nevra lightly gripped her reins as she passed through the open gates of Alvillia. The soldiers at the city entrance paid no heed to a pair of riders. Nevra glanced at Andreas before bringing her horse to a halt. The guards standing at a brazier finally looked over at the companions. Nevra pulled back her hood to reveal her ivory mane.

"I have come for the negotiations," she called.

"Then you may be too late," one of the men replied as he approached. "The war is over."

He looked happy. For years soldiers such as he had been used in the political games of barons and their enemies across the river. That time had come to an end. The guard and his brothers-in-arms could stay home with their families. Nevra barely kept at bay the grin that threatened. Her heart soared. She looked to Andreas and could see the same joy burn in his eyes.

But what of the autieyar?

Had she reached Alvillia?

"In which house will I find my kin?" Nevra asked.

One of the soldiers gestured further into the town as he gave Nevra directions. She branded them in her mind and nodded her gratitude.

"Thank you."

They followed the winding roads. The streets of Alvillia were far from empty. Though the market stalls were long closed, people still flocked the city for drink and celebration. Taverns overflowed with clientele, and many drank in the street. Some danced to the sound of music, while others played dice. All were merry. The word of peace had spread, and it had spread fast.

The war was over.

The riders dismounted beneath the sign of The King's Key, the tavern named by the guards at the gate. Nevra tied her horse to the railing and made for the door. She extended her fingers towards the handle. She froze.

No sound came from the other side.

No singing.

No laughter.

No raucous sound of drunken revelry.

Nevra glanced at Andreas with a frown and then finally took hold of the handle. She gently pushed on the door.

Locked.

Nevra's frown deepened, her heart racing. Without a word, Andreas stepped to her side and pulled forth his knife. He worked the lock for but a moment before it clicked open. The elf silently drew her knife and eased the door open. Her boots were light upon the wooden floor, her eyes keen even in the darkness. Andreas followed her inside and slowly shut the door behind them. A hint of smoke still hung in the air from freshly smothered candles.

Then she saw the blood.

White blood.

An elf lay face down upon the floor in the ivory pool. There was no sign of struggle. His throat had been cut.

Voices flowed around Naidra as she sat before the flames of her fire. Her eyes were closed to the world. The voices whispered to her. They caressed her ears with sound. Unending sound. They spoke her name. Murmured to her heart. They helped her think, helped her see clearly. Her legs were crossed, and her arms folded over her chest. Her breathing was steady as she lost herself in the vortex of sound.

They lie.

There is no peace here.

Only death.

Only treachery.

They will hunt you.

Cage you.

A rope around your neck.

Racing hooves cut through the void. Naidra's eyes blazed open. She leapt to her feet, her glaive flying into her waiting hand. She turned.

Valmoar.

He fell from his horse with a gasp. The glaive slipped from her fingers as Naidra ran towards her friend. His breathing was ragged, and his face drawn back in pain. Naidra took him in her arms and within moments her fingers were stained black with his blood. It covered his shirt and dribbled from his lips.

"We were attacked," Valmoar growled, barely able to speak. He winced as pain rolled through his body. "Solan Aloys is with them … They betrayed us here … just as they did … at Monocena."

Pain.

Anger.

Rage.

All things were awoken in the dark. They sparked inside Naidra. They burned bright.

"The humans move on our people …" Valmoar gripped her arm.

"The delegation," Naidra murmured, realising.

The barons had gathered to kill the Salvaari. They had gathered to send a message east. A message to Harkan. A message to all who called themselves elf or ruskalan.

This land was *theirs*.

"Rest," Naidra told Valmoar as his eyes burned bright.

She called upon her power and closed her friend's wounds. Skin patched and blood stopped flowing. Valmoar took a slow breath and then his consciousness left him. His chest rose and fell steadily. Naidra laid him down gently.

In her eyes, in her heart, in her soul, all she could see was Monocena. She could feel its flames on her face. She could see her friends fall. Naidra had been right – she had been right all along. There could be no peace. Not with them. Never with them. Her fists curled as she rose to her feet. The fire hissed and was snuffed out. Smoke filled the air as the voices returned.

You were right about them.

You have always been right about them.

Her glaive found its home in her hand again. Memories, memories of Monocena, of fire, of her sister, flashed through her mind. Naidra leapt on her horse and turned towards Alvillia.

Dawn wasn't far away when Duran rose. He put on his cloak and armour and reached for his sword. It wasn't on the shelf he had left it.

"With the barons in line with Aureia, there will be no war," Kaladin said as he extended Duran's sword. "Whatever the inquisition has decided, it does not matter. What matters is the peace we forge today."

Duran took the blade. "With the deal of land, we must return home," Duran replied, buckling on his sword.

"And once my brother the emperor has agreed – and he will agree – you will be free to follow your heart. Both of you."

Kaladin reached out and gripped Duran's shoulder. The young knight gave his mentor a smile and returned the gesture. Despite all the pain he had caused Kaladin with his decision, the love of his mentor was unconditional. He was the father Duran never had. Together they walked from the room side by side and joined their companions. Stefanos. Arne and the Arkin Garter. Leona. They made for their horses and mounted up. Duran pulled himself up into his saddle beside Kaladin and the company made for the amphitheatre.

The streets of Alvillia were emptier now than they had been at midnight. Dawn's light was only moments away when the riders arrived at the great stadium. Without a second thought, Duran helped the princess down to the ground. Her eyes shone with joy as their hands lingered together for a heartbeat longer than was appropriate. Eyes so full of love. So full of hope. Soon it would not matter what people saw. Soon it would not matter what they said. She gave her husband a radiant smile and then joined with Kaladin, Arne and Stefanos as they made their way into the tunnel of the amphitheatre.

Nevra stared at the dead elf. There had been no struggle. The wound was precise. Whoever had killed him had been well trained. The floorboards above creaked. The attackers were still here. Nevra glanced at Andreas and raised a finger to her lips and motioned to the staircase. Together they climbed the wooden steps without daring to make a sound. Nevra held her knife steady. She could still hear the revelry in the streets. Moonlight streamed in through the glass, the only thing providing light. They passed another body at the top of the stairs, a human clad in the garb of Salvaar. Nevra peered into the first of the bedrooms. More dead greeted her eyes. They had been slain in their sleep. Red human blood was mixed with the black from that of a ruskalan woman. Her grey eyes stared emptily towards Nevra. Hushed voices came from another of the rooms. Nevra crept through the hallway. The entire delegation was dead. Every man and woman. A shadow appeared through a doorway. He wore black clothing, and a mask covered his mouth and nose. Blood dripped from the dagger in his right hand. A bag of spoils was held in his left. More men appeared at his back. The bag of spoils rang as it hit the ground.

"Take them," the assassin hissed.

There was no room to move freely in the narrow corridor. No room for a sword. The thin blade of a steel knife darted at Nevra's throat. She slid to the side, deflected the thrust with her left arm and drove her own blade up into the assassin's neck. Blood wet the walls as she tore her dagger free. Nevra kicked the dying man to the ground. He crashed straight into the path of the second assassin. The body knocked him back and left the third alone. He attacked. Nevra moved fast. His knife missed her twice. On his third swing, Nevra opened his lead arm with her dagger. The man cried out, his weapon hitting the ground. Nevra drove him into the corridor wall and plunged her knife into his heart. The next man leapt at her back. Andreas caught him in a vice grip and thrust his blade home into the assassin's neck.

That left one.

One assassin.

Nevra turned to face him, the red blood of her enemies hot upon her skin. Her eyes blazed with anger. She walked him down. There was no escape. He had nowhere to turn, nowhere to run. Nevra's blade sliced him twice. He fell back against a wall as she came at him again. He raised his blade but Nevra was faster. Steel met flesh as her knife drive through the palm of his hand and slammed it into the wooden wall. The man screamed, his nerveless fingers dropping his dagger. Blood poured from the wound. The small bones within were shattered. Pain emerged in his eyes.

Pain and fear.

Nevra met his gaze. So close she was that she could feel his breath on her face. She could see every pore in his skin. Nevra tore the mask away and pressed her forearm against his throat.

"Who are you?" she hissed.

There was no reply.

"Do you have any idea what you have done?" Nevra snarled. "There was supposed to be peace tomorrow."

Still nothing.

"This is not the act of a common man," Andreas said from behind.

"Who gave you the order?" Nevra growled. "WHO GAVE YOU THE ORDER?"

She twisted her knife and forced herself closer to the man. He was trapped. He cried out in pain as the steel opened more of his hand.

"He came with gold and promises," the assassin said at last.

"Enough to start a war?" Andreas demanded from Nevra's side.

"Who paid you?" Nevra commanded. "Which baron set you upon this path? WHO?"

"No baron," the assassin hissed. "One of yours."

Confusion gripped Nevra. She fought against it.

"Give me a name."

The knife twisted further. Blood flowed. Bones cracked. The assassin grimaced. A groan fled his lips.

"Eyes … red as the devil. He wore black clothing now as then. He never spoke his name, but I heard it whispered long ago."

"*A name.*"

"Valmoar …"

No longer could Nevra hold her emotions in check. No longer could she keep all but rage from her face. Surprise. Confusion. Shock. At the farm she had been the only survivor.

The *only* survivor.

"Valmoar is dead," Nevra growled. "Three years ago."

"A ghost did not pay me to kill these people."

"You've met him before," Andreas stated.

"Yes," the assassin answered.

"You've *worked* with him before," Andreas continued.

"Yes."

Nevra could barely speak. She could not believe what she was hearing. In pain and on the edge of death, the assassin had no reason to lie.

"When?"

"Monocena. Three years ago."

Nevra nearly staggered to her knees. Her grip on the knife kept her standing.

"It wasn't Aloys who betrayed a company of Salvaari, was it?" Andreas growled. "Speak!"

"Aloys knew nothing. It was a ruse … a ruse to start a war."

"And when it failed?"

"He told me that it worked far greater than he had intended."

"What meaning did he carry?" Nevra said at last.

"I do not know."

"You lie."

"It's not a lie," the assassin rasped.

"YOU LIE!"

"It's not a lie! Valmoar paid me to bring war and I have. There will be no peace when the blood of your people runs in the amphitheatre this day."

Nevra tore her knife free and jammed it up against his neck. Even so close to the assassin, Nevra could barely see him. Her mind swam with questions and answers. Steel tasted blood. The assassin crumpled at her feet. The dagger rang as it hit the floor. Nevra raised a hand to her temple.

"There was no lie in his eyes, was there?" Andreas asked.

Nevra shook her head slowly.

"Who is Valmoar?"

"He led us to Monocena. He promised us peace … He died with my sister."

Andreas' face paled as he at last understood.

"If Valmoar is alive … then …"

"My sister is alive."

And if she was alive then, because of her connection with the Veil, she knew that Nevra was as well. The thought almost broke her. Valmoar had betrayed them. He had betrayed everything that they stood for. On the war path and with an iristysi at his side, there would be no stopping him.

There will be no peace when the blood of your people runs in the amphitheatre this day.

The amphitheatre. The human delegation. All of the barons and their emissaries. The princess of Aureia. All of them were in the same place at the same time … and Valmoar wanted war.

Nevra gathered up her knife and turned to her companion. Her friend. The one who had torn her from the darkness. The one who had given her a new life.

The one who had given her hope.

"Thank you," she told him.

No other words were spoken. None needed to be said. Nevra stepped close, wrapped an arm behind his neck and kissed him hard. She tasted his lips. She felt him. She felt his heart. A tear tumbled from her eye and the pommel of her knife cracked into the back of his head.

Andreas fell.

The world had changed. She had to go on alone. No one else had to die for her.

Kaladin watched as the mounting unrest continued to grow. What had begun as hope-filled conversation soon turned to whispers of irritation. The barons and emissaries were losing patience. The first light of dawn crept over the horizon, joining that of the braziers burning bright around the stage. Whispers soon turned into discussion.

"They will be here," Leona told Stefanos as they waited. "They have to be here."

"The sun is rising," called Solan Aloys, taking an angry step into the heart of the theatre. "And as we can all see, there is no sign of our new ally."

"Where is Aeslin?" asked another of the barons. "Peace cannot be made without all of us."

"She will come," spoke another.

"We were supposed to meet before the sun rose," Solan said. "That is what she told us, and here we are."

"It is as I have foreseen," Gior Meridia cried. "Why should me and mine make a deal with those who will not show us the most basic of respect?"

"They will be here," Leona said again, this time louder, for all the world to hear. "Have a little faith."

A shout came from one of the tunnels. Kaladin turned. They all did. Even through the clammer of voices, Kaladin heard the shout for what it was.

A scream.

The wind stirred. Confusion ran through the ranks of nobles. A strong gust blew through the amphitheatre. Those closest to the tunnel were hurled into the walls of the stage and the stone pillars within. Bones broke and blood rained. Kaladin staggered back. The flames of the braziers flickered and died. Smoke rose in a haze. The wind scattered dust. It became harder to see. Harder to breathe.

Naidra strode down the corridor, eyes burning with blue light. Dust and smoke filled the stage before her. The shouts of the traitors within were like a lullaby. Her glaive moved absently at her side as she drew closer to the stage. The voices in her head rose in a crescendo. In the back of her mind, she could hear the song her sister used to sing her. She began to hum it.

Tears of life and tears of snow,
gifts from the Mother for the Iceborn to grow.
Tears of life and tears of snow,
we will find home where the north wind will blow.

Her feet crossed the threshold into the amphitheatre.
Her glaive tasted blood. Men began to fall.
We will find home, we will find home,
we will find home, where the north wind will blow.

We will find home, we will find home,
we will find home, where the north wind will blow.

Naidra's eyes shone like blue fire as magic whirled all around her. It picked up screaming men and crushed them against walls of stone, against pillars.

Tears of pearl and tears of sapphire,
hope is born at the Great Queen's desire.
Tears of pearl and tears of sapphire,
songs that echo across our new empire.

Barons fell to her glaive. They fell to her magic. To Naidra, it mattered not. They were unarmed. Helpless. Prey. A soldier wearing the purple of the empire was cut in half by her magic.

We will find home, we will find home,
we will find home, where the north wind will blow.
We will find home, we will find home,
we will find home, where the north wind will blow.

The dead lay scattered along the cobbled floor of the amphitheatre. Blood stained stone. They had been unarmed but none could survive. Not for this treachery. Few still remained. Her eyes flicked to the company of nobles gathered together at the far end of the theatre. A woman stood with them. The princess of Aureia. A knight bearing the sun and moon stepped before her with an arm extended as a shield. Naidra knew that symbol and she knew it well. The symbol that had turned her people into monsters. Magic swelled within her, rage growing in tandem. Her arm extended. Her fingers curled. Cracks appeared in the pillar. It shattered. Stone shards sliced through the humans, sending blood flying. They were all cast down.

Kaladin's head rang. His vision flickered. The elf had her back turned as she cut down the last two standing barons with her glaive. It was over. They had failed. This was Salvaar's answer to peace. This is why Aeslin had not come. Most who had stood with him had been killed by the stone shards. Some had been crushed beneath the pillar as it had come down. A large fragment had fallen atop the baron of Granjaen. His eyes were empty, body broken. Another stone had fallen on Leona. Kaladin stared at her. His niece. His blood. He had failed to protect her. Another noble fell to the autieyar's steel. The elven woman drew his gaze.

A groan came from behind.

Kaladin looked back.

Leona.

Her eyes flickered open. She cried out as she stirred. She tried to move the stone. She couldn't. Kaladin dragged his battered and bloody body towards her. Leona met his eyes and her cries stopped.

Footsteps.

The elf must have heard them. Leona stretched out an arm with a groan and reached for her boot. She pulled her kukri free and with bared teeth extended it towards her uncle. Kaladin held her gaze as he took the blade. She was his niece. His family. His princess. His left hand found hers. He squeezed it tight.

"Delaureia," Kaladin told her fiercely.

With a snarl he planted his hands firmly upon the ground and heaved. Stones fell from his back, and he forced himself to his hands and knees. His fingers wrapped around the wooden handle of the kukri. He rose to his feet.

Naidra looked behind her as she heard the knight rise. A long dagger was clasped firmly in his hand. She watched him curiously and for the first time noticed that the woman behind him stirred with life. The knight charged with a roar upon his lips.

There was no fear in his eyes.

Naidra extended an arm, her magic engulfing the knight. It wrapped around him and lashed him hard against one of the stone pillars. His spine shattered and he fell, dead before he hit the ground.

Dust filled the tunnel as Duran ran for all he was worth. Men of the Garter were with him, all with swords in hand.

They had heard the screams.

His father.

His friend.

His wife.

All three stood within the stone walls of the amphitheatre. All three were trapped by whatever had emerged from the darkness. The haze of smoke and dust thinned as Duran left the tunnel behind. Enough light from the sun broke through the mist to reveal the bodies. They were everywhere. Blood covered the ground like a lake. Stefanos lay amidst the corpses. Duran saw Leona trapped by fallen rubble. He saw Kaladin charge at a lone woman. A white-haired elf. He saw her extend an arm. Duran had no time to do anything but shout. He saw his mentor crushed against a pillar. He saw Kaladin fall lifeless to the ground. Only Leona remained. A bellow ripped through Duran's lips as he ran at the autieyar.

Towards the monster.

Her eyes of blue and white turned towards him. He raised his sword.

Then he was airborne.

The ground vanished.

He came down hard.

Naidra watched the second knight and the Aureian soldiers fall. Tears of white blood streaked from her nose and the corners of her eyes. Pain screamed inside her head as the magic began to take its toll. She swayed as she fought to keep her footing. Biting back a grimace, she turned her burning gaze to the sound of stone hitting stone. The woman. The Aureian princess. She had fought free of the rock that had pinned her and now rose to her feet, blood dripping from cuts over her entire body. Her weight was on her right leg, for her left had been crushed by the pillar. She could not move. Could not run. All hope had left the human's face. Tears ran freely from her eyes and sobs shook her trembling body as she stared at the fallen knight. Perhaps he held meaning to her. Naidra twirled her glaive and began her approach. With this woman's death came the death of treachery. The death of the lie that was peace. There could *never* be peace. Not with these people. Naidra tilted her head as the whispers of fate spoke to her. She raised her arm, raised her glaive. In a single movement, she stepped forwards and sent the weapon forth with a cry.

Steel sliced through air.

Boots rang on stone.

The glaive drove deep into flesh.

Blood spilled.

White blood.

The eyes of her victim widened.

A woman fell.

Nevra fell.

Time slowed as Naidra saw her sister crash to the ground. The sister who had died three years ago had taken the blow in place of the cornered princess. Naidra leapt to Nevra's side and pulled the glaive free. It *was* Nevra … She wasn't dead. Valmoar had told her she was dead. Nevra stared up at her, no anger, pity or hate in her eyes. There was only love. Blood rolled from her lips and spilled down to her chest. Her touch was gentle upon Naidra's cheek. Naidra placed her hand over her sister's.

"Naidra," Nevra whispered. "Naidra …"

The hand slipped through Naidra's fingers. Blue eyes faded to grey as the light of Sylvaine left her. Tears flowed as what little remained of Naidra's heart shattered.

Lies.

Valmoar had said none had survived. He had told her that all of her friends were dead. That her sister was dead. Lies.

What else had he lied about?

Naidra stared in horror at her hands covered in the blood of her sister. Her fists curled in pain. Her teeth made bare with rage. Her breathing grew ragged with sorrow.

She wanted to see the world burn.

Magic channelled deeply within. Her breathing grew faster. Naidra's scream echoed through the stone of the amphitheatre, echoed to the Veil. Naidra let go of everything she felt, everything within. Tears and blood streamed from her eyes as the magic took her.

A gasp broke Duran's lips as he came to. Pain. It was all he felt. He could feel the break in his left arm. He could taste blood. Two of the Garter moved. They were barely conscious.

The autieyar.

She cradled a dead woman. An elven woman. Leona was trapped, her back pressed up against stone. Her hopeless eyes stared at the destroyed amphitheatre. Dozens of the unarmed dead. Dozens who had voted for peace dead. That peace itself was now dead. Everything that they had worked for was gone. Duran gritted his teeth and bit back pain as he pulled his dagger free. He tore the small vial from beneath his shirt and ripped the cord from his neck. The stopper fell free. Poison kissed steel. The autieyar's fists curled.

Her eyes blazed.

She screamed.

Wind howled as the autieyar's magic roared.

Duran heaved himself up and hurled his knife.

The full might of the elf's magic hit Leona, engulfing her. She tried to scream but no sound came out. Blue flames burned through her clothing, stripping flesh from bone. Duran's dagger connected with the elf's back. The light in her eyes died. Her magic died.

No woman stood before her.

Only ash.

It drifted through the air to the ground piece by piece.

Leona was gone.

Nothing remained.

Duran cried out like an animal. His limp arm was forgotten as he took up his sword. His eyes, awash with pain, turned to the elf. He had to kill her. He must kill her. Step by step, he drew closer. Step by step, he moved faster. She had killed Kaladin. She had killed Arne. She had killed Leona. His wife. His love. He raised his sword over his defenceless enemy. He cried out in agony and brought the blade down.

Arms took him before it could land. Steel rang as the sword fell from his fingers. The soldiers heaved him back, sobbing and in tears. He couldn't stand anymore. He couldn't fight. His soul was as shattered as his heart. In the flickers of his dying vision, he saw men of the Garter take the elf. He saw the few survivors of the massacre rise. He saw Stefanos.

Then he saw darkness.

TWENTY-EIGHT

His arm was tied in a splint. The fires of a dozen braziers burned but all he felt was the cold. Duran stood in the great throne room of Aureia, alone except for the emperor. His armour was gone, much of his will to fight gone with it. He had seen his friend, his mentor and father die. He had seen Kaladin's life taken before his eyes. He had seen Leona butchered … slaughtered until nothing remained.

Duran barely saw the emperor as Janus made his way towards the knight. A kukri was held in his hands. Leona's kukri. Janus looked exhausted. He had not slept. He had barely eaten. In the end, the peace he had fought so hard to achieve had claimed two of his own family.

"I have sent birds to every corner," Janus told him. "My armies will assemble and then march north. Together we will see the Salvaari fall."

There was true rage in his voice, but behind it there was agony. The grief of a brother. The grief of a father.

"I hear that you are to be named Sword of Kil'kara."

Duran could only nod. That had been the order. When he returned to Rovira, he was to be given his mentor's title.

"Kaladin saw you as a son. You were my daughter's closest friend."

"I loved her," Duran told him without care. "We married in the north."

Janus took a breath. There was no anger in his eyes as he gazed towards Duran. No malice. Only heartbreak. Duran knew that the emperor could have him killed for such a thing. He did not care. A part of him wished for it.

"We were going to leave," Duran continued. "Once peace had been won, we were going to leave."

Janus squared his jaw and took a step towards the knight. Instead of heated words or a cry for the guards, the emperor extended Leona's kukri.

Duran met his emperor's eyes and slowly took the blade. It was all that remained of her. Ash, memory and a single Delion knife. Janus placed a hand on Duran's shoulder.

"Together we will bring Salvaar to justice," the emperor swore.

Duran stared at the dagger and then closed his hand tightly around it. His gaze went to the wedding ring on his finger. He thought of Leona. He saw her in every waking moment. He saw her when he slept.

"Now go, my son," Emperor Janus bid the knight.

As Duran made for the entrance, Janus summoned his steward.

"Send word to Estevan Bailon," the emperor commanded. "Tell him he can have his Medea."

The ride to Rovira was long. Longer still with a broken arm. Duran made the journey without complaint. Before the stone faces of his gods, he was named Sword of Kil'kara. Before them he was granted his mentor's title and armour. He sent forth the call to every garrison and every citadel. The Order was to muster. Knights in their dozens joined him as he crossed the stone floor of the courtyard of Rovira towards a great statue of Durandail.

Duran fell to his knees before the god of war and spread his arms wide. He wept openly. For Kaladin. For Leona. For the thousands about to die. This was his fate.

Valmoar's eyes flashed open. No longer was he in the Northlands. Now he stood in the Veil. The wind whispered in his ear. It called to him. Mist hung in the air. It was thick, as thick as the magic that ebbed and flowed through the Plain. He was not alone. Rune-covered stones filled the undergrowth of the great forest. Mist hung in the air. Magic was everywhere. He could almost taste it. Ravens cried out.

"You have no idea," a cold voice called. "You have no idea what you have done."

The first tendril of fear edged itself into Valmoar's blood. The air grew colder, the mist thicker. He turned to see another standing opposite. His clothes were dark and his skin pale. Dark hair hung past his pointed ears. His skin was stretched over his sharp bones. Black runes were etched upon the skin of his face and a jagged scar stretched from his crown to his chin. Red eyes blazed with crimson light.

"Firstborn." Valmoar bowed in deference as Harkan approached.

"Shame," Harkan hissed, glaring at his fellow ruskalan. "Valmoar, shame on what you have done."

His voice was calm and as icy as the depths of winter. His steps were graceful and as measured as his words. His gaze was piercing as he stared at Valmoar, as he stared *through* him. The firstborn ruskalan circled Valmoar.

"I have only done what was right," Valmoar replied. "What was necessary."

"Are you so blind that you cannot see?" Harkan questioned.

The air itself seemed to follow the firstborn child of Tanris.

"I have only done what I have done to defend my people."

"I hear everything. I see everything. I *feel* everything. You are trying to shift the earth itself. You sent assassins into the heart of the Aureian palace to kill an emperor. You sent a message on the eve of the new year that the time of peace is over. You traded gold for treachery when you paid humans to attack you at Monocena. Both started this war. Both will lead to the deaths of our people. But perhaps most vile of all, you broke an autieyar to forge a deadly ally who would bow to your will. I know what you have spoken in the dark. I know what you have seen. You broke an autieyar, used her to stir hate and resentment, before finally sending her to destroy the peace that I had brought to our people. The black art of creating iristysi was forbidden after Idrisir. You learnt how the iristysi were born. You learnt how to control them, to use your own dark magic to separate her from the Veil and bend her to your will. You defy the spirits."

"No," Valmoar snarled. "No, I honour them."

"Once, there were as many autieyar as fingers on your hands. One has been taken by the humans at Alvillia because of your actions. One was killed before the Silver Throne because of your actions. Tell me, do you truly believe that those who remain have the strength to contend with both the armies of the north and south?"

Valmoar looked him in the eye as his rage burned bright. Harkan knew it was as he had suspected, yet it had been too late to stop the attack.

"For centuries, the plague of their gods has spread across the world and now infects our borders ... but we still claim to be of the Old Blood." Valmoar seethed. "The heretics stole our gods and defiled them with new names. That cannot be forgiven."

Harkan stopped before him, staring into Valmoar's soul.

"You go too far, Valmoar," he said. "Ten mortal lifetimes you have walked this Plain and yet you are nothing but a child compared to me. War. That is the song that will be sung. A song that you have written."

"And it is a grand song, my brother," Valmoar replied. "A song long in the making. We must take this chance and we must take it now. It is our *last* chance. Idrisir abandoned us. The Wolf of Black and White died a long time ago. The humans are fractured and divided. This may be our only chance."

"You have united them in common cause," Harkan countered with a growl.

He stepped towards Valmoar and glared at him with venomous eyes. He was the Firstborn. The greatest of the ruskalan.

"The humans are many. We are few. You have led us to war, a war that will see our people slaughtered," Harkan told him. "Every elf, every ruskalan, every human who calls themselves Salvaari must stand side by side. Every one of the strong. Every one of the loyal."

His voice never rose in anger. It never showed the emotion within, yet Valmoar could see it in his burning gaze, and it terrified him.

"And that isn't you."

Harkan stepped close. His eyes met Valmoar's and they blazed with crimson light. Valmoar was strong, but the Firstborn was stronger still. Here in the Veil, magic was at its greatest. The Veil gave birth to magic. The Veil *was* magic. Valmoar fought back as Harkan's power drove through him. Something shattered within. Valmoar fell to his knees. There was no blood. No sign of struggle. He collapsed to the ground. Life left him.

Naidra's blue eyes ignited. She saw Valmoar fall in the darkest part of her mind. A gasp left her lips as though she had been drowning and could finally breathe. A thousand feelings assaulted her. She could sense everything. She could see everything. The power of the Veil burned through her blood. Every presence in the palace, every elven soul in faraway Salvaar – she could feel them all. In that moment, she knew it to be true. Her connection to the Veil hadn't been shattered at Monocena. It had been stolen. Stolen by Valmoar.

He had taken her connection to the Veil.

To her people.

To the world around her.

Liar.

Deceiver.

The only friend she had ever known had been no friend at all.

What else had he lied about?

Without her connection to the Veil, Naidra had been certain that her sister was dead, but she had been alive the whole time.

Why had Nevra not come for her sooner?

Why had she left her alone with Valmoar?

Naidra shivered. She had been stripped of her clothing and now only wore a thin shift. It did nothing to keep at bay the cold and the dark of the stone and steel cage. Her face was bloodied and bruised from the beatings. Naidra tried to call upon her gift to tear off the tight chains that bound her arms and wrists.

Nothing.

Whatever the humans had done had taken her magic. She felt the presence of the guards and the man with them before the dungeon doors boomed open. Two soldiers came inside and behind them walked a man who could have only been the emperor.

Janus Delaureia. Yes, that was his name.

Naidra had killed his brother. She had killed his daughter. The thought warmed her. A thin smile crossed her lips. She chuckled as she rose to her feet. Darkness crossed the faces of the three men. Naidra grinned at her enemies, showing her bloody teeth. They were going to kill her. They were going to end her pain. If the last thing she saw in this world was the agony on the heretic emperor's face, then that would be enough. Janus stopped barely a foot from her cage and opened his fist to reveal a small vial.

"Such a small thing," he said quietly, "that can bring one so strong to her knees."

So, it was poison that had taken her power. Poison that had

led to her capture. Naidra still felt the knife. She felt the scabbed wound on her back. The first wound in decades she had been unable to heal. The emperor looked up and met her eyes. His dark gaze was sad. Naidra could read his feelings. She laughed.

"I am told that, unless slain, your kind never pass," the emperor stated coldly. "I want you to remember that I alone fought for peace between our people."

Naidra wrapped her fingers around the steel bars of her cage and watched the emperor closely.

"They say that the autieyar can feel everything around them for a mile. They say that they can always feel their kin."

Naidra frowned. Her smile faltered.

How could a human know so much?

Who had spoken to him?

How much did he know?

"I hope that this is true, for I want you to feel it all as I kill your people one by one. Every blow. Every drop of blood. Every scream. I want you to know that everything that is about to happen will happen because of you. You will live with the knowledge that you are the *last* elf. That is my vow."

Janus' fist closed around the vial as he turned and made for the doors. Naidra could only stare at him. For the first time, she felt the cold tendrils of fear close around her. She could not escape without her magic. She could not help her people. She was helpless, powerless for the first time in her life. With Valmoar gone and her connection to the Veil restored, she could feel every elven life. She would feel every elven death.

The emperor paused at the door. His words were colder than winter ice.

"May you live forever."